FIREPRINT

GEOFFREY JENKINS was born in Port Elizabeth in South Africa in 1920. He has combined a successful career in journalism with a life-long interest in the sea, and his knowledge of ships and sailing has provided the background to many of his novels.

Geoffrey Jenkins now lives in Pretoria.

Other recent titles from this best-selling author are: *A Bridge of Magpies*, *Southtrap*, *A Ravel of Waters* and *The Unripe Gold*.

Available in Fontana
by the same author

A Bridge of Magpies
Hunter-Killer
A Ravel of Waters
The River of Diamonds
Scend of the Sea
Southtrap
The Unripe Gold
A Twist of Sand
The Watering Place of Good Peace
A Grue of Ice
A Cleft of Stars

GEOFFREY JENKINS

Fireprint

FONTANA/Collins

First published in Great Britain by
William Collins Sons & Co. Ltd, 1984
A continental edition first issued
in Fontana Paperbacks 1985
This edition first issued
in Fontana Paperbacks 1985

Made and printed in Great Britain by
William Collins Sons & Co. Ltd, Glasgow

This story takes place a few years into
the future.

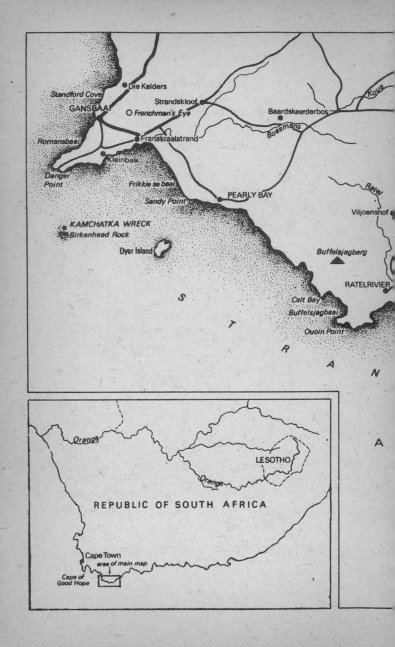

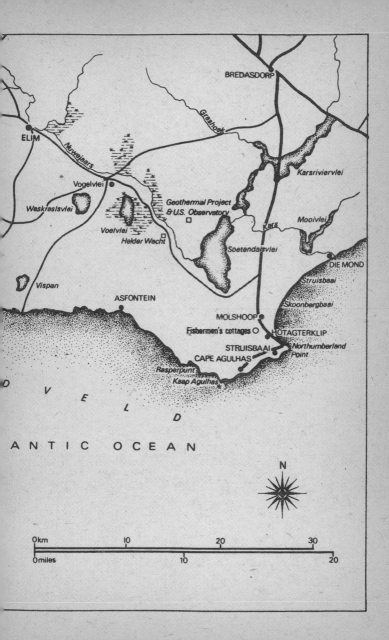

PROLOGUE

Comets are omens of evil, and the year after Halley's Comet had spread its tail across southern Africa's sky from the Cape of Good Hope to Mozambique was a time of shattering upheaval for the sub-continent.

As dramatic as the appearance of the great comet itself – and far more unexpected – was a Russian announcement that a Soviet oil drilling rig had struck a rich undersea gas field on the Agulhas Bank three hundred and thirty kilometres south of the Cape.

The Soviet news brought a flood of protest from South Africa, which for more than twenty years previously had systematically – and at great expense – explored the oil-promising continental shelf known as the Agulhas Bank, with encouraging results.

South Africa first objected by invoking the Law of the Sea Treaty, which gives a 'pioneer' prior rights for offshore exploration of undersea minerals. When the Russians ignored these objections, South Africa took her claim before the World Court of Justice. The court ruled in favour of the Soviet Union. This was followed by the Russians establishing an offshore 'gas atoll', or floating gas liquefying plant. Here undersea gas was converted and loaded into special supertankers. The product was supplied mainly to the Soviet's Black African surrogates south of the equator.

The United States was gravely concerned about these developments since they established a Russian presence athwart the strategically vital Cape Sea Route, along which sixty per cent of the West's oil from the Middle East is shipped.

Almost coinciding with the gas strike was the news that the United States was to establish a naval base at Kosi Bay, only a few kilometres from the South African–Mozambique border, Mozambique was one of the Black Marxist states which was being supplied with Soviet liquefied gas. It has one of the finest harbours in south-east Africa in Maputo; the Soviet fleet has the use of it.

Kosi Bay, once an idyllic unspoilt tropical paradise, was situated about eighteen hundred kilometres northeast of the Soviet offshore gas atoll and its cession to the Americans was part of a complicated land deal involving both South Africa and Swaziland. Swaziland is land locked and for many years had sought an outlet to the sea via a corridor (of South African territory) to Kosi Bay. South Africa, in an unexpected gesture of good neighbourliness towards Swaziland, ceded the corridor and undeveloped Kosi Bay, whereupon Swaziland gave the United States the right to construct a commercial harbour for her use. Paralleling this, Swaziland permitted the construction of a major US airfield and naval base.

By this move, the United States secured a dominating position in the Indian Ocean from which she could patrol extensive sections of the Cape sea route and thus protect her oil interests in the face of Soviet encroachments on the Agulhas Bank south of Cape Agulhas, the ultimate land point of Africa.

I

The crude graffiti of spraypaint splotched her naked left breast from shoulder to nipple. It made a suggestive, erratic loop and continued down past her bare navel to the skirt she was busy slipping off. Another red daub branched across her cleavage towards her other breast, which was only partly clear of her blouse. Her face was a curious compound of guile, expectation and incredible beauty. Her long delicate hands seemed to freeze in their undressing of herself as the car's headlights pierced the fog and revealed her.

They also revealed a man lying senseless at her feet. His wrists and throat were slashed.

Hallam Cane gave a startled oath. His woman companion, who was driving, stood on the brakes and stopped short of the rain-streaked prefab which was their destination.

Cane jerked open his door.

'Hold on!' exclaimed the driver.

But Cane had already covered the ground to the prefab entrance and the two figures. They remained immobile, the woman in her seductive stance, the man still.

Cane saw, now that he was close, that it wasn't a live woman but a statue carved from wood. Even without the fog's theatrical effect, she was so lifelike as to appear human.

The unconscious man was real enough. The blood on his wrists and throat was likewise real.

The driver jumped out and joined Cane. She was almost Spanish in her petite beauty, not as tall as the lifesize statue.

She recoiled from the scenario in horror. 'Not another tragedy!'

Cane dropped on his knees on the waterlogged ground to test the injured man's pulse.

'What is going on here?' he demanded.

The fog swirled; the smell which rose from the surrounding marshland was raw, age-old, primitive.

'He's alive?' asked the dark girl hesitantly.

'He's alive all right, but I don't like the way his heart is fluttering,' he replied. 'Know him?'

'Of course – Paul Bosch. My boss. He was in charge of the project until you arrived.'

Cane gave a low whistle. 'So this is Paul Bosch, eh? No wonder he failed to turn up at the airfield to meet me.'

He eased Bosch's head from side to side to examine the throat wound. The injured man groaned.

'If only I'd had an inkling that something was wrong, I would have called here on my way to the airfield . . .' said the girl.

'Forget it – you couldn't possibly have guessed,' replied Cane.

As he spoke, Cane's hands were exploring Bosch's body for broken bones. He indicated the statue with a movement of his head.

'This, I presume, is the Accursed Figurehead?'

'It is – why do you say it like that?' asked the girl.

'Supposed to exercise an evil influence over men, not so?'

'That's the legend.'

'I heard about her from Charles Grimmock when he was interviewing me for the job.'

In the mining magnate's wood-panelled office in a Johannesburg skyscraper, fifteen hundred kilometres to the north, Grimmock's derisory reference to the legend made it seem no more than a fairy story. The story was that years before a sailing ship's figurehead, named Alcestis after its ship, had been washed ashore and that it exercised a malign influence over men's emotions. Grimmock had dismissed it contemptuously: 'An old ship's figurehead which the locals have blown up into a sexy legend for the purpose of attracting tourists to their godforsaken part of the world. It now stands on the drilling site to titillate the work force.'

Godforsaken was indeed a correct description of the countryside which Cane had driven through at dusk that

Saturday afternoon from the rural airfield. He had been met there by Maris Swart, secretary/dogsbody to the project, in the absence of Bosch. Maris, a flying enthusiast herself, acted as flying controller at the tiny airfield when an aircraft was expected – it was too small and remote to have a full-time controller.

Where they now were was close to the ultimate land point of Africa. Named Cape Agulhas, it was situated about two hundred and twenty kilometres southeast of Cape Town. The peninsula of which Cape Agulhas formed the tip was a triangle of land about one hundred kilometres long and forty kilometres wide which signposted the meeting-ground of the Atlantic and Indian Oceans at the farthest point south of the Dark Continent. It was a low-lying, sandy, gale-swept region of marshes, swamps, tussocky grass, sand dunes, and constellations of small salt and freshwater lakes, plus short rivers which rose and vanished again within kilometres.

Cane, a British shaft drilling and marine oil well expert, had been given the job by the Johannesburg magnate of taking charge of a completely novel undertaking in the Agulhas area. Only one other of its kind had been attempted in the world – in Cornwall. Called a geothermal electricity generating project, its purpose was to tap the vast power of subterranean hot rocks near Cape Agulhas. The giant pool of potential unused energy was to be employed for the generation of electricity. Charles Grimmock had invested twenty-five million dollars in the unique project.

The undertaking had been dogged by bad luck and unexplained accidents, including the attempted suicide of Cane's predecessor, a Texan named Lloyd Howells. Howells had a fine background of drilling oil wells in the Gulf of Mexico and shaft-sinking on the South African gold mines. The Accursed Figurehead had been at the centre of the Howells affair – the Texan had been found unconscious at her feet suffering from an overdose of drugs.

Now, with a virtual photocopy of the Howells tragedy in front of him, it seemed to Cane that Grimmock's sneers could have been a little premature.

'Is he – dying?' Maris asked Cane.

'He's not bleeding to death, if that's what you mean.' He eyed her keenly. 'Bosch doesn't look the type to attempt his life for any woman, real or imaginary.'

The unconscious face was rugged and weatherbeaten from a life spent in the open. He was about forty. He and another member of the geothermal drilling team, Jan Stander, jointly held the world's deep drilling record on an upcountry mine.

'I wouldn't have thought so either. But the Accursed Figurehead has a reputation in these parts. It all began when she was first washed ashore last century. A sailor saved himself by clinging to her and being carried ashore. In his dying moments on the beach, he left an emotional letter addressed to her. There have been other tragedies connected with Alcestis over the years. My father got rid of the figure-head off our estate because of the trouble she caused.'

Cane had almost completed his examination of Bosch.

'When did you see him last?' he asked Maris.

'Yesterday afternoon late, when the drilling team returned to Bredasdorp.'

Bredasdorp, with a population of six thousand, was the only town in the Strandveld. It had no claim to the *Guinness Book of Records* beyond the fact that it was the southernmost town in Africa. It lay about thirty kilometres north of the geothermal project among rolling wheatlands, in contrast to the marshes and lakes of the coast.

'Was he – quite normal?'

'Completely. We checked about being at the airfield together to meet you.'

Cane stood up and wiped Bosch's blood off his hands with his handkerchief.

'We must get him to a doctor – where's the nearest? Before that, though, we must try and staunch the bleeding.'

'The nearest doctor is at Bredasdorp. He'll bleed to death before we can get him there.'

'He won't,' replied Cane. 'These wounds are messy but superficial.'

'Superficial?' she echoed. 'They look awful. Why then is he unconscious?'

'That is what I have been trying to establish. I'm not a doctor. But in any event, we have to stop the bleeding. There must be a first-aid post for the drilling team right here.'

'Of course,' said Maris. 'The sight of Paul Bosch drove it out of my mind for the moment. The main post is at the shaft-head excavation. There's also a small first-aid box here at the office.'

'Let's get it then.'

'I've thought of something else,' went on Maris. 'Let's first patch him up and then take him to my home – it's only about six kilometres from here.'

'What good would that do?'

'Every farmer's wife in these parts is a para-medic,' she answered. 'My mother has looked after all the minor injuries on the estate all her life. We can do a rush job here and she can fix him up enough for us to transport him to hospital.'

'Splendid.'

'I'll get the first-aid box.'

A light went on in the offices, and soon Maris was back with a box containing bandages and remedies.

They knelt down together and bound Bosch's wrists. When Cane reached his neck and moved his head, Bosch groaned again.

'Something here needs medical investigation,' he remarked. 'Wider bandages, please – are you all right?'

Maris nodded, but her face was pale.

'Hold the light – I'll manage by myself. I don't want you passing out on me.'

She gave him a wan smile and directed the flashlight for him to work by, turning her face away. The light in Bosch's eyes, which were half-open, produced no reaction. His breathing was stertorous.

Finally, Cane said, 'That's it. I wonder how long he has been here?'

Maris was able to look at the injured man now that his wounds were covered. 'It looks as if it has just happened.'

'Maybe we were meant to think that.'

'What are you implying?'

'The blood at the back of his neck is partly congealed, despite the rain. That means that the wound is not fresh. I'd say that whoever staged this scenario for our benefit was caught out unexpectedly by rain.'

'It can't be – for our benefit!'

'Were you present when Howells was discovered – here, at the figurehead's feet?' he demanded.

She stared at him. 'No. It was also a Saturday evening. Bosch and he had a mutual appointment, but Howells didn't show up.'

'Points of similarity, aren't there?'

'What are you inferring?'

'This isn't the first accident, as you well know – there have been all the other minor ones, mishaps, so-called, which have bogged down the project. Part of my brief from Mr Grimmock was to find out what – maybe who – has been the cause.'

'You're saying that there is a deliberate vendetta against the project?'

'First Howells, now Bosch,' he answered. 'I know Howells had a record of emotional instability. He'd been divorced, a messy affair. This site has no compensations – it's damned lonely. There are no diversions, no women. There was even a hint in Howells' past of a fondness for teenage girls.'

'Who told you all this?' she demanded in surprise. 'Howells was a Texan, tough as they come. He loved the good things – yes, but he wasn't the type to become a druggie and attempt to do away with himself.'

'I'm very interested – tell me more later,' said Cane. 'Our immediate priority is to get Bosch proper attention. How long will it take to get to your farm?'

'It's called *Helder Wacht* – "Clear Watch". About twenty minutes to half an hour, I reckon. The track is rough, as you know, to the turn-off to the main road. After that it is tarred.'

'Hold his head steady while I lift him into the back of the car. Careful – maybe his upper spine is damaged.'

They levered the unconscious form gently on to the back seat.

'Why not telephone your parents and warn them?' suggested Cane.

'It's quite clear that you have not experienced the Strandveld's telephone system,' smiled Maris. '*Helder Wacht* is on a party line and it would take almost as long to get through as to make our way there.'

Maris was already in the driver's seat when a thought seemed to strike Cane.

'Wait a moment,' he said.

He went to the trunk, opened a suitcase, and pulled out a deadly-looking Colt Commander automatic. He reseated himself. He snapped an eight-shot magazine into the weapon. The clack of metal against metal sounded unnaturally loud because of the confining effect of the fog.

'Just in case we are being watched,' he said.

2

In its fog-bound state, Clear Watch was a misnomer for Maris' home. Cane and Maris pulled up on the gravelled forecourt fronting the old homestead. Swirls of fog entangled themselves in tall bluegum trees flanking the place and dripped moisture on to the driveway's ochre surface. A regiment of waist-high aloes looked as if they had been gift-wrapped in plastic. Even in the poor light the majesty of the *Helder Wacht* complex was plain – a thatched roof, walls as white as an angel on either side of an open square. Flights of white-washed steps on either side led to green-painted doors. At ground level there was a teak door which looked big enough to have been a ship's hatch – which it was. A brassbound ship's lantern fitted with electric light hung over the main entrance.

Maris cut the car's lights. 'How is Bosch?'

'I don't imagine the rough journey could have done him any good,' Cane replied.

He had tried en route to keep Bosch's head from rolling about from the jolts and jars. The track had followed a waterway called New Year's River for most of the time. This was one of the Strandveld's main rivers. It rose somewhere in the northwest of the region and dragged in its wake across the entire width of the peninsula a constellation of pans, shallow little lakes and marshes, until finally it gave up, unable to reach the nearby sea, in a big inland lake close by called Soetendalsvlei.

'He hasn't made a sound for quite a while,' observed Maris. Cane turned in his seat to support Bosch's lolling head. Maris noted his strong, sensitive hands, like a surgeon's. They would need all their competence for the skilled and dangerous job of fissure blasting, she thought. Not that he lacked the academic side either – she'd seen a brief run-down in the file of Hallam Cane: aged 37, English born, a brilliant career at Cambridge, followed by post-graduate studies at the Massachusetts Institute of Technology. A man of his age – about ten years older than herself – didn't get one of the top jobs in a pioneering project like the Cornish geo-thermal electricity project (which had the backing of the Camborne School of Mines, the British Government and the EEC) without having proved himself also in the field. He was completely unlike her two previous bosses – the rip-roaring Texan Lloyd Howells and the taciturn South African Paul Bosch.

'Go first and warn your parents,' said Cane. 'Bring a blanket. We'll sling him in it – it's the best thing if he's got a bad neck injury.'

'I'll get Dad to help you. You wait with him.'

She went indoors. Cane took the opportunity to return his pistol to his suitcase.

Maris was back soon with her father, Dirk Swart, a stocky tanned, powerfully-built man wearing a faded green smoking jacket. He looked strong enough even in middle age to be a Rugby lock forward.

'What happened?' he asked briefly. 'Is he bad?'

'We don't know how bad – the whole incident is a bit mystifying,' Cane replied. 'We found him at the foot of the figurehead.'

Dirk Swart addressed Maris. 'Not again! I'll start to believe in Alcestis myself if this goes on!'

'Maybe you should have got rid of the wretched thing altogether at the time instead of merely throwing her off *Helder Wacht*,' answered Maris.

Swart shone a flashlight at Bosch. Some blood had started to ooze through the bandages.

'Who cut him up?'

'I'd like to know,' said Cane. 'Those wounds aren't the real trouble – I think it lies at the base of his neck.'

'Jeannette is the one to check,' said Maris' father. 'She's got her gear ready in the hall. Ease him out on to the blanket – gently, gently.'

Together the two men carried the unconscious man into the house. As they crunched across the ochre gravel, Cane, eyeing Maris' slim figure in a mole-coloured corduroy skirt, wondered whether her mother would be the prototype of her slender dark beauty.

She was, in fact, the opposite. Jeannette Swart was fair, tall and large-boned. Her warmth and expansiveness paralleled that of her splendid home – in the hallway's unaccustomed bright light Cane had a first impression of thick carpets, showcases containing coins and sea-things, prints of old wreck scenes, and of dark furniture as mature as fine wine.

Her competent hands stripped the first-aid bandages. 'Nothing much here. What about his neck?'

She removed the bandage and tested the wound with her fingers. 'A stitch or two will fix this. Hardly calls for a doctor.' She asked Cane. 'You agree?'

Cane noted that she, like Maris, gave a hard value to the 'r' sounds in her words – an individual kind of pronunciation which sprang from the isolation of generations which had carved a life from the inhospitable Strandveld and its iron coastline littered with more wrecks than would ever be known exactly.

'I reckon the real trouble isn't the wounds,' volunteered Cane. 'Can you take a look at the base of his neck?'

Jeannette's fingers explored the place Cane indicated. Bosch writhed and groaned.

'That seems to be it – but there's not a mark, not a bruise,' she said in a puzzled voice.

'He's a hospital case,' said Cane.

'For certain,' answered Maris' mother. 'Dirk, give Dr Joubert at the hospital a ring and tell him to expect a casualty. A bad one.'

'What makes you say that?' asked Maris.

'I reckon one of his neck vertebrae is either broken or damaged,' she replied.

'Could it have been caused by a fall?' asked Cane.

Jeannette Swart shook her head. 'It's only an outside chance. He must have hit something – but in that event, there would be a mark or a bruise.'

'Or something hit him,' remarked Cane.

'Why do you say that?' she asked. 'The same evidence would be visible, whatever it was. It would leave a mark.'

Maris outlined their discovery of the injured man. At her mention of the figurehead, Jeannette Swart sucked in her breath in a kind of stifled condemnation.

'This is the second accident involving Alcestis,' she said. 'Anything as serious as this is a police matter. You'll have to report it after you've taken him to hospital. Meanwhile, can you help me while I stitch the throat wound and stop the other bleeding? I can tell you in advance that Maris is no good at it – she'll pass out.'

'I'll distract myself looking at the Birkenhead showcase while you do your worst.'

Dirk Swart returned from the telephone. 'Jeannette, I caught Dr Joubert just as he was leaving the hospital – he wasn't too pleased, being Saturday night.'

'This will keep him out of mischief,' she rejoined.

'Try and find mischief in Bredasdorp on a Saturday night – or any other night,' commented Maris.

Jeannette Swart worked quickly with a needle and gut from her medical case; Cane assisted. Maris stood at the showcase pretending to examine relics which Cane was sure she must have seen scores of times. Above it hung a large painting depicting a wreck scene – red-jacketed soldiers lined up on a canting deck, wild waves, distraught women, life-boats casting off.

When Maris' mother had finished, Dirk Swart asked, 'What is the most comfortable and least risky way we can convey him to hospital – in my station wagon?'

Maris rejoined the group. 'My car's probably softer sprung than your station wagon, Dad. He seemed okay on the back seat coming here.'

'Need my help to hold him?' asked her father.

Jeannette Swart intervened. 'The worrying thing is his breathing. There's nothing we laymen can do about that. You two go off and get him as quickly as you can to Dr Joubert.' She addressed Cane. 'Your plans must have been disrupted. Come back here with Maris after you've finished with Bosch and have something to eat.'

'I'd like that.'

Maris gave her mother a quick glance of appreciation and added, 'It will take an hour or two. We've also got to report to the police.'

'Take it easy in the fog, Maris,' cautioned her father. 'We don't want any more accidents tonight.'

Cane and Dirk Swart carried Bosch, slung again in the blanket, to the car. Jeannette and Dirk Swart watched as it pulled away.

'I like that boy,' remarked Maris' mother.

'He's not a boy – he's a man,' her husband said.

'Man,' she echoed abstractedly. 'So does Maris.'

3

The car containing Cane, Maris, and the injured man drew clear of *Helder Wacht*'s weeping, tree-lined avenue and took the main road to Bredasdorp. Gum trees are as much a feature of the Strandveld as the pellucidly clear days which follow its fogs and storms. The name *Helder Wacht* – 'Clear Watch' – derived from just such days. Then one could see from the homestead beyond the ten kilometre strip of low sandy land to where the great oceans met, and far, far out to sea. Ashore, fields and farm boundaries were demarcated by the tall, branchless trees with their wind-distorted crowns. They gave a Corot-like effect to an otherwise entirely un-French landscape.

This farthest extremity of the Dark Continent has from time immemorial exercised a particular mystique on men's minds. Two millennia before it was even physically discovered it was given a name in anticipation – the Promontorium Prassum. It was the prime objective of the intrepid Portuguese explorers who blazed the sea route to India round it five centuries ago. Ironically, however, the true ultimate point of Africa was so undistinguished in appearance that it was by-passed by its discoverer Bartholomeu Dias, who believed that in the nearby majestic Cape of Good Hope he had discovered the legendary end of Africa. Upon its real extremity, however – the Agulhas Peninsula, which he saw from the deck of his caravel as a low, bleak, sandy, windswept shoreline – he merely bestowed the name of the saint of the day.

For the first few kilometres, Maris and Cane's road cut through marshland – in places a mere twenty-five metres above sea level – and then rose to follow a spine of land which ran like an aquaduct above the swamps and small lakes for the next fifteen kilometres. Cane had a mental picture of their route from his map studies.

He said to Maris. 'Mr Grimmock has given me a free hand to investigate why the project has run down the way it has. The Bosch and Howells incidents seem to me to be only the tip of the iceberg – there must have been other, smaller happenings which didn't percolate through to the top echelons of management. You've been on the spot. What else has taken place?'

'Yes, I've been on the job since the grassroots,' she replied. 'I – and everyone else – liked Howells. He was big and friendly and easy-going, with a laugh you could hear from here to Texas. His vitality and drive were like a shot in the arm. The men would have done anything for him. He accomplished wonders in the early days of the project, getting the machinery transported to the site, setting up things initially, and so on.'

'But he didn't carry it through,' added Cane.

'At first it was all energy and drive and achievement. Then something went sour.'

'What was the reason?'

'I don't know,' she said in a puzzled voice. 'Afterwards they said it was when Howells hit the drugs. Before that, however, all sorts of things occurred.'

'Such as?'

'Things broke that had no right to break. Accidents happened in a way which they never should have. Previously Howells would have swept them aside as mere incidents. Then they got him down. He didn't laugh like he used to. He once was accustomed to go out drinking with the boys – he was a kind of roustabout without a roustabout's crudity. Latterly, however, he only went out with the other Americans.'

'Other Americans?'

'From the observatory.'

'Oh, that.'.

Next door to the drilling site, whose name was *Helderwachtvlei* – Clear Watch Marsh – was an American geomagnetic observatory. Its purpose was to study a major magnetic anomaly which affected radio communication and navigation. This anomaly lay between the Cape, Antarctica and Rio de Janeiro. The name Agulhas itself (meaning compass needle) owed its origin to the same magnetic phenomenon, which had first been observed by the earliest Portuguese navigators.

The observatory had been financed by Fordhamn University, in the USA, and incorporated a similar previous station belonging to the South African authorities. This had operated for many years at another venue nearby, the holiday resort of Hermanus, west of Agulhas. In addition to geomagnetism, the American observatory, named Soutbos (Salt Bush) was a tracking station for space probes fired both by the Americans and other countries to trace the orbit of Halley's Comet from the time it was first sighted in 1983, past the earth in 1986, and subsequently to the limits of its orbit in the solar system.

'Howells lived alone on the site – after the Alcestis affair, it was said he was affected by the loneliness,' she went on.

'I don't buy the Accursed Figurehead story,' retorted Cane bluntly. 'I think the legend of her influence – alleged influence – over men is being manipulated by someone.'

'I'd go along with you – if it weren't for Alcestis' track record. I've told you the story of the sailor who was washed ashore with her. Another one of her early admirers kept her in his bedroom for years and finally shot himself in front of her.'

'Maris,' went on Cane in the same uncompromising tone, 'I know the Strandveld is special to you. To me it has the same sort of aura as the west of Ireland – misty, spooky, lending itself to an extra-sensory build-up. Leprechauns, all that sort of . . .'

'Bull?'

'Maybe,' he replied. 'In any event, lonely, frustrated men become fixated. They transfer their fixations to a beautiful image near at hand – in this case, Alcestis. And she *is* beautiful, I admit. She provides a kind of focus for their problems. You told me yourself that your father was forced to get rid of her.'

'That wasn't burning desire but burning religious zeal.' Maris was amused at Cane's expression. 'Most of *Helder Wacht*'s farm hands come traditionally from a village nearby called Elim. The place was established by puritan missionaries. The inhabitants all have deep religious convictions. Dad bowed to their feelings and threw out Alcestis. Where the drilling site now is once belonged to us.'

'I'm surprised to hear that *Helder Wacht* land was ever sold.'

'It's another story,' she said briefly, unwilling to elaborate.

'Those unexplained accidents,' he prompted her.

'I was here when the men started work on the project by routing and dumping for the shaft collar,' Maris explained. 'Everything went fine, as if whoever intended us ill was watching and biding his time . . .'

'Aren't you being a little fanciful?' interrupted Cane. 'The preliminary phase of shaft sinking is always fairly simple.'

'We had more men then than now on the job,' went on Maris. 'About sixty. Now there are about twenty-five left.'

'Left?'

'Left,' she repeated. 'Morale in the early days was high. Howells was everywhere. Bosch was also in his element – he and his workmate Jan Stander were like a couple of long-distance runners getting into their stride for another record.'

'Two kilometres deep at first, then more to follow. My time schedule is two years.'

'Do you intend to go as deep as that?'

'That's the estimated depth of the "hot" dome of slightly radio-active granite we want to employ for the water-heating process,' Cane answered.

Maris went on. 'The men were just starting the process of forcing liquid cement through the initial boreholes for sealing cracks and water-bearing faults when one of the feeds broke. That gave the first serious casualty.'

'Hell's delight!' exclaimed Cane. 'At a pressure of six thousand pounds per square inch!'

'It blew off one man's hand at the wrist,' Maris shuddered. 'I imagine I can still hear his screams.'

'It shouldn't ever have happened,' said Cane.

'But it did,' Maris continued. 'No one at that stage thought it was more than an accident, or that the project was jinxed . . .'

'Is that what they say?'

'You'll find out for yourself. The men were a little shocked, and Howells went for the cause like a beaver. I typed his report to the authorities. He reckoned the gear had been tampered with.'

'Deliberately? By whom?'

'If Howells suspected anyone specific, he never said. But it was only when there were the subsequent "accidents" that he began to be a very, very worried man.'

'Did he report them to management in Cape Town – Mr Renshaw?'

'Yes, of course. Mr Renshaw is a difficult man – I've never met him, although we've spoken many times on the phone. I suspect that Mr Grimmock leans on him, and he leans harder on those beneath him.'

'The man on the site isn't necessarily under Renshaw, in that sense,' replied Cane a little off-handedly.

'Sorry, I put it badly,' said Maris. 'I know the chain of command. But Renshaw as management chief holds the purse-strings.'

'Tell me more about the "accidents",' Cane said.

'Teething troubles.'

'That's a nice euphemism.'

'The next bad happening was when the cable on the big construction crane slipped when it was hoisting a kibble . . .'

'For crying out loud!' exclaimed Cane.

A kibble was a huge steel bucket used for bringing up rock from the excavation and for conveying men and equipment below the surface.

'The kibble dropped about seven metres to the bottom of the excavation – how no one was killed, I don't know, because the blasting team was there, about to start work. Maybe that is what saved them – they were working at the sidewall when the kibble struck. A couple were injured by flying rock, nothing serious. Everyone – Howells I think most of all – was badly shocked.'

'Things like that simply don't happen on a well organised job!' exclaimed Cane.

'There was a post-accident check on the crane, of course,' went on Maris. 'It was something to do with the clutch plate, which had been interfered with. It failed when it took the kibble's load.'

'What about security?' demanded Cane.

'I told you, in the beginning there was a carefree atmosphere about *Helderwachtvlei*,' said Maris. 'It's a very remote place. No one believed that there would be attempts to sabotage the machinery.'

'Sabotage?' echoed Cane. 'That is a very strong word, Maris.'

'Right from the start the team never liked the idea of sleeping overnight at the drilling site – they've always commuted from Bredasdorp. After the crane business, Howells couldn't prevail upon them to change their minds. So he took up residence himself – alone. After that, things really started to go downhill. He was a changed man. Something preyed on his mind. You know how he finished up.'

'At Alcestis' feet.'

'Do you know where he is now?' asked Maris. 'The last I heard was that he had been shipped back to the United States.'

'To an institution – exactly where, I don't know,' replied Cane.

'Look – there are the lights of Bredasdorp,' interjected Maris.

They had reached the junction of a main road from the west about ten kilometres from Bredasdorp. From a slight elevation Cane could see the town's lights.

'How is Bosch?' asked Maris.

'No change that I can detect.'

They drove into the town, its outskirts guarded by more of *Helder Wacht*'s crowned gum trees, and on through the main street, where there were a couple of lighted hotels and filling stations. A handful of strollers, clearly under the influence of Saturday night, were the only signs of life.

Maris said deprecatingly. 'That's the way our metropolis is – the end of Africa, the end of the world. Nobody has ever heard about it.'

Cane offered no comment. The place looked unwelcoming and dour. He was grateful to be returning to *Helder Wacht* for dinner.

As if reading his thoughts, Maris said. 'I don't know what arrangements Bosch had made about your accommodation – one of the hotels, I suppose. Why not stay at *Helder Wacht* for the weekend until you can get yourself sorted out?'

She wasn't looking at him but pretending to concentrate on the approach to Bredasdorp's single set of traffic lights.

He replied lightly, and she appreciated his letting her out of her shyness at taking the initiative by making the invitation. 'That means you can't have any excuses for being late on Monday – not with the boss on your doorstep.'

'You'll come then?'

He gestured at the unfriendly frontages. 'It'll be a double pleasure, Maris.'

For a brief moment, the constellation of sinister forces which surrounded the drilling project seemed far away. Then they were at the hospital. Dr Joubert, a whitecoated young man, was waiting for them at the casualty entrance with two stretcher-bearers.

'Not another casualty from the drilling project!' he exclaimed. 'You're the new man in charge, aren't you?' he asked Cane.

'Hallam Cane.'

'Take my advice and get rid of that figurehead before anything happens to you too,' remarked the doctor half-jokingly.

He opened the rear door and glanced at Bosch. His easy friendliness took a nosedive into professional rectitude.

'We suspect something to do with his neck,' said Maris.

Dr Joubert investigated Bosch's head cursorily, then said briefly to the stretchermen. 'Get him out gently – easily, easily!'

'How bad is he?' asked Cane.

'It is impossible to say before I have made a thorough examination.'

'We have to go and report to the police – may we come back afterwards?' Maris asked. 'Will that give you time enough to form some opinion?'

'Depends. I don't like the look of him at first glance.'

The constable on duty alone at the police station – only a couple of minutes' drive from the hospital – seemed at first more interested in hearing a radio commentary on the afternoon's major Rugby match in Cape Town than in an accident report. Then Maris explained in Afrikaans the reason for their visit. He gave a whistle and said formally that Bosch would have to be examined by the district surgeon. When Maris went on to say that Bosch was already in hospital – Dr Joubert doubled as police doctor – the man said that a policeman would be sent to the site in due course to take statements.

When they returned to the hospital, Dr Joubert, terse and remote, emerged from an anteroom of the operating theatre wearing surgical gear.

'He's bad – very bad,' he said. 'I can't even offer a prognosis until I've checked him further. Telephone me in the morning.'

4

'Maris – it means, "of the sea". I was given her name. No one ever knew who she was.'

Back from leaving Bosch in hospital at Bredasdorp, Cane and Maris stood after dinner in the spacious hallway at *Helder*

Wacht. Maris was indicating the striking wreck picture which Cane had noted previously. The display cabinet below it contained a variety of sea relics – Spanish pieces-of-eight, ducatoons, East India Company gold mohurs whose metal remained untarnished even after years of immersion in the sea. There was also a miscellany of other objects recovered from Agulhas wrecks, from navigator's brass dividers to a battered old pay chest in which money and sea-bottom conglomerate had been fused and indistinguishable from one another.

Maris' parents made up a foursome under the portrait. They all held long-stemmed wine glasses, which they had brought from the great old yellowwood table next door where they had had dinner. The noble ruby-red wine, named Rubicon, was a gift to Dirk Swart from a master Cape winemaker named Nico Myburgh who had an estate in the Strandveld as well as his ancestral home in the winelands of the Western Cape.

Cane felt relaxed by the gracious elegance of *Helder Wacht* – its dark old furniture, a wine cabinet salvaged from a wreck, ship's carbide lamps made of polished bronze and copper which had been converted to electricity, and on every hand fine woodwork which seemed to have absorbed the centuries.

Maris had surprised him on the drive home by telling him that, apart from her job as secretary/dogsbody to the geo-thermal project, she was a qualified architect. However, she practised only part-time for an organization named the Strandveld Restoration Trust. Its function was to renovate to their original state the architectural showpieces of the region. He could appreciate, from the elegance of *Helder Wacht*, where Maris' love of old things had originated.

Now Maris' dark, almost Spanish beauty was offset by a severely-cut long white-sleeved blouse, long black skirt and gold slippers. There was no doubt about her blood-line link to the young woman in an old-fashioned dress in a portrait flanking the wreck scene.

'What is the connection between her and that wreck?'

Maris' smile illuminated a face which was thoughtful – almost withdrawn at times, in repose – and made her green eyes full of light.

'It's a very famous wreck – it's the *Birkenhead*.'

'Sorry,' replied Cane. 'My history doesn't run to it.'

'Why should it – it happened a very long time ago,' interjected Dirk Swart. 'We Strandvelders think the world begins and ends on our doorstep.'

'But the ship was British, like he is,' exclaimed Jeannette Swart.

'Give the man a chance!' smiled Maris.

In 1852 the troopship *Birkenhead*, carrying nearly five hundred British soldiers to reinforce garrisons in the Eastern Cape against Black incursions, as well as women and children, struck a submerged rock about a kilometre off a notorious promontory some seventy-five kilometres from *Helder Wacht* in the direction of Cape Town. The place was aptly named Danger Point. The tragedy occurred in the early hours of the morning in a calm sea. There were about six hundred and thirty-eight people on board and of these a mere one hundred and eighty-four survived. Only three small boats got away from the doomed ship; they carried mainly women and children.

As the vessel went down under their feet, the regiments lined up in formation on deck; their calm courage in never breaking rank as the water rose passed into legend. Queen Victoria honoured the *Birkenhead* heroes; the German Kaiser Wilhelm is said to have quoted their example to his troops as the supreme exhibition of courage.

Dirk Swart took up the story: 'The news of the *Birkenhead*'s sinking spread through the Strandveld like wildfire next day. All the farmers rushed to the beach to try and help. My great-grandfather, who was also named Dirk, assisted in burying some of the bodies. Look' – he indicated the contents of the relics cabinet – 'that watch and some of those coins came from the drowned. Those silver spoons, too – you can tell they were British government property from the broad arrow insignia on them.'

'A broad arrow somehow makes me think of convicts,' said Cane.

'You're right,' replied Maris' father. 'But it was also a general kind of government hallmark in the old days.'

'You've told me about the ship, but you haven't told me about the girl in the painting,' observed Cane.

'It's for Maris to tell – seeing she has her name,' said Maris' mother.

'As Dad said, all next day after the wreck Dirk Swart helped bury casualties and retrieve flotsam. Then, the following night, Dirk and his wife Alma camped on the beach.

'During the night Alma woke her husband to say she could hear a child crying. They searched in the dark, but found nothing. When the sound persisted at intervals, they almost came to believe they were hearing a ghost. At daybreak they combed the beach, but there was no living being.

'Then Dirk Swart spotted a copper vessel lodged in the rocks. An occasional wave broke over it. It was, in fact, one of the troopship's big mess containers for food. The crying was coming from inside it!

'The container was sealed watertight by means of sliding covers. Dirk and Alma prised them open. To their astonishment, inside they found an infant girl, warmly dressed, wrapped in a blanket. There was nothing to identify her.'

'Think of that poor mother!' exclaimed Jeannette. 'The agony of wrapping up your child to die!'

Maris went to her mother and put her arm round her shoulders.

'Perhaps the father was one of the soldiers – who knows?' said Maris' father. 'Perhaps the parents prepared the baby's sea-cradle together – and then went down with the ship.'

'Alma and Dirk had two children of their own,' Maris continued. 'They brought the infant back to *Helder Wacht* after notifying an officer survivor. Of course, all communications were in chaos. Later, the Swarts did everything they could through the Royal Navy and the authorities in Cape Town to try and establish the child's parentage. All their enquiries failed to reveal who the sea-waif was. She grew up as one of the family, and finally married a Swart.' She gestured towards the portrait. 'They named her Maris – of the sea. It's been a family name ever since.'

Maris' father broke the emotion the story had generated. 'I breed sheep and every so often one finds that the characteristics of one fine animal emerge later in the blood line. I say that every now and again nature throws up a Swart girl who looks like the original Maris.'

Maris laughed and looked embarrassed, especially when Cane raised his glass and said. 'I'll drink to that.'

Then Maris added her own toast. 'Here's to the original stranger from the sea.'

'What we need is more wine,' said Maris' father.

They adjourned to a sitting-room whose ceiling beams were teak from a wrecked windjammer. There was also a sumptuous tapestry from China on a wall, recovered from some forgotten East Indiaman.

Dirk Swart poured fresh wine into their glasses and raised his.

'I drink to the damnation of the present operators at Birkenhead Rock.'

5

'Operators – what sort of operators deserve damnation?' exclaimed Cane.

Before anyone could speak, Jeannette Swart broke in. 'I can't go along with a toast like that. Too much life has been lost at Birkenhead Rock already – even if they are Russians.'

'Russians – in South Africa – you must be joking!' Cane said incredulously.

However, Dirk Swart was not joking. A team of four Russian divers was camped near the site of Birkenhead Rock at a cove named Birkenhead Bungalows with the reluctant approval of, and under stringent safeguards by, the South

African Government. Head of the team was Vladimir Yasa-kov, a Soviet representative on the International War Graves Commission.

The reason for the Soviet operation was to protect the remains of anti-Czarist rebel sailors who were drowned in a Russian fleet tender which sank in 1905 after striking the same rock as the *Birkenhead* had done half a century before. This vessel, named the *Kamchatka*, was part of a Russian fleet of warships which was later annihilated by the Japanese at the great Battle of Tsu-Shima, off Japan, in May 1905.

The thirty thousand kilometre voyage of the Russian fleet from the Baltic to the Far East was dogged by misfortune and ended in tragedy. It became known in history as 'The Voyage of the Damned'. Totalling more than one hundred ships, the fleet was in fact a collection of relics, rusting, decrepit and top-heavy, manned mainly by a rag-tag bunch of untrained and undisciplined peasantry and officered by effete aristo-crats. In the course of the six-months' voyage, a number of mutineers were shot on orders from the commander-in-chief, Admiral Rozhestvenski.

When the cumbersome fleet reached the Mediterranean on its outward voyage, Admiral Rozhestvenski divided it into two squadrons, despatching the older and smaller ships via the Suez Canal while he himself took the newer vessels round the Cape of Good Hope. The admiral guessed – rightly – that the older ships would not survive the wild seas of the Cape of Storms. The two sections of the battle fleet were to rendez-vous at Madagascar.

One Russian vessel did not survive the Cape. She was the *Kamchatka*. She was not a fighting unit but a fleet main-tenance and repair ship. In addition, the *Kamchatka* was a floating prison for scores of revolutionary anti-Czarist ele-ments, dissidents and mutineers who surfaced during the long voyage. After coaling his fleet at Luderitz, in Namibia, Admiral Rozhestvenski attempted to round the Cape. He ran into one of its notorious gales and the *Kamchatka*, after first losing its way, struck Birkenhead Rock. She sank with all hands.

The wreck of the *Kamchatka* had, of course, been located long previously (along with remains of the *Birkenhead*) by South African skin-divers. The ship lay in relatively shallow water – about thirty-five metres – but due to the fact that she carried nothing of value and that diving in the vicinity of Danger Point was extremely dangerous due to unpredictable underwater currents and sets, the wreck was not considered worth further investigation. There were, in fact, scores of other wrecks round the Agulhas Peninsula which offered far better rewards.

Cane's interest and surprise grew as Dirk Swart continued.

'The Russians explained that their object was to protect and prevent desecration of a war grave. . . .'

'A war grave!' echoed Cane.

'None of us in the Strandveld was ever aware that the *Kamchatka* was a war grave,' replied Maris' father. 'The contents of the wreck and its bodies were, the Reds said, protected by protocol in the same way as those of the World War II British cruiser *HMS Edinburgh* – you remember all the publicity there was a few years ago about salvaging her gold from the Barents Sea.'

'The Russians referred to the *Kamchatka* dead as "the remains of martyrs of the 1905 anti-Czarist rebellion",' interjected Maris ironically.

'Anticipating the Russian Revolution proper by more than ten years,' added Cane.

'Anti-Czarist martyrs my foot,' remarked Jeannette Swart. 'Why suddenly start to take an interest in skeletons which have been there for over threequarters of a century? I say there is something more behind it than that.'

'There certainly is,' said Maris' father. 'Gold. Golden sovereigns. The Russians said so themselves.'

'I don't believe that either,' answered Maris' mother heatedly. 'Whoever allows twenty five million dollars in golden sovereigns to lie around for all those years and make no attempt to recover them? That yarn doesn't wash with me, I'm afraid.'

Cane listened to the exchange between Maris' parents and said. 'I'm not with you. Where did the *Kamchatka*'s treasure come from?'

'If I sound like a book, it's only because I'm quoting the media – so much has been written and broadcast recently about the *Kamchatka*,' said Dirk Swart. 'Naturally, I am more than interested, being on the spot.'

'That goes for the entire Strandveld,' added Jeannette Swart. 'We know our wrecks and I say . . .'

'Just a moment, my dear, until I've told Hal here what the treasure story is.'

'Not is, but said to be,' added Maris' mother tightly.

Dirk Swart grinned at his wife's vehemence. 'As you now know, the Russian fleet was divided into two squadrons. The section that sailed via Suez contained an old armoured cruiser of eight thousand five hundred tons named the *Admiral Nakhimov* which was the flagship of the cruiser division. . . .'

'Hold on,' said Cane. 'I thought you said that only the ships that wouldn't have made it round the Cape went via Suez. How does that tie in with an old vessel being a flagship?'

'It illustrates how rotten the entire fleet was, that's all,' continued Dirk Swart. 'For reasons we will never know, the Czar selected this obsolete warship, the *Nakhimov*, as a treasure ship.'

'Treasure ship?'

'It has been well known for decades that the Czar shipped in the *Nakhimov* fifty million dollars in English golden sovereigns to pay his Far Eastern fleet. She also carried some platinum ingots for the same purpose.'

'How are these details so well known? – the Russians don't usually publicise anything, let alone treasure news. Look at the fuss they made about the gold aboard *HMS Edinburgh*,' said Cane.

'You may well ask,' said Dirk Swart, sipping his wine. 'The *Nakhimov* was torpedoed in the Battle of Tsu-Shima and was scuttled about eight kilometres off the island of

Tsu-Shima itself. The salvage operation was beyond the technical skill of either the Russians or the Japanese until recently, when new techniques made it possible. The Japanese were first off the mark.

'When the Japs succeeded in raising the first bar of platinum from the wreck, a major diplomatic row erupted between Russia and Japan. The Soviet claimed that the treasure was theirs – Japan retaliated by saying that they could have the treasure in return for four islands in the Kuril chain which had been grabbed by Russia.'

'I hope this shows you how possessively we Strandvelders regard our wrecks,' Jeannette Swart said. 'They're part of our lives. They belong to us, just as the oil does that the Russians have stolen.'

Cane looked from Maris' mother to her father in further puzzlement. 'Oil?'

'Have some more wine,' Dirk Swart said. 'Russian oil!' he muttered. 'Russian gold!' Having filled Cane's glass, he said, 'Listen!'

6

About two and a half years before, the Russians had electrified the world – South Africa in particular – with an announcement that a Soviet drilling rig had made a major ocean-bed gas strike on the continental shelf off Cape Agulhas. This shelf was known as the Agulhas Bank. It was a potential oil-bearing area which had been systematically explored at great cost for about twenty years by South Africa. During this time several promising strikes had been made, notably of natural gas.

The South African explorations had taken place relatively close to the land, whereas the Soviet strike was no less than three hundred and thirty kilometres offshore. This distance represented the extreme outer edge of the continental shelf, well beyond the limits of South African exploration.

The gas strike created an international furore, especially when the Soviet Union announced its intention to establish a floating gas liquefying plant, or 'gas atoll', at the site of the strike. Liquefied gas, transported by supertanker of special design, would be supplied mainly to Red surrogates in Africa, principally those Marxist states in southern Africa such as Mozambique, Angola, Tanzania and others.

South Africa immediately invoked the controversial United Nations Law of the Sea Treaty. The treaty defined and made specific provisions regarding the continental shelf in general and established an International Seabed Authority to govern the harvesting of ocean minerals.

The most important aspect of the treaty as far as the Soviet offshore gas strike was concerned was that it laid down an exclusive economic zone in which the coastal state – in this case South Africa – had the exclusive right to manage the resources of the sea. The limit of this zone was set at three hundred and twenty two kilometres offshore.

Although the Law of the Sea Treaty had been signed by one hundred and seventeen nations, the most notable exception from its signatories had been the United States. The Soviet Union was among the signatories; South Africa was not.

The United States had refused to sign the treaty on the grounds that it would place control of seabed mineral exploration in the hands of a coalition of Third World countries which, it feared, would try and use such control for political purposes.

American interests had, and were, investing large sums in deep-sea mining technology and considered the treaty obligations to share in mining revenues particularly unfair to these companies.

In the Agulhas strike, the United States' worst fears were realised. Neither South Africa nor the USA were slow to point out that it seemed more than coincidence that the strike was merely a few kilometres beyond the limit of three hundred and twenty two kilometres laid down by the Law of the Sea Treaty. South Africa also argued that she in any event had the exclusive 'pioneer' rights to any oil or gas.

The Soviet Union, backed by all Third World countries, categorically rejected the South African claims and protests and announced its decision to go ahead with establishing the floating gas atoll.

The United States, which regarded the gas strike as a test case, backed South Africa's claims.

South Africa then took her case against the Soviet Union to the World Court. Feeling not only ran high in the two parties directly involved, but the confrontation led to a polarization internationally between West and East.

The World Court, whose membership was heavily loaded by Third World countries, ruled in favour of the Soviet Union and gave Russia the go-ahead to proceed. Relations between the Soviet Union and South Africa, which had been hostile for many decades, deteriorated still further. South Africa banned all communication between the mainland and the gas atoll as well as refusing all servicing facilities.

Russia retaliated by introducing naval patrols; South Africa in return declared a 'no-go' zone of one hundred and fifty kilometres offshore.

The potentially explosive situation was defused from a most unexpected quarter – Russia itself. The Kremlin announced that in regard to Japanese attempts to salvage the fifty million dollars treasure from the *Admiral Nakhimov*, further searches had been made of records at Kronstadt, the port from which Admiral Rozhestvenski had sailed. These had revealed that the Czar's treasure had, in fact, not been shipped in its entirety – as had been generally accepted – in the *Nakhimov*. The gold had been divided, half being conveyed by the *Kamchatka*. This had been done, it was stated, for safety's sake so that half would go via Suez and the other half via the Cape.

The Soviet Union made a formal approach to South Africa via the neutral state of Switzerland with a proposition which, it was stated, would avoid the kind of diplomatic row which had blown up between Russia and Japan over the *Nakhimov*'s treasure. The Russians proposed that they should be allowed to salvage the *Kamchatka*'s gold on the basis of a

50/50 split with South Africa. The only condition was that any skeletons of prisoners found in the *Kamchatka* should be treated with due respect since they were 'the remains of martyrs of the 1905 anti-Czarist rebellion'.

South Africa was extremely wary of the proposal. The United States, however, saw the offer as a means of reducing tension on the vital Cape Sea Route (round which sixty per cent of the West's oil was shipped from the Middle East) and brought behind-the-scenes pressure to bear on South Africa.

Finally, South Africa agreed to allow ashore a small team of four Russian skin-divers to explore the *Kamchatka* wreck in order to produce concrete evidence of the Russian gold. The South Africans also laid down a strict time limit of one month for the operation; the team would be subject to continual police supervision; any relics recovered had to be surrendered to the resident police officer. No communication – except through South African Navy channels – would be allowed with the gas atoll.

The Russians took as their precedent for treating the *Kamchatka* as a war grave the British War Office's view of *HMS Edinburgh* – for many years it had refused permission to salvage the cruiser's gold. Finally the ban had been lifted: the Soviet Union was willing to do this in regard to the *Kamchatka*.

'Have the Russian divers found anything?' asked Cane.

'Not yet,' replied Dirk Swart. 'They've been ashore for only about a fortnight.'

'We've got our own private eye on the spot,' commented Jeannette Swart. 'The policeman guarding the diving team is a friend of Maris' from Bredasdorp – Captain Cassie Wessels.'

'He came here for a drink last week,' said Maris. 'He described the job as the most boring he'd ever done. The Russians aren't friendly – and only two of them speak English.'

'I was in America when the news of the gas strike came through,' said Cane. 'I was specially interested because I had some early experience of marine oil drilling with the South African rigs.'

'So you're not a stranger here,' exclaimed Maris, obviously pleased.

'I never visited the Strandveld – my time was spent mainly at sea.'

'What was your opinion of the gas strike?' asked Maris.

'The South Africans believed that if there were any marine oil or gas, it would be much closer to the land. Scientifically, it is remarkable to find gas where the Russians did – it's beyond the boundaries of the continental shelf itself, in very deep water called the Agulhas Basin.'

'I always said there was something very fishy about it,' remarked Jeannette Swart.

'Come, Mum – they *found* gas – that's the proof of the pudding,' said Maris.

'Marine oil is a gamble,' went on Cane cautiously. 'You can never tell in advance what you will or you won't find – or where. Take the North Sea, for example.'

'You've been there too?' asked Maris.

Cane laughed at her interest. 'It's not at all romantic. Yes, my last job before I went ashore for the Cornish geothermal project was on a production platform in the Maureen field off Aberdeen. It was the newest of its kind and cost thirteen hundred million dollars.'

Maris' father cocked an ear as a gust of wind rattled *Helder Wacht*'s old-fashioned wooden window frames. 'What I'm saying is nothing personal – we Strandvelders are a conservative lot, but the world seems to be crowding in upon us – first the American observatory with all its fancy radar dishes, antennae, telescopes . . .'

'And security,' added Jeannette. 'Armed guards, and electric fences . . .'

'They even obtained some of my land,' Dirk Swart went on. 'Next came the gas atoll and the Russians. Now . . .' he glanced at Cane, uncertain how diplomatically to voice his disapproval.

'What Dad is trying to say is that he doesn't fancy a power station either on his doorstep,' smiled Maris. 'Nor do any of us who love the Strandveld and its architectural treasures.

We don't want it to change into something we can't control.'

Cane deliberately sidetracked the conversation. 'Like the Accursed Figurehead's attraction for men,' he said lightly.

They all laughed, and Jeannette Swart said. 'We prefer to call her Alcestis. That was her ship.'

'It sounds somewhat classical,' observed Cane.

'You're right,' answered Maris. 'Alcestis was a girl in a Greek myth. She died for love, and the gods brought her back to life because of her sacrifice.'

That wasn't the way Cane saw Alcestis in his dream later that night. He was drowning, trying frantically to pluck himself free of redcoat, bandolier and heavy boots like those worn by the soldiers in the Birkenhead picture. Alcestis was swimming alongside him, one exquisite breast bare, taunting him to shed his uniform and make love to her. . . .

He awoke sweating, and listened to the gale rattling the windows, and aware of the faint stirring, like disembodied ghosts, of the bedroom's long mohair curtains.

What Cane could not hear, however, was the passage of coded radio signals pulsing through the fog over his head. They were not ordinary radio signals. Their designation was top secret. They were being transmitted by a unique system which even the world's finest code-masters could not crack. It was known as frequency-hopping – a system which hopped automatically from one frequency to another every split second, making it impossible to tune in to the transmissions.

Somewhere out in the fog, too, other men attempting to monitor the unmonitorable signals cursed as they eluded them with the guile of a surface-hugging Exocet missile. The only way to pinpoint the signals would be by leg-work done by a human. That man was already busy with his mission.

Somewhere else in the fog, too, the same man listened with satisfaction to the gale. It presaged fog again the next day. He laid out his clothes for the sortie – dark pants, sneakers, a body-hugging black shirt, nothing on which an opponent could get a grip. He added to the pile a balaclava to mask his features, and, finally, a pair of wire-cutters and a knife.

7

Fog wreathed the base of the red-and-white tower of the one-time Seventh Wonder of the World like jet contrails; higher up, it obscured the 'glasshouse' containing the great light which for more than a century had warned ships to stay clear of the sea graveyard which is Cape Agulhas. Here, Africa's land ran out; there was only ocean to the South Pole.

Hallam Cane and Maris were viewing the old lighthouse situated on Cape Agulhas. A long spit from its summit would take it clear of Africa and finish, on the right, in the Atlantic or, on the left, in the Indian Ocean. The lighthouse was regarded by Victorians as one of the wonders of their age: it was launched with champagne and named eulogistically the Pharos of the South after the world's first-ever lighthouse on the Mediterranean end of the Dark Continent. It was now out of service, but was preserved as one of the Strandveld's most valued monuments.

This made it special to Maris. It was inevitable that, with her love of historic architecture, the subject of the lighthouse should have arisen the previous night. She and Cane had been housebound by fog for the first part of Sunday morning. When it had lifted partially, Maris had suggested that they drive the twenty kilometres from *Helder Wacht* to the famous structure.

Cane had agreed readily; two telephone calls he had made that morning had left an unpleasant aftertaste. The first had been about Bosch to Dr Joubert at the hospital. The doctor had been curtly professional, clearly worried. Bosch was still unconscious; he suspected brain damage. Dr Joubert had said that since the nature of Bosch's wounds made the case a police affair, he could not discuss them. He had told Cane briefly to come and see him next day.

Cane's second call was to Clive Renshaw, the geothermal project's management chief in Cape Town, to report on Bosch. Renshaw, a successful businessman who sported an overweight belly and tight, tweezered mouth which absorbed gin and regurgitated venom, had been intercepted by Cane's call on his way to Sunday golf. He and Cane had been antagonistic towards one another ever since their first meeting.

Cane's news gave him a chance to pull rank. 'For Pete's sake, Cane – *another* accident!' he had exploded. 'I thought we were getting in you a new man who would put a stop to these blasted so-called accidents! Your outfit is losing money hand over fist, Cane. You won't last long if this sort of thing goes on!'

Cane had pointed out that he had found Bosch immediately on his arrival to take up the job, but Renshaw had cut the conversation short by telling him to telephone the next day when he had a *full* report on Bosch.

Maris' suggestion that they should visit the famous old lighthouse offset Cane's cares. Maris had a quality of shared enthusiasm to which he responded; he scrapped his original idea of making Sunday a working day by going to the drilling site, arguing rightly that the thick fog over the marshlands would make it useless anyway. He had told her briefly about Dr Joubert and left Renshaw's abrasiveness to scrape away inside himself only. It was, after all, his responsibility as boss, he reminded himself.

Now, at the lighthouse, Maris stopped the car: their onward road was blocked by a high fence.

'Security!' exclaimed Cane in surprise. 'What security does a disused lighthouse need?'

'The lighthouse is a kind of adjunct to the American observatory,' Maris replied.

'How is that?'

'The lighthouse is the tallest structure in these parts and the scientists need height for their observations. The observatory site is only about twenty-five metres above sea-level,' she explained. 'Still, I don't like to see such a beautiful old place used for such a purpose.'

The lighthouse tower formed the centrepiece of a complex which included two smaller towers. At its base was a solid building with a sharply-pitched roof. A spine of brickwork topped it. Between the security fence and the lighthouse the ground was rough, rocky, and covered in wind-trimmed aromatic heaths and heathers. A sentry-box guarded the road where it went through the fence.

'We'll be able to see the glasshouse on top in a moment – the fog's starting to clear,' said Maris.

They both looked up; Cane exclaimed, 'Maris, look! Quick!'

A man in figure-hugging black pants and sweat-shirt, wearing a balaclava to hide his features, dived through one of the glasshouse's sliding panels. He fell awkwardly on to a narrow ledge which divided the metal-and-glass 'birdcage' from the brickwork tower. But he was up again in an instant, and scrambled over a wire railing encircling the summit.

'He's going to jump – he'll kill himself!' exclaimed Maris. But he wasn't. He grabbed a thin getaway rope which stretched down to the roof's brickwork spine.

Guards materialized in the glasshouse proper, casting about for the escaper. Where he was, however, was out of their sight. He went down the rope hand-over-hand like a sailor, reached the brickwork, sprinted along it. The guards spotted him, but before they could use their carbines, he reached one of the two smaller towers. He used it as a shield by grasping a lightning conductor on its blind side and sliding down it like a circus acrobat.

The guards stood poised, weapons ready to shoot when the escaper emerged to view on the ground. From his enclosed sentry-box, the gate guard was unsighted for the drama being enacted.

Luck was with the masked man. As he hit ground level, the fog clamped down again over the glasshouse. The marksmen were blind.

The escaper started at a running crouch for the security fence.

An unconsidered reflex threw Cane out of the car – he had

spotted a couple of cut bottom strands of the wire. He sprinted for the gap.

Cane reached it first, by a fraction of a second. A shot crashed out from the glasshouse – the swirl of fog had passed – and it whanged off a rock a pace from Cane's face. It was good shooting – too good.

Cane came between the man and his escape route. The knife he held had its tip advanced so that it pointed at an angle at the sky. He rocketed through the gap in the wire. His stiff-arm punch caught Cane like a hydraulic ram in the back. A second blow chilled him the length of his spine. Cane side-and-backstepped. The point of the knife raked the air where a split second before his eyes had been. It only scored the bridge of his nose.

The faceless man was off-balance: Cane got a half-nelson on him. He tried for a full nelson or a Boston Crab. They rolled over on the ground. The man swung his right knife-hand at Cane, but he leaned backwards and let it pass. His left fist followed, catching Cane on the side of the neck. The wheeling lighthouse tower and its uncertain wreath of fog became a blurred flood of light.

Cane broke away and threw a looping armlock round the knifehand. The masked man was strong, very strong. On his knees, he dragged Cane across the rough ground, but he retained his hold. He surrendered the knife. This gave him new power with the hand. Cane rolled sideways, but he kicked him in the back. He then lifted Cane by brute strength. Cane switched his grip, transferred it to the back of the man's neck. The balaclava moved slightly askew, but not enough to make out his features.

The man raked Cane's eyes with a five-finger Liverpool Kiqq. Cane freed him as blood from the ripped nose-slash blinded him. Cane went into a kneeling stance. A fist exploded against the base of his neck. The force of it sent him forwards and upwards, his senses trying to get a focus on the wobbling sky and gyrating lighthouse. Another blow fell from behind. The tiny heather bells of the bush he fell into looked as if he were seeing them through greasy water. He felt steel hands take hold of his head; perhaps he was out before they cracked it against a stone.

Cane jerked back to consciousness unwillingly. He thought the crash of the sentry's gun was another sickening overhander targeted against his head. The back of his neck felt as if it had been palpated by a bulldozer. The air was full of American oaths.

Cane hauled himself to his knees, like a boxer trying to beat the mandatory count. He couldn't get further. He fell on his face; Maris caught him as he hit ground.

He heard an authoritative shout. 'Hold your fire, you stupid sonofabitch! This is a public road – do you want to kill someone? The game's over and the ref's gone home! Off your asses and get after him – all of you! Burn the breeze!'

Another voice answered. 'We ain't got a snowball's chance, cap. We'll never find him in the fog.'

'Hold everything – silence all!' snapped the first voice.

Cane thought the distant engine sound was blood whirring in his brain.

'That's him, getting clear in his auto!' rapped out the first voice. 'After him!'

Cane, with Maris' help, managed to get to his knees. He wasn't sure which was real fog or brain fog. There were pink strings in front of his eyes. Blood.

'Do something for him!' cried out Maris. 'He's hurt – he's badly hurt!'

Cane was aware of uniformed trousers at eye-level and the captain's authoritative voice. 'You deserve a Purple Heart, fellah! We sure appreciate your trying to stop him when we yelled.'

The Purple Heart seemed redundant; he was unaware of having responded to an American call when he leapt out of the car. It all seemed to have happened long ago; in real time, it couldn't have been more than minutes.

'That guy in the mask sure was a bumpman,' the voice went on. 'I wish you'd been able to hold him.'

Cane raised his eyes to the speaker. There was a pink screen between them and him.

'He's blind!' burst out Maris. 'He's blind – he can't see!'

Cane shook his head. The exercise cleared his vision and his brain. 'I'm not,' he replied. 'I'm okay. Help me up.'

The operation unsteadied him. When he was upright, he was overcome by a wave of nausea and a wave of shame. He'd gone for the masked man like a fanatic trying to stop a train by throwing himself in front of it. He should have known better.

Maris was saying, 'Hal – oh God, Hal, are you all right!'

Suddenly everything sprang into sharp focus – there was the lighthouse, with only a tiny scarf of fog round the glasshouse now, a captain with a pistol in his hand still, the security gate wide open, a car racing towards it from inside the fence – and Maris. Cane steadied himself on her shoulder – he could feel her muscles kicking.

'I'm okay,' he repeated, mainly to kill his sense of humiliation for demonstrating such a lack of fighting expertise. What a fool he'd been! What an idiot to have blundered at the escapee – he, who knew how to look after himself in a fight. One would have thought that all those near-real contests aboard the oil rigs on which he had served would have taught him a thing or two. The iron musclemen he had wrestled with were tougher than the lean body he had felt under his hands shortly before. Inwardly, he cursed himself.

'Your eyes!' exclaimed Maris. 'Your eyes!'

They weren't that bad – the raking fingers had, in fact, missed them altogether. The blood was coming from the way they had torn open still further the knife-cut across the bridge of his nose.

8

Cane saw Dr Joubert the following morning; nurses flitted past the office like unwinged angels of mercy. It seemed an undue amount of activity.

Dr Joubert gave him the reason. There was compassion in his eyes and competence in his hands, which he clasped on the desk in front of him like a blunted prayer pose.

'If I don't get Bosch out of here today, I think he could die. There is brain damage – how much, I can't assess. Maybe I should have moved him yesterday to the intensive care unit in Cape Town. But,' he added with a deprecatory smile, 'sometimes with a doctor it's more a matter of medical pride than the best interests of the patient.'

Cane drew up his own neck muscles uncomfortably. The gesture did not go unnoticed by Dr Joubert. He also eyed the plaster across Cane's nose. 'You been in trouble too?'

Cane laughed it off. 'The fog came up and hit me.'

'Want me to look at it?' The offer was all-embracing, Cane felt. Dr Joubert was shrewder than he thought.

'No. Rather tell me about Bosch.'

'There's a Medicare helicopter from Cape Town on its way here now.'

'Isn't that sending a man on a boy's errand? Why not an ambulance?'

'The Medicare chopper is a specialized, self-contained unit. Doctor, couple of specially trained nurses. They can cope with an emergency. Great name in these parts,' he added, as if by way of endorsement and prefacing his next remark. 'It will cost your company a lot of money, Mr Cane.'

Cane thought of Renshaw's predictable reaction. He shrugged it off.

Dr Joubert was saying, as if in extenuation, 'My job is to save life – at all costs. Bosch will die if we don't get him specialized attention.'

'You've told me the bill, but you haven't told me the reason.'

Dr Joubert eased his fingers apart. 'In my opinion,' he said cautiously, 'Bosch was hit – deliberately hit – with some sort of instrument which was designed specifically not to leave a mark. The man who hit him was a professional.'

'What makes you say that? One bruise is the same as another.'

Dr Joubert stared straight into Cane's eyes. When he was older, thought Cane, and looked across his glasses at a patient, the effect would be near-oracular.

'There is no bruise.'

'You must be joking.'

Dr Joubert bridled. 'I never joke about medicine.'

'Sorry. A figure of speech. How could a blow which has caused the kind of damage you say to Bosch's brain leave no bruise?'

'I thought I could solve that riddle myself all day yesterday, then later in the day I realized' – Dr Joubert said it so diffidently that Cane believed his motives – 'that I was suffering from a lack of humility. I telephoned a neurosurgeon in Cape Town who had been my university professor. I'm passing on what he said. He said he thought Bosch could have been hit by a special weighted blackjack – made usually of leather or rubber – which would leave no mark.'

'Do the police know this?'

'Not yet. My first task is to get Bosch on his way.'

'The wrists and throat wounds are not material.'

'Even you could see that.'

'Maris' mother, too.'

'She did a good job. It's a fine family.'

Dr Joubert was talking like an old man. Cane wondered whether Maris' dark beauty had ever sent his hormones chasing. If it had, maybe he had something in his pharmacopoeia to quiet them. Medicine would always be more than the man in Dr Joubert's life.

Dr Joubert was watching him, perhaps trying to fathom his thoughts. 'I think you should know this about the instrument.'

'A cosh, a blackjack, what the Americans call a sap?'

'Yes. That's it.'

'Will this be in your police surgeon's report?'

A ray of something illumined Dr Joubert's young-old face like the fog unscarfing itself from the old lighthouse.

'I'm telling you this for your own good, Mr Cane. There

are times when you may be alone at the drilling site.'

'Thanks. I appreciate that.'

After that hint, he was doubly glad that he had insisted that morning that Maris should not go alone to the drilling site. She had jibbed at being treated like a schoolgirl, she said. However, her mother had backed him, and he had won.

Now he would liked to have reassured Dr Joubert that if he were to stay at the drilling site, he would not be alone – his pistol would be his companion.

9

A cloud of cigarette smoke and frosty breath hung over the group of oil-skinned men under Bredasdorp's dripping trees like a presentiment of trouble. There was something in their stilled attitude – like marionettes awaiting the puppet-master's cue – which warned Cane, subconsciously at least, that he would have to watch out.

The men – about twenty-five of them – were his drilling team. They were waiting at the town rendezvous to be driven to the drilling site. Behind was a low building with crewcut thatch and adjoining it was a church-like structure. This was Bredasdorp's famous wreck museum containing one of the best collections of figureheads and ship relics in the world.

Cane drew up in Maris' car after his hospital interview. A man in a white waterproof jacket – the type worn by drillers underground – and a hard hat fringed with rubber sheeting, came forward.

'Stander.' He introduced himself in the South African way. His grip was like a cactus grab.

Before Cane could respond, his next words followed like a pressure burst.

'Where's Paul Bosch? Why isn't he here? Why didn't he turn up for our date yesterday? He's never let me down in twenty years of friendship. Where's he, eh? What's this about the hospital, eh?'

Jan Stander was Bosch's workmate; Grimmock had boasted that in the two men he had the country's two finest master-sinkers. Not just shafties – master sinkers. At four thousand metres below the surface, they had clawed their way with steel and dynamite into the gold-bearing guts of the goldfields deeper than men had gone before, a world record.

A man whose skin was only slightly darker yellow than his oilskin and which stretched across high Tartar cheekbones (testimony to Hottentot blood) said in a characteristic high sing-song voice. 'My girlfriend at the hospital tells me in bed Satterday night that Mister Bosch is there – hurt bad. Eh?'

That 'eh' seemed standard calibre ammunition used by the team.

The group closed round Cane. Theirs was the same stink of waterproofing and bodies that one encounters in the close confines of a drilling shaft.

'Bad,' reiterated another man. He was a head and a half taller than the Hottentot, black, from Lesotho, a traditional mine worker.

The Hottentot went on. 'My girlfriend says it was a *klip* – stone. On the head.'

'How come?' demanded someone from the rear. 'We never blast weekends – you know that.'

Cane eyed the motley faces – every one a witness by extravagant emphasis of some otherwise insignificant idiosyncrasy, an eye tic, a pull of the mouth, a drawing-back of lips to inhale fag smoke, to the threat of danger and death daily. He hoped that the squad would not fall to pieces now that its kingpin had gone.

He started. 'Men . . .'

There was a clatter in the sky overhead.

'Jeez!' exclaimed the Hottentot. 'A choppie! I never seen a choppie in these parts yet!'

Nor had most of Bredasdorp. The town's faces were to the sky as the white Medicare machine with its big red cross

52

emblazoned on its fuselage passed low over the town to the hospital. It was to land in the botanic gardens adjoining.

Cane said above its noise. 'That helicopter is from Cape Town. It has come to take Paul Bosch to hospital. He is hurt – how badly, we don't know. I found him when I arrived on Saturday evening.'

The men watched him.

Stander's flood of words continued. 'Hurt? How was he hurt? Where did you find him? He was going to pick you up at the airfield. He told me. . . .'

'He didn't pitch up.' Cane found himself falling into their cryptic word-pattern. 'Miss Swart was there. She drove me to the site. We found Paul Bosch unconscious.'

When some things go wrong on a drilling site, they say, other things follow suit. Cane could see what an impact his news was making. Bosch, the iron man, in their view was beyond injury. If Bosch could crack, they could crack too.

'How? Where?' demanded Stander. 'A rock from a side-wall – is that what hit him? Something fell on him, eh?'

He was talking to convince himself.

'None of those things,' Cane replied tersely. He decided to give the truth from the shoulder.

'Miss Swart and I arrived at my office door,' he said. 'Paul Bosch was lying outside, next to the figurehead. He was unconscious. His wrists were bleeding, and he had a cut on his throat.'

'Jeez!' exclaimed the articulate the Hottentot. 'Just like Mister Howells.'

'I don't believe it,' said Stander in a flat voice.

'It wasn't like Howells,' Cane snapped. 'Get that clear. Bosch had head injuries – bad injuries.'

'I don't believe it,' Stander repeated. 'Paul could take a rock or two on his head. Once I saw one make a hole in his hard hat, and it only stunned him. . . .'

'We brought him here to hospital,' Cane went on. 'Dr Joubert said he needs better treatment than this hospital can give. That's the reason for the Medicare chopper.'

'Why didn't you call me?' demanded Stander angrily. 'I

could have spoken to him – he is my mate – he would have told me about it. He wouldn't have, to a stranger.'

'He couldn't have talked to you or anyone else,' replied Cane. 'He never came round. He is still unconscious.'

The men drew back from him, shaken. He realized in a flash that it would take a lot to remotivate the team.

Stander finally said quietly. 'Will he die?' Without waiting for a reply, he rushed on angrily. '*What hit him, man?*'

'I don't know. It's a police matter now.'

The Lesotho man, whose name was Moshesh, said. 'It is not good for this to be a police matter. It was an assident, and the police don't come into assidents. . . .'

'I should have seen Paul, even if he was unconscious,' went on Stander. 'I would like to have seen for myself.'

'There was nothing to see,' answered Cane. 'That's what puzzled me. And Dr Joubert.'

'*Nothing to see?*'

'Except the superficial cuts, there was nothing.'

'That bladdy figurehead bitch!' The way the Hottentot, whose name was Giepie, got it out with a fag held between his teeth drew his lips back into a snarl.

Which is the way whoever hit Bosch wanted it to be taken, thought Cane.

'What did the statue hit him with – one of her tits?' Moshesh asked sarcastically.

'I wouldn't mind if she hit me with one,' leched Giepie. 'Better tits than my girlfriend's.'

That defused the tension – for the moment. But not for Stander. He remained dour while the other shafties laughed. Cane noted that several of them looked bleary-eyed and hangoverish.

Motivate. He had a big job ahead of him.

'Let's get going,' he said.

Cane followed the convoy until the fog cleared on high ground and then pulled ahead to collect Maris at *Helder Wacht*. He made a mental resolve that to get results from his team he must stop the daily commuting and make them live on the site.

He found Maris in her studio sketching.

'I thought I was getting a bonus holiday,' she said. She noted his strained look and indicated a sketch on the drawing board.

'This is the way I fantasize. Guaranteed therapeutic.'

'You'll have to teach me.'

'Was it bad – at the hospital?'

'Not good. They've flown Bosch to Cape Town . . .' he explained briefly. He kept the team and Stander's reaction to the news to himself. It was something he, and not she, would have to cope with. He'd also have to cope with Renshaw's reaction; there would be the police also, due that afternoon. . . .

He found himself staring sightlessly at Maris' sketch of a tower. Maris was saying, 'It's not all fantasy. It's a real place I'm interested in – it's called Frenchman's Eye.'

'That in itself sounds like fantasy.'

She did not pursue the subject. She felt that he had more on his mind than he admitted. She put her arm through his and they went down the whitewashed steps together to her car.

'Drive?' she asked.

'I'd rather familiarize myself with the scenery.'

After they had left the main road they turned along the track in the direction of the drilling site. Cane was startled to see, on his side, a huge white golfball-like dome on steel struts, two parabolic antennae about fifteen metres high, and two circular revolving radar dishes rooted into massive concrete stalks.

'What on earth is that?' he asked.

'American observatory. It's called Soutbos – Salt Bush.'

'That round object looks like a radome.'

'What is a radome?'

'It's a housing for a radar antenna. The material it is covered with admits radio waves.'

In proximity to the scientific equipment were a number of prefabs and, apart from them, a group of buildings in the same crewcut style as the town's wreck museum.

'It all looks pretty futuristic,' he observed. 'There seems to be one sizable building isolated quite a way from the others.'

'That's the security gate,' she replied. 'There's an electrified fence right round the property, as well as all kinds of sophisticated electronic checks, I'm told.'

'An outfit like that must be an asset to a small community like Bredasdorp.'

'Economically, yes. But socially the Americans keep themselves to themselves.'

'Are there many of them?'

'Quite a few scientists and technicians, and guards as well. The chief is Dr Brad Testerman.'

'Know him?'

'I've met him.'

'Just that?'

'We invited him to *Helder Wacht* when he first arrived. I reckon if you're an electronics wizard and have even been trained as a spare astronaut, you must find the Strandveld a dead loss.'

'Spare astronaut?'

'So the story goes. Whatever he is, he is an egg-head.'

'And lets you know it?'

They both laughed. They were letting each other know things.

Further on the track divided, one branch heading for Soutbos and the other for the drilling site.

Stander was waiting at the office. 'I've put the men on to greasing and checking the boom rigs and cactus grabs,' he said briefly. 'A weekend of this sort of weather plays hell with them.'

'Give me a few minutes – I have to phone Cape Town,' replied Cane.

In his blue boiler-suit, white waterproof jacket and fringed helmet, Stander looked as aggressive as a Legionnaire going into action.

'After Howells went the Cape Town office clamped down,' he said sourly. 'No unauthorized expenditure, no drilling.

Paul Bosch and I did our best, but machinery is made to work, not sit on its arse and rust in the fog.'

'Later, I want to see everything for myself,' said Cane.

'That bugger Renshaw wouldn't allow us to use diesel to run them,' grumbled on Stander. 'Save. That's all he understands.'

'Where do I find you?' asked Cane.

'At the change-room by the shaft-head.'

Cane's office was separated from the shaft-head excavation by about four hundred metres. This was necessary because of the racket made by the shaft-sinking and drilling machinery, bulldozers and trucks. Now, an unhealthy quiet hung over what should have been a scene of vibrating activity.

'Mr Renshaw on the line for you,' Maris informed Cane.

The previous day's ginny golf had stirred up Renshaw's flabby gall.

'Helicopter! Medicare! Intensive care unit! This company's not a medical research unit, Cane! What do you think this is going to set us back by?'

'Five hundred rand a day. Still, Dr Joubert says the helicopter can be regarded as an accident mercy flight – charge, nominal.'

'Five hundred rand a day!'

'A man's life is at stake,' Cane retorted. 'Bosch is one of the finest master-sinkers in the country.'

'We've got to claim – have you never heard of the Workmen's Compensation Act, Cane – of course you haven't. It makes provision for this sort of thing.'

'I've just arrived. I haven't even inspected the drilling site yet.'

'Not inspected the drilling site.' Renshaw's trick of repeating words was like a boxer's left flick in the face. Worrying, but not a knock-down. Both scored points.

Cane said. 'You asked me to report on Bosch. He's in Cape Town now – he's your pigeon. I'd like to know when I can expect him back.'

He rang off. It might have been easier to have thrown the lighthouse muscleman than the flabby management boss.

10

'Give me granite any day. The harder the rock, the better I like it. This soft stuff is as dangerous as shit.'

Stander was showing Cane the progress that had been made with the shaft-head excavation. This was the preliminary from which deep-drilling operations would be launched deep into the earth – two kilometres down, initially. The two men stood on the brink of a square hole about fifteen metres across. To seal off water-bearing pockets in the immediate vicinity, cementation rigs – grouped like surgeons awaiting the go-ahead to operate – were sited round the hole. Through them, liquid cement was forced under very high pressure. Concrete-impregnated mesh and massive ground anchors kept the sidewalls of the excavation from collapsing. In the centre of the squared hole was a smaller, circular one enclosed by metal sheeting. This marked the beginning of the shaft proper. The first excavations had been carried out by ripper-equipped bulldozers, but later on specialized machines known as cactus grabs and boom rigs (the latter with six drill arms to automatically bore seventy-five blasting holes at a time) would go into action.

At this site the shaft was being sunk on the basis of a novel plan: when the excavation had reached a depth of about 12.5 metres, a mobile headgear on a floating 'raft' of steel girders would move over the hole to provide the means of operating 'kibbles' – giant steel buckets. However, it was too early for that yet and meanwhile a tall construction crane had been substituted for hoisting and cleaning out the hole.

'Water – there's so much bladdy water here,' went on Stander. His tough face was unsmiling. 'We could lose the shaft early on if we're not damn careful.'

'Did you strike any water-bearing pockets which gave you hassles?' asked Cane.

Stander spat. 'I'll say. Fifty thousand litres an hour came out of one borehole like an elephant pissing. Pressure of 35 bar.'

Cane did not disbelieve him – there was marshland on all sides, although the shaft-head itself stood at the base of a low ridge. Prefab changing rooms, workshops, maintenance and storage sheds were sited nearby. There was also a large machinery park. The ridge had also been cleverly employed for the construction of the mobile headgear or 'floating raft'. A half-constructed array of steel girders on rails rose against the side of the ridge; when complete, it would be slid along the rails into position by means of a couple of bulldozers.

The idea of using the ridge's height for building the structure, as well as the 'floating raft' itself, had been Howells'. It was an example of the Texan's expertise which would save about three months – and money – usually taken for the construction of a conventional headgear. Cane found himself asking the question, would a drug addict have been capable of the skill and ingenuity involved? On every hand there were other lesser examples of Howells' know-how.

The shaft was planned to be sunk in five major, complex stages: after the final one, Cane's skill in probing and blasting fissures to open up the 'hot rocks' deep down would come into play. The job Cane was now surveying had only begun its second stage – in short, nothing more than the preliminaries had been accomplished so far.

'There's a couple of feet of water – not much – on the floor of the excavation,' Stander went on. 'I'll put the pumps to work and clear it. It accumulates every weekend. Odd thing, though – I would have expected more. It seems to drain away, somehow.'

'A fissure?' asked Cane.

Stander shrugged noncommittally.

'Okay – we'll take a closer look when it's dry,' said Cane. But his mind was on the vast amount of work which lay ahead. 'I want you to test-run the truck engines, bulldozers, compressors – the lot. Give 'em all a go. See how they operate.'

'It'll be a pleasure,' answered Stander. His face showed the first signs of animation since Cane had met him. 'The damn things haven't run since Howells left – management economy. We'll have to fuel 'em all up first – I had all the fuel drawn off into the big storage tank when Cape Town instructed us not to use it until we were authorized to. It'll be good to have some life come back into this place – it's like a bloody graveyard.'

'Where is the explosive kept?' asked Cane.

Stander pointed to a red-painted shed at the ridge near the floating raft and machinery 'laager'.

'Tons of it there – never had much chance to use it.'

'Let's go and see,' said Cane. 'How many blasting certificates are there amongst the crew?'

'Myself, Bosch, that's all. Howells had one, of course.'

'That seems mighty few.'

'You can't be too careful about who blasts in this tricky rock,' replied Stander. 'I hear you're a *fundi* with explosives.'

'*Fundi?*'

'It's a South African way of saying expert – Zulu.'

'I'll have to learn the men's jargon. Drillers in the States have their own way of saying things, and the North Sea rigs have another.'

'Yeah.' He strode on.

As they neared their objective, Cane asked. 'Isn't this shed a bit close to all this gear? What if something happened?'

The back of the shed had been sunk into the side of the ridge.

'Department of Mines clearance – that's good enough for me,' replied Stander. As if it wasn't, he added, 'we've got a new type of double safety fuse. Made by the wet spun process. Black powder paste.'

Stander produced a key.

'How many keys to the shed are there?' asked Cane.

'I have one, Bosch had one, and you have one. I expect

yours is in the office safe. Bosch's is probably among his things at home. I'll check and let you have it.'

He opened the door. Cane eyed the neat, brick-like stacks of explosive and capped fuse. He weighed one in his hand. These were his tools for the complicated and dangerous job of fissure blasting. If he used too much explosive, the rocks round the fissures would melt and seal them off; if he used too little, the fissures would stop short of the natural faults. Either way, no water heated by the 'hot rocks' could be brought up to run the turbines in order to generate electricity. The operation would be more art than science – his own intuition and judgement would be at stake.

What the project envisaged was the drilling of two parallel carrying wells more than two kilometres deep. Down one cold water – to be drawn from the nearby freshwater lake of Soetendalsvlei – would be forced until it reached the deep, slightly radio-active rocks. Here the rocks would heat the water to about two hundred degrees Celsius. This hot water, destined to drive turbines, would then be forced up the second well to the surface generating machinery.

'Okay,' he told Stander. 'Carry on and get the machinery going, will you? I'll be at the office.'

Maris greeted him with a wry smile. 'Power failure – it happens all the time,' she said. 'It seems to be getting worse rather than better.'

'Worse – since when?' The way she had spoken was full of implications.

'The more progress the shaft makes.'

'I see.'

'Our power comes on a branch set of poles from the main supply to Cape Agulhas,' she explained. 'The repairmen's excuse is that all the fog and condensation causes short circuits.'

He looked into her green eyes. 'Perhaps Alcestis rubbed her back against a pole and it fell down.'

They both laughed. Then Cane changed the subject.

'Is my key to the explosives shed in the safe?'

'Yes. I checked it out when we arrived. Do you want it?'

61

'Not now – later, perhaps.'

'I'll show you your office set-up.'

Their offices led into each other. His own office had a big safe in a corner, geological and seismic maps on the walls, and a table heaped with long, salami-shaped drilling cores from test drillings. The place had an air of non-occupancy; there was little clue to Howells' personality, and none to Bosch's.

'When are the police due?' he asked finally.

'Shortly before or after lunch,' she replied. 'Don't expect much punctuality in our country places.'

She left him to a mound of paperwork, but the silence – the absence of mechanical noise – worried him. He wondered why Stander had not started the machinery. He debated whether he should contact him by means of a field telephone whose big bell was designed to be heard above the racket at the excavation site.

He did not wonder for long. Stander burst into his office with a stomp of heavy boots.

'Can you beat it?' he shouted. 'Water in the diesel fuel! I'm beginning to think myself that this place is jinxed!'

'How can water get into fuel?'

'That's what I'm asking!' he exploded. 'We filled up the crane engine, a ripper bulldozer and some trucks for a start – I wanted the crane for hoisting once I'd pumped the water out of the shaft bottom so we could examine it. Then . . .'

He seemed on the verge of apoplexy.

'What happened?' Cane asked quietly.

'A few bloody coughs – hiccups! They died, each one after the other! It'll take days to strip 'em down. . . .'

'Where was the water, man? Every vehicle's tank couldn't have had water in it.'

'In the bloody main storage tank – a thousand litres of fuel, all fouled up! It'll take days to clean – useless, unproductive work!'

Stander's news crystallized the thought which had been in his mind ever since the tedious drive back alone from Bredasdorp that morning.

'You're saying that someone deliberately contaminated the main diesel storage tank?'

'What else?' rejoined Stander. 'Rain can't get in a tank of its own accord.'

'See here. I don't like the idea of the site being deserted at night. I want you to pick three good men as night watchmen. We start a weekly rota – as from tonight.'

'You're asking for trouble, Mr Cane. The men don't like this place. It gives them – and me – the heebie-jeebies. There's something queer about it. That's all I want to say.'

Cane continued. 'As soon as possible, I want the whole team sleeping and working on site.'

'Are you going to tell 'em that?'

'Are you afraid to?'

Stander ground out his half-smoked cigarette. 'Yeah. For the sake of the project, I am.'

'Say what you mean.'

'This team's morale has gone to hell – ever since the Howells business,' he jerked out. 'What happened to Paul has made it worse. They're not half the men they were when we started – I *know*. That is when accidents happen. They're talking amongst themselves, whispering. I don't like it.' He gestured towards the office entrance. 'Get rid of that damn figurehead. That's my advice. She's at the bottom of it.'

'The police will be here shortly. It stays until they have completed their investigations. After that, I'll have it cleaned up also.' He added. 'If the men catch someone messing around here at night, it will debunk this evil spirit business.'

Stander laughed ironically. 'I tell you, if you leave three of 'em behind here tonight, they won't be around in the morning. Let the situation cool before you start riding 'em.'

'Is that what you call riding?' demanded Cane.

'Under the circumstances, yes.'

'I'll think it over, Stander. If I decide to go ahead, I'll inform the men myself.'

'It's your project.'

Maris came in. 'The police have arrived.'

'Show them in.'

Her eyes were very bright, although she kept a straight face. 'Not them. Him. One policeman.'

She saw his uptight look. 'Listen,' she added quickly. 'Things work differently in these parts from cities and towns. It's only one very young constable – not the one we met in town. Let me stay and I'll translate into Afrikaans – that will put him at his ease.'

'I'd like that. You'd better be present anyway, seeing we found Bosch together.'

The young policeman's colour flared as red as his hair at having to inspect the daubs on Alcestis' breasts. He shied like a horse when Cane suggested fingerprints on the shapely curves. He tangled himself between his pencil, notebook and .38 Smith and Wesson and cannoned into the figure-head.

Cane was surprised to see that it rocked to and fro.

'What's this?' he asked Maris in surprise.

'The figurehead is hollow inside,' she explained. 'You see, it used to be fixed to the ship's bowsprit by a spar which ran through the base.' She rocked Alcestis again to demonstrate. 'It's actually off balance standing in a normal position. So someone in the past weighted the base with a couple of old cannon-balls – see for yourself.'

The red-haired representative of the law helped Cane – as if he were touching the great whore of Babylon – push Alcestis over until Cane could make out the hollow base and counterweights.

When the policeman spoke, he looked past Maris' shoulder as if he were frightened to project the image of Alcestis' breasts on to a living woman. Maris offered fair competition in this regard.

'I'll take statements.'

They went inside, out of Alcestis' immediate sphere of influence. With the help of Maris' Afrikaans, the policeman achieved a cryptic outline in police jargon of Cane and Maris' discovery of Bosch.

Then he fled.

'Sex and the single cop,' said Maris.

They laughed together. It was the first time that day he had felt like laughing.

'I wish I had even him to guard the drilling site – maybe I'll sleep here myself,' he said.

'No,' she replied. 'Don't do that. Why not stay on at *Helder Wacht* until things have stabilized here? At home you'll be right on the project's doorstep, as it were. . . .' Her voice trailed away; they stood looking at one another.

'That's the best thing that has happened to me today,' he said at length.

'Me too, Hal.'

He saw little of her for the rest of the afternoon. He spent frustrating hours with Stander and the machines. The Bredasdorp garage which supplied diesel could not find a replacement for the contaminated tank at short notice. The site continued to be without electricity – the engineers had more pressing commitments nearer town.

It was a bad afternoon.

At dusk, Cane and Maris arrived at *Helder Wacht*. They entered the homestead via Maris' studio. The sketch of the tower which Cane had seen when he had collected her for work was still on her drawing-board.

Cane stopped and looked fixedly at it. The tower and its association with another tower – that of the old lighthouse at Cape Agulhas – sparked a sudden hunch in his mind. Had he got his priorities right? he suddenly asked himself. Was he making a mistake by waiting passively until the enemy struck at the drilling site rather than going out and looking for him? He thought of the unknown force which had caused so many mishaps collectively as the enemy, reinforced by his own physical encounter at the lighthouse. Tower – hide-out – the micro-chip circuits hummed in his brain.

'Is that real?' he asked abruptly.

Maris was surprised. 'Yes, I told you. It's a place called Frenchman's Eye.'

'Near here?'

'On the other side of the peninsula – near Birkenhead.'

'Anyone could reach the drilling site from it?'

She put down her bag and coat and stood at the drawing-board with him. 'Of course. It's a little off the main road – about an hour and a half's drive from here.'

'What is this below ground?'

She sensed something of his intense interest and replied, 'Frenchman's Eye was a martello tower – that's the powder magazine. It stands on top of Dune Fountain peak and has a tremendous commanding view in all directions. The French built it as a fog and navigation warning post. A cannon was fired to warn ships.'

'It still stands?'

'Partly. The upper part and the adjoining semaphore station are in ruins but the powder magazine is very well preserved.'

'Will you take me there?'

'When?' she asked in surprise.

'Tomorrow.'

She burst out laughing in astonishment. 'I thought I was keen! It's my ambition to restore the old place! What fascinates *you* about it?'

There was a boyish sense of fun about his reply which made her warm to him. 'I'm the boss. If I decide to take the day off and instruct my secretary to accompany me to show me an architectural gem, it's my business.'

She laughed delightedly and bewilderedly. 'I don't get it!'

'It's to do with the drilling project, although Mr Renshaw might not agree,' he replied. 'Must I make it an order?'

She spread her hands as if she could not believe his words. 'Of course I'll take you! Nothing would bring me greater pleasure.'

'It's a question of priorities,' he added enigmatically.

'Priorities? Again, I don't get you.'

'I'll tell you at Frenchman's Eye.'

She was excited and smiling, like a girl. 'We'll have a picnic! We'll get away early! This sketch isn't complete – I need more details of the semaphore mast!'

Cane for his part knew what he would take on this particular tower expedition – a gun.

It had been a bad day. All at once it was a good evening.

II

It was a good day also, next day.

Maris and Cane were approaching Frenchman's Eye by road.

The brilliant morning light colour-coded their holiday mood. It was one of the pellucid, sparkling days after bad weather which had endowed *Helder Wacht* with its name. Maris sparkled too. Cane's hunch about the place was as strong as ever.

'Keep your eyes open!' exclaimed Maris. 'You'll spot the tower soon!'

Whoever had chosen the peak called Duinfontein – Dune Fountain – on which to build Frenchman's Eye had known his business. The place was at the western extremity of a mountain range and from its three hundred and fifty metre high summit there was a view to all points of the compass. Southwestwards from its base stretched a low tongue of sandhills which terminated at Danger Point, the notorious shipping deathtrap. A little offshore from Danger Point lay Birkenhead Rock.

'We can't get right up to the tower by car,' Maris went on animatedly. 'We'll have to leave it and walk a kilometre or two. It's pretty lonely – Dad won't let me come here on my own. Today is different!'

'Different!' he laughed. 'Guess what Mr Renshaw would say!'

They grinned at one another for playing truant. Stander had been morose when Cane had phoned to say he would only be in later. He gave no reason. But, he justified it to himself, his presence was not needed for the thankless task of stripping engines and filtering fuel.

'Let's go first to the cliffs from where I can show you Birkenhead Rock,' said Maris.

'How do you know where the rock is situated in the sea?'

'Even in a slight swell the sea breaks heavily over it. We've also got a double means of checking its location – the Russians diving to the *Kamchatka*.'

She broke off to indicate a road fork: one branch led towards Duinfontein peak, the other to a resort at a river mouth.

'That's our road – look, you can see Frenchman's Eye now!'

She slowed, and Cane caught a glimpse of the ruined martello tower on the summit. The car then headed towards the toe of the Danger Point peninsula – a rockbound coast with cliffs jutting out of the land like a giant black knuckle-duster. Finally, they reached a clifftop overlooking the sea about a kilometre short of their immediate objective, Birkenhead Bungalows, where Captain Wessels was stationed.

'There's a boat out there,' remarked Cane, using binoculars. 'Four people in wet suits in it – I wonder if they are the Russians? They don't seem to be diving. They're fixing something floating to the stern.'

The boat was too far away to make out exactly what the team was doing.

Cane expected Maris to drive on, but she hesitated for some reason. She sat, hands on wheel, staring out over the sea. She was wearing a warm, loose dark green top and tracksuit pants. The colour was a foil to her dark beauty. The casual clothes and flat-heeled sneakers made her seem smaller than she really was.

At length she said obliquely. 'It all happened a long time ago. The sea should bury its dead.'

'And its gold?'

'Gold has brought the *Kamchatka* back into the present – very much so,' she said. 'Whoever had heard – or known – of the *Kamchatka* before now? she continued rhetorically.

'A few Strandvelders, no-one else. Now we have stories in the media reliving old brutalities, dead-and-gone hatreds, mutinies . . .'

'And courage – immortal courage,' he interrupted. 'I'm now talking about the *Birkenhead*.'

'Hal,' she went on as if talking to herself. 'We Swarts keep the *Birkenhead*. Did you know that the anniversary of the tragedy is on Friday?'

'I did not.'

'It's a family tradition going back generations that every year on the anniversary the Swart family drops a wreath over the spot.'

'Still?'

She nodded. 'The ceremony used to be from a boat – now we do it from an aircraft. On Friday I'll fly the club's light plane with Dad and Mum and we'll carry out the remembrance.' She went on. 'It's strictly a family affair.'

'I guess so.'

She said diffidently, not looking at him. 'Will you come too? Dad and Mum would love to see you again, particularly as they're going away on holiday immediately afterwards.'

His mind raced. He wanted to accept, but by Friday what sort of demands would the drilling project and its snowballing problems be making upon him? Yet he knew that if he refused Maris, something would have gone out of their relationship.

'I'll come.'

'I'm glad.'

Captain Cassie Wessels, the police watchdog, wasn't a glad person. As they drove up, he was sitting on a camp chair on a grass strip in front of a bungalow facing out to sea. A transistor radio blaring pop music, a heap of reading matter, and a pair of powerful binoculars were his companions.

He emerged from boredom and a pile of magazines.

'Maris!' he exclaimed delightedly. '*Wat maak jy hier* – what are you doing here?'

'*Ons kom die waghond dophou* – we've come to watch over the watchdog,' she laughed, and then switched into English to introduce Cane. She thrust a parcel of goodies into Wessel's hands from Jeannette Swart.

Cane liked the strong grip of the Strandvelder's handshake. He shared with Dirk Swart an emanation of inner strength, an uncomplicated assurance that his path in life was right. He'd carry that through in his police duties – tough, incorruptible, humane. A good man for a tight corner.

'Hell,' went on the policeman. 'Anything to break the monotony! I thought when they gave me this job that Russians were beings from another planet. I've found out differently. When they're not in the water, they're playing cards – endlessly.'

'What about the language barrier?' asked Maris.

'Two of them speak good English. But they don't communicate much. I think they're under orders not to. Anyway, the boss does what talking is necessary.' He eyed Maris and Cane warmly. 'It's good to have my own people.'

'What does your wife think about all this, Cassie?' asked Maris.

'I phone her every day – it helps pass the time,' he grinned. 'But a man with a wife and two kids runs out of sweet nothings to say after a while.'

'Do you *stay* here?' Maris eyed the camp air of the place.

'No, thanks be. I live at the Gansbaai hotel. It's only a few kilometres away. The Russians aren't prisoners. They can travel within a radius of one hundred kilometres of here unrestricted. Beyond that limit, they have to ask permission from me and I check with the colonel. So far they haven't asked. They've got diplomatic status, did you know, Maris? Diplomatic number-plates for their vehicles, too.' He indicated a Kombi and a half-ton pickup, similar to the one Cane himself drove. 'With the compliments of the South African Government,' he added ironically.

'There can't have been a Russian on South African soil since – since . . .' said Maris.

'The *Kamchatka*,' added Cane.

They all laughed, and Maris said. 'After the fuss about the

gas atoll, it's a wonder our people didn't shoot them on sight.'

'I think it was a sort of olive branch the Russians extended – we'll share in the *Kamchatka*'s gold. Twenty-five million altogether. Cheap at the price, for an oilfield,' said Wessels.

'Gas,' corrected Cane.

'You know about undersea oil?' asked Wessels.

'He's a *fundi*,' interjected Maris. It was the second time recently Cane had heard the expression. 'North Sea rigs, and all that.'

Wessels eyed him with renewed respect. Cane said. 'I saw the diving team as we approached. They seemed to be busy fixing something to their boat. Maybe they've brought up some gold.'

'All they've landed so far is some old junk – bits of waterpipe, some broken clay pipes, broken bottles, a bit of sounding lead,' answered Wessels. 'They'll have to pull finger out if they hope to bring up gold – they've been ashore now for nearly two weeks.'

'There's a time limit set for them, isn't there?' asked Maris.

'A month – not a day more.'

'Perhaps today will be different,' said Cane. 'I wonder about that floating object. . . .'

'I can tell you what it is,' replied Wessels. 'It's their donkey. They must be coming ashore.'

'Donkey?'

'It's a kind of special underwater craft – sort of midget submarine. They hang on and it takes them down to the wreck.'

'What other salvage gear have they?' asked Cane.

'This isn't a salvage job,' replied the policeman. 'It's a pilot operation. If they locate any gold, the authorities will take the situation from there.'

'How do they know whereabouts to investigate?' asked Maris. 'The *Kamchatka* must either be silted over after all these years, or been broken up by the underwater currents. I

71

remember that divers who went down to the *Birkenhead* found sections of the ship strewn all over the sea-bottom.'

'Come and have a look inside here before the Russians return,' said Wessels, leading them indoors.

The central bungalow of the complex was a kind of mess-cum-office. Several South African Navy charts of the Danger Point area were pinned on the walls, as well as a mosaic of very large-scale land maps of the Strandveld.

There was also a very large blow-up of a contemporary photograph of an old-fashioned ship in port with two high funnels, towering superstructure, and small guns mounted in revolving barbettes.

'*Kamchatka*,' said Wessels. 'The team spends hours studying these old photos – I suppose to familiarize themselves with the lay-out when they're underwater. But this is what they really work on. . . .'

A striking model of the *Kamchatka* – the finest model Cane had ever seen – had a table to itself. It was over a metre long and was cut away to show every interior detail.

'Who made such a beautiful thing?' asked Maris. 'You could practically find your way about by it.'

'Vladimir Yasakov told me,' replied Wessels. 'It comes from the Heeresgeschtliches Museum in Vienna – the Austrian State National Archives.'

Supplementing the model were half a dozen detailed design drawings of the *Kamchatka*. The Russians had certainly done their homework.

'When the team has been weather-bound, Yasakov has spent a lot of time explaining about the *Kamchatka*,' Wessels went on. 'Except the one thing that matters.'

'Where the gold was kept,' said Maris.

'Yeah,' said Wessels. He indicated a complex of compartments below the bridge deep in the bowels of the ship. 'Could be anywhere here.'

'Twenty-five million in sovereigns would take up a lot of room,' said Maris thoughtfully. 'What part of the ship do the things they've already recovered come from?'

'Yasakov clams up when I ask anything like that.'

Maris pointed to a midship section plan which had been heavily circled in colour. 'What's this, Cassie?'

'You must lower your voice as if you were going into church when you speak about that part of the *Kamchatka*,' he said derisively. 'That's the prison – where the anti-Czarist elements were housed. The prison. The Czar's officers had a nasty practice – so Yasakov tells me – of encasing their prisoners' ankles in concrete and allowing it to set. If the unfortunates didn't die of gangrene, they were shot anyway. That is why the Russians insist that the ship should have all the respect of a war grave.'

'Now look at this,' Wessels went on ironically. 'This is the holy of holies – the engine-room. It was the sanctuary of the *Kamchatka*'s chief engineer, a man named Monomakh. He ran a revolutionary lending library from here. Yasakov tells me he kept a copy of *Das Kapital* stashed away behind his icon of Saint Nicholas.'

'I wonder what anti-capitalistic treasures the diving team has found today?' asked Canc in the same tone.

'Let's go and see,' said the policeman. 'I'll introduce you to them.'

They left the bungalows and descended a cliff path to a small sandy beach in a cove.

The Russians' boat was already in the breakers. Two of the four divers – all in frogmen's suits – slipped over the side to hold it steady. A third was getting the outboard hoisted clear of the sand. The fourth was securing the 'donkey' to the stern. It resembled a stubby torpedo or a minesweeper's paravane.

The diver in the stern turned and pulled off the black helmet encircling the face, revealing long hair styled back over the ears.

It was a woman.

12

There was something almost theatrical about the way she held the pose – tall, slim, well-breasted – as if she realized the impact a feminine presence in such a team was making. It was a gesture to upstage the team leader. Which of the three men he was, Cane and Maris could not judge. Their wet suits bestowed an anonymity like uniforms.

The woman held Maris' eyes and spoke to her as if she were the only one present. 'You seem surprised to see a woman.'

She had a slight foreign accent, which enhanced her low attractive voice.

'But why not?' She smiled – a warm, attractive smile, still directed at Maris. 'It is a liberated age, no? You are liberated too?' The remark was in context, but not its innuendo.

She moved towards the shore party.

'I am Anna Tarkhanova. I work on the gas atoll. We' – she gestured at the three men as if they were slightly lesser mortals – 'have the job to continually check the rig and the hulls and the anchor chains. Your rough Cape seas need watching.' She added, by way of an afterthought. 'Of course, we monitor the gas pipes and underwater electronic valves also.'

She jumped ashore and stood in front of Maris.

'What is your name?'

Maris edged towards Cane. She found Anna Tarkhanova overwhelming in an uncomfortable way she could not define.

'Maris Swart.'

'Maris Swart,' repeated the Russian. She held Maris' eyes with hers. They were wide and amber-coloured; below were high Slav cheekbones. There was no doubt about Anna Tarkhanova's charisma. Perhaps she was aware of it.

'I have not heard either before. They are charming.'

Maris edged still closer to Cane. Anna addressed him, but her eyes remained on Maris.

'The rig is a semi-submersible, plus 1A1 column stabilized unit, truster assisted.'

'That will be enough, Anna.'

Anna might have done the upstaging, but the command structure was plain. The man who spoke had pulled off his diving helmet: the anonymity vanished. He had been watching Cane intently while the exchange had been going on between Anna and Maris. Like Anna, his English was good but slightly nasal.

It was a lean face for which the eyes seemed too large. They were slightly out of alignment and the left seemed slightly bigger than the right. His mouth twisted rightwards at an angle below a rather lumpy, disproportionately big nose. It was the colour of his skin, however, which Cane noted – it had a tincture of yellowness which offset the paleness of his eyes, which were as cold as the *Kamchatka*'s sea-grave. He was about Cane's own age.

'Captain Wessels . . .' he began, but the policeman had already begun the introductions.

'Mr Vladimir Yasakov, leader of the diving team.'

The two other divers stood stiffly by the boat like marionettes. Their names were, in fact, Josef Suvorov and Stefan Rostovzeff.

Wessels remarked in Afrikaans to Maris. '*Hulle praat nie Engels nie* – they don't speak English.'

The use of Afrikaans seemed to trip a switch of anger inside Yasakov. He said in a whiplash voice. 'Captain Wessels, I demand to know what is being said. Who are these people? What is their status? This is not a circus. I will not have the public gaping. . . .'

A shadow of anger mounted in the policeman's neck, but his reply was controlled. 'I am in charge here, Mr Yasakov. If I say they are good enough to be here, that is it.'

'Who are they?' He said 'they', but he was concentrating on Cane.

'Friends of mine.'

'I have heard the lady's name, but not the man's.'

Wessels supplied it, and added, 'Mr Cane has just taken over as head of the geothermal project next door to the American observatory.'

'I see.' What he saw, Cane could not fathom. He went on. 'I still do not wish the public present when we bring ashore *Kamchatka* relics.'

The relics Yasakov was agitated about lay in the boat – a ship's lantern shaped like a seahorse, a sounding lead with a length of decayed rope attached, some clay smoking pipes, a section of an old-fashioned ship's mercury barometer, a copper steam tap, and a handful of tarnished silver buttons emblazoned with the insignia of the Czar's navy.

Wessels said, in Afrikaans again, to Maris as if trying to reassure her in the tight, uneasy atmosphere which prevailed.

'Somar 'n klomp ou rommel – just a lot of old junk.'

She replied. *'Cassie, ek dink ons moet loop. Ek hou nie van hierdie mense nie* – Cassie, I think we must go. I don't like these people.'

Yasakov broke in roughly. 'Captain Wessels, I demand to know what is being said behind my back.'

Wessels laughed. 'It is not being said behind your back, Mr Yasakov. Miss Swart says they are just leaving.'

'Good. I require you to make an immediate inventory of what we have recovered.'

Wessels eyed the relics. *'Now? That?* Have you nothing else – no gold?'

'There are things more important than gold – to us, who are not capitalists,' Yasakov answered tersely. 'I am talking about the remains of the revolutionaries who were martyred by the pigs of Czarist officers aboard the *Kamchatka*. Wait until you see a "concrete shoehorn" and you will know what I mean. We should penetrate into the prison section of the wreck within the next few days.'

'I will make an inventory of them too,' Wessels answered levelly.

Yasakov missed his innuendo and went on arrogantly. 'Of course you will. But the remains are to be treated with all due respect. In terms of the convention entered into between the Soviet Union and South Africa, all martyrs' bones are to be handed over for reverent reinterment in the Soviet Union.'

'If there's anything left of them by now,' remarked Wessels in an aside in Afrikaans to Maris.

'The concrete shoehorn is the symbol of the tyranny which led to the Baltic Fleet's destruction at the hands of the Japanese at Tsu-Shima,' went on Yasakov as if addressing a party rally.

'The Voyage of the Damned,' added Cane.

Yasakov stared at him as if he had uttered a blasphemy.

'How do you know, eh? It is not the function of a geo-thermal engineer. . . .'

'I heard the expression the other day for the first time,' Cane retorted. 'Today the world at large doesn't really give a damn what happened to your Baltic Fleet over eighty years ago.'

'It should – the United States in particular,' responded Yasakov ponderously. 'The strategic lessons of the Voyage of the Damned – the lack of world-wide supply and refuelling bases for the Red Fleet – have been absorbed and rectified by our modern naval experts. And by no less an authority than Admiral of the Fleet Sergei G. Gorshkov himself.'

Cane and Maris felt as if they had absorbed a broadside from the Red Fleet itself.

In the awkward pause which followed this verbal knock-down, the South African group almost welcomed Anna Tarkhanova's over-eager question to Maris. It was one of those conversational gambits uttered when there is no rap-port, but one party is trying hard not to let the other go.

'I was chosen for the gas atoll job because I am a fine athlete,' she said rapidly. 'I have represented my country in the Olympic Games in swimming and diving. But I am also a runner – I came third in the 5000 metre event. I have heard that there is a big – how do you say it? – marathon, in these parts. Not so?'

Maris felt she was being quick-talked into something.

'Yes,' she answered, eager to leave. 'It is a cross-country race which is quite famous in its way. It is called the Foot of Africa marathon.'

'Foot of Africa marathon!' exclaimed Anna enthusiastically. 'What a fine name! How romantic! The end of Africa!'

'I don't think any of the entrants think that,' replied Maris.

'Will they accept me? Can I run in the event?' Anna pressed her. 'I am a stranger, a foreigner, here – I do not know how to set about entering. Will you do it for me?' She put her hand on Maris' arm.

'I'll do what I can.' Maris replied coolly. 'I will let Captain Wessels know and he can pass the information on to you.'

'Thank you,' said Anna, but she was clearly disappointed.

Maris' feeling of discomfort grew; Cane had his share of it from another quarter – Yasakov. The team leader's eyes seemed never to leave him.

There was another pause, and then Cane and Maris turned to go.

Yasakov jerked at Cane. 'You live at the geothermal project?'

'Not yet. I will soon.'

Cane and Maris left and headed for Frenchman's Eye.

Their route to the peak took them some way back the way they had come before a branch gravel track led to their objective. They travelled in silence.

Finally, Maris said. 'I'm glad to be going high – I feel the need to breathe fresh air again.'

'I couldn't get the measure of either Yasakov or Anna Tarkhanova,' Cane answered thoughtfully.

'I felt I was being suffocated – by what, I don't know,' Maris went on.

'Suffocated?'

'Something started to close in on me the moment Anna started making . . . making – '

'Advances?'

'I don't know, I really don't know how to describe it,'

Maris said. She flushed slightly. 'I don't know whether advances might not be too strong a word.'

'It has connotations.'

She flashed him a glance. 'If you mean sexual, all I can say is, I don't know.'

'Does she repel you, Maris?'

'No, not exactly. She was overwhelming – that's the best word I can think of. You must admit yourself that she had considerable charisma.'

'Unlike Yasakov. *He* also never took his eyes off me. Seemed as if he were trying to get at my innermost thoughts – with a laser probe.'

'A very blunt one, or a very sharp one?' asked Maris lightly. She was rapidly regaining her equilibrium; Duinfontein peak and Frenchman's Eye were above and ahead of them: the car made a sharp right-hander towards it.

They both laughed, and she added, 'Poor Cassie. Fancy being stuck with that crowd every day!'

'I imagine Cassie could be very tough, if he chose.'

The track rose steeply and twisting; Maris' spirits rose with the gradients. 'Look back at the view, Hal!'

The panorama was grand; it became superlative once they had left the car and started on foot up the ridge on which Frenchman's Eye stood. The ground was rough and the wind, from the usual winter southwestern quadrant, was stronger than on the beach. But even so, Maris was surprised when Cane insisted on taking his jacket. It felt uncomfortably heavy with the automatic in the pocket. They also had a flashlight and Maris' sketching-pad.

They scrambled up a gully: suddenly Frenchman's Eye was in front of them.

'Wait, Maris!' Cane slipped on his coat so that the gun was handy to his right hand. The wind and exertion had brought the colour to Maris' cheeks: she looked very lovely and ridiculously young in her dark green jump suit matching her green eyes. Her dark hair blew loosely round her face.

'What a fine example of architecture – French, among all the Strandveld's other types!' exclaimed Maris.

'It's smaller than I thought,' said Cane. His eyes were all over the tower for any sign of movement. It was built of blocks of stone quarried from the mountain itself. The summit had partially collapsed; there were firing slits in the sides. Adjoining the stone structure was the base of a semaphore tower constructed of big baulks of timber. The upper section had disappeared, but the lower part was still reasonably well preserved.

Cane felt they were exposing themselves unnecessarily to anyone's sight who might be inside the ruin. 'Let's get on,' he said briefly.

The entrance door hung in pieces.

'I'll go first,' Cane said. He moved in quickly, shifting aside the broken planks but keeping his gun hand unclut-tered. Sunlight filtered through from above; the intervening woodwork – three successive floors reached by a winding stone stair – had partly crumbled away.

'You moved as if you'd seen a snake!' Maris exclaimed.

'Where's the old magazine?' Cane asked.

'Down there.'

There was a heavy old teak door at the bottom of a short flight of steps cut into the rock. It was in an excellent state of preservation. It was metal reinforced and the bolt, although rusty, was sound and worked.

If there was anyone holed up at Frenchman's Eye, this would be the place, Cane told himself.

Cane took the flashlight, threw open the door and stood back, hand in gun pocket. It was empty.

'It won't bite you,' Maris laughed.

He felt a fool. The association he had built up in his mind between the martello tower and the Agulhas lighthouse evaporated like a drop of water on a hot stove.

'I expected it to be wet and nasty,' he answered lamely.

'The French were very skilful,' said Maris, on her hobby-horse. 'This was a powder magazine for the warning gun – powder had to be kept dry. They hewed this place out of the solid rock and then cut these ventilation-cum-drainage ducts through to the outside.'

The ducts were far too small to permit the passage of a human; nor were there any signs of occupation.

'What is that?' asked Cane, indicating a smaller room leading off the magazine.

'Cannonball store,' answered Maris. 'Powder and shot were never kept together. There was always the danger that a dropped shot could cause a spark from the stonework. An additional precaution was to hang a felt curtain between the shot and powder stores.' Maris went on, 'You've sidetracked me, inspecting the magazine first. I meant to start our tour at the top. Let's go up – it's the finest view in the Strandveld.'

It was. To their right was the great sweep of Walker Bay running round to the millionaires' resort of Hermanus, which had been the original site of the geomagnetic observatory before its acquisition by the Americans. Almost below them, it seemed, was the small picture-postcard harbour of Gansbaai, where Captain Wessels resided. Nearer still, the grim pedestal of Danger Point dominated the coastline.

'It's a dream,' enthused Maris. 'Think, when I've restored the tower, everyone can share this.'

'Fire a gun!' grinned Cane.

'Flash a semaphore signal,' she grinned back.

'No one in the space age can read a semaphore signal,' he chaffed her.

'I don't care. I'm happy. It's pure magic!'

The rest of their day was magic. They had a picnic; Maris sketched, Cane admired. Cane put away his jacket with the gun. There wasn't a soul for miles. They laughed together, revelled in the small things, which became big, for them. The magic grew between them.

At the end of it all, they stayed too late for Cane to make it before the drilling site closed for the day. He shrugged it off, just as he had shrugged off the shadow of fear with which he had approached Frenchman's Eye – an intuition that had been born out of something that had left its impact from the immediate past.

You weren't wrong in your hunch, Cane. Only it didn't come from the past. It came from the future.

13

'Check it out – check, check, check! Keep that kibble clear of their heads, blast you!' yelled Stander. 'Pump, there! Pump it, dammit!'

Next morning Stander and Cane stood at the control desk in the cockpit of the drilling site's corrugated iron engine-room. Both wore standard blue boiler suits, Wellington boots, tough white tarpaulin jackets, and rubber-fringed hard hats. Stander had to shout above the racket of the diesels. Some engines drove the high overhead construction crane, whose cables dipped into the shaft-head excavation, other machines powered pumps sucking out water which had accumulated in the central cylindrical section of the excavation.

Then – bells rang and lights flashed on the control panel. Operating it was Giepie, the Hottentot with the Tartar cheekbones.

Alarm!

'Blast! Hold it!' shouted Stander.

The man's fingers stumbled uncertainly over the switches; a drop of sweat or condensation dripped off his forehead. The man's eyes were yellow, streaked with bloodshot veins.

'Hold it! Hold everything! Hold, hold, hold!'

The machines cut. Stander jerked his head for Cane to join him outside.

'Giepie – hangover,' he said tersely.

'Is he fit to work the crane?' demanded Cane. 'If he makes a slip and that kibble plunges. . . .'

'You don't have to tell me!' barked Stander. 'Goddam those bloody Americans!'

'Americans?' asked Cane. On his arrival that morning, he had ordered a detailed inspection. Now it looked as if one of the key men, Giepie, would be incapable of operating the crane which hoisted the big metal bucket, or kibble, in and out of the embryo shaft-head. He had no stand-in. Immediately he had met Stander bringing the drilling team from Bredasdorp he had realized that something was wrong. Now the problem had reared its aching head.

'Last night some of the team went out drinking with off-duty guards from the observatory,' snapped Stander. 'They were muttering in the bus this morning – they're being fed stories of exploitation and low wages – hell, as if we didn't have enough hassles without that! Giepie's a good man, but give him brandy or a woman, and he's a goner.'

'Why should the Americans put their oar into our outfit?' he demanded.

'You can't stop the men doing what they wish in their spare time,' said Stander. 'Damn all Americans!'

'You convince me all the more – I am going to stop the men living in town,' said Cane.

'I warned you before, take it easy on that score – these guys' morale is not up to this job,' answered Stander. 'Make them live on the site, and you'll have trouble – lots of trouble, man.'

'I've got it already. From tonight, I want three men sleeping here.'

Stander tilted forward his hard hat.

'You name 'em,' he said bluntly. 'I won't.'

They eyed one another. 'When a team's morale is rotten like this lot, accidents happen,' Stander asserted.

'Can Giepie operate the crane so that we can get with inspecting the floor, or can't he?'

'Not on my responsibility, Mister Cane. That's flat. Giepie is still too shot to know a switch from a swizzle-stick.'

'The water's disappearing too fast for the pumps alone to be responsible. As I said before, my guess is there's a hidden fissure somewhere,' said Cane. 'We've got to locate it.'

'You're the geologist,' replied Stander defensively.

'But you're the man who's had more field experience than anyone in this country – except Bosch. Mr Grimmock said so.'

The tough master-sinker seemed a little mollified. 'See here. The sort of formations I've drilled through in the Transvaal and Orange Free State goldfields weren't anything like this. This soft stuff is like cow-dung. It falls to bits once the drill bites.'

'What about putting down a deep test drill from the floor of the excavation to establish what is below? I know that preliminary holes were sunk – I mean something much deeper.'

'It will mean rescheduling operations, and we'll have to have the crane. Today is hopeless with Giepie as he is.'

'Are there others in the same state?'

'Three. You could kick 'em up the arse and they'd think it was a cactus grab come alive.'

A bell, which sounded like a fire alarm, burst into life above their heads.

'Office!' bellowed Stander. 'The office wants you. . . .'

As if to underscore his words, Maris' voice, distorted and metallic, came through on a loudspeaker.

'Telephone for Mr Cane. Mr Cane required urgently on the telephone.'

'It's Mr Renshaw,' Maris said when Cane reached the office. 'He's very impatient about something.'

Renshaw said. 'Why the devil can't I ever get hold of you, Cane?'

'Ever is a long time – I've only been here three days.'

'Yesterday – I tried all day yesterday to contact you. Where were you, Cane? Stander didn't know. There is such a thing as keeping your superiors informed. . . .'

'Renshaw,' said Cane quietly. 'Mr Grimmock gave me a double brief when I accepted this job. One, to put the project into orbit, and two, to find out what or who was causing the so-called accidents. I decide which has priority, and when.'

'Which was it yesterday?'

'I said, I decide the priorities.'

'That's the kind of answer which could cover a multitude of sins.'

Cane's anger rose. 'Is this call to monitor my activities? I'm not a schoolboy.'

Renshaw gave a small cough, a breather to win time.

'Is it about Bosch?' demanded Cane. 'If it is, hurry up – I've got a below-ground inspection ready to go.'

'It'll have to wait,' replied Renshaw pontifically. He had evolved a fine-honed technique which asserted his rank and at the same time twisted the arm of the person he addressed.

'Well?' snapped Cane.

'There has been an important development which affects your future with the project,' answered Renshaw. 'Mr Grimmock has been in touch with me.'

Cane said nothing. If Grimmock intended to fire him, he thought quickly, he wouldn't use Renshaw as his hatchet man. He himself had fired too many in his time to spend sleepless nights over a dismissal.

'Aren't you interested?' asked Renshaw in his maddening way.

'It depends what you have to tell me,' responded Cane.

Renshaw gave a long-suffering sigh. 'On Monday afternoon,' he went on, deliberately dragging it out. 'I had an important visitor from your area.'

'I can't guess who.'

'Of course you can't,' Renshaw said. 'Even I was a little surprised.'

'Go on.'

'I am truly glad to see you displaying some interest in my news,' resumed Renshaw. 'Mr Grimmock was very interested in what my visitor had to say.'

'Would you prefer me to telephone Mr Grimmock so that we can get to the point, Renshaw?'

Renshaw always believed in being two jumps ahead of his opponent. The world was his opponent.

'Mr Grimmock has already commissioned me to speak to you.'

When Cane again did not respond, Renshaw continued. 'My visitor was your neighbour. From the American observatory – the head of it, in fact. Dr Brad Testerman.'

'What did he want?'

'You are well aware of the fact that the observatory operates some very delicate electronic apparatus?'

'I am not aware. I've seen – from a distance – some things which look like radar dishes, antennae, and a radome.'

'Dr Testerman made the point,' Renshaw went on, 'that when eventually' – he laid stress on the word – 'the geothermal power station becomes operative, all its power grids, generators, cooling towers and other equipment may well interfere with the American observations.'

'That's their problem, isn't it?'

'It could be to our advantage, Cane, as I was not slow to point out to Mr Grimmock when I spoke to him about Dr Testerman's offer.'

'Offer?' Cane had said the right thing. He had expressed ignorance. This was Renshaw's opportunity – and pleasure.

'Offer.' Cane was becoming used to that echo syndrome.

'You may know that Fordham University in the United States is the backer of the Soutbos observatory. The station requires an environment uncluttered by the appurtenances of modern cities.' Cane wondered where he had coined the phrase. 'That is, in fact, why such a remote spot as the Strandveld was chosen in the first instance.'

'Presumably at that stage there was no geothermal project.'

'No. It was some years back. The station was built remarkably quickly in order to track the approach of Halley's Comet towards the earth in 1986.'

Cane said. 'I wasn't aware of it.'

Renshaw said. 'Fordham University – at the suggestion of Dr Testerman himself, I am informed – has decided that it wishes the environment to continue to be uncluttered. Accordingly, it has decided to make an offer to acquire the drilling site and all land eastward to the shore of Soetendalsvlei lake.'

'For how much?'

'Aren't you interested in your own future, in the light of this?'

'Aren't you? You're on the management side. If the project folds up, so does your part of it.'

Cane had a feeling that this is what Renshaw had been waiting for. 'Not at all, my dear Cane. You forget that Mr Grimmock's interests are very diversified – mining, township development, diamonds, base metals. Good management has a universal application. There will be no problem in accommodating my skills elsewhere in the Grimmock organization.'

'In other words, you've cleared your yardarm.'

'It's not an expression I care for, Cane. But we'll let it pass.'

'How much did Dr Testerman offer? Has it been accepted?'

'The nature of the offer was – a little roundabout, shall we say. Dr Testerman merely indicated that if we were to accept in principle, we would not be the losers.'

'We – you mean, Mr Grimmock.'

'I represent his interests here. Or, at least I thought I did until I spoke to him after Dr Testerman had left.'

'Tell me what you're trying to say.'

'Mr Grimmock considered that you, as the man on the spot, should act as intermediary between ourselves and Dr Testerman. Mr Grimmock wishes you to see him as soon as possible and sound him out regarding the logistics of his offer.'

'And then?'

'Ah, I forgot.' Renshaw never forgot anything. 'Mr Grimmock is flying to Cape Town this afternoon. You will arrange to see Dr Testerman immediately. You will ascertain what is in his mind. You will proceed to Cape Town and consult with us.'

'How long will I be expected to stay in Cape Town?'

'As long as Mr Grimmock thinks fit. Why?'

'I am concerned about the drilling project. My absence for any time won't help the team's morale.'

'Didn't you think of that yesterday when you were away the whole day?'

'I told you about that.'

Renshaw couldn't resist making the thrust. 'Listen, Cane – there has been so much unproductive expenditure on the drilling project that the American offer – if favourable – might be our salvation before further expenditure, possibly unjustified, takes place.'

'I've scarcely had a chance to justify myself,' said Cane.

'Perhaps that won't be necessary, if the American offer is satisfactory.'

Bastard, thought Cane, you've fixed yourself up and now you're all for abandoning a hot potato.

He said briefly. 'I'll see Testerman as soon as he can see me. I'll report back in person.'

'This afternoon,' repeated Renshaw. 'In person. At my office. Is that clear?'

'I'll be there.'

Cane put down the phone and stared ahead of him. Was this the end of the line for him? And also for a project whose novelty and challenge had stirred his imagination? Had Grimmock chosen him to be his own executioner by assigning him the task of acting as intermediary?

He was so lost in thought that he did not hear Maris come in. She looked at his uptight face. For a moment she thought he was going to unburden himself, then she saw his expression harden.

'Maris,' he said briefly. 'Mr Grimmock wants me to see Dr Testerman at the American observatory – soon. Will you fix it? It must be this morning. Within the hour, if possible.'

She nodded and turned to go.

'Maris.' She paused. 'I'll be leaving this afternoon by car for Cape Town.'

She said in a neutral voice. 'Shall I arrange accommodation?'

'Renshaw's already done that.'

She hung back uncertainly for a moment. There was a kind of emptiness, an exclusion, which she papered over with a show of businesslike efficiency.

'If anyone calls, shall I say when you'll be back?'

'Tomorrow. Probably by lunch time.'

She said, trying to penetrate the shut-off look on his face.
'When you go to Soutbos, remember the American security.'

'It'll be okay. I'm seeing the boss.'

14

'No admittance! Can't you read! Haul your ass, fellah! Nix
out! Get going!'

It wasn't okay seeing the boss, as Cane had remarked to
Maris. He was encountering at the entrance to the observatory what Maris had stressed, that security was ultra-tight.
The metalled approach roadway past the gatehouse ran dead
into a funnel-shaped arrangement of security fencing – like a
big game trap. There was a high outer mesh gate with sharp
edges top and bottom. It was reinforced with razor-tape and
twin electrification cables. Flanking the road, two further
mesh fences topped with barbed wire converged on an inner
gate – a heavy steel affair mounted on rollers – which formed
the centre section of the gatehouse. Windows, barred with
heavy mesh, faced the inner roadway.

A thickset guard, in similar uniform to the lighthouse
guards, strutted forward. A heavy baton strung from his
waist gave him a pelvic swing like Marilyn Monroe or a
nightclub bouncer.

He whipped out the baton from its leather sheath and
rapped on the inside of the notice which faced Cane.

'Jeezy-peezy!' he exclaimed to the world at large. 'Do I
have to spell it out? Beat it!'

He beat the notice.

Cane waited for the racket to subside. He said. 'Dr
Testerman is expecting me.'

'Dr Testerman is expecting me – where in hell did you get
that fancy voice from, fellah?'

Cane got out. 'I got it from my mother. Any more personal questions?'

The tone of Cane's voice stopped the man short. He resorted to pulling his minor rank. 'Keep away from this gate! You'll get yourself hurt!'

'I've come to see Dr Testerman.'

'Says who?'

Cane got near to the ugly razor tape on the fence, but not too near. He noted that the mesh had been electrically fused at every joint. It was designed to pre-detonate a rocket.

'Why don't you ask?'

'I don't waste time bumping my gums. I know my job – keep 'em out.'

The guard continued to stare hostilely for a moment, then did a smart about-turn.

'Lew!' he shouted. 'Guy here says he has a date with Brad.'

Two sentry-boxes protected the inner gate. 'Name?' came the disembodied reply from one of them.

The question was repeated by Cane's bully-boy.

'Hallam Cane.'

The guard shouted it back; a return order was emitted from the sentry-box.

'Admit him to the security area.'

The guard seemed disappointed. 'See here – when I open the gate, drive that bag of bones through and put it right here – see?' He indicated white lines painted on the tarmac. 'Unnerstand? Right here, where the TV monitors are focused. And don't try to monkey with the buzz-saw, see?'

'If I knew what the expression meant, I'd try and carry it out.'

'I don't appreciate humour – limey humour in particular,' snarled the toughie. 'Do what you're told – no tricks.'

Cane got back into his pickup. He had to wait while the guard did a hip-strut back to his own box. He had, presumably, gone to neutralize the electric fence and carry out some wizardry which would disengage the electric locking device which held the two halves of the wire gate together.

The gates opened as if of their own accord. The baton-trussed guard signalled Cane in, square between the white lines of the wire trap. At the activation of more hidden thaumaturgy, two TV camera monitors on extension booms swivelled about like lovers' tongues seeking each other blindly, until they locked on Cane behind his steering-wheel.

He switched off the engine and was about to get out.

The guard revolved his baton about his wrist like a drum-majorette on parade. 'Stay!' he barked.

That baton! Bosch had been struck by a blunt weapon, a rubber truncheon, perhaps. It had been a deliberate blow, and it had left no mark. The way the man threw the thing about — was that mere showing-off or was he capable of striking the kind of blow which had felled Bosch?

Cane was so engrossed that he almost missed the approach of the second guard. His name was Lew. Lew's strut was underscored by a .38 in an open holster. He too assumed a non-interference camera position.

'Identity?' he demanded. Police dogs respond to that tone. Cane didn't.

'Dr Testerman is expecting me.'

'That's a hill row of beans as far as I am concerned. Anyone can say that,' he retorted.

Cane began to wonder how Maris had managed to arrange the interview at all.

'Hallam Cane. From the drilling site next door.'

'A hard-rocker we have here, eh?' commented Lew to the first guard. 'Says who? Prove it.'

'I forgot to bring my birth certificate along.'

The baton-man said, 'That limey sense of humour burns my gut.'

'You can't prove it?' went on the three-eighter aggressively.

'Ask Dr Testerman.'

'Hold him here,' ordered Lew. 'This is a job for Tom Widdows.'

He and his three-eight banged their way back to the gatehouse.

It took Tom Widdows about five minutes to pick up cue. Cane had a feeling that he was the prima ballerina of a carefully orchestrated gatehouse ballet. Except that no ballet stage could have stood up to a gut-bucket like Tom Widdows.

Finally, Widdows took up position out of the cameras' line of fire also.

'Name?'

'My guess is that you know it as well as I do.'

He consulted a piece of paper. 'Hallam Cane?'

'Yes.'

'The boss will see you.'

'I know that already, or else I wouldn't be here.'

'Limey humour again,' complained the baton-man.

'Out of your seat,' ordered Widdows. 'Leave your keys. We'll see to it.' He addressed the baton-guard. 'You and Lew check him out. Security check,' he informed Cane.

'I'd be half-witted if I didn't realize that.'

Widdows glared at him. Cane noticed the swollen veins in his eyes. Had he been one of the culprits responsible for Giepie's state?

'Lew!' bawled the baton-man. 'Security check. Check him good.'

'See here,' broke in Cane sarcastically. 'Wouldn't it be a lot easier for everyone if I simply stripped – in front of the cameras, if you like.'

'This ain't a drag act,' answered Widdows. 'Security is a serious business.'

Just how serious, Cane realized during the next half an hour when he was put through a series of sophisticated electronic and X-ray tests for weapons and explosives via a succession of cubicles which finally threw him up on the observatory side of the gatehouse. The Americans had their own landrover waiting; he sat sandwiched in between Widdows and Lew as they drove to an isolated open square of four crew-cut thatched buildings – in the 'Arniston style' of the town museum – situated well away from the radome, radar antennae and lofty radio masts. It was clear that the siting of the buildings was designed to keep visitors well away from the working heart of the observatory.

Widdows pulled up. 'In there – Brad's waiting.'

'Aren't you afraid I might attack him with my bare hands?' Cane asked.

Lew managed a cross between a boffola and a belch and heaved himself and his .38 out of Cane's way.

Cane's first impression of Brad Testerman was that he could probably have coped with an attack without aid from the two bully-boys outside. He was stocky, of medium height, with a full jaw – like a reversed boxing glove at the chin. He carried it the way no fighter would – thrust well forward. He looked about forty.

He waved Cane perfunctorily to a hard chair in the bare room. He blinked his eyes as if to retain a preconceived stereotyped image which he was unwilling to surrender in the face of the real man in front of him.

'What can I do for you?' It was more a challenge than a question.

'I have been speaking to Mr Renshaw in Cape Town,' said Cane, feeling his way. 'Mr Grimmock in Johannesburg was in touch with him about your offer to acquire our drilling site land.'

Cane's comparison of a boxer's jaw on the man was reinforced by its blueness and the way Testerman clamped the lower part shut and screwed up his eyes at the same time, as if expecting a punch.

'I saw Renshaw – what is your status in this matter?' he demanded aggressively. 'As I understand it, you're only the straw boss at the site.'

'Listen,' he came back. 'I don't care for the sneer under the slang. I'm not the foreman of a bunch of manual labourers.'

'Then what in hell are you?'

'Mr Grimmock seemed satisfied with my qualifications, and that's all that matters,' he retorted. 'Mr Grimmock has asked me to act as intermediary in this proposed deal.'

'I put my proposition to Renshaw in principle. Is this a trial balloon from your side?'

The man was as prickly as a porcupine.

'I'm not putting forward any proposition – you have. I'm here as intermediary.'

Testerman shrugged. 'In my scene, discussion of price is a face-to-face deal by principals. No go-betweens.'

'Shall I tell that to Mr Grimmock – I am seeing him later in the day.'

Testerman gave a movement which seemed to move his shoulders inside his thick sweater while the garment stood still. It was a gesture which could be construed any way.

'Why does your observatory want still more land?' Cane went on. 'You've already got more than you can use.'

'I explained that to Renshaw. When your power station goes operative, it will cause electrical interference with my observatory's instruments.'

'That's a generalization. Can you amplify?'

A closed look came across the tough American's face. 'I have in my charge the most sensitive collection of electro-optical instruments outside the United States.'

'That still doesn't answer the question.'

Testerman got up abruptly and went to the window. If it hadn't been open, his short jabbing gesture would have broken the glass.

'Look – those two are twin parabolic radar antennae,' he said. 'Know what they are for?'

'Not a clue.'

Testerman seemed to relax. His voice took on a less strident note. It seemed to Cane that what followed had either been said before or carefully rehearsed.

'Their job – day and night – is to keep track of a telescope which is floating out in space,' he said. 'It is known as IRAS V – infra-red astronomical satellite. It weighs one ton. It maps heavenly bodies by the heat they emit. It is so sensitive that it could detect a baseball from a distance of a couple of thousand miles away purely by the heat the ball gives off. This sensitivity is critical – unlike ordinary light, infra-red rays travel easily through the clouds of interstellar dust which have previously blocked man's view of deep space – even to an instrument like the Kitt Peak Mayall telescope in

Arizona, which has a diameter of four metres and is equipped with a sensitive electronic camera.'

Testerman had unconsciously taken up a lecturing pose; he had it all by rote.

'The IRAS telescope is helium-cooled – in fact, its detectors are stored in a giant vacuum flask filled with liquid helium to a mere five degrees above absolute zero.'

'Why?' asked Cane.

'Because the satellite's own heat would normally overwhelm the faint celestial signals it picks up. And, boy, space is cold enough without getting down to 456 degrees below!'

Cane noted with surprise the change in the man; for a moment, as he spoke, the aggressiveness and defensiveness seemed to disappear and another person emerge. A much more likeable person.

'How do *you* know?' asked Cane.

'I know because I trained as a spare astronaut.' Then, as if he realized he was opening up, he went on curtly. 'That's got nothing to do with what we are discussing. I am merely illustrating that we at Soutbos are dealing with highly sensitive instrumentation.'

'The instruments are orbiting in space, according to your own remarks.'

Testerman screwed up his eyes and clamped his lower jaw.

'Twice a day a satellite passes overhead here, and twice a day over the Rutherford Laboratory in Oxfordshire in England. It transmits automatically to the ground all the data it has recorded. We then pass it on to the Jet Propulsion Laboratory in California for analysis.'

'Is that what you use the old lighthouse at Cape Agulhas for?'

Testerman rounded on Cane in a blaze of suspicion. 'What makes you say that, eh? What has it to do with you?'

'You may remember that I tried to waylay an intruder your guards couldn't handle.' He indicated the mark on the bridge of his nose. 'He did that – with a knife.'

If Cane expected any sort of retraction or apology from the

tough American, he was mistaken. All he said was, 'It proves you can look after yourself.'

'I'll remember that next time.'

'If there is a next time,' snapped Testerman. 'Look, Cane, tell Grimmock we need his land. I've given you part of this laboratory's space function. But I haven't told you what we scientists regard as more important – observations of Halley's Comet.' He paused, and again Cane had the impression he was rehearsing his lines.

'Halley's Comet has a history going back several hundred years before the birth of Christ, when it was first recorded by the Chinese. It could have been the star which guided the Three Wise Men to Bethlehem. In 1066 it shone down on William the Conqueror's army invading England. In 1682 Edmond Halley observed it and made careful observations and predicted its return seventy-six years later – and, in fact, it appeared on Christmas night 1758. . . .'

'Why are you telling me all this?' demanded Cane. 'It is simply a rehash of what the media has already said and written.'

'I'm coming to that,' he replied offhandedly. 'We have the job here – despite the fact that Halley's Comet has been and gone – of tracking the four rocket probes which were launched at the comet back in 1985. Two of them were Russian. They are still transmitting valuable data. In fact, the comet will remain under observation until 1990 at least – it was first spotted by two astronomers in California as long ago as 1982. That means that the comet will have been monitored for about a decade. There has never been a scientific study like it before. Soutbos is critical to it. We cannot have interference – even in the disappearing stages of the comet's visit. Scientifically, in fact, this could be the most valuable stage of all.'

'Dr Testerman, you've wrapped up your package in a lot of scientific tinsel,' said Cane. 'Your objections are based on an assumption – that the geothermal power station will interfere with your observations. How do you *know* that?'

'It must – it must!' retorted Testerman heatedly. 'How can it be otherwise?'

'I'm asking you.'

Testerman remained silent, and Cane followed up his advantage. 'What do you bid for the drilling site land? Your asking price?'

'I don't talk price through an intermediary. That's for across the table with Grimmock himself.'

'You're assuming that Grimmock will give an open-and-shut answer. Negotiations could take months. I shall go on drilling in the meantime. . . .'

Testerman's face became angrier. 'I'll have no tie-in deal,' he snapped. 'When we start talking turkey across the table, all drilling must stop. Your machinery and men must go. That's flat.'

'You don't expect us to leave millions of dollars' worth of machinery to rot?'

'My guards can take care of it – it's no problem.'

'I think it is – apart from personal considerations.'

'Listen, Cane,' said Testerman in his overbearing way. 'Grimmock should be grateful to us for our offer. Your project is down on its axles, run down – and, from what I hear, things are getting worse. There's not been much sign of revival since you came.'

'I don't care for that remark, Dr Testerman. I've been here only a couple of days. I worked on the world's first geo-thermal project in Cornwall and I know the potential of the Helderwachtvlei project.'

'Are you trying to bid me up?'

'No. What I am saying is, that if the decision whether or not to sell rested with me, I would see that the potential of Helderwachtvlei was realized.'

'Brave talk, Cane,' answered Testerman. 'However, big business doesn't operate on unrealized hopes. You may find that to your cost.'

Cane shrugged. A silence fell between the two men. Then Testerman said in dismissal. 'You know my feelings and my reasoning now. You can acquaint Grimmock with them.

Once you've done so, a mutual top-level meeting can be arranged. I will then be prepared to put forward a price.' He scribbled on a scrap of paper. 'Give Grimmock this telephone number. It's my private number. It's better than using the general switchboard.'

'I'll be in touch when I return from Cape Town.'

'That won't be necessary. The number is for Grimmock's use.'

15

'Two million dollars – that's four times what we paid for the land!' exclaimed Renshaw.

'What do you say to that, Cane?'

It was late that afternoon. The three men sat in Renshaw's soul-less boardroom in Cape Town.

'If that is what Testerman intends, why didn't he give me the figure this morning when I saw him?' Cane replied warily.

Renshaw brushed aside Cane's reservations. 'Perhaps he had his reasons – the point is, he telephoned Mr Grimmock after his meeting with you and offered two million dollars for our site. Two million for a piece of useless marshland and swamps! I'd go for it!'

Grimmock sat at the head of the table with his jacket draped over the back of his chair. He said tightly.

'I was asking Cane his opinion.'

There was a sense of power and purpose about the mining magnate which had appealed to Cane from the first. At fifty-one, a thousand financial skirmishes had left its toll only in two silver patches of hair at his temples, which a skilful hairdresser had turned to distinction. He looked physically fit, as if he played squash.

Before Cane could reply, Grimmock went on thoughtfully.

'I wonder what prompted Testerman to come up with his offer *after* you had left him, Cane. I don't like my arrangements being pre-empted – even for two million dollars. I wanted you as intermediary, and I mean it to stay that way.'

Whatever Grimmock might say, Testerman had effectively sidelined Cane and put his career on the line. He had arrived in Cape Town to find Grimmock – to whom Testerman had spoken directly by phone – already in possession of an over-generous offer for the drilling site.

Cane had left the American scientist as coolly as a brush-off and two loutish guards could make him feel. His temper had not been improved when Stander stalled yet again when Cane nominated three men as night watchmen for that night. Eventually he had ordered Stander to get on with it.

Now he was confronted with the situation of an actor who had been adroitly upstaged.

Cane chose his words. 'I tried to establish straightforwardly from Testerman why the observatory was so keen not to have the geothermal project go ahead. He simply asserted that a power station would interfere with the delicate electro-optical instruments installed at the observatory. He gave me a long spiel about monitoring a helium-cooled space telescope and probes which were fired years ago to track the course of Halley's Comet.'

'That is a reasonable assumption,' said Renshaw.

Grimmock ignored the interruption. 'You say, asserted. Did he give reasons?'

'He stated flatly that it was so. When I asked for reasons, he couldn't give them.'

'Do you consider that our power plant will interfere with the observatory?'

'I don't see why. I saw various types of radar and what I think was a radome. If the radar were used for tracking ground-hugging objects, I might consider that he had a point – perhaps. Also, all of them are kilometres away from where we will have the thermal power plant.'

'Power lines?' Grimmock asked.

'We can site ours where we wish. The Americans don't

seem to have any objections to the present power supply from Cape Agulhas.'

'They don't carry the sort of voltages that ours will.'

'True. But we're not transmitting anything. Generation of power is a passive operation. There may well be a local field round the generators, but I am pretty sure it won't cause the interference Testerman claims.'

'I see.'

There was a pause, and then Grimmock said incisively.

'Testerman's offer tempts me, Cane.'

Cane could feel Renshaw's appreciative vibes.

The magnate went on. 'Two million dollars – open and shut. A handsome profit on my original outlay. To date the geothermal project has been a one-sided balance sheet – all outgoings, no return. The entire operation seems to have got bogged down. The sensible thing seems to be to sell out at a nice profit.'

There was another tight silence. Grimmock broke it. 'Apart from the financial aspects, the project has been a headache in other ways. Endless accidents. The Howells affair, and now Bosch. How is Bosch?' he fired at Renshaw.

'Bad. He's still in intensive care. Semi-comatose. Can't speak. The specialists can't make up their minds whether or not to risk an operation.'

'I've had more than my fair share of this sort of thing, Cane,' Grimmock went on testily. 'I'd be glad to free myself of the project for these reasons. Have you made any progress with your investigations?'

Cane thought quickly. What had he to show for his visit to Frenchman's Eye? A man like Grimmock – especially one like Renshaw – would view the visit to the ruin as simply an excuse for an outing with a pretty girl. The lighthouse affair? The contaminated fuel? It would be useless trying to fool Grimmock with generalities.

'I can't prove what I am going to say,' he answered. 'But I believe that all the accidents, the unexplained accidents which normally would never have occurred in an enterprise like this, have been engineered.'

'Engineered?' exclaimed Grimmock.

'Engineered. And ruthlessly carried through.'

'By whom?'

'Someone who is determined to get rid of the geothermal project at any cost.'

Grimmock came alive. A fight was what appealed to the man.

'If it had been in a city, I could have understood – and handled – industrial sabotage. But out here in the backwoods – who wants us out of the way?'

'The same outfit which is prepared to make a ludicrous offer of two million dollars for about ten square kilometres of swampland which has no value to anyone except us.'

Grimmock gave a quick drum-beat with his pencil. 'Why should the Americans want us out of the way? – tell me that.'

'I can't,' answered Cane. 'To me, the offer – and Tester-man's tactic of by-passing me – smell. I don't know why. I intend to find out.'

'If you remain on,' Renshaw intervened.

Grimmock seemed not to hear the interjection. He was eyeing Cane keenly. 'What are the Americans after? Something of ours? – no, it can't be. Soutbos is an academic, not commercial, outfit. Even if there were something valuable we don't know about, they couldn't exploit it.'

'I agree,' went on Cane. 'Give me a chance, and I'll put the geothermal project into orbit. I believe it has enormous potential – greater than the Cornwall project. If it works, there are twenty-one other sites in South Africa where similar projects could be established. You said so yourself. I haven't had a chance yet to prove myself.'

'This is what I like to hear, Cane,' said Grimmock. 'The geothermal idea is something special as far as I am concerned. The experts were sceptical when I launched it. If for nothing else, I want to prove them wrong. What do you intend to do to get it going?'

'First the whole team will live on the site. They will work shifts, day and night, twenty-four hours a day. This business of commuting daily from Bredasdorp and working eight hours a day is for the birds. Their working morale is sapped every time they get back to town. I'll reconstitute the team, fire the trouble-makers and back-pedallers. I'll make a major effort to complete the shaft-head excavation so that we can put down really deep drills.'

'I like it,' said Grimmock slowly. 'I like it, Cane.'

'I need a replacement master-sinker to assist Stander,' Cane went on. 'The choice may be tricky. His is the sort of mutual trust job where you simply can't thrust one man upon another.'

'That's what made the Bosch–Stander team so good,' added Renshaw, who seemed determined not to be left out of the discussion.

'I'll consult Stander, and if necessary send him up to the goldfields to interview prospective workmates,' Cane continued.

'All this is going to cost a lot of money,' said Renshaw carpingly. 'I'll need your authority, Mr Grimmock, to spend still more on unproductive expenditure, and Cane will have to get mine. . . .'

'Forget it,' snapped Grimmock. 'Cane, you will act on your own initiative and cut red tape, see? I want results – soon.'

'Does this mean you are side-tracking the management side of the project, Mr Grimmock?' Renshaw asked weakly.

'For the moment, as far as Cane is concerned, yes. He has my authority to act as he thinks fit.'

Renshaw threw Cane a venomous glance and consoled himself by scribbling some notes.

Cane pulled from his pocket the slip of paper on which Testerman had noted his telephone number. He passed it to Grimmock. 'Dr Testerman gave me this number for you, Mr Grimmock. It was to communicate your acceptance of the two million offer. He regarded it as a foregone conclusion.'

'Did he, by heavens!' exploded Grimmock.

Renshaw asked uncomfortably. 'How shall we communicate your refusal to Dr Testerman?'

Grimmock tossed Testerman's scrap of paper back to Cane.

'Cane will. He remains my intermediary. Tell Testerman any way you think fit, Cane. If your suspicions about the Americans are correct, make sure that you don't bring further trouble on your head. I won't take it as an excuse for failure.'

16

Cane knew it was big trouble the moment he came in sight of the drilling site. The diesels were silent. The place was as still as a morgue. There wasn't a soul in view.

It was shortly before lunch the following day. Cane had motored from Cape Town.

The first cloud of doubt had arisen in Cane's mind the previous evening when he had telephoned Maris at home to ask her to arrange another meeting between himself and Testerman the following afternoon. Maris had been subdued. He had asked how things were at the project; she had replied noncommittally that Stander would inform him next day. Cane's elated mood at the outcome of his talks with Grimmock had foundered on Maris' flat response. He had found himself unable to tell her – as he had intended – that he had won a reprieve for the project. He had been abrupt, businesslike, with her, and had in consequence detested his stiff dinner with Grimmock and Renshaw later.

Cane jumped out of his pickup at the office. In his haste, he bumped the Accursed Figurehead. She swung on her axis. Even Alcestis' axis was sexy.

Maris was at her desk typing; Stander was sitting in a chair smoking.

'Hello, Maris.'

Her face lighted up with pleasure. She was wearing pale

yellow corduroy slacks and a gaily-patterned sweater of local wool.

'I'm glad you're back.' Her look said more.

'Where is everyone?' Cane's question was directed at both of them.

'Everyone – there's no one.' Stander was sunk in gloom. 'The men have gone on strike.'

'Strike?' echoed Cane. That was something he hadn't taken into his reckoning when he'd been so confident with Grimmock.

Stander seemed masochistically set to enjoy the situation. 'I told you not to force the men to stand watch here at night. I named the three who were to start the rota, like you said. Within half an hour, the whole team downed tools. Noways, but noways, will they sleep at this place. You can take it or leave it, Mister Cane.'

'I'll leave it,' snapped Cane. 'I'll fire the lot. I'll hire a completely new team – a crew that will work round the clock and not behave like a bunch of prima donnas. . . .'

'It's the figurehead.' Stander chewed the gloom and a piece of loose tobacco in his teeth. 'They say. . . .'

'I know what they say,' retorted Cane. 'You told me. What did you do about it?'

Stander seemed as negative as the men. 'What could I do? I took 'em back to Bredasdorp. Luckily we'd got the excavation pumped out before I gave 'em your orders.'

'Today's Thursday – I'll pay 'em off tomorrow, which is payday anyway. I'll need your help to muster a new team, Jan. Once we've got that, we'll break this project wide open. Round-the-clock shifts. Weekends. Special bonuses. Incentives for initiative. . . .'

Nothing seemed able to lift Stander out of his glumness.

'Better go and make peace with the men before you start talking like that, Mister Cane. These lads were hand-picked by me in the first place – me and Paul. They're a special breed, are shafties. They're not just hands you hire and fire and get along with the next lot just the same. It takes time and motivation to build a team.'

Cane realized how worried Stander was.

He repeated quietly but forcefully to Stander. 'I'll need your help – a lot of help, Jan. You know the goldfields set up – where to look for the best men. Promise them top pay. . . .'

'Who says?' he demanded truculently. 'Renshaw – that bladdy skin-flint?'

Eyeing Maris, Cane replied, 'Mr Grimmock gave me a blank cheque to do what I thought fit to get the project into orbit again. I want the best, and am willing to pay.'

'Pay alone doesn't motivate men,' argued Stander. 'And its motivation the strikers lack. Something knocked it out of them.'

'There's another thing,' Cane went on. 'I want you to find another master-sinker you can work with. We all know your magnificent track record with Paul Bosch. . . .'

'How is Paul?' Stander jerked out. 'What did he say to you in hospital? What actually happened to him?'

There was a pause. As if to emphasize the silence, Maris typed a single full-point.

'He is still semi-comatose – the surgeons can't make up their minds whether to operate yet or not.'

'Did he give you any message for me?' It was the plea from a man who wouldn't hesitate to go down into the fiery hell of a shaft explosion to pull out his mate.

'You've got me wrong, Jan. I didn't go to the hospital. There wasn't time. I came straight back. Renshaw gave me the latest news.'

Something surfaced inside master-sinker which gave Cane a brief – and startling – view of what a driller's loyalty could be.

He got up, ground out his cigarette on the floor.

'*You didn't go to the hospital? You couldn't find time to see Paul?*'

'No.'

Maris sat frozen in her chair.

'That finishes it!' said Stander thickly. 'I'm quitting, see? No good can come of all this. No good, I say.'

He started to stalk out; when he got abreast of the figure-head, he said over his shoulder. 'Mark my words, there's a hoodoo over this outfit. I'm getting out before something happens to me like it did to Paul.'

There was a long silence, broken only by the sound of Stander starting up his truck and driving away.

Maris got up and put her hand on Cane's arm. 'I'm sorry, Hal – you sounded so elated and enthusiastic when you phoned from Cape Town. I hadn't the heart to tell you what had happened. What transpired with Mr Grimmock?'

He sat on the edge of her desk. He decided that even the original Maris could not have had eyes as beautiful a sea-green as hers.

'Maris . . .' he began, and then the thought struck him, should he involve her in his own hopes for the project when it was now in serious danger of folding up? He marked time; the expectant look in her face faded.

'What time is my appointment with Dr Testerman?' he asked lamely.

'Two o'clock – in about an hour and a quarter,' she replied quietly.

He still stalled, wondering how much or how little to tell her. He said, 'Maris, I don't want you to stay alone while I'm away. You must go home.'

There was a quick surge of rebellious colour into her face. 'That's ridiculous. Why shouldn't I be here alone?'

'Just say I'm scared of the hoodoo.'

'There's no such thing; and you know it!' she retorted angrily. 'Don't tell me you are being infected by Stander and the others!'

He answered so gently that she found herself taken aback by his concern. 'I'd never forgive myself if anything happened to you, Maris.'

The distance which had been between them dissolved. They were back again in the mood of Frenchman's Eye. Her anger evaporated; there was a twitch of laughter at the corners of her mouth.

'You've got a lot on your mind which you consider your own business,' she said. 'But if you take it upon yourself to molly-coddle me, that's another matter. I have a say. I'll make a bargain with you – I'll go home while you're busy with Dr Testerman on one condition.'

'What is it?'

'Despite the strike and all the other problems, you will still fly with us tomorrow to drop a wreath over Birkenhead Rock. I know you said you'd come, but in view of what has happened, you'd have every justification in going back on your promise.'

He hesitated. He knew that he would have to see the strike leaders and hear their grievances – yet, he could manage that later in the day after his meeting with Testerman, which should not take long. In any event, without a team, he reasoned, there would be little point in sitting around idly at the site next day . . .

She mistook his hesitation and her face started to close.

He took her hands in his. 'It's a deal!'

'That's wonderful – quite wonderful!' she smiled at him. 'I want you to take part in some of *Helder Wacht*'s story.'

'Part of Maris,' he corrected her. 'It's a part I want to know.'

She disengaged her hands and said. 'Thank you, Hal.'

Cane's previous hesitation about confiding details of his Grimmock–Testerman interviews vanished. 'I would also like you to know about the drilling site crisis, Maris. Yesterday we came within an ace of losing the project.'

'You were light years away with worry. Was it as bad as that?'

'Testerman bid two million dollars . . .' He gave her details of the proposed deal, of Testerman's devious strategy, and Grimmock's decision to carry on in return for a re-doubling of effort.

When he had finished, Maris said. 'The men decided to strike just about the time all this was going on. It's a good thing neither Mr Grimmock nor Renshaw knew.'

'We'd be packing our bags today, if they had. In any event, I have to inform Renshaw of the strike.'

'Leave it, Hal. What good can it do at this late stage? Tomorrow's the end of the week anyway. You can make your plans, have something positive to tell Renshaw when you do speak instead of passing the initiative to him now.'

'Maybe you're right, Maris. Come what may, I intend to put this project into orbit.'

'How do you think Dr Testerman will take the rejection of his offer?'

'He was so sure of himself yesterday that he even gave me his private phone number for Mr Grimmock to phone him confirmation. As far as he was concerned, the whole thing was cut and dried. I don't expect he'll be pleased.'

It certainly wasn't pleasure, the way Testerman greeted Cane's rejection news that afternoon – it was plain fury. Cane himself was in a less than amiable mood after being put through the security hoop again.

Cane did not beat about the bush – he informed Testerman of Grimmock's decision. Cane was reminded again of a boxer the way Testerman's tough chin came up with the characteristic champ of the jaw and narrowing of the eyes.

He crashed his fist down on the table. 'Reject! What the hell do you mean – reject? This is heavy sugar I'm offering, man – two million dollars! Don't you understand?'

'We understand all right,' replied Cane. 'It's not on – two million or not.'

'You could all go shit in high cotton with that amount for a parcel of useless wasteland,' the American got out savagely. 'Is this a trick to upgrade my offer, Cane? Why doesn't Grimmock talk to me direct, eh?'

Cane got to his feet. 'It's off,' he repeated. 'We're going ahead with the geothermal project. Nothing you can do will change it.'

'Don't give me that kind of brush-off,' the American snarled. 'It isn't the end of the line, by a long chalk – see?' He put both his fists on the table and tried to control the fury in his voice. 'Your outfit will be the loser if you don't accept our offer! I'll approach the South African authorities – who originally owned the observatory when it was sited at Hermanus before the environment became too cluttered – and they'll expropriate all your land from our boundary to

Soetendalsvlei lake. The lake is state property already, so it will be a logical extension. You won't get the sort of price I'm offering if the matter goes to arbitration, especially' – he couldn't restrain his sneer – 'when the court takes into account the lack of progress you've made with the drilling project.'

Cane's suspicions regarding the 'accidents' which had dogged the drilling project welled up inside him.

'What makes you so keen to get rid of us?' he demanded.

The answer came sharply, angrily. 'For fifty years the South Africans patiently accumulated invaluable data about the strange magnetic anomaly Cape Agulhas is known for. Then came the space age and we discovered that the phenomenon was linked to radio communication. Understanding this could be of enormous significance scientifically. Now I don't intend that Soutbos should be chased away by a mushroom outfit like yours. Mark my words, Cane, if you don't accept, I'll do everything in my power to make it impossible for you to continue.'

'I – and Grimmock – aren't the sort to be pushed around,' Cane retorted. He was eager to get away from the vicious American broadside.

'I'll institute expropriation proceedings immediately,' continued Testerman roughly.

'That won't stop us – and you know it,' replied Cane. 'Even if the site is under threat of expropriation, our work will continue. We'll fight you all the way. The legal proceedings and court action could run to years.'

'I won't let the matter rest. Tell your boss that, Cane.'

Cane shrugged. The rugged American added. 'Think it over carefully, I warn you. The noose is hanging, if you refuse.'

17

Vladimir Yasakov cursed as the light plane came in low, circled the Danger Point lighthouse to check its bearings, and then headed for the Russian divers' boat. The pilot was clearly using the lighthouse and Birkenhead Rock with its telltale patch of breakers as his datum-point; the *Kamchatka* wreck, over which the divers were operating, lay a little to the southwest. Yasakov had been on edge ever since Cane and Maris' visit on Tuesday – it was now Friday morning.

'Get those things out of sight under the thwart!' he snapped at Stefan and Josef.

The two men gathered several heavy slabs of concrete together. They were slimy and barnacled, about fifty centimetres long, edges neatly squared. But they were ragged in the centre: projecting were what looked like bits of old broken piping.

They were not pipes, but human bones – leg bones.

The slabs were examples of the infamous 'concrete shoehorn' used by the *Kamchatka*'s officers to torture revolutionary and dissident prisoners to death.

The method was as follows:

The prisoner was forced to sit and his ankles were encased in liquid concrete, which subsequently set. Within hours, excruciating cramps would set in as the circulation to the feet was cut off. After a few days, gangrene would follow, and the captive would die in intolerable agony.

These relics were the reason why the *Kamchatka* had been declared a war grave and now, that morning, Yasakov and his team had penetrated the *Kamchatka*'s prison. Anna Tarkhanova, swimming like a barracuda through a ragged doorway, had made the first discovery.

'Anna!' ordered Yasakov. 'Get that other stuff out of sight also!'

Anna looked surprised. 'It's nothing, comrade – just a few leg-irons and . . .'

'Do as I say – throw something over it. The plane will be overhead any minute. I don't want anyone to see what we bring up from the wreck.'

The plane was much lower now as it approached Birkenhead Rock.

'What the devil are they up to?' asked Yasakov.

'They're opening a window!' Anna exclaimed. 'They're dropping something – flowers!'

'A wreath,' Yasakov corrected her. 'Why should they drop a wreath?'

'They're heading here!' Anna went on.

The plane was very low. It came at the boat.

'Blast them – what do they want . . .?' began Yasakov.

It was Anna who first recognized the occupants. 'It's the girl Maris piloting it! Look, her beautiful hair!'

The four divers in their wet suits stood in the boat. Anna whipped off her diving helmet and waved it at the plane.

'Stop it, you idiot . . .!' began Yasakov. Then he froze. The plane swept by and Yasakov recognized the pilot's companion.

It was Cane.

And Cane was the man who had come with her as if on an innocent outing and she and the policeman had chatted in a language he did not understand. Now the man was back, spying on his activities. . . .

Anger – and fear – welled up inside Yasakov. Cane must know something! That wreath-dropping ceremony – it was patently a blind, a clever ruse to try and lull him into a sense of false security about the operation. . . .

Yasakov was a spy.

The *Kamchatka* salvage operation was a fake.

Shortly after the Soviet gas atoll had been established off

the southern extremity of Africa about two years previously, Russian communications experts had been greatly puzzled by a stream of signals emanating from the South African mainland. These signals defied all efforts by Red experts of the Soviet Ocean Surveillance System – code-named SOSS – who had been taken specially to the gas atoll to pinpoint them.

This they had been unable to do because the signals were being transmitted by a highly sophisticated method known as frequency-hopping, well in advance of anything known to Red technology. Top Red communications experts had established that the system – one which the Soviets for years had sought to develop but (in common with the rest of the world) had failed – hopped automatically from one frequency to another every split second, thus making it impossible to tune in to, or pinpoint, the origin of, such signals.

To try and lick the problem, the Reds had installed on the gas atoll a top-secret high-frequency direction-finding system, an HF/DF station, as it was known. When this also failed to nail down the mysterious signals, SOSS resorted to using two types of special satellites employed for ocean surveillance, with a special downlink to the gas atoll. The first of these, an electronic intercept ferreting vehicle, known as ELINT, was designed to lock on electronic signals, providing the location of their origin, and possibly the type of station (from radar interpretation).

When ELINT failed to break the frequency-hopping secret, SOSS brought in a second type of sophisticated satellite known as RORSAT – radar ocean reconnaissance satellite – which employed active radar to pinpoint stations, especially at sea. When RORSAT missed supplying the answer, SOSS ingeniously linked the two satellites to permit the passive ELINT satellite to key the RORSAT to areas of interest. This outstanding electronic achievement also fell on its face. The mysterious signals continued to flow.

SOSS argued that where electronics had fallen short, man might succeed.

The man they chose was Vladimir Yasakov.

Yasakov, now 41, was a member of the KGB. In this dreaded organization his drive and skill had attracted the attention of the late President Yuri Andropov, who himself had once headed the KGB. SOSS came to appreciate Yasakov's talents through his reorganization of the system by which SOSS collected and collated intelligence information on Western naval activities at the four Red Fleet headquarters and naval headquarters itself in Moscow. Apart from updating the existing somewhat top-heavy communications system, Yasakov had introduced alternative emergency facilities as a back-up which ensured the rapid intake of intelligence and equally rapid dissipation of that information to fleet and tactical commanders.

When Andropov had succeeded Brezhnev as head of state, Yasakov – a fluent linguist speaking English, French, Portuguese and German – was transferred to the Soviet diplomatic service. This was simply a cover. First posted to Marxist Angola and subsequently to Mozambique (because of his knowledge of Portuguese), Yasakov's assignment was to gather information from the Red state-owned and controlled fishing and merchant fleets which made use of the great harbours of Maputo and Luanda. Soviet hydrographic survey vessels, apparently engaged in innocent oceanographic research, especially in the Indian Ocean, were an important source of intelligence information, which Yasakov relayed to Moscow.

Yasakov's Maputo assignment took on a significant dimension with the establishment by the United States of a naval base and airfield at Kosi Bay, one hundred and twenty kilometres south of Maputo itself. This port, situated on the boundary of South Africa with Marxist Mozambique, was a South African possession in the early 1980s and at that time was an unspoilt sub-tropical wonderland of four interconnected lakes, palm-fringed, idyllic, hardly populated.

All this was changed by virtue of a complicated diplomatic-cum-territory deal involving the United States, South Africa, and the adjacent landlocked state of Swaziland. The United States had become increasingly concerned at the presence of Soviet warships in the Indian Ocean, and their use of the strategic ports along the African shoreline fronting that ocean. Nearest American base was at Diego Garcia, in the Chagos Archipelago, far to the north towards India. From Maputo alone the Red Fleet was able to dominate one flank of the vital Cape Sea Route, round which flowed sixty per cent of the United States' oil supplies from the Middle East. No less than eight thousand of the eleven thousand kilometre oil route was without any port or airfield from which Western naval forces could operate.

The second, or western, flank of the Cape Sea Route was likewise dominated by the Soviet Fleet from the major port of Luanda, in Angola, a Red surrogate of the Kremlin like Mozambique. If the Red Fleet chose to close this strategic pincer round southern Africa, it would constitute a stranglehold on the United States' oil jugular vein.

Because of international political implications and hostility, especially from Third World countries, the United States dared not seek use of the great South African naval base which would enable it to adequately guard the Cape Sea Route, namely, that at Simonstown, near Cape Town.

To circumvent this, the United States accordingly did a secret deal with South Africa, in return for behind-the-scenes international diplomatic backing, and in the United Nations. This deal covered the port of Kosi Bay, a South African possession. At the instigation of the United States, South Africa ceded the undeveloped port and a land corridor to it to adjacent Swaziland, which was landlocked. The acquisition of an outlet to the sea had been an issue for Swaziland for many years. In terms of the agreement, the United States was given the right to develop Kosi Bay as a commercial harbour for Swaziland as well as a naval harbour for the United States fleet. An airfield, capable of taking long-range American maritime reconnaissance aircraft, was also included in the deal.

Yasakov's outstanding services in monitoring developments at Kosi Bay brought him strongly to the notice of the head of state himself. Yasakov possessed a total dedication to his task which appealed to the Soviet leader, coupled with a ruthlessness which sprang (some said) from his Uzbek blood – he had been born in the Central Asian city of Tashkent, famous for the burial place of Genghis Khan, the Mongol world conqueror. This had given him a legacy of wild mountain blood and the faint yellow skin pigmentation of the Tartar.

The *Kamchatka* salvage operation was a bluff.

Shortly after the offshore gas atoll had gone into operation – it doubled also as a stationary 'tattletale' surveillance station athwart the Cape Sea Route – Russian suspicion regarding the frequency-hopping signals fell on the American observatory at Soutbos. Its signals and passive electronics were extensively investigated by the ELINT and RORSAT satellite 'twins'. They were found to be 'clean' – the signals were what they purported to be.

The mysterious frequency-hopping signals continued unabated.

The Russians became seriously worried.

It was Yasakov, while processing SOSS data in Moscow on a return visit from Maputo, who first put forward the idea of holding out the *Kamchatka*'s gold as a carrot (ostensibly a dove of peace, in view of the gas atoll furore) to South Africa. Where electronic marvels had failed to detect the origin of the frequency-hopping signals, human legwork might succeed.

The scheme received enthusiastic support from SOSS, and was rubber-stamped by the Kremlin. Whether South Africa would buy the idea remained to be seen.

The *Kamchatka*, in fact, carried no gold. All the Czar's fifty million in English golden sovereigns had been – as history had it – conveyed by the small old armoured cruiser *Admiral Nakhimov* which was badly savaged by the Japanese in the Battle of Tsu-Shima, beached, taken in tow as a prize, and finally scuttled by her crew in about seventy metres of water eight kilometres off the island of Tsu-Shima itself, in the Straits of Korea.

The plan for the declaration of the *Kamchatka* as a war

grave (and thus still Russian state property) and his personal appointment as Soviet representative on the International War Graves Commission, was Yasakov's own brain child. This would give him the status required in South Africa's eyes to investigate the *Kamchatka* wreck.

The problem of the gold hoard aboard the *Kamchatka* was a trickier proposition. The obvious question was, why had the Soviets sat on such information for over eighty years? The gold hoard carried by the *Admiral Nakhimov* had been common knowledge, and even formed the focus of a major diplomatic row between Russia and Japan in the 1980s regarding its recovery.

Again, Yasakov came up with the answer. He had worked at the command centre of the Baltic Fleet at Leningrad, streamlining the supply of SOSS information to Fleet Headquarters in Moscow. It was from the port of Kronstadt, adjoining Leningrad, that the Czar's ill-fated Baltic Fleet had sailed to its doom.

Yasakov produced a skilfully-faked document, purporting to be contemporary, from the Baltic Fleet's archives which stated that the Czar's gold had been divided equally between the *Kamchatka* and *Admiral Nakhimov*. The document also claimed to give details of maltreatment and torture of sailors by the Czar's officers prior to the 'Voyage of the Damned'. This latter document gave the Soviet Union all the ammunition it needed to submit it to the International War Graves Commission with a passionate plea for the honouring of these 'martyrs of the 1905 revolution'.

Simultaneously, the report regarding the Czar's gold was passed on, via the War Graves Commission, to South Africa (with whom the Soviets had no diplomatic links) with a proposition for a joint salvage operation to recover the bullion, to be split on a 50/50 basis.

South Africa sniffed at the bait, rejected it. No Russian salvage ships would be allowed in South African waters, it was categorically stated. However, South Africa would be willing to allow ashore, for a limited period of a month and under stringent security safeguards, a small team of divers. If these divers were able to produce tangible proof of Czarist gold from the *Kamchatka* wreck, South Africa might be willing to reconsider the matter.

It was all that Yasakov needed – except that the time limit would squeeze him unmercifully. He had the answer to the gold – he would take ashore with him from the gas atoll a small number of genuine English golden sovereigns of contemporary date. With these he would 'salt' the wreck and eventually produce them to prove the Russian story of the *Kamchatka*'s gold. He would, in terms of the security protocol, hand these over to the South African police watchdog.

South Africa had been lukewarm about the plan, but had finally agreed.

Of Yasakov's team, only Anna Tarkhanova had an inkling of what the true purpose of the salvage operation was. Anna had been briefed that it was a cover for a secret mission to which Yasakov had been assigned – that was enough for her, as a good Russian. Anna was a prominent member of the Komsomol (Young Communist) organization aboard the gas atoll.

When Yasakov first landed, he was full of confidence that he would soon find the source of the frequency-hopping transmissions – Red surveillance experts felt that they emanated from the Agulhas Peninsula. He decided to go first for high, unfrequented places as a possible venue of a secret transmitter. He was jubilant to find soon just such a place within easy reach of the diving team's base – Frenchman's Eye. It had the right ingredients – a ruined tower, a commanding position on the highest peak in the area, an isolated situation where few people went. He was disappointed. It was clear that Frenchman's Eye had never been used for transmissions.

Yasakov then tried the next high place close to home – the 45 metre Danger Point lighthouse. When he explained that he was one of the Russian team diving off Danger Point, a friendly and bored lighthouse-keeper took him on a conducted tour. It was as clean as a whistle. Yasakov moved systematically round the coast, investigating another notorious wreck-strewn promontory known as Quoin Point, about halfway between Danger Point and Cape Agulhas. It turned out to be a harmless automatic light mounted on a framework tower.

Yasakov and his team had been ashore about a fortnight by the time he had eliminated other likely places ahead of the old lighthouse at Cape Agulhas. A prior visit had revealed the guards and security fence; it was no secret that it was part of the Soutbos observatory. Yasakov waited his moment for a foggy day to attempt his break-in.

That day happened to coincide with Cane and Maris' visit.

Under cover of the fog, Yasakov had cut the fence, climbed up on to the roof, eluded the guards, and made his way into the glasshouse on the summit.

The place contained highly sophisticated electronic equipment.

Yasakov was triumphant. He knew he had found what he had been sent ashore to locate – the frequency-hopping transmitter, although its abstruse mechanism was beyond his knowledge.

Yasakov had been unlucky. At the moment of his discovery, a two-man American guard squad had entered the glasshouse on a routine two-hourly round. Yasakov took to his heels; his savage encounter with Cane served to plant in his own mind the fact that somehow Cane was associated with the American security set-up. This was reinforced by Cane's visit to Birkenhead on his way with Maris to Frenchman's Eye. Yasakov had recognized him and become alarmed. He became convinced that Cane had been assigned to spy on him, and that he was using the geothermal project as a front.

Now, Yasakov watched the disappearing plane with narrowed eyes. If Cane were genuine, how could he take time out from the geothermal project on a normal working day with the pretty girl he knew to be his secretary? This was the third time he'd seen them together. Obviously, she was involved in his spying activities. He felt sure that a camera in the plane had recorded everything visible in the boat – he congratulated himself on having hidden the 'concrete shoehorns'.

Yasakov was, of course, unaware of the strike that had paralyzed the drilling project, or of the fact that Cane's stay at *Helder Wacht* had been extended because of it, or that Maris' parents were leaving that afternoon for a vacation up-country.

'Do you think the plane will come back?' Anna asked Yasakov eagerly, like an excited child.

'Be your age – they've seen all they want to see for today.'

Anna's smile wilted under his biting tone. 'You don't really think so?' she persisted.

They wouldn't come – but he would go to them, Yasakov told himself incisively. He'd go to the drilling site. He'd search the place and find out what Cane was up to. Tonight.

18

Yasakov peered into the murky darkness, every nerve taut strung. Where was he? Where was the drilling site? Where was the turn-off to it among these sodden, god-forsaken marshes? They seemed to generate fog like theatre smoke-machines. He both cursed and welcomed the murk: it would conceal him during his projected search of Cane's outfit, but it could also prevent him from finding the place at all.

It was dusk that Friday afternoon. When the weather had started to deteriorate later that morning, Yasakov had cut the diving operation. The cloud had socked in, a thin cold rain had started, and the team and Wessels had spent a long, prickly day cooped up together. Finally, Wessels had departed to Gansbaai, leaving Yasakov free to undertake his mission.

Just when Yasakov had begun to fear that he had overshot

the combined turn-off to the drilling site and American observatory, the sign loomed up out of the fog.

Yasakov got out of his pickup, made a quick reconnaissance. His problem now was to find a safe place to park his pickup for a quick getaway, if need be. With swamps flanking the road, a turning place seemed out of the question. Two roadways branched leftwards as the sign indicated, but a third track – in shocking state – continued straight on. This, he knew from maps, led to a ruined farm. It was clear from the state of its surface that it was never used.

Yasakov explored this old track on foot, and eventually found a place some way along it firm enough to turn round. He returned to his vehicle and drove to the spot – he marked it by leaving his flashlight burning there. From here he intended to walk to Cane's offices.

Now for it! Yasakov cut the headlights, reached into the cubby. He took from it a skin-diver's knife and lethal blue Makarov automatic. He smiled cynically to himself as he checked the weapon. The diving team had been forbidden weapons by the South Africans – a KGB man without a gun! He had carefully dismantled his favourite weapon and secreted it among the electric motors and portable generator and batteries of the 'donkey' before coming ashore. The South African authorities had been naïve enough not to search the diving team's gear more than cursorily. The need for concealment had, however, left him short of ammunition. He had no more than twenty-five rounds, some of which had come ashore in Anna's personal belongings and some in his own sponge bag.

Yasakov started back along the potholed track to the signpost. He wore the same dark clothes, boxer-type canvas boots and balaclava as he had for the lighthouse sortie. The boots were soon soaked.

After the turn-off, there was not a sound. There was no intrusion of anything at all upon Yasakov's senses except the cold, decaying smell of marshland. He followed a winding route slightly downhill, steering by the feel of the soles of his feet rather than by sight – he dared not risk the flashlight.

Suddenly something – he hadn't heard a sound – loomed huge and amorphous in front of Yasakov. He dropped into a crouch, pulling out his knife and pistol.

Then he almost burst out laughing with relief.

It was a building!

He had stumbled upon Cane's office prefab. Now he groped forward towards the vague outline, hands outstretched, hoping to locate a door or window to give him access to the interior.

He was almost up against the structure proper when his hands lighted on something solid. It swayed away from his fingers.

Yasakov's knife went forward into an attacking position.

It wasn't human, from its feel – but what in hell was it?

The thing moved back at him, scraped the point of his knife. But it didn't recoil from the sharpness.

Yasakov took a pace back, shaking. Had he triggered off some kind of special sensitive burglar alarm? He had to risk the flashlight!

He transferred it to his right hand – his knife hand – to work the switch simultaneously while holding the weapon, and employing his left for aiming the Makarov.

Now!

If it hadn't been for the fixed posture, Yasakov would have sworn that the face and breasts were real. As it was, he – like so many others – was astounded at the lifelike beauty of the figurehead.

The light also revealed a door beyond the figurehead; the place seemed completely deserted.

Yasakov gave the figurehead a trial shove. She swung backward and seesawed seductively forward again. He drew the immediate – and correct – conclusion that the base on which Alcestis stood was counterweighted.

Yasakov's mind began to race as an idea took shape. Alcestis could be the way in to Cane's secret! He could prove his suspicions – if. . . . It all depended on the amount of space in the statue's base.

Yasakov pulled Alcestis towards him to investigate. She came forward as willingly as any half-naked whore would. Yasakov knelt and checked the counterweighting layout. Immediately he spotted the two old cannon-balls in the hollow interior.

Yasakov leant back, excited. One could not have found a more suitable and unlikely place in which to secrete a highly sophisticated electronic 'bug' and minute, ultra-sensitive microphone in order to tap conversations. The thin prefab walls would offer little interference to electronic eavesdropping.

The gadget itself – a model of which the KGB was specially proud – had been brought ashore by Yasakov, and was now at Birkenhead. No one had thought of looking twice at his electric razor, in the head of which the 'bug' had been hidden to escape South African scrutiny.

Yasakov's mind raced on the logistics of the bugging operation. It would mean a return visit. The figurehead would have to be removed and carried to a safe spot nearby. This would require the assistance of one of his team. He almost automatically decided on Anna – she had the brains and initiative.

However, the operation would have to wait for later. His immediate task was to break in and case Cane's offices.

Yasakov turned his attention to the door. The simple, standard lock was child's play to the KGB man. He didn't even bother to employ his special stainless steel picklocks – his knifepoint was enough.

Once open, the flashlight revealed the reception area with Maris' desk and, beyond, Cane's own office. It looked more promising, especially the big safe in the corner.

Close to it, Yasakov's lips curled – it didn't even have a combination lock. It was the kind of old model the KGB practised its kindergarten trainees on.

Yasakov put away the Makarov, knelt, laid the knife next to him on the floor.

He was about to slip a beautifully fabricated masterkey into the lock.

He heard the stealthy tread of a footstep, almost upon him.

It was Cane.

19

Yasakov's reactions were like lightning. He did not even consider how Cane had come upon him. In fact, Cane's pickup had slid off the track up to its axles in bog. He had come on foot.

Cane came at him.

Yasakov did not attempt to get to his feet. He grabbed his knife and snapped out the torch in one swift action, rolled past the desk.

His sole thought was to get clear – the consequences of being nailed as a KGB man were too horrendous.

Cane flung himself at the safe, hands out to grab the balaclava-ed figure – his split-second identification was that he was the same man as at the lighthouse.

He found nothing.

Yasakov spun on his shoulder on the floor, making for a gap between desk and wall which would take him to the door. Cane heard the movement in the darkness, just touched Yasakov's tight black jersey. It was no more than a fingerhold. Yasakov wrenched free, snapped the flashlight full into Cane's eyes. It blinded him. All he was able to spot was a black-clad figure crouching; it launched itself up; there was the wicked gleam of a knife-point, advanced and pointing upward. That was how it had been at the lighthouse.

Cane kicked, unsighted. Yasakov grunted with pain as Cane's shoe connected with the Russian's wrist – the knife went spinning.

Yasakov was fast – and skilled. In a flash he had cupped his free hand round Cane's ankle. Hopelessly off-balance, Cane was an easy target to upend and send crashing against the safe.

Then Yasakov was gone.

Cane knew that it was crazy to go after him unarmed. He needed his gun lodged in the safe – and light to unlock it. He would have to risk exposing himself by using light. Cane did not hesitate. He snapped on the switch – the sudden illumination blinded him momentarily – snatched his keys from his pocket, whipped open the safe door.

There it was – his customized .45 Colt Combat Commander with its set of high-accuracy Bo-Mar competition sights and special stainless steel butt. He had bought it while studying in the United States for competition shooting.

Cane snatched up the gun, some extra shells, smacked the safe closed, pitched the keys into his pocket, and flung himself after Yasakov.

Which way had the intruder gone?

Yasakov had escaped; he had also blundered.

Directional orientation was hopeless in the fog, which as so often in the Strandveld had fallen like a blanket after dark. Even if Yasakov had used his flashlight, its tiny beam would not have helped him. But he was certain of the one thing that would – the feel of the hard track. There was a rough parking area in front of the offices. The approach road entered from one side.

Yasakov moved swiftly across the parking ground, the way he thought he remembered approaching. A light – blurred but still strong enough not to be wholly obscured by the fog – jumped up in the office behind him.

He must get out!

Yasakov found a track. It was firm – he was on his way!

After a short distance, he sneaked a look back. The tell-tale light had vanished.

Yasakov hurried on.

Cane slipped out into the darkness – he'd put out the light. He stood hard against Alcestis in order to fox his attacker should he be waiting for him.

Cane tried to project himself into the place of the man in

the hope of trying to establish in which direction he might have gone. There was nothing in the safe of value to an outsider, even in the interests of industrial sabotage.

Sabotage!

That was it! That was what the man had been up to. The attempt on the safe was, Cane reasoned, merely a secondary operation. His main purpose was to create one of those 'accidents' which had played such hell with the project. If he were correct in his assumption, the intruder would head for the excavation site. The sole escape road led to and from it past the office. But there was another possible exit beyond the normal route via the road junction – towards the American observatory, although the security fence blocked the way. However, it would not be a barrier if his attacker were an American, one of Testerman's men, and the fence had been neutralized for his escape. . . .

Cane didn't hesitate further. He headed for the shaft head.

Yasakov knew he was off course the moment he stumbled over a thick polythene cementation rig hose on the outskirts of the excavation.

He stopped. Panic surged through him. Did the track lead to a dead end where he would be trapped by Cane . . .?

Yasakov pulled himself together. Cane had no idea in which direction he had gone – perhaps he was at this moment racing up the real exit road. If that were so, should he retrace his steps and try to locate that route? Maybe bushwhack Cane in the process?

Such a course would be too dangerous, Yasakov decided. What was needed was a cool head and nerve – and some kind of shelter where he could use his flashlight to consult the small illuminated boat's pocket compass he had brought along with him. He would press on for a limited distance, see what lay ahead, and try and find such a spot to get his bearings.

Yasakov went on, his unease growing at every step. He sensed the presence of objects – what they were, he could not define – about him in the fog. He was, in fact, passing within metres of the open excavation, overhung by the tall construction crane. The smells also puzzled him: the unique odour of wet cement sidewalls, then the acrid reek of diesel fuel and anti-rust paint.

Although Yasakov did not know it, he was heading straight into the machinery park in the lee of the low ridge. This, by virtue of the order in which the machines were employed, formed a natural laager: trucks and bulldozers on the periphery, more exotic machinery such as six-boom and two-boom rigs and massive cactus grabs in the centre.

Somehow, Yasakov passed through the outer line of machines without bumping into one. Then something touched him lightly on the shoulder. He leapt sideways like a shot buck, cannoning into a tangle of rubber pipes. They were on his face and neck like an octopus' tentacles.

Yasakov froze, consciously dropped the pistol barrel which he had instinctively aimed at a central steel column which supported the boom rig's arm hydraulically.

Yasakov moved sideways, encountering more rubber and steel.

Where was Cane?

Yasakov stood rooted, fearful of creating any giveaway sound by moving. His need to consult his compass – a few seconds would be enough – became more imperative still.

He pocketed his gun and used both hands outstretched like a sleepwalker to feel his way. His fumbling fingers banged into a pyramid of stacked ten-litre empty fuel and paint drums. They went down with a crash. It seemed to Yasakov that the sound could be heard as far away as Cape Agulhas.

The racket and Cane's shot were almost simultaneous.

Like an old-fashioned submarine firing on a sonic bearing, Cane could range his shot only in the sound's general direction.

Yasakov noted subconsciously the heavy clap of the shot – a man-stopper calibre – and the slug screeched off a solid piece of machinery into a hysterical ricochet. It ended in a metallic thud of white-hot metal against something unyielding.

It was only seconds before both hunted and hunter knew what it had hit.

The blazing ricochet had acted like an incendiary bullet: it ripped into a small drum of either fuel or paint.

A small glow cut through the fog; in seconds it turned to glowing incandescence. Then into a lightning bolt – the contents exploded like half a dozen grenades. Flaming liquid spewed in every direction.

The intense heat surrounding the drum cleared the fog like a flarepath.

Yasakov, gun at the ready, gasped at what it revealed. It was like a walkway into a nightmare world – huge machines resembling prehistoric monsters, steel arms and claws, massive jaws capable of biting tons of earth at a snap – they were on every side. Scalding light flamed through a forest of pipes and hydraulic arms.

Yasakov kept his head. He went down on his knees to present the smallest target. He consulted his compass by means of the unexpected gift of light, equating its readings with the map picture in his mind. Now he knew exactly where he had gone wrong. He had headed north from the office instead of south. The latter course would have put him back on the correct exit track. Deliberately now, like a missile silo targeting itself on a firing bearing in line with the compass, Yasakov faced the way he must escape.

Cane was athwart that route.

Yasakov equally deliberately took the Makarov and aimed it the way the compass showed.

The Russian pistol, loved by a generation of terrorists and assassins, had a lighter, more thoracic cough than the deep lung-note of Cane's Colt. The shot was, in point of fact, useless since the slug hit some metal object on the fringe of the laager. Cane was warned that his man was armed, apart from the knife he'd dropped.

One round gone from each man's eight-shot magazine.

Yasakov both welcomed the blaze and feared it. Had he intended to slug it out with Cane, he would have risked another shot in the direction of the drum in the hope of igniting another, but his first objective was escape. Now he headed the way he had come. Strange surrealistic shapes on every hand. He felt safer. The chance of a bullet – even a snap shot – hitting him seemed less likely.

Undefined shapes loomed ahead, blocking his route south. He must get south! He also knew that somewhere close was a hole in the ground deep enough to break his neck.

Yasakov edged ahead.

Two shots answered the move.

Could he be seen? No ricochets – surely Cane wouldn't fire at random.

Another deep-throated cough.

This time Yasakov saw the gun-flash – leftwards. Cane seemed to be circling towards the burning drum, firing at something he mistook for his quarry.

Facing firmly on his predetermined heading, Yasakov waited with the Makarov levelled.

It crashed out a split second after Cane's next flash.

Cane went silent, perhaps reorientating and targeting himself on Yasakov's pistol-flash.

He'd have to be very careful, Yasakov told himself.

Just how careful, he was reminded immediately and forcefully. There was a crash above his head a little to his left. Glass from a truck windscreen showered down upon him. He could now identify what the shapes were ahead.

He crept forward on hands and knees. He was reassured by the touch of a heavy tyre. He crept underneath the vehicle and tried to fathom what was ahead.

Blackness.

The drum blaze began to die down; Yasakov again drew out the compass and just managed to confirm his heading – spot on! If he could locate the road used by the dumper trucks, it would lead him to the excavation – and after that a single track led to Cane's office.

Another shot rang out. This time it was further round still to his left and, it seemed to Yasakov, from a higher elevation. He was not to know that Cane had by-passed the constellation of machinery and was now halfway up the ridge backing it. His plan had been to gain vantage height on the intruder and at the same time cut him off from his escape route to the observatory.

Yasakov crawled forward on hands and knees, steering by the deep tread-marks of heavy tyres. He started to move more confidently. He broke clear of the laager. The fog masked the dying drum fire. It was only a glow now.

Yasakov rose into a low crouch. He started on more quickly. Suddenly, the smell of wet cement was in his nostrils. He stopped, felt.

His hands scraped empty air.

He was poised on the lip of the excavation!

Yasakov broke into a sweat. One step more and he'd have been into a hole God knows how deep.

Yasakov pulled his kicking nerves together. If this was the shaft-head excavation, the office block must lie on its opposite side. All he had to do, he assured himself, was to work his way round it. . . .

Yasakov felt instinctively that he should try left, which he did. Inch by inch, he groped his way along the brink of the excavation until finally he located a track with heavy tread-cuts. He knew he was safe on course.

He hurried on.

In minutes, he was at Cane's office. Although he was convinced that Cane was in his rear at the machinery park, he took no chances. He went down on his belly, gun in hand, and edged past the prefab, silent and furtive as a snake.

Then he was clear – safe.

He hightailed up the exit road to his getaway vehicle.

20

Cane reached his objective – the top of the ridge backing the machinery laager – as Yasakov was probing his way through the machines to safety. The rising ground formed a kind of dyke against which the fog accumulated. However, Cane's purpose was not to use the ridge as a vantage-point. It was to cut his man off from where he believed he was headed – towards the American observatory. From the ridge a poor path ran to the electrified security fence. It began near the half-completed headgear 'raft'. Cane aimed for this structure. The girders would also give him still extra height for a firing platform.

In minutes Cane reached the scaffolding. He took up position, his Colt ready.

Blackness. Blackness.

The glow from the burned-out drum had vanished. He could not see the excavation, although he knew where it was beneath him.

Not a sound.

Five minutes. Ten minutes.

Had a chance bullet accounted for his man? It was unlikely. In the kind of exchange which had taken place between them the odds were a million to one against either being hit. But chances could happen – that drum, for instance. His heart had been in his mouth during the whole blaze for fear that it would spread to the entire machinery park. It would have been another 'accident' – king-size, of his own making.

Cane waited. The night was colder, the fog thicker. He began to freeze on his perch.

Should he risk a shot to where he believed the intruder still lurked? He rejected it. A blind one might start another conflagration. However, a shot might draw the intruder's fire as a giveaway.

Cane loosed a bullet into the air. It sounded as flat as audience response to a corny stage crack.

There was no answer.

Was his man lying doggo? If so, which of the two of them could stick it out longest? Cane felt that he had already betrayed his impatience by his shot.

He waited.

His ears became accustomed to the non-human sounds the machines made in the icy dampness – a creak, a contraction, a groan.

Then – a sudden thought struck Cane. What if Maris became anxious and decided to drive over from *Helder Wacht* and see what had happened to him? She could have phoned the office, and when there was no answer suspected that he had got bogged down – they had even discussed the possibility. That meant she could walk straight into the gunman in his office. There was nothing to stop him entering – Cane had left the door ajar in his haste. The thought made him feel for his office and safe keys. They were gone! They must have fallen out of his pocket during the hide-and-seek among the machinery.

Without admitting it consciously, he realized that the bird had flown. He decided to get back to the office.

Knowing the lay-out, it took him less than half the time it had taken Yasakov. He had his gun out all the time. Now, when a passing gleam from a window revealed his destination, he dropped into a firing crouch and waited.

He gave himself ten minutes. When there was no sound, he made a short rush to the doorway, slipping behind Alcestis and holding his gun under her shapely breasts. The coast remained clear.

Finally, Cane sidled into Maris' office. Gun poised, he snapped on the light.

The place was deserted.

He shut the door. A reflection on the floor near the door of his own office caught his eye. A knife!

Cane recognized the weapon that his assailant had used at the lighthouse and in their skirmish in front of the safe. It was the sort of instrument a skin-diver used.

Cane crouched low behind his desk so as not to offer a target through the lighted window and telephoned Maris.

'Maris?' he asked.

'Hal – what's wrong?' One word had been enough to give away his tension.

'Nothing much – my pickup slid off the track into the marsh. I'm at my office. Can you come and fetch me?'

'Are you hurt? You sound so . . .'

'Nothing – just a bit damp. We'll have to pull the pickup out later with a tractor.'

'I'll come right over. Wait at the office.'

A new danger loomed in his mind. If the gunman, lurking on the track perhaps, heard Maris' car approaching, he could hold her up . . .

'No,' he replied. 'I'll walk up to the road junction. I'll wait for you there.'

'*What is wrong, Hal?*' she demanded.

'I'll meet you at the fork,' he replied tersely. 'If by any chance I am not there, you are not to drive on here, do you understand, Maris?'

'I don't understand.' Her voice rose. 'Hal, there hasn't been – another – Alcestis *happening*, has there?'

He tried to play it lightly, but his attempt misfired.

'No, the lady has been trying her charms on me as the only male around, but without success.'

'I'll be over like a bat out of hell,' Maris said.

'You won't, or you'll finish up in the marsh like me,' he said. He glanced anxiously at the light. It might be serving at that very moment as a beacon to home the gunman in on him.

'Take it easy, Maris. See you.'

'Hal . . .' But he had already put down the phone. He slipped outside and up the twisting track to the road junction.

His only moment of anxiety on the way was passing his bogged-down vehicle. It loomed unexpectedly as a grey mass with two bright headlight patches. This was the ideal place to bushwhack him.

In a flash, Cane was down on his hands and knees. He crawled by, every nerve tingling.

He reached the road fork, stood guard.

The gun and the knife in his fists were the first objects Maris' headlight illuminated. He had, of course, heard her car long before it appeared in sight.

Cane went forward at the double and swung himself into the passenger's seat before Maris had brought the vehicle fully to a halt.

'*For God's sake, are you all right!*' she exclaimed.

Until then, he hadn't given a thought as to how he might look – sodden shoes, mud-streaked tan corduroys, sopping to shin height, one arm of his sweater ripped from an encounter with some edge of machinery, hands filthy, face daubed with rust or mud, or both.

'Get the hell out!' he snapped. 'Quick! Make a turn here where you've got room! Stay away from the road to the drill site.'

Before he could stop her, she snapped on the car's interior light. Her eyes were all over him – wide, distraught eyes, and an already beautiful face made more beautiful by its taut-strung muscles and framed by long black hair. He thought he had never seen anyone look more lovely. He knew in a flash, this was the woman for him.

He reached up for the light switch, but paused with his fingers on the switch. His eyes locked with hers. They both wanted the moment to last for ever. They both knew.

Then, he killed the light. He laid the knife down and held her. He could feel the uncontrollable kick of a muscle in her neck and the fine bones of her shoulder.

He said, gently and breathlessly. 'This is not the time. Not now, my darling. There's a man with a gun around.'

Her hand came across to take his, but recoiled from the touch of the Colt. She said in a strangled voice. 'I've never been so scared – so happy – so . . .'

'Quick – go!' he urged her.

She rammed the car into gear and accelerated away in the direction from which she'd come.

It was not until they reached the main tarred road after the twisty run along the New Year's River that either broke the silence. Then Cane said, holding the knife by its razor-sharp point. 'I got his knife – he came at me the same way as he did at the lighthouse. Point up.'

'The same man?' Her voice was subdued.

'The technique was like a signature tune. A complete giveaway. So was his balaclava and outfit.'

He outlined the evening's events, and finally she asked, trying to make the question sound reasonable, although she could not keep her voice level.

'How many shots did he fire at you?'

'Three – four, perhaps. I didn't count.'

'He meant to kill you?'

'Of course.'

She slowed the car to a walking pace. 'What is happening in our Strandveld, Hal?' she demanded. 'Killings, sluggings, men with guns and knives. . . . Who is behind it? Who was – is – the man who attacked you, Hal? You must have suspicions!'

What had passed between them at the road junction gave her a different dimension altogether. She was now someone to share with, confide in, draw upon, trust with secrets.

Cane said quietly. 'Maris, we've scarcely had time to speak. . . .' He told her about Testerman's violent reaction at their second meeting when he had passed on the news of Grimmock's rejection to him, and added, 'I haven't dared formulate this even to myself – I suspect Testerman. I am convinced he wants to get rid of the geothermal project. Why, I don't know. I believe he has been behind all the so-called accidents which have jinxed the project. I can't prove it, but I suspect he put our men up to their strike.'

She replied thoughtfully. 'You know what you're saying, don't you – that he traded on Howells' weaknesses and fed him drugs, that he beat up Bosch within an inch of death, and rigged a series of "accidents" which could have caused serious injuries, even deaths? It isn't a very pretty picture of a scientist.'

'That's why I've kept my suspicions to myself until now. Make no mistake, Testerman is very tough. Tonight was the last straw. But it wasn't he who attacked me – the build was different. If only I could have nailed the man! I've got to find out, Maris! I'm lacking the key to what it is all about! I haven't got a starting point to work from! What could he have been after in our safe?'

'There's nothing there of much value,' she replied.

They had now reached the entrance to *Helder Wacht* and Maris drove through the gates to the homestead's lighted courtyard.

'A little money, nothing really worth breaking in for, staff registers, inventories of machines, that sort of thing.' She pulled up short and eyed Cane. 'Wait – there *was* something, I'd forgotten. But what you suspect about American involvement may give it some meaning. Last week, a few days before you were due, Paul Bosch dictated a memo to me. It was technical, but broadly to the effect that he had located a deep fissure in the shaft-head excavation. It ran, he said, in the direction of the American observatory. Most significant, however, was that he suspected the fissure gave access to a cave under the observatory. . . .'

'*What!*' broke in Cane. '*A fissure – a cave – under the observatory!*'

'The memo was quite short,' went on Maris. 'It's there, in the safe. I typed it and locked it away myself, with a map illustrating its whereabouts.'

'A map also! Great heavens!' exclaimed Cane. 'Bosch must have kept it dark – Stander never mentioned a fissure to me. But it would account for the way the water drains away. I couldn't understand it, nor could Stander. What did the map look like?'

'It was a rough sketch – I didn't examine it closely.'

'We must get back there – now!' Cane went on excitedly. 'Now, tonight! I must see this thing! I'll have to borrow your safe key – I lost mine during the shoot-out. A fissure, an underground cave!'

'I haven't a spare safe key´– it's kept in the bank safe deposit in Bredasdorp,' answered Maris. 'All I have is an office door key.' There was, however, relief in her voice, and she added. 'Even if I'd had a key, it would have been very risky to have gone back tonight.'

'True,' admitted Cane reluctantly.

They left the car and walked into *Helder Wacht*'s spacious hall. A mirror revealed his scarecrow appearance.

'We'll go back to the site first thing tomorrow morning – my keys could be lying about somewhere. If so, we can investigate the excavation on the strength of Bosch's map! A fissure and a cave – maybe this is just what we've been looking for!'

21

Hidden eyes watched Cane and Maris next morning as their car pulled up in front of the drilling site office. Further back on the track they had passed Cane's pickup. It certainly was beyond their ability to remove it. The day was watery thin, with sunlight diffused through blowing cloud.

'I used my keys to get my pistol out of the safe,' Cane explained. 'I remember grabbing them just before I started in pursuit. . . .'

'Maybe they're still in the lock,' said Maris.

'No need for your key to the door,' he smiled at her. 'I had to leave the place open.'

Cane took his gun from the glove compartment. The move was not lost on the watcher, who also noted the professional way Cane made for the door, using the figurehead as cover; Maris waited in the car.

Cane kicked open the door, paused. 'Okay – all clear,' he called to Maris.

Maris said with a shudder. 'It seems so alien, Hal – precautions, dodging into your own office gun in hand. . . .'

He looked into her eyes. 'I didn't start it, Maris.'

No you didn't, Cane. It was started in the Kremlin, and by men you'll never know hidden deep under a famous mountain in the United States. You're in the grip of something bigger than yourself, bigger a thousand times than the Strandveld itself. . . .

The hidden watcher slipped away.

'The keys aren't in the safe,' remarked Maris.

'We'll search the path to the shaft head and machinery park,' said Cane. 'They can't be far.'

'Is it safe?' Maris asked uneasily. 'Think of what happened last night.'

'He'd be mad to hang around in daylight,' said Cane confidently.

Maris still hung back. 'Are you going to report last night's incident to the police? Perhaps the burglar came back and opened the safe after you'd left.'

Cane tested the safe handle. 'Snug as the Bank of England. I certainly shan't inform the police. What good would it do?'

Maris looked towards the shaft head and, beyond, to the brontosaurus-like machines dripping condensation.

'The whole place seems to be watching, Hal.'

'You're being fanciful,' he reassured her.

There was no sign of the keys anywhere. Cane tried to recreate his route but it was mainly guesswork. From the headgear raft on the ridge they looked down into the excavation ripped out of the marshland.

'Before we go to Bredasdorp for the spare safe key, I'm going to take a look at the floor of the excavation for Bosch's fissure,' said Cane. 'I wonder how he happened on it in the first place?'

'I really would have expected Stander to have known about it,' added Maris.

'The fact that he doesn't means that the mouth must be well hidden,' went on Cane.

'Wouldn't it be less risky to wait until we can study Bosch's map first?' asked Maris.

'You know more about it than I do.'

'If it hadn't been so technical. . . .' She shrugged. 'Let's go and look, then. But' – she checked her watch – 'the bank closes at 10.30 on Saturdays. Already we're cutting it fine.'

They positioned themselves on the edge of the excavation's square section. The shotcrete-coated walls of the upper part, about twelve metres deep, looked grim and prison-like. This was known as the founding or 'toe-in' level over which, in due course, the temporary headgear raft would operate. Sinking had been continued inside the square excavation in a smaller, round section. Its walls were of heavily reinforced metal shuttering. On its floor stood several mechanical loaders, specialized boom-rigs, dumpers and kibbles. Hoisting was by means of a crane which towered high above.

'Look how comparatively dry it is down there on the floor,' commented Cane. 'Otherwise that machinery wouldn't be there. Normally, there would be a couple of feet of water. The fissure must be draining it away.'

'Where could it be – there's no sign of it from up here,' said Maris.

They descended into the hole by means of one of the many ladders used by the workers. Cane led, guiding Maris' feet into the rungs. They reached a rock shelf overlooking the circular shaft. It was about eight and a half metres in diameter. This was the spearhead which would penetrate deep into the earth and the platform from which steel probes would plunge into the 'hot rocks' more than two kilometres under the surface.

Cane cast round, trying to locate his objective.

'The mouth of the fissure must be pretty inconspicuous,' he started to say. 'The master-sinker's job is to seal off any fissures at this level. Yet, Bosch must have either explored it himself or probed it somehow to have suspected the existence of a cave beyond. . . .'

'To have deduced that, he must have been inside,' commented Maris.

Cane started to examine the metal shuttering.

'Hal,' Maris interrupted. 'If we don't move soon, the bank will be closed. We'll then have to wait until Monday.'

'True,' Cane agreed reluctantly. 'But to have to wait even until this evening seems such a hell of a waste.'

'Pity you're tied to my car.'

Cane realized that they would not be able to return directly to the drilling site from the bank because Maris had made an arrangement for the plane she had flown over Birkenhead Rock to undergo a minor repair. This was to be carried out at the rural airfield where Cane had landed by a fellow member of Maris' flying club. He was the only person in the area competent to do it. It meant that he would have to travel with Maris first to Bredasdorp, on to the airfield, and only afterwards back to the drilling site.

'Okay – let's go. The site's as empty as a discarded beer-can.'

He was wrong. Later that day, men with sophisticated skill in their fingers would descend the same two ladders that he and Maris had used and work among the heavy machinery. They had selected these as their targets.

The drilling site had also been chosen that night as a target by the Russian diving team. Yasakov had named Anna to accompany him once it was dark enough. The plan was to carry the Accursed Figurehead to a spot where they could operate without fear of detection. There they would install the sophisticated 'bug' to eavesdrop on Cane's office. After the installation, Alcestis would be restored to her position by the door. There would be no danger of encountering anyone at the drilling site on a Saturday night, Yasakov reasoned.

Yasakov's reasoning was wrong. At dusk, Cane and Maris were ahead of the Soviet pair at the site. Fog and thin rain made the time a blurred indeterminate between day and night. Cane had the spare safe key from the bank. The plane repairs had taken longer than anticipated. It was late before they left the airfield. Cane's pent-up frustrations were aggravated by the forty kilometre detour they had been compelled to make round the lake of Soetendalsvlei to reach the drilling site.

Now, Cane opened the office safe.

Maris said. 'Nothing has been touched.'

'The memo and the map?'

'Here.'

She handed him a single page of typescript with a pencilled

map attached. Cane reached for it like an alcoholic for a drink.

'Ah!'

His eyes devoured the page, then he flicked back to refer to the sketch.

'Hal – what does it say?'

His eyes held hers. 'If what Bosch surmises here is correct, it is of the utmost significance to the project – and in other directions too.'

'What do you mean? Is there a fissure?'

'Too damn right, there's a fissure! And it's easy to find. Bosch says here that he marked the entrance by bolting the shuttering over the place instead of welding it, as is the case with the rest. It's on the western face of the cylindrical section, almost at floor level.'

'Why keep it secret by wrapping it up in jargon that I couldn't follow?'

'My guess was that he was waiting for me to arrive in order to discuss its significance, geologically speaking, and how it would influence the project.'

'A fissure is a fissure.'

Cane slid the map in front of her. 'Not this fissure – if it's a sort of umbilical cord to a cave.'

'Is a cave possible? I know that there are caves at places like Arniston on the coast as big as an aircraft hangar. Long ago, some farmers made small fortunes out of bat guano from caves on their properties.'

'The entire Strandveld is geologically unstable,' said Cane. 'That is one of its basic characteristics. That means that fissures and caves form as the earth heaves. . . .'

'We're always having earth tremors,' said Maris. 'The biggest earthquake South Africa ever experienced happened in the Western Cape nearly twenty years ago. It destroyed an entire town called Tulbach.'

'Bosch doesn't state specifically that he found a cave. The memo goes no further than saying that there is a fissure inclining downwards in a general westerly direction.'

'In other words, towards the American observatory.'

'We'll come to that aspect in a moment. If Bosch was able to state that it inclined downwards he must have explored it if only for a short distance.'

'How far is the cave from the mouth of the fissure?'

'His sketch is not to scale. There's no way of measuring. In any event, Bosch is hypothesizing about its location – even existence. You can see that from the vague outline of the sketch. If he had had anything firm to go upon, he surely would have noted it.'

'If there is a cave, what will it mean to our project?'

'It largely depends *where* it is. If it is situated under the American observatory, there would be all sorts of problems of ownership and drilling rights. There's bound to be a legal squabble. A cave would also pose all kinds of problems for deep drilling.'

'A kind of launching-pad into inner space.'

Cane was excited, keyed up. 'Smart girl! That's just about what a cave would be. We'll find out soon enough. A couple more flashlights and two hard hats with cyclops lights, and we're ready for the launch.'

'Tonight? You mean you are going to look for the fissure tonight?'

'Now! This minute! Nothing is going to stop me now from seeing what this is all about!'

'Hal – are you sure?' Maris asked uncertainly. 'Is it safe to go looking for something as dicey as a fissure in darkness – plus a cave to fall into at the other end?'

He took her by the shoulders and held her face up to his. 'Maris, a lot of things have happened at the project – Bosch's "accident" in itself – which have to be sorted out. The sooner the better. I believe we have here the key to some at least of these mysterious happenings. The fissure and the cave would be in darkness anyway during daylight. Night makes no difference underground. If you'd care to stay. . . .'

'I don't care to stay at all!' she replied so fiercely that he grinned. 'If you go down, I go down. That's all there is to it.'

'Thank you, Maris. That's what I wanted to hear.' He held her and kissed her. 'Since you're nervous, my Colt will go along too.' He laid it on the table. 'Now – quick! Let's organize lights and things and I'll double-check the magazine.'

At that moment, Yasakov and Anna sidled up to the lighted window. They saw the gun in Cane's hand: Yasakov silently and imperatively flagged down Anna into a crouch. Fog swirled. It had done so all the way along the track from where Yasakov had parked the Russian pickup at its previous hide-out. They had already been close to the office when the light had showed up through the murk. Yasakov, who had come unarmed, never expected to find Cane in occupation. Nor Maris with him.

The sound of Cane's voice through the prefab's thin walls underscored Yasakov's earlier certainty that his 'bug' would log conversations inside.

'That's the lot – let's get going!' Cane's voice pulsed with anticipation.

Yasakov, risking a look, took in at a glance the open safe, the torches, the Colt, the sheet of paper in Cane's hand, the pair's white hard hats each fitted with a blue-rimmed cyclops light and cable to a belt battery. The inference was clear – they were going underground.

'Shall I leave the light on?' asked Maris.

'Why not?' replied Cane. 'It will serve as a guide when we return. We shouldn't be too long.'

'Depending on what we find.'

'Depending on what we find,' he echoed.

Yasakov sank out of sight. He and Anna watched the cyclops lights make strange swathes through the fog as Cane and Maris went down the roadway towards the shaft head.

'Quick!' Yasakov ordered. 'The figurehead!'

'Wouldn't it be easier to bug it where it stands?' asked Anna in a whisper. Anna's eyes were alight: excitement of any kind was adrenalin in her veins.

'Too dangerous,' replied Yasakov in low tones. 'If they come back unexpectedly soon, they'd be right on top of us before we saw or heard them. Cane's a bastard with a gun – I should know.'

'Shows he's up to something.'

Yasakov and Anna conveyed Alcestis up the exit track. Once the office light was well out of sight, they would set about the bugging. They had their flashlights for the job.

Cane and Maris had their lights also for their descent into the earth by means of the ladders Cane had positioned earlier. Their cyclops 'eyes' eerily lit a scenario fit for a Hitchcock thriller – water gleamed on the subterranean labyrinth of black rock, snaking hoses as thick as pythons, heavy earth-moving and drilling machines with macabre shapes.

'I feel as if I'm blind and groping my way into something that scares me anyway,' said Maris with a shudder.

'The shaftie with an imagination is no good to himself or anyone else,' Cane replied reassuringly. 'All that's here is rock and water. It can't bite.'

They climbed down. Cane had with him a spanner which he had collected from a tool shed on the way. Finally they squelched along the excavation floor to a halt on its western face.

Cane went down on his hands and knees. 'This is it, Maris. Look! Bolts – no welds. This is where the fissure starts.'

He handed the Colt to Maris and went to work with the spanner. In minutes he had unbolted two sections of metal sheeting big enough to admit a man crouching.

'My oath! Look at that! It's a fissure all right.'

Maris joined him. Their twin cyclops lights lit the mouth of a dark hole at knee-level, half-obscured and blocked by a large boulder.

Cane found a small rock, pitched it through the opening. They heard it bounce – once, twice, three times, then silence.

'No splash,' commented Cane.

'Hal,' said Maris urgently. 'We've found the fissure – okay. But must we risk going further in these conditions? What if either of us falls – gets hurt – gets trapped. What then? It's half a nightmare to me already. Why not wait until you can muster a proper team.'

'No,' replied Cane. 'If this had been a straightforward

thing, Bosch would have done all that already. I can't turn back – not now, when I'm on the threshold of finding out . . .'

'Finding out – what, Hal? You've got nothing to go on, nothing! It's not only the hole that scares me – there's something evil here. My intuition tells me that. . . .'

Her voice trailed off.

The time was 6.45 p.m.

'I can't ask you to come – I can't ask you to stay. Not here. Not alone,' said Cane.

'I'll come. I'd rather be with you, either way.'

'Just keep your imagination in check. It's nothing but a hole in the ground. I'll lead. Hold on to my belt.'

Cane squirmed through the narrow gap. When it came to Maris' turn to enter, he reached back, gripped her hand and guided her inside.

6.50 p.m.

The fissure's floor was muddy and slippery. Cane and Maris had to brace themselves not to slide downwards. Cane's initial progress was on his belly: soon he was able to rise on his hunkers. Further on, the fissure broadened still more so that they could move side by side. The roof rose a little too. It became easier not to keep bumping their hard hats.

6.55 p.m.

They squatted on an intrusion of rock. Cane directed his flashlight beam and cyclops light this way and that. Maris clung to his belt like a biker on a pillion.

'This passageway is definitely natural – look at the formation,' he said with satisfaction.

'How far do you intend going?' Maris asked in a small voice.

'As far as it goes,' he answered. 'There's plenty of guts in these lights – they're good for another hour at least.'

'Will we ever manage to get out again?'

'It's a bit slippery, but it's negotiable,' replied Cane confidently. 'The way this fissure is fashioned and its downward slope makes me think it could have been caused by one of those upheavals of the earth we were talking about earlier. Maybe Bosch realized that too, when he saw for himself. Then, maybe he went on to deduce that there must be a cave at the end of it. I wonder how far he penetrated?'

The timing device which would trigger the explosion was set for 7 p.m.

It wasn't one of those primitive alarm clock affairs used by terrorists in the seventies whose accuracy was far from pinpoint. The bomber knew that his device would fire on the second. He had had no problem finding explosives – he had broken into the blasting shed near the machinery laager and helped himself. The mechanical dumpers, loaders, drills and kibbles on the excavation floor – through which Cane and Maris had threaded their way to the fissure mouth – were all primed with individual charges connected to a central detonator – an unobtrusive little thing about the size of a cigarette pack, mud camouflaged, and hidden under a mechanical loader.

7 p.m.

The earth under Cane and Maris bucked once, twice.

The shockwave of the blast and its ear-stunning thud followed almost simultaneously.

The eight and a half metre diameter of the circular excavation with its steel walling served to concentrate the multiple blast; kibbles, machines and drills became flying dismembered chunks of shrapnel which destroyed each other and the sidewalls.

The narrow mouth of the fissure and its winding, downward incline protected Cane and Maris just as a foxhole does against a near-miss shell-burst. One moment they had been perched side by side in tomb-like silence; the next they were hit in the back by a blast and a roar which pitched them head first down the fissure. Their cyclops lights gyrated in mad arcs.

The ground slipped, loosed, opened up. . . .

What the bomber had not bargained for was the unstable geological nature of the terrain. He had not been aware, perhaps, of the area's long case-history of earth-tremors, shakes and rock falls. He was not to know that the concentration of blast in that confined area only eight and a half metres across, coupled with the presence of a fissure which had been probably caused by some natural ground instability anyway, would provoke an artificial tremor.

Inside the fissure, the earth split, tore, ripped. Rocks ground together with a roar like Antarctic icebergs mating.

Maris and Cane crashed together. Maris snatched him by the belt.

'God! – Hal! – what!'

He held her. His light showed her face streaked with mud and muck, her eyes wide and terror-stricken. 'Darling!'

The tremor struck again. It ripped the fissure ahead of them wide, like a can-opener splitting a tin. Rock elbowed rock, widening the passageway. Loose debris, small rocks and jets of water squirted from the roof. The floor under them dissolved.

They fell. Their lights went.

The distance, in darkness and terror, seemed eternal, incalculable.

Their passage into the bowels of the earth was a bruising, terrifying one; but their landing was soft – in water. It was, in fact, a stream-bed. For them, it might have been their death-bed. Or the end of the world.

22

To Yasakov, busy with Anna bugging the figurehead, the explosion was not the end of the world: it was an inexplicable act of carelessness or madness on Cane's part. He automatically blamed it on Cane – he himself had seen him leave for the shaft head.

Yasakov and Anna had carried Alcestis to a spot out of range of the office light and therefore safe. They had first to remove the counterweight cannonballs. The interior of the lifesize statue was hollow – far too large for the compact little electronic device with its recorder which would be set in action once Alcestis was restored to her place by the door.

Yasakov and Anna were discussing the most unobtrusive place to rig the ultra-sensitive microphone. Anna favoured a spot under the arm; Yasakov one lower down (with less wire showing, therefore) where Alcestis' dress formed a series of drapes.

The explosion ripped aside the fog.

There was a time lag. Then the muffled roar reached them. The interval was short enough for them to be able only to gape at one another in stunned surprise.

Yasakov leapt to his feet. 'What the hell! That fool Cane!'

Anna was up too, eyes transfixed on the spot where the flash had leapt up momentarily through the fog.

'He couldn't have blown up his own machinery!' she exclaimed.

'Unless it wasn't his own,' Yasakov retorted.

'What do you mean?'

'Cane's a spy – that's why we're here, isn't it? He's not genuinely part of the drilling outfit. To destroy it would make sense in that context, wouldn't it?'

'For what reason, comrade?' asked Anna. The way she used the term comrade had an edge to it which rattled Yasakov.

'If I knew the reason, I wouldn't be bugging his conversations,' Yasakov replied acidly. 'The point now is, Cane has blown up something at the shaft head – and we've got to find out what it is.'

'Then let us go and look,' said Anna. She certainly didn't lack guts, Yasakov admitted.

'I go – you stay, right here,' ordered Yasakov.

'Wouldn't it be better first to put the figurehead back in position?'

'Cane's not the sort to blow up himself and his girl-friend either by accident or design,' answered Yasakov. 'They might return at any moment to the office. It's the certain place after they've completed the job.'

'They also left the light burning,' Anna reminded him.

'Stay here – we'll play it by ear, depending on what I find at the shaft head,' said Yasakov.

'Are you sure it was the shaft head?' asked Anna.

'No. All I can say is that the explosion seemed nearer than at the machinery park.'

'How long do I wait?'

'You are under my orders, comrade. You take no decisions on your own – understand? You will be here when I return – until I return.'

'Shall I finish the bugging?'

'Fix the mike on the dress at the back.'

'Yes, comrade.' Again, that irritating scrape she gave to the word.

Yasakov took a flashlight and in a moment was swallowed up by the fog.

He wished, as the office light reappeared through the murk, that he had the Makarov. Being forced to follow a single track was like being channelled into the muzzles of a firing-squad – and he knew Cane wouldn't miss.

He edged past the light on hands and knees.

Silence.

He pressed on.

From ahead came a sudden metallic sound. It sounded like a junked car being rolled over. Yasakov froze, waited. It did not reoccur. Finally Yasakov decided that it must have come from some piece of damaged machinery settling.

Yasakov was puzzled as he neared the excavation site by the complete absence of sound, or of light. Had Cane annihilated himself and the girl? Or had Cane indeed been responsible for the explosion? If not Cane, then whom? Had Cane triggered a booby trap?

Yasakov decided to risk using his flashlight. He found himself close to the edge of the excavation. A waft of pungent, burnt-metal-oil stench greeted his nostrils. Keeping the light burning, he moved rapidly to the rim of the hole and threw the beam downwards.

The place looked like a junk-yard. Machinery in pieces

and in various stages of decrepitude lay about – an arm of a multi-drill rig had been driven by brute force into the sidewall, from which it projected like a Frankenstein limb. Steel shuttering had been ripped apart – it lay everywhere. Some pieces projected still from the sidewall – in contorted, fantastic shapes.

But it wasn't upon these that Yasakov's beam steadied and probed in defiance of the risk involved in using a light with a dangerous enemy about.

The earth on the far side of the excavation looked as if it had been chopped open by a gigantic axe blow. The ground lay riven and newly opened. Yasakov was not to know that this was where Cane had found the mouth of the fissure.

Yasakov's flashlight beam held steady. He thought the reflection was coming off a chunk of metal shuttering which had been blasted into the opening.

He clicked off the light. Darkness swamped the scene of devastation.

Except in one place. The reflection was still there, despite the fact that there was no light to feed it.

The faint glow was coming from the fissure mouth.

23

Light – and the sound of voices – jerked Maris out of her trance.

She hauled herself on to one elbow in the shallow stream bed in which she lay.

'Hal! Hal! Listen! People!'

Cane lay without answering. Maris half got up, splashed to him, shook the inanimate figure. As she gripped him by the shoulder she realized – she could see! Yet both their torches had vanished in the fall.

'Hal! Hal! Please! Are you all right?'

Cane got his eyes open and his head up.

'Hal! Wake up – for God's sake – try – there are people –'

'You must be crazy,' he muttered. 'People! We fell through the world.'

Maris levered his head and shoulders round to show him what she meant. Further down the watercourse, which was ceilinged with rock, was a funnel-shaped aperture.

'Look, Hal! You must look! Light – voices!'

Cane shook his head. 'It can't be, Maris. We're dead. We fell through . . .'

'We fell – *but there are voices*, Hal! Voices! That means help!'

Cane got on his hunkers and stared in disbelief. The sight seemed to clear his brain.

'My oath!' he said in a different tone. 'You're right, Maris! Let's get on.'

They heaved themselves into a crouch and made for the source of the light.

Now the rock ceiling allowed them to stand upright, but they held back for a moment in stunned astonishment before making their way to the lighted place beyond.

They wondered, indeed, whether they had not been translated into another existence.

The cave looked like the bridge of *Star Trek*'s USS Enterprise. The walls were lined with consoles, glowing TV monitor screens reflecting eerie green and orange-red light from thirty centimetre dials bisected by yellow revolving tracking lights. Men with clip-on headphones, microphones and telephones on flexible cables to hand, played with sensitive fingers across keyboards set with galaxies of switches – red, green, blue and white – plus levers, toggles and buttons. There must have been over twenty men in the cave but fewer than half that number were operating the consoles themselves and their intricate keyboards. The others seemed to be either seniors standing by interpreting the screened displays, or technicians. Some of the consoles had a single large screen in the centre, with arrays of print-out figures and letters on smaller adjoining blue screens, while others had the same centre screen flanked by smaller similar ones on either side.

Maris and Cane debouched on a scene of chaos. The explosion had stirred up the place like a hornets' nest. Some of the men were standing by the operators yelling and gesticulating at swinging needles and fluctuating lights on the monitor screens; some of the operators themselves were cursing fluently and dancing their fingers across the keyboards to try and stabilize the gyrating pointers. One man, apparently in a position of authority, was bellowing into a red-painted phone which he had snatched from a group of others – green, blue , black, and boudoir-pink.

The double line of consoles against the walls was divided in half by a remarkable display. It looked to Cane like a big lighted cricket scoreboard with computer-type lettering and figures. It had slots numbered 1 to 9. The first of them, No 1, occupied bottom place. Next to it was the brightly illuminated word, APPLEJACK.

The cave was, in fact, a small replica of another cave hidden deep under five hundred metres of granite below the Rocky Mountains of North America, thousands of kilometres away from the Strandveld. This nuclear-safe bunker was the headquarters of the North American Aerospace Command – NORAD. Here, far beneath Cheyenne Mountain in Colorado – once the hide-out of Butch Cassidy and the Sundance Kid and where Buffalo Bill wrote himself into history by shooting 4000 buffalo in eight months – was the nightmare heart of red alerts, killer satellites, retaliatory nuclear strikes, and all the hideous panoply of nuclear annihilation. Twenty-four hours a day, every day, men hunched over screens and computers watched Soviet submarines cruise the Pacific and Atlantic Oceans, monitored Soviet planes and satellites and nuclear tests, and maintained unsleeping vigilance against nuclear attack.

NORAD's task was to warn against an impending nuclear attack, estimate the number of incoming missiles when the attack took place, assess where they would target home, alert the President of the United States, and send missiles and planes on retaliatory strikes.

NORAD HQ – or Doomsday City as it was known – was entered at the end of a long dank tunnel, whose rock dripped condensation, via two huge twenty-five ton steel blast doors cushioned on shock absorbers to withstand a nuclear blast. Beyond the giant doors were five buildings – one of them three storeys high – which comprised headquarters. These structures were grafted on steel springs to protect their delicate instruments against the concussion of nuclear explosions.

Part of the chilling nuclear scenario was a jumbo jet bomber of the US Strategic Air Command which stayed constantly airborne. It was code-named LOOKING GLASS. This flying headquarters was designed to take over should the White House be obliterated by a nuclear blast.

Centrepiece of the Cheyenne Mountain set up was a huge lighted board among the TV screens and monitors similar to the one which astounded Cane and Maris. It was, in fact, what was known as an Alert Code Status Board. It depicted the nine stages of nuclear attack. APPLEJACK – at the bottom at Cheyenne Mountain as at Agulhas – signified that the situation was neutral. Other gradations had the innocent-sounding codes, LEMON JUICE, SNOWMAN, BIG NOISE, COCKED PISTOL, FAST PACE, SAFETY CATCH, and DOUBLE TAKE, leading to the eventual apocalyptic number 9, FADE OUT.

Feeding data to, and in instant voice contact with (if necessary) were a far-flung chain of United States early warning anti-missile stations throughout the world. There were four major stations, called Sites 1, 2, 3 and 4. Site 1 was situated at Thule in Greenland; Site 2 at Shemya Island, Alaska, only seven hundred and eighty kilometres distant from the Russian coast itself; Site 3 was a Fylingdales Moor, England; and the newest, Site 4, at Soutbos Observatory, Cape Agulhas, code-named Dolla's Downes.

The so-called American geomagnetic observatory was, in fact, a front behind which anti-missile and satellite activities were carried out. The station had been established with the full knowledge and cooperation of the South African author-

152

ities in return for secret American support in world forums, especially in the United Nations. By allowing the early warning station to be set up on the highly strategic southernmost tip of Africa, South Africa had enabled the USA to complete its world-wide chain of early warning stations. Without Dolla's Downes, an important gap would have remained in the American system. Dolla's Downes' position enabled it to carry out surveillance over the great empty reaches of the Southern Ocean from which, before its establishment, Red submarine missiles could be fired undetected. Now that important Achilles heel was closed.

Cane and Maris walked forward into the light.

The explosion of silence was as tangible in the opposite way to what the explosion of the dynamite had been.

A second before, agitated voices had crackled like automatic fire. Now, console operators and assistants, TV screen operators and technicians manning recondite instruments froze as they sat or stood. The man yelling into the red telephone bit back his words. Incredulity swept through the operations room like a nuclear shock-wave.

Brad Testerman was near the fissure end of the station with Ed Weinback, his second-in-command, a wiry little man with hard eyes and greying hair.

At the sight of Cane and Maris – mud-and-water bedraggled, blinking in the unaccustomed light – Testerman's boxer's jaw came up and it champed in characteristic style.

'*Cane!*' he burst out in disbelief. '*Cane*, by all that's holy! *Here!*'

Cane addressed him through what seemed to be a corridor of gaping men.

'I – we – the explosion – ' he gestured behind him at the streambed aperture from which they had emerged. 'It threw us down – from the shaft head . . .'

Testerman strode down upon them. 'Don't lie to me, Cane! *How did you get in here – how!*'

Without waiting for a reply, he turned and shouted the length of the cave to two bruisers standing by steel doors – a smaller edition of NORAD's Cheyenne Mountain blast doors.

'Grab 'em!' he snarled. 'Grab 'em – and keep 'em grabbed!'

He spun on Weinback. 'Quick – blindfold 'em! Anything will do – so long as it keeps them from seeing more than they have done already.'

The two toughies lived up to their name. The grip one laid on Cane's arm felt as if he had doubled his sub-machine-gun barrel in half and bent it round flesh and bone.

'Listen to me!' expostulated Maris. 'We're not here because we chose to come. We never suspected such a place. . . .'

'Shut up!' snapped Testerman. 'There's a guilty bumper-sticker message plastered all over both of you!'

'Rubbish!' retorted Cane. 'We were exploring a fissure on the floor of the excavation when suddenly there was one hell of an explosion and we were thrown into the bowels of the earth. . . .'

'I'll run you out of here on a rail,' went on Testerman, his voice rising with anger. 'Jeez, Ed, what the hell's keeping you? Look at them! Their eyes are going all over the place!'

'Trying to find some cleaning cloth – the best I can do for blindfolds,' replied Weinback, searching one of the console cabinets.

'Hurry!' snapped Testerman. 'A leaker can do as much damage as a whole nuclear burst!'

'What are you talking about, Dr Testerman?' demanded Maris. She gestured at the cave and its instruments. 'What is this all about?'

'About?' His response was harsh and overbearing. 'She bursts into a classified place and asks, what is it all about? Okay, I'll tell you what a leaker is – it's one single nuclear missile which penetrates the defences and creates hell. That's what you've done – what you are.'

'We've done nothing,' retorted Cane. 'I've told you, we were exploring a fissure . . .'

'Ah, stow it!' snapped Testerman. 'Exploring a fissure – in

pitch darkness, on a Saturday night, fog to hide your move-
ments, not a man of your team in sight. Bullshit! Don't try
and kick field goals by moonlight, I warn you!'

'That's the way it was,' repeated Maris.

'Here's some cloth,' interrupted Weinback, joining the
group. 'It ain't too clean.'

'Don't be particular about the hygiene,' answered Testerman. 'We didn't ask 'em here.'

Cane held Testerman's eyes with his. 'You can't do this,
Testerman, I warn you. By whose authority. . . .'

Testerman laughed derisively and indicated the guards'
sub-machine-guns. 'That's my authority, Cane. I warn you,
don't argue with it.'

To underline his words, the man gripping Cane's arm gave
it a savage twist so that his head came forward as if to meet the
bandage in Weinback's hands. 'Spanish walk him, Brad?'

'In a moment. Get 'em both upstairs to my office. I don't
want them to see any more than they have.'

Cane's last sight of the cave, as the oily rag was whipped
round his eyes, was of the operators still staring at them in
bewilderment, against a surrealistic backdrop of consoles,
dials, switches, screens and moving patterns of multi-
coloured lights.

The guard, whom Testerman called Clint, was purposely
rough; the eye bandage was too tight, but when Cane tried to
ease it, Clint struck away his hand. 'Leave it!'

'Brad!' It was Ed Weinback. Cane recognized him from
his deep, resonant voice.

'Yeah – what is it, Ed?'

'Before you leave with these two, I'd like to check what
this screw-up has done to the instruments. We may have
to . . .'

'Keep it to yourself, Ed,' cautioned Testerman. 'These
two still have ears.'

'Okay, okay,' replied Weinback reassuringly. 'They don't
know what it's all about. We're obligated first to checking.
That's the way I see it.' There was a slightly deprecating note
in his voice.

'Okay – make it quick.'

'Fellahs – any problems?' called out Weinback. 'Anything busted by the explosion?'

There was a chorus of replies, and Weinback laughed, which seemed to lower the tension. 'I've only got one pair of ears – now, Biggs, Merrell, Suggs?'

'No hassles, Ed. We thought at first the monitors were all shook up, but they've settled back to normal.'

Another voice said. 'Proves we need steel springs under this outfit, like Cheyenne Mountain.'

'We didn't expect to be honoured by the first explosion,' replied Weinback with the same note of humour in his voice. 'Any other guys got problems?'

'Cracked dial on the satellite monitor, but she seems steady on the reading, Ed.'

'Good. Communications?'

'Phones okay.'

Weinback addressed Testerman in a more formal voice.

'Reporting, sir. Minor damage. Nothing material. All systems okay.'

Cane detected the relief in Testerman's reply. 'Good. Now listen, Ed. If what these two say is correct, the station is open to the sky. We've got to do something about it – damn quick.'

'You believe their story, Brad?'

'I'll check it, you may be damn sure, but how else did they get in here? We gotta guard against all eventualities.'

'Sure, sure,' answered Weinback.

Testerman went on. 'Ed – Tom Widdows is still on the gate, isn't he?'

'Yeah.'

'Tell him to stay on duty until I order him off. No one – but no one – is to pass in or out, understood? Unless he can identify personally to Tom or by documents.'

'Tom's a springbutt about security anyway,' replied Weinback. 'I'll tell him.'

'I want the three section leaders – Preston Biggs, James Merrell and Marc Suggs – to each take four men. Preston and his boys will investigate and report whether or not there is a fissure and whether it links up with the shaft head – clear?'

'Three teams of four will leave us only eight men on the instruments, Brad.'

'It's enough for an emergency stint,' Testerman replied incisively. 'It won't be for long. It's Saturday night, and the main signals for the day have gone out. The rest is routine. Eight men can cope. They don't have to bust their asses – nothing's cooking.'

'That we know of,' replied Weinback sombrely.

'We will never know until eight or twelve minutes before,' answered Testerman enigmatically.

'Just time to put the world in the pressure cooker,' added Weinback. They sounded to Cane like doctors discussing a patient whom they knew was sure to die.

'If you start thinking like that, Ed, you'll go out of your skull,' Testerman said tightly. 'Now – James Merrell to lead the second party. They are to take the path across the marshes to the shaft head . . .'

'The security fence is across their route . . .' Weinback started, but Testerman interrupted him.

'I know, I know. When you call Widdows, tell him to discontinue power to the fence. James is to cut the fence by the drill site boundary and go through. We can fix it again later.'

Weinback gave a low whistle.

Testerman went on. 'Marc will take a truck and beat it by road to the drilling site. Warn Tom not to hold 'em up at the gate. Report to me as soon as you hear anything. Now – get moving!'

Weinback began to muster the three teams. 'Preston, Marc. . . .'

'Clint,' ordered Testerman. 'Get these two up to my office. March!'

24

Put your head down, Vladimir Yasakov – you're seeing things which no other KGB man has ever seen before.

The Russian was crouched on his knees at the streambed entrance to the American early warning station, the way Cane and Maris had entered the cave. He had picked his way along the same route from the surface that they had followed via the explosion enlarged fissure. He had been guided at first by the faint glimmer of light which initially had caught his eye. This grew stronger as he progressed downwards – it was impossible to judge how far – and, as it did so, he became warier. Finally the batteries of consoles, TV and radar screens, monitors and other instruments had burst on his astonished gaze. The sound of voices was equally staggering.

Yasakov knew that he had hit upon a secret far weightier than anything he had been assigned to discover. He might have had second thoughts that the place was simply an underground extension of the surface observatory complex – the TV screens, consoles and the rest might well have operated as the Americans claimed. However, one thing negated that so absolutely that Yasakov could have shouted aloud his conviction – the Alert Status Board. It blazed the answer from each one of its nine coded slots. Yasakov had no more idea than Cane or Maris of its purpose. APPLEJACK stood proclaimed in lights. Yasakov knew code when he saw it, *and this was code*! What it all meant, he intended to find out.

Yasakov had been within an ace of missing out. Had Testerman marched off Cane and Maris upstairs immediately they were blindfolded as he intended before Weinback's request to wait in order to check the instruments, Yasakov would have arrived too late to have spotted them.

Also, he might have been trapped by Preston Biggs' four man team deputed to investigate the fissure.

As it was, the Russian reached the cave entrance simultaneously with Testerman's orders to check the fissure, to cut the electric fence after first neutralizing it, and for the third American group to race by road to the shaft head. He had a camera-flash image of the cave's sophisticated instrumentation, of the Alert Status Board, of the two captives. He eavesdropped on the final terse exchanges between Testerman and Weinback.

Overriding everything but his awareness that he must get the hell out quick was his certainty that in front of his eyes was a strategic secret of priceless importance to the Kremlin. He lingered long enough to see Cane and Maris led away.

Then, silent and furtive as a snake reversing into its hole, he slid back out of the light into the shadows of the fissure on his way back to the shaft head.

He had to find out what the cave was all about!

His mind went into orbit as a plan shaped itself. Even the brutal roughness of the ascent – rocks, debris, mud, darkness, sweat, gasps for breath – could not hinder the birth of the concept in his brain. First, he had to get to Anna and the figurehead before the American team racing by road spotted her. He had to get the statue safely out of sight.

The fissure's exit came almost before he realized where he was in the darkness. In a moment he was through the gap and standing on the excavation floor among the wrecked machines, every nerve and ear strained.

The place was as silent as the grave.

Yasakov sped up a ladder he had previously positioned to descend. He used his flashlight freely, knowing no one was around, to find his way to Cane's office. The light there still stood out. He raced past, and up the exit track.

Suddenly, a roundel of torchlight showed through the murk ahead.

'Comrade?' It was Anna.

Yasakov pulled up, his gasps like a man's rescued from drowning.

'Out!' he said. 'We must get out! A squad of Americans is coming this way. . . .'

'Americans!'

'Yes, Americans,' he panted. 'Four of them are on their way right now to the shaft-head from the' – he stumbled over the word – 'observatory, in a truck. They will pass this way. If they catch us, we're done.'

'How do you know all this?' Anna asked in astonishment.

'No time now to explain – I'll tell you later. You take the figurehead's head and I'll carry the base. Quick! Follow the track to the junction and then on to our own vehicle!'

'I don't know what all this is about, but why not simply dump the statue in the marsh?' asked Anna.

'It would mean removing the bugging apparatus, and we haven't got time for that,' Yasakov answered. 'Move, move!'

Together they hefted up Alcestis. Anna led, using her flashlight. The pair stumbled and slipped up the greasy track. On the final slope leading to the road fork the weight told and slowed them down.

Then Yasakov slipped, came down on his knees.

'Comrade . . .?'

'Keep going,' snapped Yasakov, getting up.

'Let me take the heavy end for a spell,' said Anna. She had never seen the cold, imperturbable Yasakov in such a state of nerves.

The reversed positions helped; Anna was strong and fit. They kept going at a brisk pace.

'Comrade Yasakov,' hissed Anna. 'I hear something – a motor engine, perhaps.'

Yasakov halted. 'I don't.'

Again they slogged up the steepening incline. Then Yasakov's torch picked up the roadsign.

'There it is again!' whispered Anna. 'It is a car engine! It's coming this way fast!'

The two Russians swung away leftwards at the fork in the direction of their getaway vehicle, breaking into a run and trying to keep step and at the same time miss the water-filled potholes. Behind them now they heard Suggs' truck and saw two vague yellow patches – foglights.

'Down!' ordered Yasakov.

They flopped down on the track's muddy surface with Alcestis. There was a rapid change of gears from the direction of the road junction and a shout from someone being thrown about in the rear of the American vehicle. Then the note changed as it started to pick its way downhill by the route they had come so shortly before.

'To the pickup!' ordered Yasakov. 'This damn figurehead is as much a danger as a real body. We'll take it and hide it well out of sight at Frenchman's Eye.'

25

'What kind of game are you playing, Cane?'

Cane eyed the tough, stocky American with his outthrust jaw. He remembered that some heavyweights have glass jaws. Testerman was behaving as if he could hand out as much as he could absorb.

Maris and Cane were in Testerman's office on the surface. They had been marched, blindfold, from the underground station by Clint and another toughie. They had heard the rumble of the steel blast-proof doors rolling back to let them pass; after that, there had been a smell of wetness as if they had passed along a corridor cut out of rock; an ascent in a lift; another long upward tunnel ascent along what felt like concrete under Cane's shoes.

When their blindfolds had been removed, they had found themselves in a well-lit office in the Arniston-type complex of buildings where Cane had first met Testerman. It was not, however, the same bare room – three telephones, an intercom, a small computer-word processor, and a TV monitor screen.

Testerman had scarcely waited for Maris and Cane to stop blinking in the unaccustomed light before he threw the question at Cane.

'I might ask the same thing,' retorted Cane.

'You could, but you wouldn't get an answer.' Testerman was abrasive, aggressive.

'You're treating us like a couple of criminals instead of innocent victims of something over which we had no control,' broke in Maris. 'Isn't our explanation good enough for you?'

'No,' snapped Testerman. In spite of her grimy state, she was very beautiful, he admitted to himself. The flash in her green eyes which followed his retort made her more so.

'Why not?' she blazed. 'That's the way it happened.'

'The way you *say* it happened, you mean.'

'Why should we lie? We have nothing to hide. You know who we are.'

'Why indeed?' the American responded. 'See here, Cane is a blasting expert, one of the top six in the world, from what I hear. He knows just how much explosive to use to accomplish what. There is an explosion. Two people fall into my cave. Neither of them is hurt. Put two and two together. The answer is that Cane equals explosion equals fissure.'

Cane was watching the American closely, and decided, from his hectoring tone, that he was either lying or bluffing.

'I was investigating a fissure,' Cane answered. 'I told you before. Mercifully, we were underground when the dynamite went up or we'd have been killed. The next thing we knew was that there was a rockfall. . . .'

'Yeah, yeah,' retorted Testerman impatiently. 'I know it all. It's a piss poor explanation, I repeat, piss poor.'

'The truth is often simple,' Maris interjected.

'I don't buy a lot of mixed up crap,' answered Testerman roughly. 'I don't buy it, Cane. You and your secretary come along on a Saturday night in thick fog to conduct a search for a fissure which must have been known to the drilling team anyway. Don't tell me this is your way of working! You'd go about an operation such as you claim in daylight, plus men, plus machines. . . .'

'Plus all blasting precautions,' added Cane.

Testerman glared at him. 'I say that what you and the girl were up to in the shaft head was a treff. . . .'

'If I knew what treff meant, I'd be able to reply,' Maris interrupted.

'Secret meeting. Transacting illegal business. Satisfied?'

'With the explanation, not its application.'

'Don't try and get smart with me,' Testerman growled. 'You two are in a spot. . . .'

It was, in fact, Testerman himself who was in a spot. He was a desperately worried man. He needed time to think; time to assess what to do with Cane and Maris. Theirs was no ordinary breach of Dolla's Downes' security system – only a very adroit mouse could have managed that. Cane and Maris had been pitchforked into the very nerve centre of one of the world's most highly secret operations. It was one of a chain on which the safety of mankind – the West in particular – depended. Not only had they seen things no outsider had a right to see, but they had opened up a way to the outside world from the cave via the fissure. The implications made Testerman's stomach heave.

Hell! If it hadn't been for the Alert Status Board and its blazing word APPLEJACK he might have talked them into believing that the computers, radar and TV monitor screens and electronic instruments were all part of the space tele-scope tracking process and geomagnetic studies – but APPLEJACK!

What to do with Cane and Maris? They weren't spies. He could – and he might still have to – refer the break-in to NORAD HQ back at home base. That, he told himself grimly, would be the surest way to blot his copy book forever. He had been appointed to command Dolla's Downes because of his qualities of initiative, toughness and leadership; they'd all be needed to solve this one. Nor could he, without NORAD knowing, call in the South African authorities. He could lock up his two captives, but for how long? Such strongarm tactics might well boomerang. He needed time.

Testerman went on savagely, his sandpaper temper roughened by the enormity of the problem. 'From the git-go your goddam geothermal project has been a pain in the ass to me,' he snapped at Cane. 'Now you've made it worse.'

'I didn't make it worse,' replied Cane levelly. 'Blame it on whoever set off the dynamite.'

Testerman took a hold on himself and said in a more conciliatory tone. 'See here, I don't deny that this thing has thrown me. The observatory has now become a clay pigeon. . . .'

He caught Maris' eye. 'Sorry.' He came almost near to being not unfriendly. 'Clay pigeon – vulnerable.'

'What have you got to hide?' demanded Cane.

'That's my problem,' he retorted. He noted the way Cane was regarding him. The bastard, he thought, he's not taking my bait. He'd only have to open his mouth about the existence of an underground station linked to aboveground antennae and radar dishes and the secret would be out.

Maris said. 'Dr Testerman, no one in the Strandveld guesses that such a thing as your underground station exists. We will give you our word. . . .'

'Why should you?' he replied. 'It's nothing to you. I have no way of keeping you to such a promise.' He addressed Cane. 'How would you propose to keep the existence of the fissure secret? Every shaftie on the job would know about it.'

'Not necessarily the connection with the cave,' replied Cane.

'Not necessarily the connection with the cave,' he mimicked Cane's English accent. 'I don't buy it, fellah.'

'You'll have to come to some understanding before you let us out of here,' answered Cane. 'You might as well think about it now.'

Testerman gave an ugly laugh. 'Forget it. You're not leaving this station until I've had time to consider. Clint!' he shouted to the guard outside the door. 'Lock 'em up – in the spare living quarters.'

'You can't do this!' protested Cane. 'Who in hell do you think you are, Testerman?'

The American ignored his outburst. 'You'll be in the building adjoining this one – we use it for relief staff when – when – we're working extra shifts. There are all facilities. You'll be comfortable. Don't try anything funny – there'll be guards.'

'Guards – lock us up – you have no right to do this!' protested Maris. 'You're not the police. . . .'

'So what? I intend locking you up until I get some sense out of you. Think it over. You'll have plenty of time. You could be here for days.'

On the other side of the Strandveld, Yasakov had other ideas. His plan would go into operation the next night.

26

'If any of them tries to escape, shove their heads underwater until they're half drowned,' ordered Yasakov. 'We've only got one gun, and I'll need that for Testerman. Everything clear? Get going!'

It was early the next evening, Sunday. The night was fogless, but cold; a sea wind brought in drifts of cloud from the ocean which from time to time obscured the new moon and the stars.

The four Russians – Yasakov, Anna Tarkhanova, Stefan Rostovtzeff and Josef Suvorov – stood by their Kombi on the wet, soggy shore of the big inland lake named Soetendalsvlei, east of the drilling site. Three of them, Yasakov, Anna and Stefan, wore black wet suits and diving caps. They looked like Middle Ages inquisitors or devils from a ballet scene. The fourth member of the team, Josef, wore plain, dark clothes.

Yasakov planned to kidnap Cane, Maris and Testerman in

a split operation. He intended to break in to Dolla's Downes via the cut electric fence. Yasakov was strung as tight as a guitar string with tension. Now that his team was under starter's orders, so to say, the things that could go wrong, the contingencies which seemed only minor when the daring plan first avalanched into his mind at the sight of Cane and Maris in the underground station, now loomed bigger than Cape Agulhas itself.

The plan *had* to work! It constituted more simply than success of the mission for which he had been sent ashore in the first place. He now knew that the frequency-hopping transmissions going out from the old lighthouse originated from the secret station deep in the ground. He could have left it at that and reported back to Vice-Admiral Strokin aboard the gas atoll, who in turn would have advised the Kremlin.

However, Yasakov hadn't risen to the top in the KGB because of a bureaucratic mentality and literal adherence to orders. The moment he had sighted the cave with its sophisticated instrumentation, he had known he was on to something big. He had realized instantly that such an establishment could not have been built without South African knowledge and cooperation. The mere fact of such collusion between the United States and South Africa would in itself be a valuable propaganda weapon. Yet Yasakov wanted more than mere point scoring. He wanted to establish what the outfit was all about – that mysterious lighted board with the equally mysterious APPLEJACK code blazing was branded on his memory.

The additional sight he had of Cane and Maris being held blindfold reinforced the conviction he had had from the start, namely, that Cane was a spy. The girl Maris was clearly part of his activities. Since Cane was a spy, Yasakov reasoned, he must have had an idea of what he was looking for in the cave – and by getting his hands on him, Yasakov meant to beat the truth out of him. He also needed Testerman as head of the station. If the operation were as top secret as it appeared, it wouldn't be easy to extract its function from Testerman alone. Information from the spy could supplement, be used as a lever, regarding what the American might say. . . .

The team stood poised on the eastern, or far, shore of Soetendalsvlei. This stretch of water, about two kilometres east of the drilling site and separated from it by a constellation of marshes and swamps, formed a natural barrier across the Strandveld immediately north of Cape Agulhas. The lake was seven and a half kilometres long and three and a half wide. Yasakov had chosen it as the springboard from which to launch his kidnap operation. The place was state property, closed to the public. The nearest habitations were farms well away from its eastern shore near the main road to Cape Agulhas. The water barrier, Yasakov had decided, would be an effective deterrent to pursuit if he were unlucky enough to be followed – he himself had provided a novel means of beating that obstacle.

'Get the donkey into the water!' ordered Yasakov.

The electric underwater craft used by the team for the *Kamchatka* salvage operation was Yasakov's trump card for the snatch. He intended to ferry his captives across Soetendalsvlei by means of it, and on the outward journey to transport his team to the operational area.

Yasakov slid the Kombi door wide and the four Russians humped it to the water's edge by its grab-handles. These they would also use to hang on to while crossing the lake. Where they were now was a place called Vissersdrift, a marshy spot on a river which rose out of the lake, at the extreme north-eastern tip of the lake. Yasakov intended to make a transverse crossing of about two and a half kilometres of Soetendalsvlei which would bring him ashore in the marshes adjoining the drilling site. The team's wet suits would enable them to negotiate water, marsh or ground itself.

The donkey lay ready in the water like a torpedo.

'Josef!' said Yasakov. 'You are to wait here until Anna and Stefan return with two prisoners – understood?'

'Understood, comrade.' Josef's reply was neutral. This was the third time he'd received the same instructions, showing how uptight Yasakov was.

'Got those two spare wet suits, Anna? – one for Cane, one for the girl?' he went on.

'Yes, comrade.'

The operation was divided into two parts. It had all sounded so fail-safe when he had outlined it that morning after making a reconnaissance of the Vissersdrift area. Now, consulting the small compass strapped to his wrist (the one he used on *Kamchatka* diving operations) to put the donkey on its heading across the lake, all the holes in the plan were too painfully obvious.

That electric fence. It must still be open. That was the key to success. He himself had seen the damage the explosion had done at the shaft head. If the Americans intended to seal the fissure – which he was convinced they must – it would be a job for a bulldozer, and he didn't see them making the long road detour when they could use a short cut from the observatory via the fence.

Yasakov found himself sweating. 'Knives?'

Both Anna and Stefan nodded. He himself checked the Makarov and buttoned it safely inside his wet suit.

He waded in, grasped a grab-handle at the nose, like a family chief taking the head of a coffin.

'Anna!'

She joined him at the front and, with Stefan at the rear, they moved the craft until they were up to their chests in water.

'West-southwest!' Yasakov orientated it on that heading. 'Anna! Go! Normal cruising speed!'

Anna threw a lever inside the tiny perspex-covered compartment in the nose, the screw bit, and the strange craft slid silently, purposefully, across the dark surface of the water.

The only real resemblance between the sleek craft and a donkey was its slowness. Normal speed was about five kilometres an hour. It could go faster, but with a penalty upon its batteries.

It took about half an hour to accomplish the crossing. Yasakov almost enjoyed the quiet passage across the calm water and the occasional sight of a star overhead. He would not be returning this way, if his plan worked the way he intended. He had assigned himself the most difficult and dangerous second phase of the operation– the capture and abduction of Testerman himself.

This part of the plan was shot through with so many imponderables that Yasakov himself felt doubts. He had no idea of the lay-out of the observatory surface complex. He hoped to find Testerman above ground in an administrative rather than an operational building – and alone. This was the biggest imponderable of all. If it failed, so did the whole plan. He was aware, as everyone was, of the security-tight gate-house – if Cane and Maris were being held there, he would have no chance of extracting them. A shoot-out would be futile. The whole operation had to proceed under an umbrella of normality. That applied most of all to his plan to snatch Testerman and get him clear of the observatory site.

Anna broke in on his thoughts. 'Looks like the shore ahead, comrade.'

She was the tallest of the three. Almost immediately again she called. 'Bottom! I've touched bottom, comrade!'

Now the low shoreline was visible: they waded waist deep towards it.

The marshes pointed like a pitted steel blade in the direction of the drilling site and, beyond, the American observatory.

'You must give me your compass, or else I'll never locate the donkey again,' said Anna.

Yasakov searched the horizon – now dim, now brighter as an odd cloud drifted across the faint moon – for a landmark by which Anna could pinpoint the craft on her return.

'A compass is no use without a datum point,' he replied. 'Try and spot something you can use as one.'

Stefan unexpectedly, spoke. 'There's something away on the left, comrade – could be a dead tree. Close to the water, I think.'

'Go and have a look – quick!' ordered Yasakov.

He'd wanted a moment alone with Anna anyway to discuss

contingencies in case his own part of the operation did not work out.

'Anna,' he said brusquely, in order not to prejudice his role as established leader. 'There are two parts to this operation, as you are aware. Yours is the easier. If mine does not succeed, you are to get the truth about the underground station out of Cane and the girl and report to Admiral Strokin – is that clear?'

'What else shall I report?' Anna was shrewd, conscious that Yasakov had only told the team enough to get by on.

'Tell him that the origin of the frequency-hopping signals is an underground, highly sophisticated American station with computers, TV screens, radar monitors.'

'What conclusions should Admiral Strokin draw from that?'

'None. Report the facts. Moscow can decide what further is to be done.'

'Are you writing your own epitaph in advance, comrade?'

'No, damn it, I'm not! I only want to make sure that someone else besides myself knows.'

'Thank you for the compliment.' There was that faint scratch in her reply which always irritated him. Maybe it was the way she was made. 'Here comes Stefan.'

Silence fell between the two black-capped figures as the burly Russian approached.

'Dead tree,' he said briefly. 'Right on the water's edge. Good landmark.'

'We'll move the donkey there.'

The three dragged it along in the shallows and parked it on the shore near the tree.

Yasakov pointed. 'That's our way.'

'How far?' asked Stefan. For him, breaking silence was as noteworthy as the dynamite explosion itself.

'About two kilometres.'

The wet suits were the key to their good progress. In clothes, or bathing costumes, they could not have pushed through the welter of mud, pools, tussocky grass and stunted scratchy bushes the way they did. When they fell, they simply floundered out of the bog again. Yasakov checked direction from time to time.

As it turned out, they were well to the north of their first objective, the shaft head, when Anna suddenly exclaimed.

'Comrade – there's something sticking up! There, to our left!'

Her keen eyes had picked out the steel tracery of the headgear raft against the ridge backing the excavation.

'Smart girl – I know where we are. Head towards it.'

They made a ninety degree turn and soon found themselves at the machinery park and explosives shed. Yasakov cast round for the marsh path leading – as he knew – towards the American fence. He located it on the far side of the ridge.

'Follow me!'

It was Anna, again, who spotted the wire first, silhouetted against a group of lighted buildings on the observatory side. The station was sited in a shallow valley; silhouetted, too were the radome, two parabolic antennae, dish antennae, and one big geniculate antenna bent like a knee crippled with arthritis.

Yasakov had no eyes for them.

Was the wire open?

He dared not risk his flashlight. The break had to be here, where the path intersected the wire!

The loose strands of barbed wire had been neatly tied back at a concrete post to form a gateway. The electric cable was still in position.

Was it alive?

'Try testing it with a knife,' suggested Anna.

'No,' said Yasakov tersely. 'Crawl under.'

'Maybe they've put sensors in the gap,' Anna went on.

In his excitement, Yasakov admitted to himself he hadn't thought of that.

'Search both sides of the wire, but don't put your hands through,' he ordered.

'What do we look for?' asked Stefan.

'Anything suspicious looking,' answered Yasakov. 'Use your head, man – it's got to *look* electric!'

There wasn't anything.

'I'll lead,' said Yasakov in relief. He ducked down, went through the gap.

The anti-climax was like crossing a bridge you believe to be mined but is not.

Nothing happened.

Anna and Stefan followed.

'Where now?' asked Anna.

They really had little option. The group of lighted buildings – which they saw now were thatched – beckoned like a beacon. In the far distance was more light, and Yasakov deduced – rightly – that it was the gatehouse. As they stood undecided, a brace of lights went out in the thatched buildings, an engine started, then headlights shone out. The Arniston complex became clearer; another parked vehicle was visible as the Russians got closer. Yasakov identified it as a landrover.

Yasakov heaved a deep sigh of relief. If that landrover belonged to Testerman, Testerman himself could be inside the building. . . .

He found out, soon enough.

The three Russians crept silently up to the window of a room from which light was shining and peered in.

Inside, Testerman was interrogating Cane and Maris.

27

'I've dismissed the guards so that you can feel anything you say won't be under duress,' Testerman said.

'Am I expected to be grateful?' Cane responded. It was the first time since the previous night that they had seen Testerman. The living quarters they had shared were comfortable. They had slept well. Much of the nightmare effect of the explosion and being precipitated into the science-fiction world of the cave station had worn off. He and Maris had discussed endlessly what its function might be. They had reached no conclusion. Both remained certain, however, that it was more than a mere observatory.

An angry flush passed over Testerman's face and his eyes narrowed in their characteristic way.

He replied, holding himself in check. 'I haven't put you through the wringer. I could, if I wanted to. You've nothing to complain of beyond a break in your normal routine. I've come to discuss the situation you've created – reasonably, between reasonable people.'

Maris had got her long dark hair tidy and had spruced up her muddy clothes. 'The only unreasonable thing being the basic situation.'

'What do you mean?'

'A cave full of sophisticated electronic instruments . . .'

'APPLEJACK,' added Cane.

Testerman got up from his chair and stalked across the room. 'Leave it!' he snapped. 'Dragging the cave into this is what we call a cheap shot. I've come to talk about *you*.'

'You can't separate the two,' said Maris.

'I can and I do,' replied the American impatiently. 'Listen to me. My men have examined the shaft head. The damage is extensive, both to the workings and to the machinery. In fact, some of the machinery is a total write-off. It will take thousands, maybe tens of thousands, to get everything going again.'

'I'll judge for myself when I see it – I don't need the opinion of non-experts,' replied Cane.

'Get hold of Grimmock and explain there's been an accident,' Testerman went on persuasively. 'You can back out of the project and not lose face. My original offer stands. We'll acquire the whole site. . . .'

Cane laughed derisively. 'You're naïve, Testerman. Do you really expect me, Grimmock, and the mining authorities to paper over an explosion which has – in your own words – caused damage amounting to tens of thousands of dollars?

What about the insurers? They won't buy it any more than I do. The whole thing stinks.'

'Of what?'

'Intimidation.'

'You're saying I arranged the explosion?'

'Could be.'

'And opened a route to a top secret outfit . . .' Testerman bit his words short.

Cane pounced on his slip. 'Top secret, eh, Testerman? That's something we haven't heard before.'

'The type of satellite tracking we do naturally has a military application,' he covered up. 'The methods are classified. Top secret.'

'Is APPLEJACK also top secret?' asked Maris.

Blast them both, Testerman told himself. He'd spent half the night debating in his own mind whether or not he should refer their case to NORAD. He had only had to pick up a phone and he could speak direct to the Director of Missile Warning Operations, or to the general himself. Yet – even by voice connection, it would be impossible to explain the background, the explosion, the fissure. . . . From the distance of Cheyenne Mountain his bosses would see it as a straightforward breach of security which he, Testerman, was trying to buck off on them. Blast them both!

'I've spent a lot of time thinking about you,' said the American. 'You can go free – on three conditions. First, Cane, you will contact Grimmock – you will use my phone here while I listen in – and back down on the geothermal project. Explain the explosion in your own rationale. Second, I need your shaft sinking expertise to seal the fissure so that the cave is absolutely secure, permanently. You'll be paid handsomely for the job. Third, both of you will keep your mouths shut – tight shut – about the cave and what you saw in it.'

'Is that all?' asked Cane derisively.

There was a knock at the door.

Testerman was startled. He had sent the two guards away with strict orders that he was not to be disturbed.

'Who is it?' he demanded harshly.

There was no reply.

Knock.

Testerman took the key of the door from his pocket, thrust it into the lock, and pulled it open.

He looked into the blue, unsmiling mouth of a Makarov.

The figure holding it looked like a devil out of hell in his black wet suit and skull-hugging cap.

Before Testerman could open his mouth, the figure crowded him back inside, slammed the door.

At the same time, there was a crash from the window, and two more devil-figures threw themselves on Cane and Maris. They held diving-knives at their throats.

'Quiet!' hissed Yasakov. 'One word from any of you, and you'll die! Close up – get close together!'

He waved the three of them into a knot and kept the Makarov on them. He snapped out something in Russian to Stefan. He withdrew himself and his knife from Cane, locked the door, and passed the key to Yasakov, who pocketed it. It took only seconds.

Anna let go Maris – she had grasped her in an underarm grip which included her breast as she had seized her from behind to position the knife at her throat – and took up station next to Yasakov. She pulled off her cap.

'Anna Tarkhanova!' Maris burst out, flabbergasted.

'Yasakov, by all that's holy! It's the Russian diving team!' Cane added incredulously.

'You are correct,' Yasakov said. Tension stilted his language. 'Keep still, if you value your lives!'

He rapped out something in Russian to Anna and Stefan. Stefan's hands went first to Testerman. His face was emotionless when he pulled a .45 Mark IV Colt military model from the American's back pocket. He passed it to Yasakov, who snapped off the safety catch and held both pistols aimed. Stefan frisked Cane equally expertly. Anna's hands held more than frisking. Maris cringed as they passed over her thighs and breasts. All the time Anna's eyes were on her. They held strange, frightening messages.

Yasakov's nerves and guns were on hair triggers. He said harshly. 'Do as I say, and none of you will get hurt. Otherwise . . .' he gestured significantly with one of the pistols.

Cane glanced at Testerman. Shock and disbelief chased each other across his tough features and seemed to rob him of speech.

To Cane, Yasakov's tight-fitting black rubber suit was as individual as a fingerprint.

'Yasakov!' he exclaimed. 'The man at the lighthouse! The bastard who also tried to kill me at the drilling site!'

Yasakov's reaction was full of menace. 'You should not try and play tricks with a KGB man, Mister Cane. Especially when it comes to spying.'

The enormity of his utterance crashed home on Testerman.

'*KGB! The KGB inside my outfit! This outfit!*'

'I hope to have some other surprises also for you, Dr Testerman,' Yasakov said grimly.

Testerman addressed Cane as if he did not believe the evidence of his own eyes.

'You say, these are the Russian diving team – it can't be, man!'

Maris supplied the answer. 'We met them at Birkenhead. They're Russians all right, Dr Testerman.'

'This man Cane is a spy,' Yasakov told Testerman harshly. 'He spied on me, tried to . . .'

'Rubbish!' retorted Cane. 'I am an engineer, in charge of the geothermal project. . . .'

'You can tell me all that later,' continued Yasakov with a rising threat in his voice. 'You are a spy. I say so, Vladimir Yasakov. And spies must pay the price.'

'That also goes for a self-confessed KGB man.'

The Makarov held steady between Cane's eyes. 'Don't threaten me, Mister Cane. It could be bad for you – and the girl.'

His eyes held Cane's, but his words were for Testerman. 'Now – quick – those guards – how long will they be away?'

Testerman seemed to be getting a grip on his shattered senses. 'Find out.'

'I have found out other things, Dr Testerman.'

'Such as?'

'Your so-called observatory is a bluff. The old lighthouse is a bluff. You operate a secret underground station from a cave under our feet. From it go out secret signals. Frequency-hopping signals.'

Cane thought Testerman was about to pass out. He went deadly pale and swayed on his feet.

'*You – the KGB – know that?*' he managed to get out in a whisper.

Yasakov laughed, an ugly, triumphant laugh.

'You can have more if you want it,' he sneered. 'Perhaps you will want to shoot yourself when I tell you – it will save me the trouble. I wonder what your bosses will say when they hear it, Testerman?'

'You goddam bastard, you filthy sonofabitch!'

Yasakov was quicker than the American. He had seen his muscles tense to jump him and had nodded like a flash to Stefan. The man's bearlike arm was round Testerman's neck in an instant, throttling him, before he had even managed to project himself forward.

Yasakov held the guns on Cane. 'Don't you try anything, Cane!'

He said something to Stefan, who relaxed his pressure on Testerman. He gasped for air, coughed, choked. His protruding eyes sank back to normal in their sockets.

All the time Yasakov stood with the pistols on the three captives; Anna watched with a faint smile, her eyes never leaving Maris' face.

When Testerman had got his breath back, Yasakov said.

'You three are coming with us – in two groups. Cane and the girl will accompany Stefan and Anna Tarkhanova, and you, Testerman, will go with me.'

'Go and stuff it, Yasakov.'

'The only thing Americans have is big mouths,' answered Yasakov contemptuously. 'That is why we in the Soviet

Union are ahead of you in the nuclear arms race, with our navy, and in the air.'

Testerman's shock seemed to have programmed his mind to a single subject. 'How did you know about the cave?' he got out.

Until now, Yasakov had had his man reeling against the ropes. Now he threw his punch for the kill.

'Because I have seen it.'

If there had been a referee for the fight, he would have waved his hand in front of Testerman's eyes to see if he were still reacting.

'*You – saw – it!*'

'APPLEJACK!' Yasakov said softly. 'What does APPLE-JACK stand for, Testerman?'

But Yasakov had pushed his luck too far. Testerman, even in his shocked state, realized that if Yasakov did not know what APPLEJACK meant, he did not – could not – know the full scope of the cave as an anti-missile early warning station.

His voice was different, stronger, when he answered – without the Russian knowing the key to the Alert Status Board and its nine fatal codes, he could still face it out that the underground station was what it purported to be – a highly sophisticated geomagnetic observatory and space telescope-cum-satellite monitoring station.

'Find out.'

'I mean to,' answered Yasakov in his sinister way. 'I mean to.'

He flicked a glance at Anna. She came to him and he passed her the American's gun. He knew he could trust her in a tight situation like the present better than Stefan. Stefan would do the job – if ordered. Anna would pre-empt it.

'Wet suits,' he ordered Stefan. 'Bring 'em in – through the window. Don't show yourself.'

The big Russian did what he was told and returned with the two wet suits.

Yasakov said. 'Cane, you and the girl will get into those and go with Anna and Stefan – understood?'

'What on earth are we supposed to do in diving suits?' demanded Maris.

'You'll discover soon,' replied Yasakov. 'Testerman, you will come with me.'

'Like hell I will, Yasakov! How do you think you'll get away with this, man? The place is guarded, day and night. . . .'

'That's my problem, isn't it?' responded Yasakov thinly. 'We got in, didn't we?'

Testerman was silent.

'You will telephone the main security gate and order them to open it,' went on Yasakov. Now that he was formulating his plan in words for the first time, his mouth was dry. 'You will say that you will be driving through in your landrover – the one parked outside now – with two prisoners in the back and you do not wish to be stopped. Clear?'

Testerman looked slightly amused. It was plain he had no intention of obeying.

'You will also telephone your second-in-command, Ed Weinback, and tell him that you are leaving immediately for Cape Town. You will say that you have extracted important information as the result of your interrogation of Cane and the girl, and that you are handing them over to the South African authorities for further questioning.'

Yasakov waited. His mouth was dry. He had drawn the conclusion that because the cave must have been established with the collusion of the South African authorities, they would also be involved in its security. It was a long shot in the dark. He'd have to browbeat Testerman somehow into doing what he wished. Force would be useless. If Testerman went missing, a hunt would be set in train and there was no knowing where it would end. The essence of his plan regarding Testerman was that his departure would have to appear voluntary.

He could almost see the thought racing through Testerman's mind – a secret signal to the gatehouse guard. . . .

'The other two prisoners won't be in the back of your landrover,' he added. 'I will. Plus a gun. If there is the slightest hint of a double-cross, I'll put a bullet through your spine. Now – get on to that phone!'

28

A bullet was the way out, Testerman resolved in a flash.

It would mean his own life, but in the great scheme of things, what did that amount to? Better by far one life rather than the Soviet Union knowing the secret of a key United States anti-missile warning station. His sacrifice might mean that the nuclear missiles might not fly or, if they did, they would not reach their target because of the intervention of the Agulhas warning station. . . .

Yasakov unknowingly gave him a breathing space.

'Strip down to your underclothes,' he ordered Cane and Maris. 'Get those wet suits on. Take your clothes along – you'll need them later.'

'No!' answered Maris.

'Damn your false modesty!' snapped Yasakov. 'If you won't – Anna!'

He said something cynical in Russian. Anna grinned and tossed her head. She advanced on Maris. She recalled the woman's groping search of her body and the grip on her breast. . . .

She recoiled. 'Very well.'

'Quick! You too, Cane. You're leaving with Anna and Stefan ahead of Testerman and myself.'

'See here, Yasakov,' said Testerman slowly, almost drawling. 'I'm not hauling my ass out of this room – under any circumstances or threats. That includes' – he nodded at the Makarov – 'that. Go ahead. Shoot. You don't get anything out of me.'

Yasakov's gun came up in response. The nicked foresight took in Testerman's right eye, then moved slightly to the centre of his forehead, and finally down to his heart. Not all Professor Barnard and his heart-transplant team would ever put it together again if Yasakov's finger tightened one millimetre on the trigger.

'What are you waiting for?' sneered Testerman. 'Afraid of the bang?'

The silence was electric. Cane had stripped off his shirt, Maris her blouse. Anna's attention seemed divided between Maris' beautiful breasts and the Yasakov-Testerman confrontation. Stefan stood immobile, knife held in one paw like a butcher.

'If you choose this way, you choose it,' said Yasakov. 'Let me warn you, though, you will not be the only one to die if you compel me to shoot you. I will see that retaliation takes place against the underground station from our offshore gas atoll.'

A second previously, Testerman had reconciled himself to the role of martyr; now a new element had been tossed into the arena – Yasakov's mention of the gas atoll. Retaliation! That meant the gas atoll was not what it purported to be, that it had the means – that implied weaponry – to *mount* retaliation.

He pulled himself back from what he believed to be the abyss of certain self-chosen death. An alternative tore through his mind with the flash-crash of an underwater missile launch. If he pretended to string along with Yasakov so that he could find out what the so-called gas atoll really was . . .

In the moment of dying, we are told, one's past life flashes before one in one instant photo-take. With Testerman, a trigger pull away from death, the American strategic masterplan for siting the early warning station on Africa's farthest land tip flashed in front of him like an instant print out. If the gas atoll were more than it purported to be, that masterplan was in gravest danger. But if he could find out what the gas atoll was all about, the United States – and the West's main oil artery along the Cape Sea Route – would remain secure.

The United States had not been naïve about the gas atoll in the first place. It had supported South Africa in its protest to the World Court – the project contravened a principle in the Law of the Sea Treaty which America had stood for and in consequence had refused to sign the treaty. Also, when the gas atoll had gone into position, its activities had been thoroughly monitored by a US spy satellite. It had been shown to be 'clean'. Passive electronics had been detected – radio, radar and the like – which were regarded as natural. The Soviets had kept foreign ships and planes at a distance by means of a small warship patrol. South Africa had in turn declared a 'no-go' area of one hundred and fifty kilometres from the coast. This US spy satellite watched all the time.

Now, Testerman had no reason to doubt what Yasakov had asserted, namely that the gas atoll was capable of retaliation. The fact that the Soviets had gone to such extraordinary lengths to get spies ashore to nail down the elusive frequency-hopping transmissions showed what significance Moscow attached to them. What the Soviets did not – could not – know was to whom those signals were being directed. By virtue of them, Dolla's Downes early warning station had become more than simply a passive monitor of nuclear firings. It had been pitchforked into the front line of a nuclear war.

The frequency-hopping signals were, in fact, the spearhead of the US Navy's new radio communications system which would order deeply-submerged US nuclear missile-firing submarines to retaliate in response to an attack against the United States. The system was code-named ELF – Extremely Low Frequency. For the first time, deadly submerged killers would know instantly of surprise nuclear attack on their homeland, and would strike back on the turn.

Until now, US missile submarines had had either to surface or trail antennae to make radio contact with their bases. This meant that they could spend days, or weeks, out of communication with their command centres. Above all, by leaving the depths of the ocean, the submarines lost their prime strategic advantage – virtual undetectability. They automatically became prey to preemptive Soviet submarine killers.

Under the ELF system, a steady stream of extremely low frequency signals was transmitted, twenty-four hours a day, to the secret patrol lines in the strategic quadrant covering the Southern Ocean and South Indian Ocean. These non-stop transmissions were monitored by the submarine strike force. If they stopped, their orders were to surface immediately and make contact with Dolla's Downes – the codename for Soutbos. A break signified one thing only – a nuclear war was on. NORAD, via Testerman, would order the cataclysmic press of the button to send nuclear missiles flying.

ELF had become a major strategic weapon by virtue of a masterly development which South Africa had pioneered and put that country far ahead of the rest of the world – frequency hopping. The South African system, which enabled transmissions to 'hop' every milli-second from frequency to frequency, was impossible to break. When undercover negotiations had begun years before between the US and South Africa for the establishment of the secret underground base near Cape Agulhas, South Africa had offered the United States access to the system in return for her goodwill and backing internationally. No wonder, Testerman thought, the gas atoll had been worried.

Testerman's stomach crimped when he thought of the gas atoll as something more than a mere supply point in relation to the great new American base at Kosi Bay, some one thousand and eight hundred kilometres away to the northeast, on the border of South Africa and Marxist Mozambique. Was the gas atoll, securely situated over three hundred kilometres out to sea off the Cape, the advance eyes and ears of the Soviet fleet, ready to annihilate Kosi Bay in the event of a nuclear war? It meant, he realized in a flash of insight, that the United States and Soviet Union, unknown to one another, were rubbing shoulders at and off the Cape by virtue of two secret stations.

The vast implications of Yasakov's remark left Testerman feeling stunned. *He had to find out more about the gas atoll.*

His throat threw up a noise something between a cough and a retch.

Yasakov gave an almost imperceptible sign to Stefan to stand aside from the shot.

'*Wait!*'

It wasn't fear that blanched Testerman's face; it was the realization that in his own hands lay the decision which could stop those end-of-the-world missiles flying – eight to twelve minutes' grace was all the time Dolla's Downes would have from the time a Red sub commander threw the firing switch to the moment the missiles crashed down on Kosi Bay and elsewhere.

Yasakov's face, with its lightly yellow pigmentation, gashed mouth, and slanting eyes, was as impassive as a death mask. Maris, who was rigid with terror, moved close to Cane.

Sweat poured down Testerman's face. 'I'll do it,' he got out hoarsely. 'I'll go with you, Yasakov. I'll instruct Widdows to open the gate. Just as you say.'

Life – in the form of contempt – came back into Yasakov's face.

'You'll do it, loud-mouth,' he sneered. 'You'll do it all right!'

Cane felt sick. He couldn't handle the choice – either Testerman dying in front of his eyes, or seeing him cringe from cowardice and go along with the Russian's plans.

'Weinback – Weinback first!' snapped Yasakov. 'Where is he right now – in the cave?'

'Yeah.'

He gestured at the group of telephones with his pistol.

'Tell him what I told you before to say. Don't try anything on, see?'

Testerman nodded. He moved like a zombie towards the instruments.

'Hold it!' snapped Yasakov. 'Get your breath back. Speak normally. Weinback must not suspect.'

Yasakov turned to Cane, Maris, Anna and Stefan, standing like a frozen tableau.

'Get those wet suits on – dress!' he said. 'Hurry – you're leaving first.'

Maris slipped off her slacks and stood in her bra and pants. Anna's eyes were all over Maris' slender body.

'I'll zip you into it.'

She held out a wet suit, smaller than the other destined for Cane. The zip ran from crutch to neck.

Maris shrank back. 'No. I know how to manage.'

Cane saw his chance. Anna was less than a metre away. She had dropped her gun-arm in her eagerness to help Maris. His reflexes tightened.

'Cane! Don't try it! Anna, blast you!'

Yasakov seemed to have eyes in the back of his head. He was already into a firing crouch, and had moved into position so that he could shoot at Cane and Testerman through an arc of 180 degrees.

In a flash the drooping gun in Anna's hand was on Cane. He'd have to be very, very fast to jump her. His ruse might have worked, had it not been for Yasakov.

'You might collect a bullet yourself, if you don't keep your mind on the job!' he said coldly to Anna.

Anna didn't face him, but said sulkily to Cane. 'Into your suit – quick.'

'You ready?' Yasakov asked Testerman.

Testerman nodded. Cane couldn't stand the sight of a coward selling himself out. Now he decided he would rather have seen a bullet do its job.

Testerman picked up a phone. 'Ed? Brad here. See here . . .' He paused fractionally as Yasakov went up behind him and held the Makarov within centimetres of the back of his neck. 'See here, fellah. I've just given these two who broke into the cave a cathaul. The guy's the case ace in this little poker game, like I thought. There's a lot else, for my ears only. The long and the short of it is, I've decided to take 'em both off now to Cape Town. This is a job for South African Security.'

The only sound in the office except for Testerman's voice was the rasp of Cane's zip as he completed donning his wet-suit. There was a crackle of surprise from Weinback's end.

'Yeah, now, right this moment. It's too important to wait until morning,' Testerman went on. 'It's only three hours away to Cape Town. Sure, the landrover. I don't need anyone to accompany me – they won't escape – I can't go into detail, but they won't. I'll be away a couple of days, maybe longer. You're in command. Everything is plain sailing. Just keep the routine signals going.'

Cane and Maris couldn't hear Weinback's reply. It took nearly a minute. Yasakov could. He moved into Cane's sight with the pistol aimed at his ear – but clear, Cane noted, of a possible sideswipe by Testerman from the earpiece in his hand.

Testerman said. 'That's the way it is, Ed. I'm leaving right away. I'll just call Tom on the gate to clear me through.'

Testerman raised his eyes at Yasakov, who nodded, satisfied. The American's performance had been faultless.

'Okay. Fine, fine. See you, Ed.'

As he put down the receiver, Testerman wondered briefly whether it might not indeed be his last goodbye to Ed. He shrugged mentally. The last long count was endemic to the missile game.

'Now the guard on the gatehouse!' ordered Yasakov.

Testerman chose another phone. 'Tom – Brad here.'

Widdows had one of those voices which don't need the services of an earpiece to carry. All in the office could overhear him.

'Trouble? You in trouble with them prisoners, Brad?'

Testerman gave a forced laugh. 'No, Tom. Everything okay this end.'

'That guy and the girl that broke in are a hot can of corns,' Widdows said. 'Never thought my security could have been busted like that.'

'It wasn't your fault, Tom. They came in from outa the earth. I told you.'

'Yeah, Brad, I know, but I still feel bad that anyone could have got through. What about that wire, Brad? I don't like the fence being cut. The power's off too . . .'

Yasakov waved the pistol in front of Testerman's face. He mouthed the word for him to say to Widdows.

'Tomorrow,' said Testerman obediently. 'We'll restore the power tomorrow and repair the fence.'

'I don't want another heist man coming through my security tonight . . .'

'He wasn't a heist man,' Testerman sounded almost naturally amused. 'He didn't hold me up. Now' – the tone of his voice changed – 'I've put these two through the mill . . .'

'They come clean after Clint and Ben left?' asked the talkative Widdows. Yasakov's face was tightening – such familiarity didn't exist in the Soviet chain of command.

'Yeah,' replied Testerman. 'They came clean – so clean, Tom, that I'm taking 'em straight through to Cape Town. Now. Tonight. I want you to open the gate so that I can ride right through without stopping. Clear? I'll be there in less than ten minutes.'

'No guards?' Widdows seemed outraged.

'What they told me makes it unnecessary.'

'Brad,' asked Widdows. 'Are you okay? You sound so kinda starched-shirt.'

Yasakov signalled Testerman to end the conversation.

'What they told me made me uptight, Tom. I'll be handing them over to South African Security in Cape Town. You don't have to worry any more about them. They won't try and escape, I assure you. Ed is taking over command. I'll be away a few days. Have that gate open for me, will you?'

'Sure, Brad, sure.' But there was something puzzled, unresolved, in Widdows' response.

'Satisfied?' demanded Testerman when he put down the phone.

'There won't be any guards on the gap in the wire tonight?' demanded Yasakov.

Testerman realized, then. 'By all that's holy – so that's the way you came in!'

'It's also the way the others are going out,' retorted Yasakov. He threw a final glance round the office and his eyes rested on the desk.

'Break it open?' asked Stefan. 'There were no keys on the American.'

'No,' answered Yasakov. 'I don't want any signs left behind that anything unusual has taken place.'

There were a few odd papers on the desk, but nothing of any significance. Yasakov guessed rightly that Testerman had deliberately removed anything which might have given Cane and Maris any information while interrogating them.

Yasakov's glance then rested on what looked like a word processor against the wall. He could not go to it while keeping close guard on Testerman.

'What is that?' he demanded.

'Relay monitor to me from downstairs – personal,' Testerman replied indifferently.

'Relaying what?'

'Routine observations – satellite and space telescope data.'

'Stefan,' said Yasakov in Russian. 'See if there's anything there.'

A perforated, telex-like reel with some writing on it sprouted at the machine's side.

'Comrade!' said Anna in an urgent whisper. 'I think I hear something!'

'Take it – give it to me later,' Yasakov snapped at Stefan. 'Quick!'

Stefan ripped off the sheet, thrust it inside his wet suit top. At a word from Yasakov, he moved swiftly to the door, opened it warily, and peered out. He nodded that the coast was still clear.

'Out! Get clear of the light as quick as you can,' Yasakov told Anna in a low, imperative tone. 'You know what you have to do. If either of the prisoners make trouble, shoot 'em.' He addressed Cane and Maris. 'She will, too.' He opened the door wider. 'On your way, Anna! See you at Birkenhead!'

29

The four black-suited figures in skull-hugging caps might have been beings from outer space as they slipped past Dolla's Downes' equally space-age radome and parabolic antennae. Maris felt that the whole chain of events since the explosion had had a quality of unreality for her; now, the forced march under Anna and Stefan's guard shared the same nightmarish feeling.

Anna led the party; she had passed Testerman's Colt to Stefan in the rear. The only everyday thing seemed to be her shoes, which hung suspended from her neck.

Anna steered by Yasakov's wrist compass. The group moved silently and fast. The captives' sole hope of salvation, a lighted building served the radome, was now behind.

Maris longed to talk to Cane. The twenty-four hours they had spent locked up had deepened their feelings for one another. She had been confident that she would convince Testerman – until Yasakov had broken in on their interrogation. Now she felt they were no more than tiny grains trapped between gigantic millstones of power – the Soviet Union on the one hand, and the United States on the other.

'Keep going – don't drag your feet!' It was Anna. She had a knife in her hand and her eyes were bright with excitement. The marsh path which the Americans had flattened to the security fence gap made no demands on their wet suits; both Cane and Maris wondered what their purpose was.

The wire loomed.

'Down – don't touch it!' ordered Anna.

Maris, who was the smallest of the four, passed through first. It was like crossing a rubicon – into unknown fears.

Cane said to her. 'We're on our own ground now – the drilling site.'

'Silence!' said Anna.

Anna then steered the group away from the fence in the direction she herself had approached it first – well clear of the headgear raft, down the ridge near the explosives shed, and then on into the marshes.

Now the wet suits came into their own. For the next two kilometres the party splashed, floundered, mud-bathed, slipped and tumbled. Cane lashed his bundle of clothes on top of his head. Anna used the flashlight and compass; Stefan, like an incarnation of retribution, brought up the rear. Once, when he slipped and came down heavily, Cane saw his chance, but the Russian was too quick and he found himself looking into a pistol's mouth.

They ploughed on. Both Cane and Maris kept their heads down trying to find easier patches.

Suddenly Anna called out. 'Halt!'

They had reached the dead tree on the lake. For a moment, neither Cane nor Maris took in the fact that what stretched ahead of them now was continuous water, water uncontaminated by mud, muck, grass and slime.

'Our journey is easy now,' said Anna. 'We go across.'

She pointed with her flashlight. The torpedo-shaped donkey craft might have been part of Maris' earlier space fantasy. Both she and Cane had seen it before at Birkenhead.

'Where the devil are we going in that?' exclaimed Cane.

'Across the lake,' repeated Anna. 'You will hold on to the grab handles. Put your clothes on top.' She added, 'Josef is waiting on the far shore. Now, get the donkey into the water.'

The craft was too heavy for Cane and Maris alone. Anna kept guard with Stefan's gun while the three of them got the craft afloat. They took up station at their respective grab-handles and waited for Anna to join them. Maris was immediately ahead of Cane, Stefan on his left at the rear; Anna was to navigate from the front left-hand position.

The escape plan dropped into Cane's mind as they readied themselves. It hinged on who took the gun, Anna or Stefan. If it were Stefan and Anna kept the knife . . .

Anna splashed into the shallows. She handed Stefan the Colt, made for her own grab-handle.

He would have to move fast, while the craft was still close to the shore. If he made the attempt in deep water, the donkey's superior speed would hunt him down. He would also have to have the dim outline of the land to guide him, or else he might go on swimming aimlessly. . . .

Anna put the knife between her teeth in order to have her hands free to manipulate the controls. She said something to Stefan. The pistol held on Cane. Cane himself leaned forward and put his hand on Maris' shoulder, as if to reassure her. That wasn't his message – he hoped she would understand later – he would come back for her.

Maris turned and held his eyes with hers. Stefan growled and Cane removed his hand.

The donkey's electric motor started to pulse.

'Bring the head round – more, more,' ordered Anna, checking direction from the wrist-compass. 'Go!' she added finally.

As the craft picked up speed, the four of them streamed their legs as if swimming. Cane tried a glance over his shoulder at the receding land. The look was intercepted by Stefan – the pistol was aimed at his head. He'd have to be very, very quick and smart to escape a bullet. He couldn't leave the attempt too long.

Like Yasakov, Cane might almost have enjoyed the silent passage across the lake's still water under the cold stars had he not had weightier things on his mind.

Five minutes.

In one lithe, ultra-fast movement, Cane let go, spun, ducked, dived.

He never heard Stefan's shot – he was going deep, deep as he could without having filled his lungs as full as he would have wished. The water was dark. Down, down. He spun on his own axis like a shark, taking his direction shorewards from his last sighting.

There was a shadow in the water. For one brief second he thought it was his own. It wasn't. It was Anna. He spotted the knife-blade, lighter in the general dimness.

Then she was at him.

The blade came in apparent slow motion – the water pressure slowed it down – at his throat. Cane kept his cool. He guessed Anna might think he would break surface; already he could feel the need of air – but instead he went deeper, writhing and twisting under her.

Cane had expected her to turn and follow. Her counter-move trapped him. She opened her legs wide, clamped them shut again under his armpits as he swept past.

The last oxygen was forced from his lungs. His head and face were crushed against her navel. Her legs tightened like a vice. She jerked his head back with one hand so that his throat stood exposed; with the other, she pushed the point of the knife against it.

There was fire in Cane's lungs. His eyes felt as if they would burst out of their sockets. How long could Anna herself go on without air?

He must have blacked out momentarily. He was half aware of being powered surfacewards by the thrust of Anna's arms and torso. Her crutch seesawed against his face as she fought her way upwards. He realized that her frantic motions were because her own air had run out.

Then – the stars, the lake surface, and the inrush of cold, life-giving air. Nothing else mattered. Not even Anna with her knife. But Anna was tough, and far more in practice than he was despite his lifelong hobby of skin-diving. The long dives to the *Kamchatka* had honed her into top form.

Cane snapped back to reality as the knifepoint burned across his cheek.

Anna coughed water in his face. 'You fool! Do you want your girl killed?' Her eyes were blazing, but Cane noted that it was more with excitement than anger.

She shouted, and Stefan replied from nearby.

Then she said emphatically, menacingly. 'Mister Cane, I'll kill your girl myself if you try that sort of thing on again – understand?'

Cane got rid of some water. He nodded. He believed her.

The donkey glided up to them.

'Hal – Hal darling . . .!' Maris began.

Anna snapped something in Russian and then barked at Maris. 'Shut up! Keep your hands on the grab-handles! I have ordered Stefan to shoot if you let go!'

She added to Cane. 'He'd like the chance to do so to you, Mister Cane. He's feeling sore about the way you got away from him.'

'Hal . . .'

'I'm okay.' His curtness stemmed from his bitterness. He knew that he'd blown his one chance of escape. He would not get another from the alert Russians.

'Get going again!' called Anna.

Josef was waiting in the Kombi, when at length they reached the far shore of Soetendalsvlei. They were rewarded with hot coffee and a set of bonds round their wrists and ankles. They were bundled into the vehicle's spacious interior alongside the donkey.

They headed for Birkenhead.

In Testerman's office at Dolla's Downes, Yasakov held his Makarov on Testerman. He was about to face one of the most dangerous moments of the kidnap – the passage past the gatehouse and Tom Widdows. Testerman would obviously have to drive. . . .

'Switch out the light – lock the door,' Yasakov ordered, his voice harsh with tension.

They went out. Yasakov motioned Testerman into the landrover's driving seat. He himself vaulted into the rear, knelt on the floorboards gun in hand behind the wide bucket seats, which gave him all the cover he needed.

'Get going – no stopping, d'ye hear!'

The vehicle jerked on starting from Testerman's state of nerves.

'No games!' snarled the Russian, jamming the pistol muzzle against Testerman's ribs. 'Lights! Move! Through the gate, quick as hell!'

Yasakov had a sudden idea as they neared the gatehouse.

'Put your lights on full!' he said. That way, they would dazzle the guards so that they would not be able to make out what was in the rear, even if they should look in.

Testerman obeyed. Yasakov lay down full length.

The landrover went for the gate.

Yasakov was right. Widdows, who had come out on to the verge of the roadway, was blinded by the headlights and shaded his eyes. Testerman went through steadily, lifting one hand in salute as he passed.

The second, outer gate, was also open.

They passed through.

'Where now?'

Testerman lifted his foot from the accelerator. His answer was a savage jab of the gun in his back.

'Keep going – until I tell you.'

The road fork. That was the critical point at which the driver switch would have to take place. Yasakov checked inside his wet suit top – the two lengths of thin, powerful nylon cord were there with which to lash Testerman's arms and legs.

Yasakov got as fully to his feet as he could and rested the Makarov's barrel against Testerman's neck. He could also now see the road ahead. So far the getaway had been almost too easy.

It wasn't easy, however, when Testerman pulled up beyond the road junction on Yasakov's orders and the Russian stood in the roadway by the driver's door.

'Out!' he said.

Testerman flung the door wide, launched himself out sideways at the Russian from an awkward sitting stance. Yasakov was half expecting him to try a break.

Had Yasakov not wanted Testerman alive to interrogate him about Dolla's Downes, he would have stepped back and shot him dead. But, above anything, he needed the information which the American possessed.

Yasakov moved forward, instead of backwards, as Testerman might have expected, and lashed at his head with the pistol. Blood spurted from a cut across his forehead. He was half stunned. As he fell, Yasakov struck him a second time. The blow, aimed for behind his ear, missed, but caught him between neck and shoulder. Pain seared through the base of his neck; the nerves and muscles of the arm he had intended to grab Yasakov with were semi-paralysed.

He fell untidily in the roadway. Yasakov ended the roughing-up with a savage kick in the rib-cage which brought a grunt of pain from his half stunned victim.

Before he could attempt any retaliation, Yasakov was down on his knees and in a flash the nylon lashing was round Testerman's ankles.

Yasakov jumped clear. Testerman's senses were still between wind and water. Yasakov stamped on one of his wrists, then brought the other by hand to join it. In a single adroit movement, he had the two securely lashed behind Testerman's back.

Even discounting the stunning blows to the head, Testerman was no threat to anyone.

Yasakov laid the pistol on the front seat, dragged Testerman round to the back of the landrover, and heaved him unceremoniously inside.

He headed for Birkenhead.

30

'What does APPLEJACK mean?'

Yasakov threw the question at Testerman. The American, Cane and Maris were tied to chairs in the mess-cum-office of the Russian diving team at Birkenhead – the room with the striking model of the *Kamchatka*.

It was nearing midnight. Anna, bringing Cane and Maris, and Yasakov with Testerman, had successfully accomplished the rendezvous. All but Josef and Testerman were in wet suits still.

Yasakov had given his gun to Anna; Stefan still had Testerman's Colt. There was hardly any need for the show of hardware – the three captives were trussed like fowls. Testerman was in poorest shape – blood had congealed on the welt across his forehead, and he sat awkwardly because of the pain from Yasakov's kick in his ribs. Cane was in a savage frame of mind; Maris' diving cap was off; her hair fell almost to her shoulders.

Testerman blinked at the question.

'It is code, isn't it – code for what?' Yasakov fired at him. In his interrogation so far, Yasakov had been unable to shake Testerman's assertion that the underground station was anything more than it was known to be – an observatory conducting geo-magnetic studies and monitoring Halley's Comet.

'Yeah – it's code,' admitted Testerman.

'*What does it mean?*' Yasakov strode angrily close to Testerman's chair.

'It's the code name for a one-ton orbiting telescope named IRAS when it was launched three, four years back,' he lied.

'Why IRAS?' demanded Yasakov.

'Infra-red astronomical satellite.'

'Why give it a code name?' persisted Yasakov.

Testerman's answer was at a tangent. 'The satellite is heat-detecting. It is so sensitive that it can pick up a baseball's heat from a thousand kilometres away. Because its own heat could overwhelm incoming signals, its detectors are housed in a giant vacuum flask filled with liquid helium chilled to only minus five degrees above absolute zero. . . .'

'Answer my question – don't talk round it,' snarled Yasakov.

Time was running out for Yasakov. He was being squeezed – and he knew it. The South African authorities had originally granted the Russian diving team a period of a month in which to produce tangible proof of the *Kamchatka*'s treasure. The team had now been ashore for nearly three weeks. The deadline for their departure was in ten days' time

– tonight was Sunday, and they had to leave on Wednesday week.

Yasakov was also being squeezed by the cumbersome communications system. Under it the Russian team could – in urgent circumstances – communicate with the gas atoll. Any communication (in plain language) had to be via the South African naval communications centre at Silvermine, near Cape Town. What he had discovered already about the frequency-hopping signals was priceless – but he could not pass it on to the gas atoll. Nonetheless, that secret in itself was tantalizingly little by comparison to what he stood on the threshold of – the real purpose of the Dolla's Downes station. Lacking that, he would have achieved only half the loaf.

He meant to get the whole loaf, even if he had to beat the three to death to get it.

'What are the other slots on the board for? Eh? There aren't so many telescopes in space.'

'There *are* other space vehicles, if not telescopes,' Testerman answered levelly. 'The purpose of all of them is to keep watch on Halley's Comet, as well as the comet called Giacobini-Zinner which preceded Halley's in 1985.'

'Go on.' Yasakov was grim-faced.

'Four other space vehicles are out there – they all have code-names,' went on Testerman. 'One of them was named Giotto – it is a European Space Agency project – in honour of the famous artist who painted Halley's Comet in the Middle Ages.'

'That makes one,' snapped Yasakov.

'There is Planet A, sent up by the Japanese, their first major space venture.'

'Two.'

'You Russians launched two probes as well,' continued Testerman, keeping his voice cool and rational.

'Four.'

'Each Soviet probe dropped smaller probes as they passed by Venus in order to investigate the planet's atmosphere,' Testerman continued. 'Afterwards, they rendezvoused and followed Halley's Comet.'

'Six. You are three short. There are nine slots.'

'You're forgetting APPLEJACK – that's the space tele-scope,' he went on. 'Instead of dropping two minor probes into Venus' atmosphere, the two Soviet satellites dropped two *each*.' It was the only chance answer Testerman had given. All the rest were watertight.

Yasakov felt he was being talked out of Dolla's Downes' true function. He'd have to be tough, very tough, with Testerman.

'And the so-called geomagnetic aspect of your so-called observatory?'

'The magnetic anomaly which exists between the Cape and Antarctica is under continual investigation.'

'And in order to do that you have to observe comets?' Yasakov asked sarcastically.

'Yes. The observatory's brief is to investigate what are known as magnetic field reversals – when the compass needle changes from north-seeking to south-seeking. Cape Agulhas is important because the first Portuguese found the anomaly right here. Agulhas means compass needle. When an aster-oid in the distant past collided with the earth, it churned up iron-rich material deep down and caused a magnetic anomaly. . . .'

Yasakov couldn't take any more. 'Shut up!' he snarled. 'Don't throw the bull, Testerman, as you Americans so rightly call it. Frequency-hopping transmissions have no-thing to do with all this scientific claptrap. You know it, too!'

Testerman went cold. He hoped his face wasn't showing what he felt. Those frequency-hopping signals – ELF – were the thin stream on which the safety of the world depended. Let them stop, for however short a while, and the deep-diving American subs would go on retaliatory alert. Missiles would be fused up, and they would surface to receive orders to press the firing button. . . . There would be no recall once that happened. Nothing, he vowed inwardly again, would extract any information about ELF from him. They could torture him, shoot him, he would keep his secret. But if he could find out what the Reds were up to on the gas atoll. . . .

He gave the only reply he could. 'I don't know what you are talking about. I am a scientist, nothing else.'

'Nothing else, eh? We'll see about that,' replied Yasakov. 'Perhaps our spy here will tell us things you won't – won't, for the moment, Testerman.'

'He doesn't know anything – he's not a spy,' replied Testerman.

Yasakov was on to this like a badger dog going down a hole after its prey.

'So – he doesn't know anything?' Yasakov echoed. 'What should he not know, Testerman? If he's not a spy, why should you keep him and his assistant locked up for twenty-four hours? Why blindfold them in the cave and march them off under armed guard?'

'*You saw!*' Testerman's shock overcame his discretion. For the first time, Cane found himself with a better feeling towards the tough American. He was clearly covering up for himself and Maris.

Cane said, to try and take the heat off him. 'I am not a spy. I am an engineer. I don't have to prove it. Maris here is secretary to the geothermal project. I know nothing of what goes on in the cave station.'

Yasakov grabbed Cane by the throat of his wet suit and shook him. 'APPLEJACK – what does it mean, Cane?'

'I have no idea.'

Yasakov struck him across the face with the back of his hand.

'You'll have to do better than that to get yourself off the hook, Cane. What were you doing exploring a passage into the earth with your – ah, assistant – at night when there was no one around to check on you? Answer me that! What were you doing at the old lighthouse, eh? Why did you try and spy on me from the air at the *Kamchatka* wreck? You *are* a spy, Cane.'

Cane held his mounting anger in check. 'It happened as I said. I was investigating a fissure which – which had just come to my notice. Maris and I were already inside it when there was an explosion. The next thing we knew we found ourselves in the cave.'

'That's the way it was,' Maris added.

'So – a fissure had just been brought to your attention – outside working hours, on a Saturday night. Bah! Do you expect me to swallow that?' Yasakov sneered. 'And then someone – unknown to you – sets off a massive explosion. I say again – bah! What were you and the woman up to, Cane?'

'He gave me those facts just as he has given them to you,' interrupted Testerman. 'That's the way it happened, I know. The two of them suddenly appeared in the cave.'

Testerman was clearly trying to draw Yasakov's fire on himself.

So far, Yasakov had not directed his attention at Maris. Cane eyed him the way one might a deadly snake waving its head about, not knowing where it would strike next.

Anna too wondered why Yasakov had left her alone so far. She watched Yasakov going to work on the two men with interest and a degree of detachment. She respected Yasakov – after all he had once had the nod from Yuri Andropov himself – and she had known all along that the *Kamchatka* operation was a cover for some wider issue for which he had been specially chosen. As a trusted member of the shipboard People's Control Committee and assistant commissar of the gas atoll's Komsomol (Young Communist Organization), Anna felt no qualms about Yasakov's methods. If the men forced him to get rough, that was their own affair.

With Maris, however, it was different. Anna felt, with a curious upsurge of feeling for the white-faced young woman, that she would not be able to bear the sight of her being smashed up. Maris' unusual beauty, the green, almost mystical eyes, her petite, beautiful figure and breasts at the thought of which Anna's pulse quickened – Maris was something apart. She was part of another world she secretly longed for – of freedom and being one's own person; what woman in Russia would dare wear lipstick and nail polish the way Maris did? Anna had never known it; she envied and admired Maris.

'Anna!' She was brought up with a start by Yasakov addressing her in Russian.

'Yes, comrade?'

'I'm putting the girl in your charge. I want information – the purpose of the cave and its frequency-hopping transmissions. I don't care how you get it, but get it. Is that clear?'

Anna drew in her breath with relief. She knew instinctively what her approach would be.

'And the two men?'

In response, Yasakov addressed Stefan and Josef. 'Go and get two spades from the garage. I'm taking them to the beach.'

'Will you be bringing them back, comrade?' Anna's question was full of implications.

Yasakov laughed mirthlessly. 'It depends. On them.'

Cane and Testerman could not, of course, understand Yasakov's orders. When Stefan handed over his gun to Yasakov, Testerman reverted to his earlier tack with him.

'Yasakov,' he said. 'Up to now you've done all the accusing about spies and spying. It's a classic trick to accuse the enemy of what you yourself are up to. *You* are the spy, Yasakov. I wouldn't care to be in your shoes once it gets to the ears of the South African authorities what you are really up to.'

Yasakov seemed amused. 'It first has to get to their ears, American. No way is that going to happen.'

Stefan and Josef reappeared with two spades. The sight silenced Testerman; Cane went cold.

'No!' Maris cried out in anguish. 'You can't do that. Stop! You must not . . .!'

'Tell everything you know to Anna when we've gone, and it won't happen the way you think,' said Yasakov. 'It's up to you.'

Maris' eyes went to Cane. He tried to convey the reassurance to her that Yasakov could not afford to kill them without finding out what he wanted to know. To merely shoot and bury them – he gave Yasakov credit for more sense.

He responded with an Afrikaans expression Maris had taught him had been a slogan of the early Strandvelders in their darkest hours. '*Hou moed* – keep up your courage.'

'What are you saying, eh?' demanded Yasakov. 'What are you telling the woman – quick!'

Cane looked the angry Russian square in the eye. 'Go and get stuffed.'

Yasakov raised the pistol barrel as if to lash Cane across the face, then dropped it. He said coldly. 'In a little while, you may regret that remark, Cane.'

He barked an order at Stefan and Josef. Concentrating first on Cane, they eased off the lashings on his ankles so that there was enough slack for him to hobble. They then freed him from the chair, still keeping his wrists secured behind his back. When they had dealt with Testerman likewise, and the two thugs had collected the spades and Cane's clothes, Yasakov ordered. 'March! To the beach!'

Maris was left alone with Anna. She was armed only with a knife. When the five men had gone towards a cliff path leading down to a small hidden sandy cove, Anna knelt down and loosened the cord from Maris' ankles.

She said quietly, in a woman-to-woman way. 'Men are savages, aren't they? I think they enjoy doing that sort of thing to one another. You've been through a lot tonight, Maris. Even with your wet-suit, the swamps and lake must have been cold. I'm used to it, with all the diving. Wouldn't you like a hot bath and spruce up. Here are your clothes. That's the bathroom.' She indicated a door.

'What is he going to do to Hal? Those spades . . .' Maris burst out.

'Comrade Yasakov won't kill them,' she answered soothingly. 'He is just trying – how do you say it? – trying to twist their arms. That is all, my dear.'

Maris felt trapped. She was terrified on the one hand of Yasakov, and scared on the other by Anna's changed attitude. A tough, no-nonsense approach would have been easier to handle than her charisma. And it *was* charisma, Maris admitted to herself. Anna had style. She could have been very attractive had it not been for . . .

Maris felt cold, outwardly and inwardly. The thought of a

hot bath – Anna had gauged her need exactly. She'd have to have her hands and ankles free for the bath; she might be able, with the door securely locked, to make a break for it via a window. . . . Testerman's landrover stood at the rear of the bungalows, and the Russians' own vehicles were close by.

Maris accepted.

The only snag in Anna's gesture was that the bathroom door had no lock.

Cane was just starting his awkward downward descent of the cliff path – Stefan and Josef were behind him, Testerman ahead, and Yasakov leading – when Maris' scream cut through the night.

31

The scream was loaded with terror, revulsion, naked fear. Naked.

Cane stopped as if a bullet had passed through him.

His reaction – blind, irrational, unwise, in retrospect, was the measure of his feelings for Maris.

He jacknifed backwards into the two guards – Stefan had the gun and Josef the two spades. It was like expecting a hobbled horse to clear a five-barred gate. The short length rope brought him crashing down against the two Russians.

Yasakov wheeled round with a startled oath. He thrust aside Testerman to get at the pile of bodies writhing on the sandy path. Stefan's gun was crowded into immobility; Josef's spade was of more use in the mêlée.

The man got on to his knees, smashed the flat of the implement down between Cane's shoulder-blades.

Cane felt as if the whole weight of the *Kamchatka*'s tonnage had hit him. As he pitched forward on his face, Yasakov also hit him, using the reversed Makarov as a club.

As his senses evaporated, Cane heard Yasakov yell. He was

saying in Russian. 'The American! Keep your eye on the American, you fools! Don't let him get away!'

Cane's moment of senselessness was as quick as the flick of a car's headlights. His nose and mouth had scarcely hit the sand before he was half-conscious again.

Yasakov grabbed him by the hair and hauled him to his knees. This time, he struck him savagely across the face with the barrel of the automatic. The foresight's sharp edge left a long cut from cheekbone to nose.

Cane slumped forward, trying hopelessly to protect his face, but his hands were tied behind his back. He finished up in a kind of praying, kneeling position.

Yasakov first threw an abrasive remark at the two Russian bully boys, then addressed Cane in English.

'So,' he said savagely. 'None of you knows anything, no one has anything to hide, but when one of the party gives a scream, her co-conspirator goes berserk to reach her – eh?'

'What is that bitch doing to her?' Cane mouthed.

'How should I know?' Yasakov retorted with studied casualness. 'I know nothing of lesbian love-making.'

Cane tried to heft himself to his feet, but this time Stefan was ready. He clamped a massive paw over Cane's neck like a yoke and held him down.

'You filthy lot of bastards!' Cane's words were slurred, as if he had had a drink too many.

'Your girlfriend has only to confess to Anna and I'm sure Anna will restrain herself,' Yasakov said urbanely. 'We will find out in due course. Meanwhile, you two will have the opportunity to tell me all about the underground station.'

The opportunity was two holes in the beach. When Stefan and Josef started digging, doubts crowded in on both the captives' minds that they were not graves. They could easily have been: the cove was secluded hemmed in by high cliffs.

The next stage of the operation was more sinister still. The two captives were stripped to their underpants – Cane had been unaware of how cold the night was until his wet suit was removed – shoved roughly into a sitting position, and their wrists tied under their knees. The hobbles on their ankles were shortened.

On Yasakov's orders, Stefan and Josef picked up the captives and seated them in the graves, shovelling in sand up to their necks.

It was after midnight.

Cane's upper back was a triangle of pain where the spade had struck him; his face seemed to be a mixture of heat and ice – heat from the wound, ice from the cold wind blowing off the sea. How long would he be able to take it? In a matter of some five hours it would be dawn. Soon after that, Cassie Wessels would come on duty and all evidence of the night's activities would have to be removed. What did Yasakov intend to do with them? They certainly could not be hidden at Birkenhead.

Yasakov and the two bully boys went and sat on the rocks close by. The two lit cigarettes. Yasakov stared.

The wind rose; sand blew into Cane and Testerman's eyes. The blood caked on Cane's face.

Still Yasakov waited.

After about an hour, Cane realized for what. A burning, muscle-probing cramp seized hold of his legs, raced up into his back, and flashed like an electric current to the lashings on his ankles. Cane gave a gasp.

It was a signal to Yasakov. He came across and squatted down.

'That is only the first of many,' he said. 'The spasms get progressively worse.'

Testerman jerked. Cane knew that the first cramp had also grabbed him. A Boston Crab had nothing on Yasakov's technique.

'Consider carefully before you answer,' Yasakov said slowly. 'What is the purpose of your underground station?'

Neither man replied. Further cramps settled on Cane's hip-bones – he would have done anything, anything, to have been able to straighten out. The nylon ropes felt like steel.

'If you are as innocent as you pretend to be, why are you putting up with all this?' Yasakov went on.

'He knows nothing – I told you before.' Testerman's words were cut short as a shudder – it was an involuntary muscle contraction – jerked his head.

'What does APPLEJACK mean?'

A pathfinder wave of the incoming tide explored the beach and sent a splash of spray into the captives' faces.

'No answer?' Yasakov rejoined Stefan and Josef. They chain-smoked to keep themselves awake.

After a time, Yasakov came back. Cane's thighs, legs and back were locked in long shuddering cramps which left him gasping in agony.

Yasakov eyed him dispassionately. 'Think of her scream, Cane – Anna is probably doing worse things to her than you're having to put up with. You only have to come clean and I will stop it all.'

'You sadistic bastard!' Cane managed to utter. 'If I get my hands free, I will kill you and – and Anna.'

'Brave words, Mister Cane, but without any basis in reality,' he sneered. 'Testerman?'

'Lay off him,' the American said thickly. 'Lay off him and Maris. . . .'

'Yes, yes, you said it before,' retorted Yasakov.

Testerman said. 'If you keep us alive, you've got problems, Yasakov – there's no place to hide. The same goes for my landrover. Once I am missed, search parties will locate it, for sure. If you kill us, you've got three bodies to dispose of.'

Yasakov gave a grim smile. 'It's my problem, Testerman. I solve my own problems. Now – what about the cave?'

They stayed silent.

The night was measured not in hours but in long convulsions. It did not feel to Cane as if he had any live tissue left in his lower body – until a searing blast of pain shot through his crutch like a branding-iron. He could not stifle his cry – it *must* stop!

Yasakov was at his side again. 'You can end it, any time. Just tell me about the cave. . . .'

'Stuff you,' said Cane weakly.

The Russian returned in a little while. Small waves had

begun to wash regularly across the captives' necks and sometimes filled their parched mouths. They dared not swallow the sea water – they would go mad with thirst. Testerman had started to mutter incoherently; he had slipped into temporary delirium.

'Yes?' persisted Yasakov. 'What is APPLEJACK, Testerman? Testerman!'

Cane realized that he was now seeing Yasakov's figure in dim outline.

The dawn! They had won!

Yasakov himself had to admit it soon. He ordered the two guards to dig out his victims. They simply lay on their sides, half in and half out of the incoming tide, unmoving, semisenseless. Their lashings were loosened and their clothes pulled on. They could not stand or walk, think even. The Russians dragged them to the shelter of the rocks. Yasakov eyed the lightening sky anxiously. He gave Cane and Testerman half an hour to recover sufficiently to stumble up the cliff path. They could not have run away even had they wished to.

At the top of the cliff, Cane staggered into the mess room.

He had a blurred sight of Maris sitting tied to a chair. The experiences of the night had burned charcoal circles round her eyes; her face was ashen. He heard her call, 'Hal! Oh God, Hal!' before he pitched on the floor.

Yasakov asked. 'Anna?'

'Nothing, comrade – she sticks to her story.'

Yasakov said savagely. 'Throw them all into the landrover. Get moving – it will be light soon. Everyone in!'

'Where to, comrade?' asked Anna.

'Frenchman's Eye.'

32

'Any normal girl would have given Anna the big kiss-off, the way you did – even this sexy cutie,' said Testerman. He indicated the Accursed Figurehead.

Alcestis presided over the three captives. It was their concluding shock of the night when Maris, Cane and Testerman were thrust unceremoniously into the old magazine at Frenchman's Eye to find Alcestis there. The 'bug' and electric wiring had been removed; there was nothing to show why the figurehead was in their prison.

Yasakov was tense with frustration and anxiety, worried to get them well clear of Birkenhead before sunrise, frustrated because he had completely failed to extract any telling information from his captives.

The Russians had used Testerman's landrover to transport the captives; Josef had followed in their own light pickup in order to take the diving team back to their headquarters from the end of the mountain track.

The landrover also served a useful purpose. It was able to negotiate the rough terrain from where the track ended to the martello tower. The ruined base of the old semaphore tower, built of baulks of timber, served as ideal concealment for the vehicle – it would have been hard to spot even by helicopter search.

Yasakov had departed leaving the three in darkness with some water and food. The heavy old door had been padlocked on the outside. Short of a blasting charge, it would have been impossible to get out of the magazine. Yasakov did not tie them up. Cane and Testerman were in poor shape still from their sandburial; Maris had been only lightly bound.

Now the first fingers of the rising sun struck the summit of Dune Fountain peak and threw long spoke-like bars of light through the ventilation ducts. For the first time they could see each other. The mess the men were in shocked Maris. Previously she had massaged their wrists and ankles; with the light, she could see to try and clean up their wounds.

'Kiss-off is the wrong word,' she responded to Testerman's remark with a shudder. 'Nothing with a kiss in it, please.'

'Do you want to talk about it?' asked Cane.

'Anna is a lesbian – of course,' Maris replied flatly.

'For sure,' Testerman said; Cane felt Maris' fingers tighten in his.

'She told me so.'

'I would have thought the bathroom alone would have been proof enough,' Cane's voice was grim.

'She apologized for *that*,' said Maris. 'She said she's been temporarily carried away – she – she . . .'

Testerman cut in. 'What had sex to do with information she wanted about the – the –' he hesitated. 'The underground station?'

'It was to form part of the bargain,' answered Maris. 'Anna really can be very charming. She apologized, as I said, most diffidently, almost modestly. . . .'

'Modestly!' exclaimed Cane. 'My oath!'

'She said that she appreciated the fact that lesbianism was a way of life for some, if not all, women,' went on Maris. 'She tried to tell me that love between woman and woman was deeper, a more spiritual relationship than between woman and man. She herself, she said, had experienced great love from other women.'

'Quote. Period.' said Testerman shortly. 'What did she want in return?'

'She kept her hands away from me,' replied Maris obliquely. 'She said I need not confess directly to Yasakov what the true purpose of the cave was. It was a secret we could share as – as – pillow-talk. She herself would pass the information on to Yasakov.'

'Where? How?' demanded Cane.

'She launched into a kind of dream world scenario,'

continued Maris. 'It really was quite pathetic, it was so divorced from reality. I would go with her to the gas atoll, where we would be alone, happy. . . . Once the secret of the cave station was out, you two would be disposed of. Aboard the gas atoll, once I had defected, I would be guaranteed safety and security. There would be no need to concern myself about what the place really was.'

Testerman was on to her remark like an Exocet making its final dive on its target.

'Gas atoll? What it *really* was? What was it? Quick, Maris, I must know!'

Cane broke in. 'Listen, Testerman, Maris and I are the ham in the sandwich – you on the one hand, and the Russians on the other. It's about time we knew what *you* are up to!'

The stocky American sat down on the stone floor next to them. 'Brad's the name, see? Right now, let me say you both deserve a Purple Heart. I know you're both in the clear. You, Hal, are no more a spy than this tower's ass.'

Cane had previously been aware of the American's sympathetic vibrations. It was better to have them formulated in words.

'Thanks for the compliment,' he replied. 'It still doesn't answer my question.'

'It knocked my socks off when I saw you two in the cave,' replied Testerman. 'Still, the less you know, the less that son of a bitch Yasakov can extract from you.'

'Meaning – there is more to it than just an observatory?' demanded Cane. 'What about APPLEJACK? And the old lighthouse?'

'See here, Hal,' said Testerman. 'I owe you another apology. It's nothing – maybe it is everything – to do with our present situation.'

'Go on.'

Testerman took a pull from a water canteen Yasakov had left them.

'I don't know how to say this – maybe it is only because we are in this tight spot together that I'm able,' he said hesitantly.

'I can take most things after last night.'

'Okay. Here it is then. Straight from the shoulder. We – I – was behind all the accidents at the drilling site. I wanted to get rid of the geothermal project. I wanted you out. It's when I monkeyed with the buzzsaw that things went wrong.'

Cane stared unspeaking at him for a long time. 'What you're saying is that you were responsible for the explosion?'

'Yeah. We set a time fuse on some of your own dynamite out of your shed. I reckoned that when you saw the smashed-up machinery in the excavation, even you would throw in the towel. But my guy who rigged it didn't know about fissures – or that a fissure led to the cave,' he added wryly. 'That set the capstone on my bad luck. You know the rest.'

'You mean that you were also responsible for Howells and Bosch?' said Maris incredulously.

'Easy now,' said Testerman. 'Howells was a bit of a psycho anyway. He only needed a push to send him over the edge. Bosch – I don't like to talk about it. He wasn't meant to get hurt like that. He overreacted and so did my men. That's all I want to say. I sure feel bad about Bosch.'

'Why are you telling me all this?' demanded Cane. 'It could prejudice you hopelessly once Grimmock hears about it.'

Testerman said quietly. 'You're forgetting something, aren't you, Hal? Yasakov.'

The seriousness of his reply sent a chill through Cane and Maris.

The American added. 'Yasakov is a spy. He is a KGB man. He is desperate.'

'What you've told us about your activities at the drilling site means you've got something big to hide,' said Cane.

'I've answered that,' Testerman retorted. 'Yasakov isn't a bush leaguer, fellah. It isn't a two-bit game he's playing. He means business.'

Testerman said after a long silence. 'One or more of us has got to escape. If it's either of you two, you are to make like a bat out of hell to Dolla's Downes and report to Ed Weinback. Ed will know what to do securitywise.'

'Meaning?'

Testerman shrugged and kept silent.

'Brad, that underground establishment could not have been set up without the co-operation of South Africa, could it?' Cane asked.

'You're welcome to make any deductions.'

'Nor the use of the old lighthouse,' Maris added.

They fell silent, each with their own thoughts.

It was a long, tense day.

It was a long, tense day for Yasakov.

The weather was clear and the sea calm. Had he had any valid excuse to Cassie Wessels, Yasakov would have called off diving operations. His team needed sleep. They were in a state of fatigue in which underwater mistakes could be easily made. He himself had only half his mind on the diving – he was in a ferment to get back to Frenchman's Eye. The team, sullen and tired, made a pretence of diving. Yasakov hoped Captain Wessels was not watching through his binoculars. There was no reason why he should. He had seen it all a hundred times before.

It was a long, tense day.

At dusk, Yasakov allowed Wessels to get well clear of Birkenhead, and then drove hard to Frenchman's Eye. He took with him two pistols, some lengths of thin nylon rope, a lantern, flashlights, and Josef. The other two – Stefan and Anna – seemed dead on their feet. Anna seemed emotionally as well as physically exhausted.

Yasakov parked the light pickup at the end of the track and soon outdistanced Josef on the kilometre and a half walk to the old tower. He was torn between the prompting of his wild Uzbek blood – the Uzbeks have always been the butchers of Central Asia – and his skill as a practised KGB interrogator to extract information by more subtle means than twisting a prisoner's body into a bloodied mess.

He decided to try KGB methods first.

Yasakov had to wait for Josef. Then he unlocked the padlock, pushed the door open with his foot, Makarov aimed. Josef stood aside, offering covering fire.

'Stand back in there!' he ordered. Simultaneously he clicked on his torch with the idea of blinding the prisoners. 'Stand against the far wall – together!'

They were there all right: Testerman, looking tougher than ever with his blood-caked wound and day's growth of beard; Cane, lean and hard with the ugly pistol-barrel welt across his face; Maris, her eyes big from the darkness.

On Yasakov's orders, Josef lit a lantern and put it in the middle of the magazine. Even a *kamikaze* attempt to jump either of the Russians would not have got as far as the doorway.

Next, Yasakov entered, and Josef slid into position like a well-rehearsed circus bear.

Yasakov knew that between interrogator and captive a curious relationship develops, even when death is the stake on the table. This relationship is a subtle thing – almost like the flow of electricity between two battery poles – and can, if the interrogator knows what to look for, often give away secrets which the prisoner would rather die than reveal. And Testerman and Cane had already shown themselves hard nuts to crack.

He addressed Testerman. 'What happened to you last night is only the beginning, unless you come clean. There is no point in subjecting yourself to what I have in store for you. Dolla's Downes observatory is phoney, isn't it?'

'I told you. It is a geomagnetic observatory which is also involved in space tracking. That is all.'

'It is significant that your underground station should have been established more or less at the same time as the new American naval base at Kosi Bay,' Yasakov said.

'Was it?' replied Testerman blandly. 'I wouldn't know – I'm a scientist, not a navy man.'

Yasakov added, giving the comment the value of a throw-away line. 'At the same time also, we Russians established the offshore gas atoll.'

What had made the KGB man say that? Testerman asked himself.

Yasakov switched his attention away from him to Cane.

'You must be a pretty valuable man for your bosses to bring you all the way from overseas to investigate the underground establishment and the old lighthouse, Mister Cane.' Before Cane had time to repeat his previous denial, Yasakov added, addressing Maris. 'Your principals have a good eye for their special agents – pretty, a member of a respected family of the region, with a good working knowledge of old buildings which could house transmitters – frequency-hopping transmitters.'

'Get this clear,' Maris rejoined angrily. 'I am not a spy or a secret agent or anything like that – for anyone. You can go on repeating it until you are blue in the face. . . .'

'You can still save your skin by telling me what the cave station's purpose is. I guarantee you indemnity if you defect and come with me to the gas atoll.'

'Gas atoll!' replied Maris contemptuously. 'Your team was suspect with us Strandvelders right from the start – we know our wrecks. They are part of our lives. We *know* the *Kamchatka*.'

'Do you?' Yasakov sneered. He put his free hand into a pocket and then extended it to Maris.

It contained a palmful of golden sovereigns.

'The Czar's treasure – twenty-five million dollars of it down there in the water.'

Maris peered at the coins, going unthinkingly closer to the Russian.

'Those coins have never been in the sea,' she burst out. 'A gold coin which has been immersed for so long and just brought to the surface has a particular look about it. . . .'

'Gold is not affected by seawater,' said Yasakov. 'See, the dates are contemporary with the *Kamchatka* – 1900, 1901, 1902 – beautiful English sovereigns.'

Maris stared at him and then said softly. 'You've salted the *Kamchatka* wreck! Those sovereigns came from elsewhere!'

Yasakov's eyes were hooded, perhaps from fatigue, perhaps from playing with her, perhaps in anticipation of the bombshell he was about to pitch into the arena which he hoped would draw an admission from Testerman.

By admission, the interrogator won admission. 'You are very clever and you are right. But no one else will guess. Those sovereigns came from a collection in the Kremlin museum. Captain Wessels will get them at the right moment.'

He turned to Testerman.

'The *Kamchatka* operation is a blind,' he said bluntly. 'The gas atoll is not a gas atoll. There never was an offshore gas strike. The liquefied gas which is supposedly pumped up from the ocean bed and shipped out by special supertanker is, in fact, sent all the way to this southern point of Africa from the Soviet's own resources in Siberia – the same source which supplies Europe by pipeline. You Americans are dumb. Your spy satellites monitored our tankers, but failed to note that they came laden – it is simply a double shuttle service. The whole gas strike business is one big fake, a front.'

'*Jeez!*' whispered Testerman. '*What for?*'

'You can now begin to understand why your frequency-hopping transmissions cause us so much concern.' The KGB man believed he had Testerman on the ropes. Any moment now, he'd open his mouth and the cave's secret would be out. He only needed a little shove. No need to remind him that with the gas atoll knowledge he now had, his life was forfeit. Like the other two. That could come later – after his confession.

Yasakov went on deliberately.

'The gas atoll is, in fact, a mid-course missile updating station for the Soviet navy's new super-secret SS-NX-20 missile. It is fired from an equally new super-secret submarine – the Typhoon.'

'The SS-NX-20 and the Typhoon! My God!' burst out Testerman.

'So,' sneered Yasakov. 'You are just a simple scientist, detached from the affairs of the world in your ivory tower under the Strandveld! May I tell you a little more?'

'More? There is more?' Only a hoarse whisper came from the American.

'The SS-NX-20 has a range of 9600 kilometres and contains twelve individually targeted nuclear warheads,' Yasakov continued. 'They are meant to be fired from submarines positioned in Antarctic waters. But, as you will appreciate, missiles at that range to be spot-on accurate require electronic updating during their trajectory. That is the gas atoll's function. You will note that the gas atoll is eighteen hundred kilometres from the American base at Kosi Bay – the optimum updating range to pinpoint a missile after it has been launched from the sub-Antarctic.'

Testerman remained deadly silent. Yasakov waited. He knew that the strange love-hate bond between questioner and questioned took a little time to develop – a pair gets into a kind of mental tandem and tells one another things on a non-conscious level, from which answers are deduced. He was aware that, in the light of this, Testerman would not reply directly but obliquely – but the hidden meanings would be there.

Yasakov waited.

Maris edged close to Cane. In the tense atmosphere, Josef swivelled his sights in their direction at her movement.

Yasakov's Uzbek blood was fast overtaking his interrogatory techniques.

'Yes? – yes? What do you say?' he demanded of Testerman. The American's head stayed down. He shook it.

'Yes?' Yasakov started to lose control.

Testerman shook his head again.

'Josef!' Yasakov's order was a savage explosion of the wild genes which had made his ancestors feared throughout Asia. 'You know what to do – the nylon shoehorn!'

33)

Shoehorn was a misnomer. It was Yasakov's name for an adaptation of the dreadful method of torture which the Czar's officers aboard the *Kamchatka* had used against political dissidents. That had been known as the 'concrete shoehorn'. Yasakov's device consisted of a thin nylon rope twisted tight to form a tourniquet, secured by a short length of wire.

Josef first tied the captives' arms firmly behind their backs; Yasakov stood guard.

'You, Testerman – sit down!' snapped Yasakov. 'Away from the others. Down!'

The American had no option but to obey. Yasakov kept his line of fire clear. Cane and Maris watched in silent horror as Josef screwed one length of nylon rope tight, then with a pair of pliers, he nipped the knot fast with wire. He repeated the procedure on Testerman's other ankle. Next, he secured the two loops with a third, short length.

'Cane!'

Cane winced as the nylon rope bit into grooves the previous night's rope had cut into his flesh.

'Now the girl!'

The three of them sat propped against a wall like trussed chickens. At a further order from Yasakov, Josef went outside and returned with some blankets. He threw them roughly at the captives.

'Not for your comfort,' said Yasakov. 'Just to ensure you don't die of pneumonia before you have a taste of the things those capitalistic swine of the Czar's did to our proletariat.'

Cane could feel his toes starting to go numb; the constriction of blood in his lower limbs felt like air being pumped into an overfull balloon.

'You'll have plenty of time to think things over before I return. You can change your minds right now, if you wish, before the pain really begins.'

'Bugger you,' retorted Testerman.

'As you wish,' replied Yasakov.

'When will you be back?' asked Maris.

'It depends on your friend Captain Wessels – and the weather,' Yasakov replied. 'I suppose you still believe in prayer – start praying that the weather is bad enough to stop us diving. Otherwise,' he replied relentlessly, 'it could be any time. Josef, lock the door!'

Darkness clamped down like a solid thing when the Russian removed the lantern; they heard the padlock click.

They were alone.

The Accursed Figurehead held her seductive pose.

They realized from the growing numbness that it would not be long before they could not move, so they arranged the blankets clumsily around themselves while they still had strength and some mobility. Maris sat between the two men.

Then the pain came.

It targeted first on Maris. She gave a tiny hiccough of agony and thrust her head hard against Cane. Then, her lips went to his mouth for comfort and her teeth clenched involuntarily. It might have been a lover's kiss – except it was pain, not passion. He tried to hold her while it lasted but his hands were fast. Before the awful visitant had done with her, it was his own turn – and then Testerman's.

Later, his half-delirious mind could not determine which was worse – the pain or cramps like strychnine poison convulsions which devastated his thighs and back.

At some stage during that hideous night, all three of them must have passed into unconsciousness; none of them was aware of the grey light of day which peeped through the ventilation ducts and then seemed to revert again to night at what it saw lying on the old magazine floor.

The door opened. It was Yasakov. Behind him were Anna, Stefan and Josef.

The Russian shone his flashlight on the three contorted

bundles mixed up with the blankets, like dogs which had scrabbled for some last comfort in dying.

Anna gave an exclamation and rushed for Maris.

'Leave her!' Yasakov had his pistol and Stefan was backing him. However, the captives were as little threat as Halley's Comet in space.

'She's dead – you've killed her!' exclaimed Anna.

'All the more reason then to leave her,' retorted the Russian, 'but it's not true.' He pocketed his pistol and ordered Josef. 'Open the door and let in some light and air. There's no danger on such a foggy day.'

Foggy, clammy and cold it was: diving was out of the question. Cassie Wessels had been only too pleased to leave Birkenhead and return to the comfort of his hotel at nearby Gansbaai.

The uncertain light revealed the awful state of the captives' lower legs and ankles – blue-black, monstrously swollen, the nylon shoehorn a line of blue ligament cutting into livid flesh.

Anna dropped on her knees. 'She is a woman, comrade – women are different from men!'

'You should know. Get up off your knees to a spy,' Yasakov said harshly. 'Drag her into a sitting position. I want to question all three of them.'

'She is in no condition to answer anything. . . .'

'She's just in the right condition, suitably softened up, I hope,' retorted Yasakov. 'Stefan, Josef, organize the men to face me.'

Cane managed to lever his head up – it weighed a ton – and saw, dimly, the group of Russians. He was frightened for Maris, whose head kept falling forward like a sleepwalker's.

Yasakov addressed them in a hard voice. 'You are lucky. The weather is too bad for diving. Otherwise, we would not have come before tonight. You still have the chance to save your legs. Gangrene usually takes a couple of days to set in and your circulations may not have been too badly affected for you to recover. Testerman?'

The American's weals had oozed more blood; Cane hoped he did not look as bad.

219

Testerman tried to speak, but could not.

'Water!' ordered Yasakov. 'All of them!'

Testerman managed to utter one word. 'Observatory.'

Yasakov held back his anger. He realized that if he pushed the three much further, he wouldn't get his answers anyway.

'Cane – now's your last chance!'

'I told you before.'

'Maris Swart!'

'I know nothing. That is the truth. Neither Hal nor I know anything!'

Yasakov's eyes had their sinister, hooded look. The realization that he was near the end of the line with the three aroused his savage instincts. He had to *do* something!

'Search them!' he snapped. 'Take them to pieces! The smallest clue!'

'We searched them when we first brought them to Birkenhead, comrade,' Stefan said diffidently.

'Don't question my orders, or it will be the worse for you!' rapped out Yasakov. 'Search them, I say!'

Anna went forward, unbidden, to Maris. Maris had not the strength to recoil. This time her hands were unseeking, gentle, perfunctory.

'Nothing here, comrade,' she reported.

Yasakov knew as well as Stefan that they would find the prisoners 'clean'. What he wanted was to give himself a breathing space to think. To think of any little clue, however insignificant, since his entry into the cave. In his mind he also traced back systematically his team's later break-in to the above-ground complex at Dolla's Downes and the capture of the three in Testerman's office. If only he had let Stefan go ahead and break open Testerman's desk drawer! Yet, he had not wanted to leave any tell-tale signs behind. . . .

Document! Suddenly he remembered.

Stefan had left the desk alone and gone over to the word-processor. Testerman had described it as a repeat monitor of any significant data received in the cave below. He recalled how Stefan had torn off the strip of telex-like paper from the machine and thrust it inside his wet suit. Testerman had seemed unconcerned at the time; maybe it was simply an act.

Yasakov barked in Russian. 'Stefan! Where is the paper you took from the machine in the American's office?'

Anna looked surprised at the note in Yasakov's voice and said. 'He thrust it inside his wet suit. . . .'

'Let him answer for himself!'

Stefan's mental processes were as painstakingly slow as a dinosaur's.

'I remember putting it inside my wet suit, like Anna says, comrade. Then we crossed the lake, and Josef was waiting at the Kombi. We then went to Birkenhead . . .'

'I don't want your itinerary! I want to know what happened to the paper!'

Stefan looked oafish, confused. 'I kept on the wet suit when we went to the beach, and then we brought the prisoners here in the landrover. It was hot with so many of us in the back of the landrover. . . .'

'Did you open your diving jacket? Did you take out the paper?'

'I – I don't remember, comrade. I may have. It was warm. . . .'

'Anna, take Stefan and Josef. Search the landrover. Take it apart, if necessary. *Find that paper!*'

'If it is there, comrade.' There again was the virtual silent insolence with which Anna endowed the word comrade.

'Hurry, blast you!' he retorted.

Yasakov sat down in the entranceway on a fisherman's canvas stool which he had brought along for a protracted interrogation. He put the Makarov across his knees – a totally unnecessary precaution.

In about five minutes, Anna was back. She handed Yasakov a crumpled, muddied piece of paper in characteristic print-out format.

'I think this is what you were looking for, comrade.' Her voice was neutral, deliberately so. She must have read its contents.

She passed it to Yasakov and added, 'The others are going on with the search.'

Yasakov smoothed the paper out on his knee and read. It might have been an anaesthetic needle which was thrust into him. He went completely still, holding his seated pose as if frozen. The hooded eyes riveted on the print-out, reading it again and again, in sheer disbelief.

At length, Anna broke his reverie. 'That is it, comrade?'

Yasakov looked at her. His pale eyes had a strange, blank look as if their owner was light years away.

She was more startled when he said. 'Cut the prisoners loose. Massage their legs. Give them some hot coffee and sandwiches.'

'Stefan and Josef have the knives.' Anna knew what had stunned Yasakov in the document; but neither she nor anyone else could have guessed what was going on behind the KGB man's remote eyes.

'Get them,' responded Yasakov mechanically. 'I have what I want.'

It was only the arrival of the full team which seemed to jerk Yasakov out of his state of total abstraction.

Stefan began to say, 'I am sorry, comrade, in all the hurry of the getaway the paper got overlooked.'

'Forget it. Cut them loose.' He addressed Anna. 'You heard – massage, coffee, something to eat to revive them.'

Anna took Stefan's knife and went to Maris. Her legs were like bloated blood-sausages tied at the bottom. The flesh was so contused that it overflowed the cords – she could not sever them without cutting Maris.

Anna eased her over on her side, sawed the knot with its wire nip loose, first the one ankle and then the other. Then she freed her hands.

Maris couldn't move. She sat immobile in the same cramped pose, unable to straighten herself out.

Stefan and Josef next cut the men loose and the team began massage.

Yasakov himself might have been a disembodied spectator. He sat on his canvas stool completely abstracted as if the main part of his mind were operating on another – completely absorbing – wavelength. No one present – or anyone in the civilized world – could have guessed at the daring and outrageous plan which was taking shape in his mind.

Finally, Anna said. 'The prisoners are free, comrade. Your other orders have been carried out.'

Yasakov blinked like a subject coming out of a hypnotic trance. Cane, Maris and Testerman had been unable to hold the coffee mugs to their mouths; they had to be fed like infants.

Yasakov addressed them in his usual biting way, but he could not conceal the overtone of jubilation that crept into his words.

'Your display of stiff upper lip has been most touching,' he said. 'But quite useless. You may be lucky in avoiding gangrene in your legs.'

'Ah, cheese it!' muttered Testerman.

'It really doesn't matter any more what you do or do not say,' went on Yasakov. He held up the print-out paper to Testerman, keeping the wording towards himself.

'Recognize this?'

'It looks like the strip your grisly bear tore off the word-processor in my office.'

'Where does this information originate?'

'From the main receivers in the cave,' answered Testerman unconcernedly. 'The processor is a relay monitor for observation data connected with the space telescope. . . .'

'You will have to be more careful in future with your so-called data monitor – if there is a future,' Yasakov went on. 'In Russia an operator would be shot for such carelessness.'

Testerman winced from the pain in his ankles as he tried to sit more upright.

'What are you saying, Yasakov?'

'Perhaps your operator fed the wrong tape into the machine. Does it matter? Let me read you what it says.'

He passed his pistol to Anna and stood up. He articulated slowly.

NORTH AMERICAN AEROSPACE DEFENCE COMMAND HEAD-
QUARTERS, CHEYENNE MOUNTAIN, COLORADO, TO
BRIGADIER BRAD TESTERMAN, COMMANDING DOLLA'S
DOWNES ANTI-MISSILE EARLY WARNING STATION, CAPE
AGULHAS, SOUTH AFRICA.

HOLD ALERT STATUS CODE APPLEJACK. THIS IS A DUMMY
RUN. REPEAT, THIS IS A DUMMY RUN. IT IS NOT REPEAT NOT
FOR REAL.

AT 2100 HOURS GMT ON JUNE FIRST ALL EXTRA LOW FRE-
QUENCY SIGNALS TO US NUCLEAR SUBMARINES IN SOUTHERN
OCEAN QUOTE SANCTUARY UNQUOTE QUADRANT WILL BE
DISCONTINUED FOR THREE REPEAT THREE MINUTES. ALL
SUBMARINES WILL THEN, IN ACCORDANCE WITH STANDING
ORDERS, INSTITUTE RETALIATORY NUCLEAR ALERT PROCE-
DURES AND SURFACE FOR COMMAND INSTRUCTIONS. DOLLA'S
DOWNES STATION WILL RELAY NORAD COMMAND ORDERS AS
FOLLOWS: THIS IS A TEST REPEAT THIS IS A TEST OF ALL
COMMUNICATIONS AND NUCLEAR ALERT PROCEDURES. NO
MISSILES WILL BE FIRED.

DURING THIS EXERCISE YOU WILL REALIGN LOCALLY YOUR
ALERT STATUS BOARD CODES FROM APPLEJACK THROUGH
ADVANCED NUCLEAR WARNING CODES BIG NOISE, COCKED
PISTOL AND FAST PACE. THIS STATUS MUST NOT REPEAT NOT
BE REPEATED TO OTHER ANTI-MISSILE WARNING STATIONS.
DOLLA'S DOWNES WILL FOLLOW ALL OTHER NUCLEAR ALERT
STATION PROCEDURES DURING TEST.

AFTER THREE MINUTES, YOU WILL RESUME EXTRA LOW
FREQUENCY SIGNALS FROM CAPE AGULHAS TRANSMITTERS.
YOU WILL SUBMIT PERSONAL REPORT ON SUCCESS OR OTHER-
WISE OF THIS EXERCISE TO NORAD HQ SOONEST.

Yasakov stopped reading. From some last muscular re-
serve Testerman found strength to heft himself upright and
project himself at the Russian. But there was no power in it.
He simply flopped forward on his face, jerking like a dying
fish on a deck.

Yasakov, who had taken his time to sidestep the attack –

well telegraphed in advance – raised his foot to kick the prostrate American. Then he drew it back and shrugged. He could afford not to.

Testerman had lost. So had the United States.

34

Yasakov felt as if a nylon shoehorn itself had been clamped round his brain. As with the torture device, he was being squeezed. Not, however, by tangible things like ropes but by time and circumstance. Time, most of all. A thousand thoughts tore through his mind, each one requiring to be dovetailed into the pattern of the masterplan which had taken shape in his mind when he had clapped eyes on the print-out ordering the American nuclear exercise.

Yasakov almost tripped over a rock along the track from Frenchman's Eye to where he had parked the pickup. Now, in direct contradiction of his earlier wish, he wanted the fog to clear. A fake dive to the *Kamchatka* to produce the 'salted' gold was a priority piece of the jigsaw. It involved Captain Wessels; he must not make the discovery appear too slick.

However, what was burning him up right now was his inner question, would the Kremlin buy his plan? Yasakov had already decided that there could be only one place to sell it – right at the top. He was only too well aware of the red tape and petty jealousies with which the decision-making segment of the naval command was shot through.

There was only one person who had the flair, the panache – and the authority – to sanction such a daring scheme. That was Admiral of the Fleet Sergei Gorshkov. The name itself sent a thrill of excitement – and of fear – through Yasakov. Admiral Gorshkov was known world-wide as the 'father' of the formidable modern Soviet navy. Yasakov was a profound admirer of Admiral Gorshkov, and was steeped in the great admiral's philosophy and strategic thinking. Now, as he hurried across Dune Fountain peak, a phrase of Admiral Gorshkov's dropped into his mind – 'working out a decision is a profoundly creative process'. His own masterplan, with its magnificent strategic spectrum, was surely an example of that creative process!

Yasakov examined his plan in the context (he hoped) of Admiral Gorshkov's thinking. It fitted the admiral's favourite topic, 'the battle for the first salvo'. The surprise it would create would achieve maximum result with minimum expenditure of manpower, equipment and time. In fact, the cost – and equipment involved – was laughably low for the ends it would accomplish. It was a peace-time surprise thrust which would achieve colossal military results – without a shot being fired.

Yasakov felt persuaded that this aspect alone would be enough to win him the go-ahead. The plan also fitted Admiral Gorshkov's publicly propounded mission for the Red Fleet during the 1980s – force projection and support for the Third World. What could be more appropriate geographically here, on the southernmost tip of Africa, the home ground of the Third World?

Gorshkov *must* agree! The admiral's huge expansion plan of the Soviet navy also had roots in the tip of Africa. The *Kamchatka* had been part of the Czar's doomed fleet, the loss of which had taught Russia such a humiliating lesson, namely, that a bluewater fleet must have world-wide replenishment bases if it were to operate as a fighting force. The strategic and logistic lessons of the Voyage of the Damned permeated all Admiral Gorshkov's strategic thinking.

Yasakov again quickened his pace. He *had* to speak personally to Admiral Gorshkov from the gas atoll. However, it was one thing to want to speak to him – it meant a voice linkup via satellite direct to Moscow – and another thing to achieve it. He could imagine the furore his request would create aboard the gas atoll. Vice-Admiral Strokin, commanding the offshore installation, was a good enough sailor but no expert in the grander aspects of global politics and naval strategy – which was just what his plan was all about. Whether he would risk a rocket – possibly a black mark against his career – by agreeing to a request to speak direct to one of the top five in the Kremlin hierarchy – was open to doubt.

Time – that was the biggest obstacle of all. Yasakov almost broke into a trot, as if that would help break the time squeeze into which he had to fit a mass of logistic detail.

Today was Tuesday – Tuesday morning. In eight days' time, on Wednesday the following week, the South African deadline for the team's stay ashore lapsed. On that day, they were to be picked up by South African helicopter and flown to a Soviet warship from the gas atoll at the 'no-go' zone boundary.

The agreement under which the diving team had been allowed ashore was strict – anything of value from the wreck had to be handed over immediately to Captain Wessels. Any communications, in plain language, had to be routed (after official clearance) through the South African naval station at Silvermine, near Cape Town. Physical communication – as witness the helicopter/warship arrangement – was equally top heavy.

Yasakov reasoned that if he could fake the discovery of the sovereigns that afternoon – he meant to try, depending on the weather – it would take a further day at least for his request to visit the gas atoll to go through official red tape. That, in turn, meant it would be Thursday afternoon at the earliest before he could reach the gas atoll. He would then have lost a day and a half out of the precious eight left to the deadline. . . .

When could he be back ashore?

Yasakov, in terms of his masterplan, needed to make a second – unofficial and top-secret – shuttle to the gas atoll. For this, Yasakov required a boat from the shore. And a skipper who would keep his mouth shut. That meant enough dollars to buy it closed for a night sortie out to sea. He knew where he would find the sort of boat he wanted – at Roman's Bay. Roman's Bay was a small indentation on the coast on the opposite side of the Danger Point peninsula from Birkenhead. Yasakov remembered seeing fishing boats anchored, nets drying, and boat sheds. He hoped now to find a skipper fog-bound who would be willing to go to sea at short notice, at a price. He would not be able to book him for a specific day – so much depended on what happened aboard the gas atoll. But sufficient dollars would keep the skipper's time open.

Yasakov reached the pickup and set off down the mountain. He was being crowded for time also in regard to his prisoners. The American nuclear test exercise was set for the day after the South African deadline expired. How soon before that would questions and investigations start about Testerman's continued absence? From the NORAD signal it was clear that Testerman himself was meant to direct it.

Yasakov smiled grimly to himself. If Admiral Gorshkov agreed to his plan, there would be no need to worry about disposing of the captives. The way he planned it, there wouldn't be a trace of them left.

Yasakov called at Birkenhead on his way to Roman's Bay and collected all the loose money he could find – about 300 dollars. At the bay itself, three or four fishing-boats were at anchor, weather-bound. Yasakov spotted the one he wanted – a sturdy seventy footer with a deckhouse/bridge aft and a tough bow to shoulder aside the Cape rollers. Its name was the *Stormgans – Storm Goose –* of about eighty tons.

Yasakov walked down to the sandy beach, where a Coloured fisherman, with a face a colour somewhere between teak and mahogany, was mending nets.

'Fog too bad for fishing?' Yasakov remarked conversationally.

Skipper Plaatjies Voogds emitted brandy and an oath.

'Be okay this afternoon. Weather's clearing.'

'You going out?'

Skipper Voogds eyed Yasakov. He wasn't sure who he was, but any friendly stranger might be a sucker for a quick touch.

'Maybe – if I can't find anyone to buy me a bladdy drink.'

Yasakov was ready, after the good news the skipper had

given him – and he would know local weather – to buy him half a dozen drinks.

He nodded towards the fishing boat. 'Yours?'

If there was anything Skipper Voogds loved as much as *withond* – the local tiger's breath – it was his ship.

'Ja. The *Stormgans*. Best on the coast.'

Time. Logistics. These were uppermost in Yasakov's mind. The fishing boat would be no good to him if she were not fast enough to bring him back from the secret rendezvous in time. . . .

'Fast?'

'Better than most. Ten and a half knots cruising – and I can get more out of the diesel if I'm in a hurry.'

'I've taken a fancy to the *Stormgans*, skipper,' Yasakov went on. 'I think we may have something to discuss? Where can we have that drink?'

An hour, five *withonds* and 150 dollars' advance later, Yasakov had the *Stormgans* lined up for early the following week. The deal was that Skipper Voogds would be ready at all times, especially at night, to put to sea. Yasakov did not trust Voogds' word, but felt that the promise of another 150 dollars would keep him available.

Skipper Voogds was not to know that he would never live to see his fee.

By the time Yasakov and Skipper Voogds had returned to the beach, the fog had started dissipating, the sun was breaking through patchily, and the sea was calm.

Yasakov headed at speed to pick up his diving team at Frenchman's Eye. Whether Captain Wessels went on duty at Birkenhead that afternoon or not, was immaterial. Yasakov had every justification to go out to the *Kamchatka* and 'reeover' the golden sovereigns.

Captain Wessels did not, in fact, return to Birkenhead. He was surprised, therefore, when late that afternoon there was a knock on his hotel bedroom door at Gansbaai.

It was Yasakov. He presented the policeman with a small bag of English golden sovereigns, in wet sand still. The coins were contemporary with the *Kamchatka*. He accompanied his find with a formal request to be airlifted as soon as possible to the gas atoll.

35

'A nuclear shell! No way! You must be crazy, Yasakov!'

Vice-Admiral Strokin's explosion was, in Yasakov's opinion, predictable. The KGB man eyed the sailor across the desk-top without flinching. Strokin's was the sort of face which seemed to recur in navies everywhere – a firm mouth, rather prominent nose, shortish hair. Had it not been for the dark Soviet navy uniform with its high collar and insignia, Strokin could have passed for an American or a German.

It was Thursday night – two days since Yasakov had taken his parcel of sovereigns to Captain Wessels. Yasakov was aboard the Soviet offshore gas atoll, three hundred and thirty kilometres out to sea off Cape Agulhas. He had come aboard less than an hour before from the frigate *Grisha III* which had rendezvoused – in accordance with protocol – on the boundary of the 'no-go' zone one hundred and fifty kilometres from the coast, with a Super Frelon helicopter.

Now that he was aboard – he had demanded an immediate interview with Vice-Admiral Strokin – Yasakov admitted to himself that the shuttle operation had really taken place reasonably quickly, although for two days he had fretted and fumed. The diving team had been without Wessels – he had had to deliver in person the sovereigns to Cape Town. Diving operations had ceased.

Strokin's office, despite the air conditioning, was clammy. Outwardly, the Russians' establishment *looked* like an oil rig – six columns on two lower hulls, a helicopter pad, eight huge twenty ton anchors holding it fast against the treacherous currents of the Agulhas Bank.

Strokin made an expressive gesture towards two men who

flanked him at the desk. When he had heard that Yasakov would be arriving, Strokin, a good bureaucrat, had decided to clear his yardarm in the light of whatever Yasakov wanted. He had invited Partala, the gas atoll's political officer, and Penzin, head of the Komsomol (Young Communist organization) aboard, to sit in on the interview. Although Partala was technically subordinate to him, as CO he wielded immense power through reporting independently through the Main Political Administration of the Navy to the Ministry of Defence Main Political Administration. Penzin, barely thirty, fresh-faced and handsome, was under Partala as political officer, but was responsible for the manning structure of the offshore installation.

Strokin repeated, as if to underscore the lunacy of Yasakov's request. 'You are asking me to deliver you a 155 mm nuclear naval shell as well as a timing detonator?'

'That is correct,' Yasakov answered.

'You don't want me to fire it as well?' he added sarcastically.

Yasakov remained unruffled. He had not – as he had reasoned previously – a high opinion of Strokin's 'creative decision-making'.

'No,' he said. 'That is why I want a timing device. One that will run for about six hours.'

Both Partala and Penzin's faces remained blank. They had never had to cope with a hot potato like Yasakov's. They'd wait and take their cue from the CO.

Strokin blew out his cheeks. 'And what, may I ask, do you want to do with a nuclear naval shell once you have it?'

'I intend to destroy the town of Bredasdorp and its six thousand inhabitants with it.'

Yasakov had been forearmed against Strokin's incredulity. Strokin himself was glad he had summoned Partala and Penzin; he couldn't cope with this sort of request alone.

There was a tight silence. 'You are serious, Comrade Yasakov?'

Yasakov's eyes were hooded in their sinister way.

'I have never been more serious in my life.'

Strokin wavered under the KGB man's cold stare. He made a helpless gesture.

'But – a nuclear explosion – I cannot take that responsibility – the shell is a short-range tactical weapon for the navy, not meant to destroy civilians. . . .'

'I know that.'

Yasakov knew exactly what he had chosen. It was the Soviet navy's answer to the American W-82 shell with its nuclear warhead. It had far less explosive power than the standard nuclear weapon, but emitted six times as much lethal radiation. The shell was the standard size 155 mm, favoured by both the Red and US navies. It could also be fired on land from the standard 155 mm artillery pieces which were commonplace in Europe. On land, its use was against tanks and infantry; at sea, it was a short-range killer of outstanding punch.

Partala repeated, tacitly endorsing Strokin's incredulity.

'You want to kill six thousand civilians with it?'

'Yes.'

Yasakov was becoming impatient; but he didn't as yet flare into anger against these three fools.

'You know the international consequences of such a massacre of harmless civilians?'

Yasakov kept his cool. He wasn't going to deal with underlings or bandy words. He wanted Gorshkov – his idol, the admiral of the fleet.

'I realize that this is a decision which cannot be taken at lower command levels,' he replied. 'Therefore I request formally to speak directly to Admiral Sergei Gorshkov at Fleet Headquarters in Moscow.'

Yasakov was not sure which caused the greater consternation – the nuclear shell request or the admiral's name.

'You can't . . .' began Strokin.

It was not for nothing that Penzin had been chosen to handle men. He said smoothly, 'I think in view of the magnitude of this request, it should be discussed in private by Vice-Admiral Strokin, Comrade Partala and myself. We will inform you of our decision in due course.'

Yasakov shook his head. He knew what a phrase like 'in due course' meant. If he allowed these bureaucrats to fob him off, he would return ashore on Monday – the day the return South Africa air-sea lift was due – with nothing to show for his visit. On Wednesday the diving team would be booted out – for good. What he had to do, he had to do before then. Time was running out.

'No. I must have your decision tonight. I must speak to Admiral Gorshkov tomorrow morning.'

'Impossible,' retorted Strokin. 'You don't know what you are asking.'

He himself knew that if the admiral of the fleet viewed Yasakov's request in the same light as he did, he'd lose his command for sanctioning a madman's call.

'I do. It will take time to set up the call via the satellite linkup.'

Strokin turned to Penzin, grateful to have a breather, for the present at least.

'We three will discuss Comrade Yasakov's request,' he announced formally.

Yasakov was a KGB man, had once been a protégé of Andropov himself, and, moreover, the job he had done ashore in locating the origin of the frequency-hopping signals – Yasakov had prefaced the meeting with that news – would put him in high favour in the Kremlin. Strokin felt himself to be in deeper waters than the cold Cape seas under the gas atoll. Yet if he managed to pass the buck to Admiral Gorshkov, it would become the famous admiral's decision and the hot potato would have been adroitly removed from his own plate. A nuclear explosion! Good God!

The three gas atoll supremos were away for an hour. Strokin walked a razor's-edge between fear of Gorshkov and fear of approving or disapproving Yasakov's request. Gorshkov was the way out, he skilfully inferred to Partala and Penzin. Both were cautiously willing to fall in line.

Yasakov for his part waited, alien, alone, in the strange environment of the gas atoll. The floor rocked in the Cape's long winter swells and squalls rattled against the soundproof windows.

At last Strokin, Partala and Penzin returned. They were as formal as if Yasakov was being courtmartialled. Penzin carried a tape-recorder.

Strokin said. 'It is necessary, in view of the seriousness of your request, to have our proceedings recorded. You agree?'

'I agree.' Yasakov added, 'But that does not apply to my conversation with the admiral of the fleet.'

Strokin ignored the anticipation in Yasakov's words.

He went on. 'Your request, Comrade Yasakov, is for me to supply you with one 155 mm nuclear naval shell?'

'With timing device.'

Partala intervened. 'Is there such a thing here as a six-hour delayed-action timer?'

'It is no problem,' replied Strokin. 'We use them for the mines the gas atoll keeps in stock in case of necessity. There are contact, coded radio or sonic detonator timers.'

'I don't want a remote-control device,' Yasakov answered abruptly. 'I want a simple delayed-action fuse.' He added thinly, 'I intend to be well clear of the blast area when the shell goes up.'

Strokin bit his lip: Yasakov was pre-empting the admiral's decision. He wished now that he had never clapped eyes on the KGB man.

'One nuclear naval shell, plus timer,' Strokin repeated for the benefit of the tape-recorder. 'Purpose – to destroy the town of Bredasdorp near Cape Agulhas and its six thousand civilian population. Correct?'

'Correct.'

Strokin said heavily. 'Since neither I nor my two colleagues are empowered to grant or even consider such a request, we have – at your own suggestion – agreed to allow you to discuss it directly with the Commander-in-Chief, Admiral Sergei Gorshkov.'

'Good,' said Yasakov briefly. 'When?'

'I have ordered a linkup by voice contact via ELINT

satellite for 0930 tomorrow morning with Fleet Head-quarters in Moscow.'

'Just outside Moscow,' Yasakov corrected him. He could not help tweaking Strokin's tail, now that he had won.

36

But had he won?

Yasakov slept badly. He dreamed he had lost Testerman's print-out. He awoke, searched frantically for it. It was safe under his pillow where he had stashed it before turning in. He naturally had not shown it to Strokin; it was his heavy artillery for his encounter with Admiral Gorshkov.

There was no more sleep for Yasakov. He could not get used to the odd motion – due probably, he considered, to a tanker laden from his own country's Urengoi gas fields being moored against the gas atoll and inhibiting its natural roll.

He spent the rest of the night formulating in his own mind what he would say to the Commander-in-Chief.

When the call came, promptly at 0930 next morning, Yasakov spoke from Strokin's office.

'Gorshkov.'

This was the voice of the man with the farmer's face, big flat ears and balding wispy hair who had outlasted seven United States naval supremos and built one of the mightiest navies the world has seen.

'Yasakov.' His mouth was dry.

'What is the meaning of this call, Yasakov? Where is Strokin? This linkup is for use only in a serious emergency.'

'This is an emergency, admiral. I want your authorization for Strokin to supply me with one 155 mm nuclear naval shell, plus timing device.'

Half the night Yasakov had spent mustering his words; now the format was going awry.

'Why?'

Yasakov answered quickly. 'Admiral, I have discovered that the Americans are operating an anti-missile early warning station from a cave on the mainland opposite the gas atoll. . . .' Yasakov succinctly outlined his discovery and the capture of Testerman, keeping a low profile himself.

There was a slightly less severe note in Gorshkov's voice when Yasakov had finished. 'Good,' he said. 'Good, Yasakov. But that still does not merit this emergency call. I would have been informed anyway.'

'No, admiral, it does not. But what I have in mind does, in my opinion.'

'Go on.'

Yasakov was thankful that the admiral had not chided him before he got into his stride.

He said carefully. 'It is a plan to outflank the big new American naval base at Kosi Bay, one thousand eight hundred kilometres from here, and establish Soviet dominance over the Cape Sea Route. At the same time, it will prejudice all Black Africa against the United States.'

'Anything else?'

Yasakov was wise enough not to respond. He continued. 'Ever since it was established, the Kosi Bay base has been a thorn in our side – it neutralizes the Red Fleet's use of the facilities at Maputo, which is only one hundred and twenty kilometres away across the South African border. As you well know, the base is the only major American one in the South Indian Ocean – their nearest is Diego Garcia, thousands of kilometres away to the north, towards India. We know the Americans are flying long-range maritime patrols from Kosi Bay. They now have a firm grip on the Cape Sea Route, which is the West's oil artery. From what I have discovered about the extra low frequency signals, I realize the Americans have missile-firing submarines deployed in the Southern Ocean towards Antarctica. The station at Dolla's Downes is a key link to these submarines in any nuclear war.'

'Your grasp of strategy interests me, Yasakov.'

'The biggest fear Black Africa has is that South Africa might possess the nuclear bomb,' Yasakov hurried on. 'If it were established that South Africa had the bomb – or had exploded one – it would bring the Organization of African Unity, especially states like Nigeria, Zambia, Zaire, Tanzania, Zimbabwe, Mozambique and Angola more strongly than ever on to our side.'

'What are you getting at, Yasakov?'

'I'm getting at this, admiral – a decade ago, when South Africa was supposed to have been on the brink of testing a nuclear device in the Kalahari Desert, there was a world uproar. . . .'

Gorshkov said, and there was a shade of amusement in his voice, 'To such an extent that both our own and United States spy satellites cooperated.'

There was a new note in the admiral's voice; Yasakov struck while the iron was hot.

'There was a similar outcry from the whole world – including ourselves – when South Africa was believed to have tested a nuclear bomb deep in the South Atlantic in 1979. I am sure I do not have to elaborate to you on that, admiral.'

'Why do you want a *Soviet* nuclear shell now?'

'The Soviet 155 mm shell is almost a cousin to the American W-82,' the KGB man answered. 'It is a weapon which has limited destructive force but which packs six times the amount of radiation of an ordinary nuclear weapon. . . .'

'Don't lecture me on the shell I was responsible for developing,' snapped Gorshkov.

'I will plant the shell in Bredasdorp,' Yasakov resumed. 'I and my team will get well clear – the shell will be detonated by a timing device after about six hours.'

Yasakov went on, deliberately, underlining every word. '*This will be the first nuclear explosion on the soil of Africa.*'

'Then?'

'The population will, of course, be annihilated. There will be a world outcry. We – the Soviet Union – will immediately join in and accuse the United States of nuclear collusion with South Africa. Already the South African missile testing station which is sited on the eastern coast opposite Bredasdorp is under suspicion. We, the Soviet, will reinforce that suspicion by producing proof positive of the American early warning station at Dolla's Downes – likewise situated in the Strandveld, close to the missile range.

'We will accuse the United States of exploding a nuclear weapon through carelessness and killing thousands of innocents. We will go further and say that the United States uses the Dolla's Downes station as an underground storage place for nuclear weapons, and supplies them to South Africa to test from their missile range nearby.'

Yasakov spelled out his earlier assertion, slowly, carefully. 'It is Black Africa's greatest fear that South Africa might possess the ultimate weapon. We will show that she does – with American cooperation and assistance.'

'You interest me, Yasakov,' said Gorshkov.

'Following Bredasdorp, there will be a wave of revulsion throughout the world at the callousness and cynicism of the United States and its double-dealing with Black Africa,' Yasakov continued. 'Our propaganda will emphasize that six thousand innocents have died through that cynicism.

'But in particular Black Africa will react. With a little prodding on our part, the Soviet Union can get Black Africa to "lean" on Swaziland and force the closure of the Kosi Bay naval base. I feel quite certain that once Black Africa realizes what is afoot by the Americans, such a base will be compelled to shut down. At one stroke, at cost of no Soviet lives and only the price of one shell, we will have removed the American naval threat from southern Africa seas. The action would constitute a strategic and political masterstroke of the first magnitude.

'It would, if I may quote your own words, admiral, fulfil the doctrine of the first salvo and at the same time the Soviet fleet's own stated mission in the 1980s – support to the Third World.'

Admiral Gorshkov said abstractedly. 'One of those shells costs about four million American dollars.'

There was a silence. Then the Moscow voice said. 'There

is one thing you have overlooked, Yasakov. The shell will destroy the underground station. We will have no proof of what we assert, nothing tangible to point an accusing finger at.'

'On the contrary, admiral,' replied Yasakov. 'The explosion will destroy only the town of Bredasdorp. The cave is situated about thirty kilometres away. It is safe underground – it will not be affected by the blast.'

There was another silence, and then Gorshkov said softly. 'This is the most outrageous, daring, and risky plan I have ever heard.'

'It is, admiral. But it is the logical extension of your own scheme for the gas atoll front. It puts the finishing touch to the Red Fleet's plan to gain control of the Cape of Good Hope. The gas atoll is a toehold – the Bredasdorp bomb is the stranglehold.'

'There is one uncertainty and one major hole in your plan,' said Gorshkov – and it seemed to Yasakov that there was genuine regret in his reply. 'The uncertainty is, those three captives of yours. Have you disposed of them? If not, and one of them should escape. . . .'

'I have a watertight plan for their disposal, admiral,' answered Yasakov. 'They will die at the time of the explosion.'

Gorshkov was friendly, almost warm. 'You know my policy of always leaving local decisions to the man on the spot, Yasakov. If you say for certain they are to be disposed of, I accept that.'

Yasakov waited in suspense.

'If I were to agree to this plan – and I admit that there are things about it which I admire, its ingenuity, its scope, its daringness – I would have to discuss it with the head of state. I say now we could not go ahead with a plan with such international, naval and political implications merely on the strength of a confession you have extracted – by means best known to yourself – from the American Testerman. It is only his word, under duress. He may be leading you up the garden path.'

239

Relief flooded over Yasakov and he replied slowly. 'I have proof, written proof, of what I say, admiral. I have a copy of an order from North American Aerospace Command at Cheyenne Mountain to Testerman giving instructions for a dummy exercise next week to test communications between the early warning station and the retaliatory nuclear submarine force stationed in the Southern Ocean.'

'*You have?*' From the amazement in his exclamation, Yasakov wondered how the admiral was looking, what he was thinking.

His next words told him a great deal.

'Yasakov,' he said tersely. 'Instruct Strokin to have a photo of that order relayed to me by satellite. Immediately. Top priority. When I have seen it, I will let you have my answer.'

37

Aboard the gas atoll, Yasakov waited – and agonized.

At Frenchman's Eye, Cane, Maris and Testerman waited – and agonized.

Vice-Admiral Strokin had come into his office a while after the Moscow call had terminated. He had found Yasakov sitting by the radio-phone, totally abstracted. From the drawn look on the Faustian face, with its twisted mouth and slanting eyes, Strokin thought for a moment that Yasakov had stopped a rocket from Admiral Gorshkov. He was quickly disabused. Yasakov informed him briefly that the admiral would be speaking to him later, and passed on his orders about the print-out of the NORAD document.

When would Gorshkov reply?

That was the question which bugged the KGB man. Today was Friday: even if the fleet admiral made his request top priority with the head of state, how soon would it be before the two supremos got together? Today? Tonight? Tomorrow?

When?

On Monday the South African helicopter would be back for its scheduled return lift, Gorshkov or no Gorshkov.

On Wednesday, the Russian diving party's stay ashore would end. Their departure day would be a write-off as far as nuclear shell operations were concerned. Everything had to be finalized on Tuesday.

Yasakov could find nothing aboard the gas atoll to occupy himself and calm his racing thoughts during the long day and night which followed. A southwesterly gale was in full flight and buffeted the gas atoll. It was impossible to keep a footing on the deck up above.

Yasakov was treated by Strokin, Partala and Penzin like a quarantine case – it depended on the diagnosis from Moscow how he would be handled in future. Meanwhile, he was kept at arm's length, a potential pariah, or a potential Hero of the Soviet Union. The three chiefs inclined towards the first.

At Frenchman's Eye, the three captives had seen nothing of Yasakov for three days. His last visit before being airlifted to the gas atoll – of which they knew nothing – had been on Wednesday evening. He had addressed only a few words to them. His concern was to ensure that they were tightly guarded, day and night, during his absence.

The fact that Anna, Stefan and Josef could be spared for round-the-clock guard duties told the captives that something was afoot. What had occurred that Cassie Wessels was no longer watch-dogging at Birkenhead? What had happened to the diving operation?

Vigilance was ultra-tight, with one of the three Russians always on duty. Often there were two. At night, the prisoners were locked in while one Russian kept watch outside the door, armed and wakeful. He or she made a check every couple of hours. The Accursed Figurehead's reputation as a bringer of bad luck hit the top of the graph with the captives.

Conditions physically eased after Yasakov had learned the

secret of Dolla's Downes. Adjoining the main magazine the smaller cannon-ball store was used as a toilet/washroom by the captives. Water, organized by Anna, was carted from Birkenhead in twenty litre plastic containers.

Anna made another gesture – aimed at Maris but appreciated by all three captives – a pile of magazines from the Birkenhead mess, including women's journals. The fact that Anna could help herself to Captain Wessels' literature meant only one thing – somehow, the amiable Wessels was no longer on duty. Why?

Anna passed a women's glossy to Maris, holding it open at an article on the art of make-up.

'It must be wonderful to enjoy all these things as if they were simply a part of your everyday life,' she said. 'We have nothing like it in Russia.'

'You could always defect,' commented Testerman.

'It makes one feel like a woman, seeing these things,' she went on wistfully. 'I suppose if you want to, Maris, you can go to a beauty parlour and have a make-up, any time.'

'Facial,' Maris corrected her with a smile. 'Yes. Bredasdorp hasn't got much in that line, however. Cape Town would be the place.'

'My figure I have made by swimming, diving, athletics,' Anna went on. 'In Russia the women with good bodies smell of sweat – their own sweat. You in the West achieve results by massages, perfumes, all the things a woman loves.'

Maris eyed her warily. She felt that the conversation had begun to assume dangerous overtones.

'Aren't you happy in Russia?'

Anna shrugged. 'You in the West say Russian women are more liberated – for example, you could point to me as the only woman aboard the gas atoll. Is this the sort of freedom a woman wants? Maybe I would rather be free to have a facial, or do the sort of things you do.'

Testerman broke in angrily. 'You talk about freedom – it isn't worth a harlot's hello. Look at us!'

'That is a different kind of freedom,' she retorted. 'If you play games which harm my country and the cause of peace, you must expect to have to suffer for it. My country comes first, at all times.'

'That sounds like a straight quote from the Komsomol propaganda machine,' sneered Testerman.

Cane remained silent during these exchanges. Despite Anna's softer attitude towards Maris – obviously motivated by her lesbian feelings – he knew that she was as single-minded about the captives as Yasakov himself. When they had been alone at night, the three of them had discussed time and again possible escape plans, ranging from fantasy to suicide tactics. They had decided that the two men, Stefan and Josef, could only be overcome by using force. They had also debated a possible soft approach to Anna via Maris.

'She sure thinks you're tablegrade,' Testerman had mocked Maris. 'But I reckon if it came to the crunch of deciding between you and Mother Russia, she'd opt for Momma.'

That had about summed it up. Yasakov's unexplained absence seemed to be a godsend for them to try and make a break to get word to Ed Weinback, but the Russian guards were more vigilant than if the KGB man had been standing behind them with his pistol.

Anna herself had remained tight-lipped about the team's boss.

Again, it had been Testerman who had summed up the situation. 'He's like an American movie producer – keeps you in the dark and feeds you shit.'

Now it was Friday night.

To Yasakov aboard the gas atoll waiting for a return call from Admiral Gorshkov, the day had been interminable. It did not come.

To the captives at Frenchman's Eye, the darkening of the ventilation slits spelled the end of another endless day. The Russians had withdrawn, leaving them alone.

'Who is the trigger-man tonight?' asked Testerman. His query was brittle with tension.

'Stefan,' answered Cane.

'Good. Then he can't understand what I have to say, even if he should overhear.'

There was a tight pause.

'Listen, you two,' he went on. 'I guess you've been dealt a poor deck in this game. There's no need for you to continue being involved. I'm going to come clean to Anna.'

'About what?' asked Cane. 'I've already said my say a dozen times – Yasakov doesn't believe a word. That's the situation. We're in this with you up to the neck, whether we like it or not. Our only hope is to try and make a break.'

'How? Any fresh ideas?' Before Cane or Maris could answer, the American hurried on. 'See here, every scheme we've mulled over up to now has been half-assed. Nothing concrete. No time, no action plan. We have got to *do* something.'

'I wonder what Yasakov is up to?' Maris asked at a tangent.

'To recap, at the risk of sounding tedious, one of us has got to get out and pass the word to Ed Weinback,' Testerman stated.

'Easily said,' answered Cane. 'You know what the consequences of failure will be.'

'Yeah – the nylon shoehorn, or they'll make a hamburger out of us.'

'If they put those cords on us again, we'll be immobile for days, even if we got the opportunity after that to break out,' said Maris.

'I know, I know,' replied Testerman impatiently. 'What I am building on is time.'

'I'd say time was our worst enemy, next to Yasakov,' commented Cane.

'The NORAD exercise is scheduled for next Thursday,' went on Testerman. 'What I say is, that soon Ed Weinback will be wondering where in hell I am, if he hasn't done so already. There is only one person who commands a test run like that – the boss. My guess is that by Tuesday/Wednesday at the latest, Ed will countercheck with South African Security in Cape Town.'

'He may have done that already,' Cane pointed out.

'Yasakov chose this place well – who would think of searching here?'

'I reckon Ed hasn't been in touch,' said Testerman. 'South African Security are smart, mighty smart. I know. They'd take the whole Strandveld apart to find us, if they were on to it.' He addressed Maris. 'Won't you be missed at home?'

'My parents are away on vacation,' she answered. 'The fact that I have not been around for some days may be ascribed' – she threw Cane a look – 'to romantic reasons.'

'What about your outfit, Hal?'

'There's a strike on – no one will be working on the site.'

'I know that, but what about your management?'

'My Cape Town chief is in the doghouse and he won't stir a finger to get in touch unless he's ordered to from Johannesburg. The way I see things, that is not likely.'

'Both of you then are more or less incommunicado,' murmured Testerman. 'So we're completely out of touch with the outside world and on our own.'

'We're on our own,' echoed Cane. 'What you're hinting at, Brad, is that we have to sweat it out until the United States Cavalry arrive – in due course?'

'Due course being next Tuesday or Wednesday, with the NORAD test on the doorstep?' added Maris.

'It's not the way I see it at all;' snapped Testerman. 'I'm simply not lying around on my corking mat in this grungy dump waiting for some goddam Red to shoot me first. I'm coming out fighting with my five-ouncers, even if I have to stop a bullet. It's a *kamikaze* plan, I know. Now listen, here it is. . . .'

Aboard the gas atoll, Yasakov sweated it out. Friday night came and went, and with it went the KGB man's hopes of Moscow approval of his masterplan. He consoled himself by telling himself that a decision of such magnitude could not be made in an hour or two; there would be an answer first thing on Saturday morning.

There was no return call from Moscow on Saturday morning.

Yasakov sweated.

As the hours passed, Vice-Admiral Strokin's attitude became more distant, more formal. By late Saturday afternoon Yasakov – still without word – began to believe that he was a candidate for a Siberian work camp.

On Friday evening, he had been Strokin's guest at dinner; tonight, Saturday, he sat alone in the general mess. No one viewing that remote, ruthless face would consider him company. He toyed with his food; it tasted like hell.

Yasakov was so abstracted that he did not hear the thump of boots alongside him. The newcomer tapped him on the shoulder. It was a sailor, with a big pistol in a holster.

Yasakov responded like a sleepwalker. This was it. Strokin had sent one of his own personal guards to pick him up at mealtime so that if he resisted there would be plenty of manpower around to assist the messenger.

'Comrade Yasakov – quick! Vice-Admiral Strokin's office!'

If it had been an ordinary call, Yasakov reasoned, Strokin would have summoned him on the mess loudspeaker intercom. The man had the holster flap closed. At least, thought Yasakov, he had been spared the ignominy of open arrest.

He got up hurriedly and made his way out, with the sailor following.

Strokin was alone in his office. He held out the radiophone to Yasakov.

'Gorshkov.'

Yasakov felt as if one of the new nuclear bullets the Red Army was said to be designing had passed through him.

He made an inarticulate reply.

The farmer's voice at the Moscow end was harsh – maybe there was some distortion, maybe it was Yasakov's own trepidation which interpreted it that way.

The admiral of the fleet said. 'I have had two meetings with the head of state – one yesterday and one today – regarding your proposition. It has been a big decision to take. We consider the plan has merit. Go ahead.'

'*Go ahead?*'

'I authorize you to go ahead and destroy Bredasdorp with a 155 mm nuclear naval shell,' snapped Gorshkov. 'Can I make it clearer? What is wrong with you, man? It was your idea.'

'Nothing is wrong,' Yasakov managed to say. He took a big grip on himself. 'Everything is in train.'

Gorshkov went on, less impatiently. 'Once we approved the plan, the propaganda chiefs had to be briefed.' He laughed brittly. 'Again, as you suggested, Yasakov. The entire blame will fall on the Americans. We are going for broke to get the Kosi Bay base shut down. Now – as to details – put Strokin on the line, will you?'

Strokin regarded the KGB man's ashen face and trembling hands. He had overheard most of what the admiral of the fleet had said – he had one of those voices which carry.

'Strokin,' said Gorshkov – Yasakov likewise could overhear – 'give Yasakov what he wants. Plus a timer. He must have a timer. We are not going to fire the damn thing from a gun.'

Strokin said cautiously. 'I am formally authorized to supply Vladimir Yasakov with one 155 mm nuclear naval shell from the magazine of the patrol destroyer *Sovremennyy* plus detonating timer normally used for mines?'

'Did I say anything else?' rejoined Gorshkov.

'No, admiral, but I would like to have the record straight. It is a big thing.'

'Record straight? Isn't my word good enough for you, Strokin?'

Strokin's inborn devotion to red tape overcame his awe of the naval chief.

'If anything should go wrong,' he stammered, 'I'd like a record of authorization – such an explosion will have international consequences. I could be accused of crimes against humanity.'

An unprintable oath spilled across the room. 'Clearing your yardarm eh, Strokin? I'll remember this. Good – you shall have my authorization by signal. Meanwhile, I order you to supply Yasakov with what he wants.'

'Yes, admiral.'

'Put Yasakov on the line again.'

The ear-and-mouthpiece were wet with Strokin's sweat.

'How do you intend getting the shell ashore, Yasakov?' asked Gorshkov. 'What are the logistics of the plan?'

Yasakov had got his breath back again. 'On Monday morning I return to the mainland by South African helicopter, after first being taken to the boundary of the no-go zone by Soviet frigate. Ashore, I have already arranged to have a fishing-boat at my disposal. I will return that same night, Monday, and collect the shell from the frigate, which will wait for me. I will convey it ashore . . .'

'Does Strokin know all this?'

'No, admiral, it hinged on your decision regarding the shell.'

'See that he carries it out the way you want – you have my full authority,' said Gorshkov. 'How do you intend to transport the shell, once you have got it ashore?'

'It is very light – it weighs only forty-nine kilograms,' Yasakov replied. He knew full well that the admiral was as well aware of its weight as he was. 'It is about the same weight as a pocket of cement – one strong man can lift it ashore from the boat. I have such a man, and a mini-bus for the road journey.'

'Good. You know I believe in trusting the man on the spot, but one thing still worries me – those three captives. How much do they know?'

'Nothing about the shell – yet,' replied Yasakov tightly. 'But too much about the gas atoll for comfort.'

'I would prefer that you disposed of them as soon as you get ashore, Yasakov.'

'Bodies offer problems, and nothing must go wrong with the plan,' answered Yasakov. He felt that he could talk that way now that Moscow had given its say-so. 'I will give them a unique and spectacular end – at the heart of the explosion.'

'So be it, then. You know the consequences of failure.' His laugh echoed all the way from Moscow. 'You know what will happen if this plan of yours aborts, don't you, Yasakov? The KGB will hunt you down to the ends of the earth and kill you, wherever you may be. There will be no place for you to hide. Is that clear?'

Yasakov felt the chill of the admiral's words. 'Yes, admiral. I shall not fail.'

Gorshkov went on, 'I want a helicopter from the gas atoll to monitor the explosion from a safe distance and report back immediately it takes place. Tell Strokin that – I will also speak to him later about communications and minor matters arising out of the explosion. Now – I assume you plan to be well outside the danger area when the blast occurs?'

'Yes. I and my team will be at sea about halfway back to the gas atoll at the deadline. There will be no radiation danger.'

Gorshkov said briefly. 'Yasakov – there is no such thing as good luck, and I do not wish it to you. Everything is good planning; you have planned this operation well.'

'Thank you, admiral.'

'A final question. What is the precise time of the explosion?'

'Dawn on Wednesday morning – 5 a.m.'

38

Monday. 11 a.m.

There was a clatter of rotors over Frenchman's Eye.

'Helicopter!' There was a wild surge of hope in Testerman's face. He threw down a much-thumbed magazine. 'By heavens!' he hissed at Cane and Maris. 'Ed's started things moving! Here's the search party!'

Stefan, on guard, drew back against the door. The scared way in which he brandished the Colt indicated that the noise spelled danger – he could not understand Testerman's English.

The door flew open. Anna and Josef bundled in.

'Don't make a sound, a signal!' she rapped out at the captives.

Josef had the second pistol. He was as edgy as the others.

'Shut the door – quick!' Anna ordered Josef. 'They can see right inside here from the air.'

Josef slammed it shut.

'It's not the door you have to worry about – it's the landrover,' Cane said jubilantly. 'Once the search party spots that, you've had it.'

The noise was coming from the Gansbaai side of Dune Fountain peak.

Six pairs of ears strained through the dimness of the magazine prison. Would the helicopter sight the landrover stashed inside the old semaphore tower, as well as the unattended Kombi parked at the end of the track? It *must* investigate!

Clatter, clatter.

Anna opened the door a crack and listened.

Then she laughed. 'Super Frelon!' she exclaimed. 'It's a South African machine! It's bringing back Comrade Yasakov from the gas atoll!'

That was, in fact, what it was.

It took all Yasakov's willpower not to peer out of the machine as it passed the seaward side of the ruined tower. What was happening there? As soon as he had landed, Frenchman's Eye would be one of his first priorities.

The Super Frelon came within range of the Danger Point lighthouse, and finally hung above the Russian mess at Birkenhead.

Yasakov pulled his anorak tight about him in preparation for going overside on the winch wire. There was a hard feel to its pockets. Fools, thought Yasakov, they didn't even search me. A second Makarov and a grenade would make assurance doubly sure that the captives didn't try anything in the plan's final stages.

In seconds, he was glad to feel the tussocky grass under his feet again. He freed himself of the 'horse collar', dodged clear of the slipstream, raised a hand in final salute.

He went straight to the mess telephone. He dialled Captain Wessels' hotel.

Cassie Wessels had also heard – and seen – the Super Frelon pass over Gansbaai. He had, of course, known that Yasakov was scheduled to return that day, but he was unaware of the exact time.

The desk clerk called to Captain Wessels on his way out to drive to Birkenhead.

'Telephone, Captain Wessels.'

'Yasakov.'

Yasakov was uneasy the moment he entered the Russian mess. It had an unlived-in look about it, the sort of neglected appearance which wouldn't escape a smart policeman like Wessels. He now had to keep up the fiction that the Russian team would depart, as arranged officially, on Wednesday.

Wessels was surprised, but amiable. 'I was just coming over. I've been involved over the gold coins since you left, and the ongoing arrangements. I haven't been near Birkenhead. I only arrived back yesterday afternoon.'

In Cape Town, Wessels had, in fact, been closely examined regarding the *Kamchatka* gold. In the end, it had been decided that the discovery was genuine.

Yasakov breathed a sigh of relief. Wessels had let fall something he wanted to find out – had the almost continual day-and-night absence of his team caused any eyebrow-lifting? On the other hand, he didn't like the sound of that phrase, 'ongoing arrangements'. As far as he was concerned, the Strandveld's world would end on Wednesday at dawn.

'Ongoing arrangements?' he echoed.

'Yes. Now that you've found the gold, is the team remaining to carry out further operations? Didn't your people brief you – I thought that was what your visit was all about.'

Yasakov hadn't been a diplomat for nothing. 'It's the sort of decision that has to be taken at higher levels than either me or you,' he said, trying to sound confidential. 'Diplomatic levels, you understand? It takes time, of course.'

'Meaning?'

'My instructions are to leave on Wednesday as scheduled. What happens after that is up to others.'

'So you're packing up and leaving?'

'That's what I phoned to say.'

Yasakov hurried on. 'You remember – the departure schedule was fully documented. I have a copy here. . . .'

'No need.' Wessels was inwardly pleased. He had rated Birkenhead as the most boring job of his career. 'I escort you by road to Cape Town and pass you into the care of the authorities. . . .'

Yasakov detected the relief in Wessels' voice. 'Mid-morning Wednesday, then?' he said incisively. 'We'll be all packed up and ready to go. There's no need to come over now.'

Wessels remembered the endless card games, magazines, radio, the boredom of whiling away the hours in company with unfriendly strangers.

'Sure you don't want any help?'

'We can manage ourselves. There's not much to take away.'

There'll be nothing of Bredasdorp to take away either on Wednesday, he reminded himself. He wondered whether Wessels would escape radiation burns. If he stayed in Gansbaai, he would. If he ventured home to Bredasdorp to his family on Tuesday. . . . That was Wessels' problem. He had enough of his own.

'Fine, fine,' replied Wessels. 'See you Wednesday.'

'Goodbye.'

Yasakov drove quickly to Frenchman's Eye. The grenade and pistol in his anorak bumped against him as the vehicle sped along. He debated whether he shouldn't follow Admiral Gorshkov's advice and dispose of the three prisoners right away. He only had to toss the grenade into the old magazine. . . .

Yasakov rejected the idea. First, the idea of giving the three a Viking's funeral at the heart of the nuclear explosion appealed to his innate cruelty. He wanted them to suffer, and suffer they would, for about five or six hours while they sat waiting for the shell to go off. He'd tell them the approximate deadline, of course.

Second, he didn't like the idea of leaving bodies about. If he killed them now, there was always the off chance that some nosy parker or hiker might find them, with only forty-two hours left. . . . Better to guard them, live, right to the end.

Yasakov parked, and half ran to the tower. No one was in sight. Only when he was close Anna appeared, gun in hand.

'Comrade Yasakov! We thought it must be you in the helicopter . . .'

'The prisoners – are they safe?' he interrupted.

'Safe.'

'Show me.'

Now that he had finally made up his mind about their fate, he intended to take no risks.

He eyed Cane, Maris and Testerman sitting on blankets, gagged.

'Take off those gags – I want to speak to them,' he ordered.

'The nylon shoehorn?' asked Stefan hopefully.

'No. Just lash 'em.'

Testerman and Cane were dismayed when they understood what Yasakov had ordered. In one moment, their *kamikaze* escape plan, scheduled for that evening when the guards finally went off duty, went down in flames. They had counted on being able to jump the man leaving the magazine by slamming the heavy door prematurely on him, grabbing his gun – even if it meant one of them being shot – and attempting to shoot it out with the other Russians. It was a crazy, odds-against plan which might have worked. Now it had aborted with their being tied up again.

Testerman tried to get to his feet, making inarticulate sounds behind his gag.

Yasakov threateningly pulled out the grenade and Makarov he had brought from the gas atoll. Stefan thrust the American roughly to the floor. At the same time he ripped away his gag.

'You goddam bastard!' Testerman burst out.

'Save it, if you don't want to get hurt,' answered Yasakov. 'Tie 'em up – tight, but not too tight. Keep 'em that way, until I return?'

'You are going away again?' asked Anna in surprise.

'Yes.' The KGB man did not elaborate. 'This time I am taking Josef with me.' He switched into Russian, speaking to Anna. 'You are in command. I will be back tomorrow evening after dark – is that clear? You are to double your vigilance over the prisoners.'

'We didn't let you down before, comrade,' Anna answered. She managed to put that slight grate into the form of address which irritated him. She waited for Yasakov to go on.

He did not. He seemed to go into a fit of abstraction when he noted the Accursed Figurehead standing in a corner. When the two guards had lashed the captives' wrists and ankles securely, he said to Josef.

'Turn that thing over.'

The old cannonballs had been removed to retrieve the electronic 'bug' when Alcestis had first been brought to Frenchman's Eye. She had been propped upright to compensate for the counterweights.

Yasakov examined the interior of the statue where once a ship's bowsprit had supported the figurehead in position in the bow.

'Good!' he exclaimed. 'Good! Bredasdorp will find out just how accursed its famous figurehead can be!'

39

Tuesday 1 a.m.
Twenty-eight hours to detonation.

It seemed such a small thing to issue the death warrant of six thousand people.

The nuclear shell hung in the Russian frigate *Grisha III*'s port quarter crane, the one she used for loading depth charges, mines and SAM missiles. A floodlight was trained on it from the upperworks, giving a sense of theatre in the pitch darkness to the rendezvous far out to sea between the Russian warship and Yasakov's hired fishing boat, the *Stormgans*.

Skipper Plaatjies Voogds edged the *Stormgans* astern of the *Grisha III*'s square transom to find a lee, a calmer patch among the long swells, in order to take aboard the nuclear shell.

Yasakov held on to a grab-handle inside the *Stormgans'* tiny bridge and watched the two ships manoeuvre. The *Grisha III* was one of two frigates which was on permanent patrol round the gas atoll; the other was named the *Mirka*. Both shared the same high flared bow – so necessary in the wild Cape seas – and clean cutaway to the stern with its clutches of depth charges and mine rails. Yasakov could make out the depth charges in the frigate's lights – evil-looking things with nose-cones like space vehicles. Amidships, a steel lattice mast, six times the height of a man, held a complex tracery of air search, fire control and navigation antennae and radio aerials.

Yasakov was grateful for the *Grisha III*'s display of illumination. She had, on the fishing boat's approach, switched off her searchlights, which she had also been using earlier. Without them, Skipper Plaatjies, a rule-of-thumb sailor, would never have located the warship. However, Yasakov had taken the precaution before leaving the gas atoll of obtaining a course to steer from Roman's Bay to the rendezvous from the frigate's captain before they had parted earlier for the Super Frelon pickup. Even so, the navigation had been a hit-and-miss affair. The *Stormgans* had been more than eight kilometres out when they had first spotted the *Grisha III*'s searchlights down-horizon.

Yasakov had chosen the rendezvous well outside the 'no go' zone one hundred and fifty kilometres offshore. It was inside the gas atoll's positive identification radar advisory zone – fifty kilometres beyond the 'no go' boundary – so that there could be no interference by South African ships. In the event, the *Stormgans* had sighted nothing.

Skipper Plaatjies screwed up his eyes at the *Grisha III*'s twin-mounted 57 mm guns and 30 mm Gatling aft. Tompions waterproofed their muzzles against the heavy seas.

'Fine ship, eh, mister? Warship?'

Yasakov nodded. He, too, thought the frigate looked businesslike and formidable, but not in the same category as the ship which had supplied him with the nuclear shell, the new 6000-ton destroyer *Sovremennyy* which, with the two frigates, constituted the gas atoll naval patrol. The *Sovremennyy* had been specially equipped with 155 mm guns in place of her previous four 130 mm guns in order to accommodate the nuclear shell. It gave the *Sovremennyy* unparalleled fire-power for a destroyer.

Skipper Plaatjies gave the wheel a spoke or two to keep her well clear of the frigate's stern.

'What business have we with a warship, mister?'

'You'll see in a minute. Bring the *Stormgans* alongside that crane.'

Skipper Plaatjies did not like the way Yasakov ordered him about, nor the secret night rendezvous. He knew about the gas atoll, of course, but had never ventured that far out – it was beyond the Agulhas Bank fishing zone.

A second floodlight snapped on astern, focused on the nuclear shell. It foreshortened the shell and made it look leaner than its 155 mm calibre. It was, in fact, about one and a half metres long and, as it stood upright in the armourer's shop aboard the *Sovremennyy* it had taken Yasakov up to the chin.

Yasakov tried to spot the rear of the shell, but it was still blocked from his view. That was where the ingenious timer had been installed which would enable him and the Russian team to get well clear of the blast area before Bredasdorp was annihilated.

The *Sovremennyy*'s armourer had been an expert in techniques of detonating Soviet nuclear mines either by coded radio or sonic signal. He had entered into the spirit of the nuclear shell idea. He had demonstrated with patent pride the delicate micro-circuitry and digital timing device (manufactured in Japan) which would detonate the shell at any specified time, from a few hours to a fortnight ahead. The armourer himself had wanted to set the timer before parting with the shell; but Yasakov had jibbed at the thought of carting about a primed nuclear shell, even if the man swore it was safe.

At the end of his demonstration, the armourer had winked and shown him another ingenious device.

'If you are not going to take it along primed, we'll include this, just in case anyone gets any ideas once the timer has been finally set,' he grinned. 'Once it is set, don't move it unless you want to be blown to hell.'

The *Stormgans* came round, Skipper Plaatjies holding her off so as not to cannon into the frigate's side – and for the first time that night Yasakov saw the rear of the shell. It was carefully wrapped in black plastic against the sea to protect its sensitive electronics.

An awareness of how much depended on him alone made Yasakov raw with nerves.

The bridge of the *Stormgans* rolled towards the suspended shell. Two Red seamen looked on anxiously.

'Keep clear, blast you!' snarled Yasakov. 'Do you want to spoil everything?'

Skipper Plaatjies' thin eyes narrowed. He made a mock gesture of taking his hands from the wheel.

'Do it your bladdy self, then.'

But his eye had gauged the distance and the roll, and in a second he had snugged the fishing boat alongside.

One of the seamen called to Yasakov, and they started to swing the crane's awesome burden outboard. Josef went forward to the *Stormgan*'s welldeck to bring it aboard.

The frigate's captain stood on the warship's upperworks.

'You ready for the other goods as well?' he asked Yasakov in Russian.

'Send 'em aboard,' Yasakov replied. 'Don't let 'em get wet.'

'No chance of that – my men know what they are doing.'

Skipper Plaatjies interrupted. 'Mister, what language are these men speaking?'

Yasakov hesitated and then replied – once the job was done, Skipper Plaatjies wouldn't have the opportunity of passing on the information.

'Russian.'

Two seamen came to the frigate's rail. They each carried an armful of PPSh-41 sub-machineguns, belts of ammunition, several pistols and grenades.

Skipper Plaatjies eyed their transfer to Josef, who had carefully lashed the shell to an eyebolt in the deck.

'Mister . . .'

'Shut up!' snapped Yasakov.

'Those guns . . .' persisted Skipper Plaatjies. He had had a simple upbringing. Russians were of the devil, guns were evil. That is what the dominie at the Elim mission station had always taught.

'Yes, they're guns – use your bloody eyes!' went on Yasakov. 'Now, if you don't shut up and get on with your job, I'll use one of them on you!'

Plaatjies continued in a quiet voice. 'That on the deck there – my deck – is a shell, eh? What do you use it for ashore, eh? And those guns – who are they going to, and for what?'

Yasakov took a sudden decision. He wasn't going to allow the scruples of a primitive fishing skipper to interfere with his masterplan.

'I'll explain in a moment,' he said curtly. He cupped his hands and shouted to the *Grisha III*'s captain.

'Give me an exact course back to Roman's Bay, will you?'

'Are you afraid your skipper won't even be able to hit the mainland?' the officer called.

Yasakov tried to reciprocate his heartiness. 'Maybe that's it.'

'Hold on a moment – I'll get it from the navigating officer.'

Skipper Plaatjies said in angry tones. 'You do not answer my questions – what are those guns for? Why do we meet a Russian warship in secret out to sea on a dark night? What is going on here, eh? Who is going to get that shell? Terrorists?'

'You were well paid to keep your mouth shut,' Yasakov retorted.

'Not well enough. I have only half my 300 dollars. Where is the rest, mister? Now that I see . . .'

The loading was complete and the frigate's crane snapped home into position. One of the seamen called to Josef. 'Ready!'

Josef looked enquiringly to Yasakov on the bridge.

'Ready, comrade?'

'In a moment.'

Skipper Plaatjies burst out. 'When I ask you something, you start speaking to others in a language I do not understand. What are you saying? What. . . .'

'You'll get your reward – soon,' Yasakov said quietly.

'My three hundred dollars. . . .'

There was a hail from the frigate's captain. 'Here is your course, Comrade Yasakov. Follow it, and you'll hit Roman's Bay right in the bull's-eye.'

'Thanks.' Yasakov jotted down the figures. 'That's everything. Cast off?'

'Cast off.'

He rapped out an order and the Russian hands cast the *Stormgans* loose. Skipper Plaatjies gunned the boat's engine and turned away.

Unexpectedly, the frigate doused all her lights. She vanished from sight like an evil god-in-the-box into the dark ocean.

Yasakov called something to Josef, still on the welldeck. He rummaged amongst the small arms. Then, there was a click like a magazine being snapped home, and he joined Yasakov and Skipper Plaatjies at the wheel. The faint binnacle light was the only illumination.

Yasakov stubbed a finger on the compass and said. 'Steer. . . .'

Skipper Plaatjies bent forward to read the figures.

Josef shot him twice through the back of the head.

When they had cleaned up the blood and brains which messed the compass' face, Yasakov and Josef took the body and pitched it overboard.

They set course for Roman's Bay.

Even with the engine throttled well back, they sighted the shore about lunch time the same day. All afternoon the fishing boat marked time offshore, as if it were fishing. Then, when darkness fell, they closed the land and anchored in Roman's Bay.

The Kombi was on the roadway above the little harbour where they had left it. There was no one about – the fishermen all lived in Gansbaai.

They landed on the beach from the *Stormgans'* dinghy. Yasakov helped lift the shell from the boat into Josef's arms – its 49 kilograms' weight was child's play to the toughie. As he did so, Yasakov's foot slipped on the wet shingle and he nearly came down.

Take care with that shell, Yasakov, it is wet with the blood of six thousand innocents. And blood is slippery.

40

Tuesday night. 9 o'clock.

Eight hours to detonation.

Yasakov stopped the Kombi at the track end on Dune Fountain peak. He switched off the headlights, waited for Josef who had followed in the pickup. It was a black night; there were a few scattered lights along the coast; far below, the bright beam of Danger Point lighthouse pulsed every so often, like a sword of conscience in a night of evil.

Yasakov clicked on the interior light. There it was! The long shell wrapped in black plastic, propped securely on the floor. He and Josef had driven with it from Roman's Bay to Birkenhead in order to collect the pickup. Yasakov required both vehicles for his convoy to Bredasdorp – there was not enough room in the Kombi for the diving team plus prisoners. Plus the shell.

Yasakov had taken a last look round the Birkenhead mess. As he did so, the telephone had started to ring. Yasakov had made for it, then stopped. Who would be telephoning at that time of night – Captain Wessels? If he answered, would there be something – something, he could not think what – which would delay him, thwart the explosion schedule at the last minute?

The phone went on ringing. Yasakov fled, jumped into the Kombi, and ordered Josef to follow.

He could still hear the ringing as they pulled away.

Josef arrived at the track end.

Yasakov's words were clipped with tension. 'We can't take these vehicles further than this. You know what the Kombi contains.'

'Yes, Comrade Yasakov,' replied Josef dutifully. 'A naval shell.' He had no idea it was other than the normal.

'I will go and bring back the prisoners in the landrover. You' – he indicated the small armoury of pistols, submachineguns and grenades – 'will guard it with your life, understand? Shoot anyone who comes close.'

'Yes, comrade.'

Yasakov could not make the sort of speed he wished over the rough path to Frenchman's Eye. He kept on telling himself as he stumbled along at a half trot that there was plenty of time. The journey to Bredasdorp would take about an hour and a half. Say another half an hour to load up the prisoners and get them to the Kombi – plenty of time. He must not make the mistake of arriving too early at Bredasdorp and having to hang around on its outskirts. The town would be deserted by 11 o'clock. It always was.

'Halt!' It was Stefan with Yasakov's original Makarov.

'Yasakov.' His words tumbled out. 'Everything is well – the prisoners?'

'Trussed like fowls, as you ordered, Comrade Yasakov,' replied Stefan.

'Take this.' Yasakov thrust a deadly PPSh-41 sub-machinegun into his hands. 'I've added to our arsenal.'

'So I see, comrade,' Stefan answered almost jocularly.

Stefan rapped on the door of the magazine and Anna opened. By the light of the oil lamp, the trio of captives looked at their worst – the men were unshaven and dirty, Maris crumpled and pale.

Anna was both glad and sorry to see Yasakov. She knew, of course, that the diving team's stay ashore lapsed next day; she realized – although Yasakov had said nothing – that the captives' fate dovetailed with that deadline. She was indifferent about the two men – one a spy and the other an American commander whose operations threatened the Red presence in Cape waters. If Yasakov planned to shoot them, it was too bad. But she could not let Maris go the same way, and she intended to approach Yasakov with a suggestion to spare her life. Looking at the pale, beautiful creature, Anna, during the long hours of guarding her, both sleeping and waking, had felt a surge of emotion which (she told herself) she had never felt for any other woman. She would persuade Yasakov that Cane had forced her into his schemes under duress. . . . There would be no disgrace in doing what she planned for Maris; Maris would like – perhaps even love – her for saving her life.

'We're leaving here – now,' Yasakov announced curtly. 'You, Stefan and Anna – get these three into the landrover.'

'The landrover, comrade – isn't there the danger that it could be spotted?'

Yasakov eyed her. Her idea to put forward her suggestion about Maris froze under the KGB man's icy commands. He looked savage, too – he had strung a couple of grenades to his belt, he had an automatic in one hand, and his eyes held that sinister, hooded look which they took on in moments of crisis and action. He wore the same type of black clothes as in the lighthouse sortie.

'You don't have to tell me my business,' he retorted.

'Where are you taking us?' Testerman demanded.

He had heard the word landrover. If Ed Weinback had set alarm procedures in motion, the landrover would be the finest giveaway. . . .

'You'll find out.'

'Yasakov – don't you think this farce has gone on long enough?' said Cane. 'Okay, you've had your fun, tying us up and treating us like shit. I am not a spy. Nor is Maris. Put an end to it.'

There was a fearsome double meaning in Yasakov's reply. 'That is just what I intend doing, Mister Cane. You won't have long to wait now.' He addressed Stefan. 'Pick 'em up, you and Anna. Throw them in the back of the landrover.'

There was nothing either man could do. When it was Maris' turn, Anna took her shoulders and whispered to her when they got outside. 'Don't worry, my dear. It'll still come right.'

Maris shuddered. All the kindnesses Anna had shown during the time Yasakov had been away pointed to one thing only. Sex. That, she reasoned, would be Anna's bargaining counter for saving her.

'Now the figurehead,' Yasakov ordered when Anna and Stefan returned from the landrover.

'The figurehead, comrade?' echoed Anna. 'It will take up a lot of room – why should we take it . . .?'

Anna wilted under Yasakov's cold stare. 'As a good Russian, you obey orders – you do not question them. *Is that clear?*'

She had realized previously that Yasakov would be difficult to approach about Maris, but now. . . . She must not antagonize the man. That Uzbek blood! She replied docilely, 'Yes, comrade.'

'Now get rid of all signs of occupation,' Yasakov went on when Anna and Stefan returned a second time from the landrover. He himself double-checked after the two had spent another ten minutes cleaning up the magazine. There must not be the slightest sign – after the explosion – of any Russian implication whatsoever.

The landrover made short work of the rough terrain to the waiting Kombi and pickup.

Yasakov checked his watch.

9.45.

Plenty of time.

The three vehicles were grouped in a loose circle. Headlights illuminated the scene. The captives were humped from the landrover and seated on the ground.

'Get the figurehead – and the shell,' Yasakov ordered Stefan and Josef. There was something he had to check before they set off.

The two Russians rolled the five-foot object wrapped in black plastic to the open sliding door of the Kombi. Anna stared in silence. She had pictured a totally different situation. Yasakov had come ashore with a shell!

'Remove the wrapping,' Yasakov said.

Both Cane and Testerman gave a gasp at the sight of a shell. Its brass casing was longer than the conventional weapon, and there was the odd piece at the rear – the timer.

But it was the nose which riveted all eyes. It was painted bright red, with a skull-and-crossbones logo in white. Under it were two words in Russian script.

'What in God's name is that?'

Neither Testerman – nor any American – had set eyes on a top-secret Soviet nuclear shell.

It was Anna who broke the spell. She read out the lettering, in English.

'Nuclear warhead.'

'*I don't believe it! It can't be!*' burst out Testerman. '*A nuclear shell! Here!*'

Maris, who was sitting next to Cane, made an inarticulate sound. Then she rolled to him, and put her lips against his. It was an affirmation of love in the face of the end of the world.

Cane's blasting knowledge told him at once what the plastic cover and numerals meant – a timer! The nerves in his stomach and groin crimped. Had this crazy Russian already set an irrevocable armageddon in train? If only he could get his hands on the thing! It appeared to be a standard Soviet timer – he was familiar with the type of Russian device from his explosives background.

'Anna has saved me the trouble of breaking it to you,' Yasakov told the awestruck group. There was a strange, cold fire in his voice. 'Yes, that is a nuclear naval shell.' He addressed Stefan and Josef. 'Stop gawping like a couple of idiots – see if it fits inside the figurehead!'

'Inside the figurehead?' Anna's voice was wobbly with emotion.

'They call it accursed – accursed it shall be,' responded Yasakov. 'Carefully – don't damage the shell!'

Cane whispered in Maris' ear. 'It can't be fused yet!'

Stefan and Josef eased the shell into the cavity which once a ship's bowsprit had occupied. The shell was a fraction too long – the primer projected several inches. Not enough, however, to interfere with Yasakov's plan. He would have hated to have had to sacrifice the final macabre touch.

'Yasakov – get a grip on your senses!' rapped out Cane. 'What are you going to do with this shell?'

'You'll find out,' retorted the Russian.

'Nuclear shells are not left lying around for anyone to help themselves to – you must have been authorized!' Testerman interrupted.

Yasakov fixed him with a cold stare. It wasn't the look of a maniac. It was the clear, calculated assessment of a man who had worked out the odds and the prize, and was going for the jackpot. A Red jackpot.

'I was authorized.'

Anna's mind raced with a thousand schemes. The sight of the shell had upset her previous Maris plans; she would have to improvise. She believed she understood the shell's purpose – Yasakov would plant it inside the shafthead fissure and destroy the American cave station. Further, Anna reasoned that Yasakov would shoot the captives at the drilling site – there would be no fear of the shots being heard – before secreting the shell in the fissure. Anna was persuaded in her own mind that Yasakov would listen to her regarding

Maris. A last-minute reprieve from execution *must* make her grateful to herself. . . .

'Load it up – get going! You, Anna, will drive with Stefan in the pickup. Follow me and Josef in the Kombi. Keep me in sight, but don't give the impression that you're tailing me. Understood?'

Stefan and Josef first hefted the shell into the Kombi, followed by the figurehead and, finally, the three captives.

Cane made a last appeal for a hearing. 'Yasakov – in heaven's name, what are you up to? Where are we going – with this awful thing . . .?'

'Gag them – all three,' was Yasakov's only reply.

Yasakov took the wheel of the Kombi. He checked his watch.

10.15 p.m.

That would give comfortable time to reach Bredasdorp a little before midnight in keeping with the explosion schedule.

The convoy picked its way slowly down Dune Fountain peak. When it reached the main road, it headed east towards Bredasdorp.

Just over an hour later, the Kombi reached a road junction about twenty-five kilometres from Bredasdorp. One branch led rightwards towards the drilling site and Cape Agulhas; the other continued to Bredasdorp.

Anna, who was following, saw the Kombi take the left fork. Surely Yasakov had missed his direction – he should have switched right, towards the drilling site!

Anna accelerated and passed the Kombi, flicking her lights to draw Yasakov's attention. She pulled up in front, went to Yasakov's window.

'Comrade Yasakov – the road to the drilling site is right – you're heading the wrong way!'

Yasakov's eyes were hooded. 'I took the correct turn. We are going to Bredasdorp.'

The enormity of the realization seemed to push Anna back bodily from the window.

266

'Bredasdorp! You are going to explode the nuclear shell in Bredasdorp!'

'Yes.'

'But – but – it is a *nuclear* shell! There are thousands of people in the town – you'll kill them all!'

'You are wasting time and interfering with the logistics of the operation,' Yasakov retorted coldly. 'It has the full approval of Admiral of the Fleet Sergei Gorshkov!'

'But – they're innocent – they haven't done anything. . . .'

Her remonstrations came through clearly to the captives, although they did not understand the Russian. Josef sat expressionless, the sub-machinegun propped across his knees.

'Anna! Obey orders, d'ye hear! There is no omelette without breaking the eggs. The annihilation of a handful of people in the interests of securing peace and stability for the Cape Sea Route under the Red flag is unimportant. This is a major strategic blow we are striking – Admiral Gorshkov thinks this way too. They are only South Africans, anyway. Now get going and follow me.'

Anna stared at him with eyes like a sleepwalker.

'Where to?'

'The town museum. Got that?'

Anna nodded, and made her way slowly to the pickup ahead.

The Kombi took the lead again. The pickup followed.

Shortly before midnight, the death convoy entered sleeping Bredasdorp.

41

Midnight.

Five hours to detonation.

Bredasdorp slept.

Yasakov's Kombi edged warily into the street where the museum was situated.

There was not a soul to be seen.

The museum fronted onto a roadway, across from which was an open space with lawns and milkwood trees. It consisted of two buildings separated by an alley – one a low thatched structure and the other a taller building which looked like a church. In fact, it had once been a church: high arched windows, now bricked up on the inside, pointed to this.

Yasakov parked opposite the alley entrance. There was a small side door halfway down through which he intended to break into the museum. Josef had been briefed for the job. What worried Yasakov was that there might be a burglar alarm. He had counted on there being no warning device in such a small town. If he were mistaken. . . .

Tension added to the harshness of his order. 'Get going, Josef! Give me that gun! Quick, man, quick!'

Now the pickup pulled up behind the Kombi; Anna and Stefan joined the group.

'Get inside!' hissed Yasakov. 'Don't stand around watching! Inside!'

The two bundled in alongside the captives. Josef took a small crowbar which he had used during the *Kamchatka* operation and slipped down the alley.

He was back in minutes. The small door had been no match for his brute strength.

'Open,' he said laconically.

'First the shell and the figurehead – hurry!' snapped Yasakov. 'Anna, stay on guard here with me. You two, keep clear of the coin display cases. They may have alarms – the coins from the old wrecks are valuable.'

Anna said in a strained voice. 'Do we loose the prisoners' legs to get them into the place?'

'No,' replied Yasakov. 'We'll carry them in.'

The two bully boys shoved Cane, Maris and Testerman aside to get at the shell. They got it out, went off at a jog-trot. They returned; the figurehead followed.

'Now – these three!' said Yasakov.

Anna slipped her gun into her waistband. 'I'll take the girl.'

Without waiting for Yasakov's approval, she picked up Maris bodily, slung her over her shoulder, and went into the museum. Josef and Stefan followed, first carrying Cane, and then Testerman.

'Shut the door!' Yasakov's voice was more brittle than before. This was his moment of truth. Now he had only to set the timer.

'Light!' he snapped. 'Torches!'

Two flashlights snapped on.

The tall shell, almost man-height, stood upright, ultra-modern and menacing amongst the wreck museum's collection of old sea things. The light scarcely reached as far as the arched window openings. In each of them stood an old ship's figurehead. Their bright colours – garish reds, blues, whites and golds – and exaggerated expressions and attitudes were as incongruous as the gags round the captives' mouths. Alcestis was different; she was a queen among them. One of the figureheads depicting a man had a ruff, tophat and beard; a woman, with a blue poke-bonnet and blue skirt had her breast outthrust to meet wind and wave – with a coat-of-arms emblazoned on it.

There were also anchors, salvaged porcelain, ships' copper kettles and utensils, a display of old weapons – even a cannon mounted on a gun truck.

Cane rolled on to his side to observe Yasakov at the shell. The Russian took a couple of fine screwdrivers, long-nosed pliers and what looked like a blank key cut from stainless steel from his pocket – these had been supplied to him by the *Sovremennyy*'s armourer to set the timer.

'Light – closer, closer!'

His nerves might have been unsteady; his hands were not.

Carefully he inserted the stainless steel gadget, turned it to match some numerals which were invisible to Cane. Cane recognized the device – a standard, well-proven Soviet design which had sent thousands to their deaths at the hands of terrorists.

Yasakov was occupied for a couple of minutes only. He then replaced the plastic cover plate, drew back and rested for a moment on his hunkers. Sweat beaded his forehead, despite the museum's chill.

Detonating was in train!

Yasakov stood up, leaving the tools on the floor.

'Stefan! Josef! Slip the figurehead over the shell – watch it – don't move it!' he rapped out.

The two thugs upended Alcestis and gently eased her into place over the weapon.

'Steady!'

Yasakov then pushed the old cannon on its wheeled truck to give extra support to the figurehead, although she was well balanced without the addition. The upright shell threw her further back at an angle than normal: the posture was more soliciting, more harlot-like, than ever.

A nuclear death pulse began to beat inside her.

Yasakov addressed the three captives lying on the floor. His voice was impersonal, like a judge pronouncing a death sentence.

'You will have several hours to think before the shell explodes. It is set for dawn. That will give you plenty of opportunity to consider the consequences of crossing the might of the Soviet Union. Think about it well!' He switched into Russian for his team. 'Out! Stefan, you and Anna will follow the Kombi with me and Josef.'

Maris lay with a wisp of dark hair across her face. Anna paused as the others started for the door. The two women's eyes locked. There was something frightening, pathetic, exalted, in Anna's face.

'Goodbye.'

Then she was gone.

The alley door closed. There was a sound of engines starting. Light was gone; darkness, fear, and utter helplessness crowded through the closed door like ghosts passing through solid wood. Inside Alcestis' wayward womb a child was being conceived – to be born at an unspecified time in a few hours – which would rip, destroy and annihilate. Not only little Bredasdorp, but the world at large.

There was a thumping noise on the old yellowwood floor. It sounded like a human body.

It was – Maris'.

Maris' bonds were looser – Anna's doing – than either Cane or Testerman's. There was a limited amount of play in her wrists. She knew that if she could get her hands – roped though they were behind her back – close to Cane's mouth, she could free his gag.

Cane himself lay half under a big table which carried a display of ship relics (including a silver drinking cup with big handles). Alcestis was a metre or two away – no immediate danger of Maris on her way to Cane colliding with the figurehead and its lethal burden.

Maris' eyes were becoming more adapted to the blackness: she thought she caught a glimmer from a wall above the display cases. It was where the weapons were exhibited. They included several old-time cutlasses – heavy weapons with a blade weighted at the back, razor-sharp on the cutting edge.

Maris steered by the gleam, rolling over and trying to find some purchase for her feet. Cane lay en route to the weapons exhibit. In a minute of effort she was gasping: pain shot through her shoulders; her breasts felt as if they were being ripped off bodily. Thump!

It wasn't a table leg but Cane's body she had struck. She tried to suck in air; the choking gag felt as if it were being drawn clean down her throat. When she had got her breath back, she manoeuvred her hands and back to try and reach his gag.

Cane realized what she was about. Slowly, like two blind worms jockeying to make love, she brought her hands into position on his face.

It was a slower – and still more painful business – to find the gag's knots. If she could have cried out when she half ripped a nail off one finger, she would have done so. All she could do was to lean forward and chew in agony on her suffocating gag.

'Maris!'

Words meant his gag was off!

'You're wonderful, wonderful! We'll get out of this yet!'

Over-confident maybe; simply to hear was everything to Maris.

'Brad,' Cane went on, talking into darkness, 'Maris has managed to free my gag. Make a noise somehow to tell us where you are – thump with your hands or feet – anything.'

There was a thump-thump answer from the direction of the door – not unlike those signalling beetles the South Africans call tok-tokkies (thump-thumps).

'Listen,' said Cane. 'First, I am going to have a crack at getting off Maris' gag. Then I've got an idea. If I can get to the weapons display on the wall, maybe I can reach one of those old cutlasses. . . .'

There was a double thump of approval from Testerman.

'Okay,' said Cane. 'Here goes.'

Cane's attempt was a frustrating, clumsy, breath-robbing proposition which had both him and Maris half sobbing. Hands were hopeless – Cane's were too tightly lashed to give him the minute amount of freedom which Maris herself enjoyed.

Finally, Cane said. 'Darling – come to me. Put your mouth against mine.'

No lover's teeth were rougher. Cane ripped and tore until in the end Maris was able to complete the job herself on the shreds of fabric left.

The effort left them both exhausted. How long it had taken was anyone's guess. If that relatively simple operation had occupied so long, would Cane reach the cutlasses before the shell's deadline ran out?

Maris said, when she had recovered her breath. 'Hal, we must do something for Brad next. The more we three can communicate, the better chance we have.'

'There is no need,' said a voice at the door.

It was Anna.

42

A flashlight beam sliced through the blackness. Anna also held a Makarov, a second pistol was thrust into her waistband, a knife completed her armament.

Her first words were the only level utterance she made. She came in swiftly, her voice rising, as if a dam of emotion had broken its floodgates.

'I can't go through with it!' Her words were jerky, half-hysterical; tears poured down her cheeks. 'I can't go through with it, I tell you! I have seen the people he wants to kill – ordinary, good people! Thousands of them – he will kill them all! I will defect! We will go to the authorities, the police – quickly – now – we will go together. I will cut you loose. Maris . . .' she choked on the word and burst out sobbing.

'Anna!' demanded Cane urgently. 'What about Stefan – where is he? Why isn't he here?'

Anna dropped on her knees beside Cane and Maris. She pulled the pistol from her waistband and flung it unseeingly next to Cane. She thrust the barrel of the second Makarov at Cane. 'Feel!' she cried hysterically. 'Feel! It is still warm – I killed Stefan. Two shots. He told me, he told me – no, it doesn't matter what he said. I wanted to come back. He wouldn't go along with me. He was a good Russian. Thousands dead – what did it matter? – I killed him. He had a gun also. He could equally have killed me . . .'

Maris said urgently. 'Anna – you did the right thing. Cut us loose, quick. Brad is still gagged – hurry.'

Anna seemed deaf to the plea. Instead, she laid the Makarov's barrel against Cane's cheek. 'It is warm, like life,' she mouthed. 'The townspeople are warm, alive – we can save them still. I am warm, I am warm. I came back. . . .'

Cane broke in as matter-of-factly as he could. *'Cut us loose!'*

Anna put the second pistol also next to Cane; she went to Maris.

'You first, Maris – I came back for you.'

She sliced through her cords, did the same for Cane.

She broke out sobbing. 'He is not my Mother Russia – Yasakov is a devil. He is cold, he has no heart. . . .'

Cane put his foot on one of the automatics and said quietly. 'Brad next, Anna. All three of us must be free before we can go to the police.'

Anna shone the torch, located Testerman. In a minute the others knew he was a free man when he exclaimed.

'Jeez – if this doesn't take the porcelain hairnet!'

Anna started back to Cane and Maris past the Accursed Figurehead.

The heavy 9mm slug caught her in the neck. A fountain of blood erupted. It was an executioner's bullet. Yasakov's.

The crash of the shot and a second bullet followed simultaneously.

Anna spun, tried to grab the figurehead for support, missed, crashed to the floor.

Cane hurled himself to the floor also with Maris on top of Anna's flashlight. He grabbed the Makarov. At the same moment he yelled, 'Brad!' and slid the second pistol in the direction of the American.

A third shot from the doorway ripped into the table top above Cane. Cane snapped out the light. In the muzzle-flash of Yasakov's shot he had a split-second view of Josef as well at the door. And the silhouette of the PPSh-41 with its 35-shot box magazine.

Cane rolled sideways and outwards, the same way Yasakov himself had beaten him in the office shoot-out. He came to rest against something solid – he could not tell what.

Silence.

The sound vacuum after the ear-blasting concussions and red stabs of a second before was unnerving.

Where was Yasakov?

Cane lay like a dead man.

He could not hear the Russian's breathing and take a bearing from it. Then something moved near him. He froze. Yasakov? Maybe. Brad or Maris? Unlikely. Josef – he had been too far away.

He detected the faint rustle again.

He knew then what it was. It was a muscle spasm from one of Anna's dead limbs.

Cane eased away for cover behind whatever the hard thing above him was. Then he realized what it was – the cannon, on its wooden truck.

Silence.

A voice, a sound – anything would be a giveaway which would invite a bullet.

How long could it go on? His ears were straining like early warning antennae; the pistol was up; his finger ready on the trigger.

A bell clanged out – madly, insanely, absurdly.

A burglar alarm on one of the coin showcases! Josef's long volley blazed out in reply. The man's nerves were not as good as Yasakov's. It cost him his life. Testerman's bullet took him in the head before the volley – which lit the garish figureheads and marine bric-a-brac – was finished. A crash followed from the direction of the showcase wall – the cutlass display had been dislodged by the spray of bullets.

Yasakov held his fire; Cane held his fire; Testerman held his fire.

The alarm bell clanged on. Nobody was to know that it had been deliberately activated by Maris. She had wormed her way along the floor and bumped her shoulders against the showcase's under surface. She had reasoned that an alarm would bring outsiders – police, she hoped – to the scene.

Then Cane heard a clink of steel. It was not from Testerman's quarter.

He tried a snap shot.

Yasakov's reply would have killed him, had it not been for

the cast-iron barrel of the old cannon. Fragments of lead screamed away in every direction, joining the clangour of the alarm bell.

Cane had spotted, in the flashes, his chance. The ridiculous tophatted figurehead stood nearby, beyond an intervening table. If he could get behind the statue, it would provide him with cover to pick off Yasakov.

The banging of the bell covered the sound of his rush: in a flash, standing upright, he had tucked himself in behind the statue.

Now!

Yasakov realized that it was only a matter of time before someone was aroused by the alarm. He had to finish off the three former captives – quick! If he killed them and got out, the nuclear explosion would still take place as scheduled. Or, let some nosy policeman move that shell. . . .

He fired in the direction where he had last known Cane to be.

Cane, safe behind the figurehead, marked Yasakov's position and pressed the trigger – only bad shooting would miss the Russian's head.

There was a click.

Empty!

He had forgotten that Anna had used up two shots on Stefan – the magazine could not have been full anyway. The gun in his hand was as useless as if he himself had been tied up.

Testerman loosed off three shots. It was clear to Cane, however, that he wasn't sighted for Yasakov – the slugs banged about and there was a crash of breaking glass. Yasakov responded with a single round in the American's direction.

The sound of glass gave Cane an idea. He knew that to his left lay the ruins of the weapons display. If he could get his hands on one of those heavy old cutlasses and rush Yasakov before he could fire at close quarters. . . .

The bell clanged on.

Someone must come soon!

Cane crawled across the room on hands and knees, probing ahead in order not to make a clatter.

Here it was!

His fingers first met the weighted back of the blade; he slid them down to the hilt and stealthily got a grip on the formidable weapon.

The bell unnerved Yasakov. He loosed off a shot – wilder, more random than anything previously.

Cane launched himself, praying that Testerman would not fire on him by mistake.

The hot blast and racket of a shot almost in his face blinded and deafened Cane. The cutlass came down on Yasakov's gun, steel on steel, sent it spinning. Cane could not have stopped his blood-lust then even if he had wanted to. The weapon went up again; there was an awful jar in his wrist and arm; the blade bit deep into bone and flesh.

Cane pivoted, dragged the blade clear with both hands on the hilt. He raised it to slash again.

There was no need. Yasakov emitted a hideous, sickening noise from a mouth which vomited blood. He pitched forward, jerking and writhing.

The museum's lights went on.

A voice roared. 'Police! Hold it! Throw down your guns! The place is surrounded! Now, now, now!'

43

'Come out! Hands above your heads! Out!'

Half a dozen men, in anti-terror squad camouflage uniforms, fanned out at a firija crouch round the major at the door. There was enough fire power in their UZI-type submachineguns to obliterate a battalion. They were stationed in this sleepy country town as much as anything in case someone should attack the American establishment with all its valuable equipment.

Cane led, blinking in the light, followed by Testerman. Blood was dripping from a shallow bullet-groove across one cheek.

'*Allemagtig!*' exclaimed the officer. 'This place looks like a bloody slaughter house!'

He stared for a moment at the American and exclaimed. 'You're Dr Testerman – there's a general alert out for you!'

Testerman grinned lopsidedly. 'Glad to hear it!'

However, the police officer's attention was riveted on something else. Maris had emerged from under the showcase where she had found cover. She was dishevelled, dirty, her long hair in a mess.

'*Maris Swart!*' he burst out. 'Now I've seen everything! How in hell do you come to be involved in this . . .!'

'Listen, Pieter, listen all of you!' She switched into rapid Afrikaans. As she outlined their kidnapping and the events leading up to the shoot-out, incredulity and admiration chased across the major's face. Then she turned urgently and indicated the Accursed Figurehead.

'A nuclear shell!' exclaimed the man in English in disbelief. 'Maris, this is a *spookstorie* – a bogeyman story.'

'I wish it were, major,' Cane interrupted. 'Quick – what is the time?'

The man seemed stunned.

'Two thirty.'

A cold shiver ran down Cane's spine. It seemed impossible that two and a half hours could have elapsed since Yasakov set the timer. Two and a half hours – subtracted from how long before the shell went up?

Cane tried to keep his voice matter-of-fact. 'There is a Soviet nuclear shell inside that figurehead. . . .'

The policeman shook his head in disbelief, but Cane hurried on. 'It has been set to detonate at dawn. What precisely Yasakov meant by dawn, I don't know. He didn't give us an exact time. You can set modern timers to the second.'

The policeman went on mulishly, eyeing the figurehead, at whose feet lay Anna's body. 'I don't believe you. Your story is too fantastic.' He seemed to wake up to the shambles around them. 'Get these bodies out of here – put 'em in the van. Take 'em to the station. I'll be right along,' he ordered his men.

'You're going to look here first, major. Here, Brad, hold the thing steady.'

Cane and Testerman, followed by the officer and his squad – they held their guns ready as if the figurehead would open fire on them – clustered round the figurehead. Cane and Testerman gripped the base of the shell while two men took hold of the figurehead itself. One of them, holding the top half, said under his breath, 'I wish these titties were for real.'

'Now,' said Cane. 'Ease it upwards – gently, for Pete's sake – don't shake it!'

The wooden envelope was withdrawn. First, the shell's brass casing showed, next the red-painted warhead with its skull-and-crossbones logo.

The major was dumbfounded. Cane indicated the Russian lettering. 'That says, nuclear warhead.'

Next, he pointed to the base. 'That's the timing mechanism. It's located under the plastic plate.'

The major said hoarsely. 'We've got to get it out of here – we'll load it in the van – throw it into the sea. . . .'

'For pity's sake, major, listen!' Cane rapped out. 'Apart from the timer, the Reds have installed a tumbler device. That means, if you move a primed explosive charge before the set time, or mess about with the timing mechanism, it goes off in your face. *Do you understand?*'

'Yes, I do. They teach it on our anti-terrorist courses.'

'Good. Now I think I know how to defuse this. It's a standard Soviet design which they've used for years for terrorist bombings. The design is refined from time to time. But basically if you know one, you know the others. My guess is, there is a digital timer as well as the tumbler fuse – I'll defuse that first, and then go for the tumbler. Okay?'

'You are a very brave man, Mr Cane.'

'Skip the compliments,' replied Cane. 'Time is running out. Leave me to get on with it.'

The major suddenly became decisive. 'What is the blast area of a shell like this?'

'Yasakov intended to wipe out the whole of Bredasdorp with it,' Testerman said.

The policeman shook his head as if he could not absorb more and said automatically. 'The bastard – he did?' Then he addressed one of the squad. 'Jan, get back to the station. Phone HQ in Cape Town. Tell 'em I want them to fly a bomb disposal squad here – fast as hell. Their best men. Nuclear shell.' He added, half apologetically. 'We have never had to cope with a situation like this before.'

A man came from the door and said. 'Major, the public's starting to arrive – they heard the firing. They want to know what's up.'

'Cordon the place off – the whole block,' ordered the officer, who was back in his own familiar element. 'Get all the vehicles and men you can raise. Don't let anyone near.' He said to Cane, who was kneeling on the floor at the shell. 'It could go off anytime?'

'Yasakov said dawn.'

'I could clear the town,' said the major. 'Send men from house to house – knock 'em up and tell them to get the hell out.'

'And start a panic rush – mass hysteria? No, rather leave it to me – I can cope.'

2.45 a.m.

Two and a quarter hours to detonation.

Cane picked up the tools Yasakov had left lying, and went to work.

In the museum office, Testerman found a telephone and dialled. It rang for some time. The answer was sleepy.

'Ed – Brad.'

'*Brad*! Where in hell have you been! I've nearly gone out of my skull with worry!'

Testerman cut him short. 'Skip the biographical events. We've got a full nuclear emergency on our hands.'

'*Nuclear emergency* – are you kidding, Brad?'

'I wish I were. Listen. . . .' He gave Weinback a quick run

down on what was happening inside the museum. 'Hal is trying to void the timer. The tumbler is the wildcard in the pack. We daren't move the shell. We don't know whether the damn thing will go up or not, but Hal reckons he knows what he's about. Now these are my orders. No American – I repeat, no American from Soutbos – is to approach within twenty kilometres of Bredasdorp until I give the all clear. Understood?'

'Sure, Brad. But what if it goes up?'

'Then you're automatically in command. Meanwhile, you are to make instant voice contact with NORAD at Cheyenne Mountain. Priority linkup. Warn NORAD that the secret of Dolla's Downes has been blown. Tell 'em the Russian gas atoll is a Red missile mid-course updating station. And switch Alert Status codes. APPLEJACK no longer applies.'

'What is to follow it?' Weinback's voice was strained.

'COCKED PISTOL – full nuclear alert.'

'God's truth!'

'That's the way it is, fellah.'

3.30 a.m.

One and a half hours to detonation.

The sweat trickled off Cane's hands as he worked. It was the only sign of the tension which lanced through him. Maris held a flashlight close for him to see the intricate mechanism, one of several the police had provided as one after another had burned out.

The Accursed Figurehead presided over the scene. The major stood by, chain-smoking.

'It is more complicated than I thought,' Cane had said. 'They've made the digital timing microcircuitry more sophisticated than the earlier models. It will take more time to sort out.'

'You reckon you can?' The major's voice was uneven.

'We won't know if I can't.'

Far out over the sea, west of Birkenhead, A Super Frelon helicopter of the South African Air Force was beating its rotors against half a gale. It raced towards Bredasdorp. The pilot was – against all rules – cutting across the sea to make time. Every minute was vital. Six crack bomb disposal experts, two still in pyjamas under overcoats, slumped on the machine's seats, withdrawn, unspeaking.

A signal came in giving the Super Frelon clearance to land on the lawns outside the museum. They told the pilot he'd identify the place because the police cordon would have its headlights on.

Deep under Cheyenne Mountain, in the massive concrete bunker known as Doomsday City, the Master Alert Status Board of NORAD Command – duplicated at secret early warning stations throughout the world, from Dolla's Downes to Fylingdale Moors and Shemya Island – blazed with the nuclear emergency code, COCKED PISTOL.

Ed Weinback's call had put into action all the fearful panoply of nuclear attack: the White House had been alerted; at strategic fighter bases in British Colombia, Oregon and Michigan, aircrews had scrambled, ready for missile interception. Near Doomsday City, also deep under Cheyenne Mountain, power was being fed to the Peacekeeper missile silos. United States submarines, keeping sleepless vigilance under far-flung, unknown seas, had been signalled and their nuclear attack alert retaliation procedure was in operation. Their grim-faced commanders awaited only NORAD's order to push the firing buttons.

That could mean a rush of missiles in both directions, to and from the United States and Soviet Union; it would spell the end of the world as we know it. The men watching and waiting knew that, too. The code signal which would blaze from NORAD's Alert Status Board to herald that nuclear armageddon would have the title, DOUBLE TAKE.

It depended on what happened inside the wreck museum.

4 a.m.

One hour to detonation.

Cane worked methodically, slowly, like a racing mechanic

unhurried by the roar of other machines passing his pit, knowing that if he were not certain of his touch at every point, the race would be lost.

Once or twice, when Maris changed flashlights yet again as the tiny collection of removed microcircuitry innards grew, he and Maris looked into one another's strained eyes. They said nothing. Love exchanged on that level would, they knew, never pass away, whatever the outcome.

4 a.m.

A Soviet helicopter rose from the gas atoll's pad into the pre-dawn darkness. Vice-Admiral Strokin had borrowed the machine from the *Sovremennyy* because the naval helicopter had a longer range than the one stationed on the gas atoll. Strokin knew the detonation time – 5 a.m.

The pilot gave himself plenty of time. In an hour he would cross the off-limits one hundred and fifty kilometre zone and push beyond that to intercept the fishing boat bringing Yasakov and his team to safety.

He had been given explicit orders to report back to the gas atoll immediately he sighted the distant flash of the nuclear explosion over the northern horizon, where the land lay.

4.30 a.m.

Half an hour to detonation.

Cane gave a long, sudden intake of breath.

Like a surgeon removing a growth, he drew from the timer's innards a thin plastic tube with calibrated figures and what could have been red liquid inside. It resembled a foreshortened wine temperature thermometer.

He got up into a kneeling position. His eyes locked with Maris'. Together they stood up.

He nodded briefly at Testerman and the police major. Then he linked his arm in Maris'.

Together they walked out slowly on to the lawn outside beyond the roadway, floodlit by police headlights for the Super Frelon's landing.

They were alone. Not even the police saw them come.

They had turned their backs to the museum as if to save their eyes, if not their lives, from the nuclear explosion.

At NORAD Headquarters, a top priority voice call came through from Dolla's Downes.

Men hunched over computers, consoles and illuminated monitoring screens suddenly relaxed and sighed. The Master Alert Status Board changed with equal suddenness. COCKED PISTOL became APPLEJACK.

At secret American and Canadian fighter bases pointed at the Soviet Union, aircrews unscrambled.

Under Cheyenne Mountain, from which Butch Cassidy and the Sundance Kid once rose to terrorize the town of Cheyenne, power to the missile silos was cut and the men poised to throw the switches – as in the deep-diving submarines – leant back in their chairs from the radar screens.

At Dolla's Downes, the nerve-stretched American team watched the Alert Status Board skip down the ladder to its bottom slot. It came alight. It read, APPLEJACK.

The world – and Bredasdorp – would lie easily in its bed again.

EPILOGUE

When the Soviet helicopter assigned to pick up Yasakov failed to report the telltale fireball signature – fireprint – of a nuclear explosion over the mainland after a fruitless search for the fishing-boat, Vice-Admiral Strokin recalled the machine and reported urgently and directly to the admiral of the fleet in Moscow. By daybreak Admiral Gorshkov knew that Yasakov's plan had aborted and that there was only one way out – Red retreat from the Cape Sea Route. The gas atoll's true purpose, he reasoned, must now be known both to the Americans and South Africans. He warned Strokin of the impending closure, after a face-saving lapse of time had taken place.

The public Soviet announcement followed a month later. It coincided, oddly enough, with the news of the shutdown of the geothermal project. The parties involved in both operations, 'gas' and geo thermal power, claimed that the end of their respective projects was 'for economic reasons'. However, Charles Grimmock's previous objections for refusing to sell the drilling site melted in the face of a joint American –South African offer. Under this deal, the whole wild marshland from the drilling site eastwards to the great inland lake was effectively scaled against outsiders.

Part of the deal involved an exchange of land situated on the expensive resort coast north of Gansbaai where there were hot springs. This had been specially acquired by the South African authorities. Grimmock was shrewd enough to realize that even if his new geothermal project should fail, he still stood to gain land worth ten times as at the original drilling site.

Maris happily joined Cane at the new project: it was within

sight of Frenchman's Eye, which she set about restoring with equal happiness.

The Soviets never claimed the bodies of the *Kamchatka* diving team. They had, according to Tass, the official Russian news agency, all been lost diving for the Czar's treasure. The four were buried secretly in the disused graveyard of an old farm where several bodies washed ashore from the Birkenhead some time after the tragedy had been interred.

Alcestis posed a problem for the museum staff once the furore of the shoot-out had died down and the nuclear shell had been sent to the United States for expert examination. The fresh bullet-hole through one arm was masked by plugging and painting, but the stain of Anna's blood on her bare breast, deeper than the red colour of the cherry wood from which the Accursed Figurehead had been carved, defied all efforts of the experts to eradicate it.

Geoffrey Jenkins

Geoffrey Jenkins writes of adventure on land and at sea in some of the most exciting thrillers ever written.

'Geoffrey Jenkins has the touch that creates villains and heroes – and even icy heroines – with a few vivid words.' *Liverpool Post*

'A style which combines the best of Nevile Shute and Ian Fleming.' *Books and Bookmen*

SOUTHTRAP
A BRIDGE OF MAGPIES
SCEND OF THE SEA
HUNTER-KILLER
A TWIST OF SAND
A RAVEL OF WATERS
THE UNRIPE GOLD
A GRUE OF ICE
A CLEFT OF STARS

FONTANA PAPERBACKS

Fontana Paperbacks: Fiction

Fontana is a leading paperback publisher of both non-fiction, popular and academic, and fiction. Below are some recent fiction titles.

- ☐ COMING TO TERMS Imogen Winn £2.25
- ☐ TAPPING THE SOURCE Kem Nunn £1.95
- ☐ METZGER'S DOG Thomas Perry £2.50
- ☐ THE SKYLARK'S SONG Audrey Howard £1.95
- ☐ THE MYSTERY OF THE BLUE TRAIN Agatha Christie £1.75
- ☐ A SPLENDID DEFIANCE Stella Riley £1.95
- ☐ ALMOST PARADISE Susan Isaacs £2.95
- ☐ NIGHT OF ERROR Desmond Bagley £1.95
- ☐ SABRA Nigel Slater £1.75
- ☐ THE FALLEN ANGELS Susannah Kells £2.50
- ☐ THE RAGING OF THE SEA Charles Gidley £2.95
- ☐ CRESCENT CITY Belva Plain £2.75
- ☐ THE KILLING ANNIVERSARY Ian St James £2.95
- ☐ LEMONADE SPRINGS Denise Jefferies £1.95
- ☐ THE BONE COLLECTORS Brian Callison £1.95

You can buy Fontana paperbacks at your local bookshop or newsagent. Or you can order them from Fontana Paperbacks, Cash Sales Department, Box 29, Douglas, Isle of Man. Please send a cheque, postal or money order (not currency) worth the purchase price plus 15p per book for postage (maximum postage is £3.00 for orders within the UK).

NAME (Block letters) _____

ADDRESS _____

_____